GLASSBORN

CURIOSITY KILLED THE COLONY

A RIVETING DYSTOPIAN NOVEL

KN TRISTAN

QUINTA

YEAR: 2179

Terra Levitt touched the Heart of Mars hanging at her neck every few seconds.

By the time Quinta Voss finished reviewing her vitals, she'd already worried her thumb across the ruby a dozen times. It was a nervous tic Quinta had noticed in a lot of wearers. She'd stopped finding it strange a long time ago – her family's initial on so many pendants, their name in every prayer, right next to Valence's. But the pendant on her patient's neck still made her aware of the digital badge over her breast pocket with her name on it.

Not that anyone in the colony needed telling that she was a Voss.

"When did symptoms begin?" she asked as she read the wall of data Valence was producing about Terra's vital signs. Three years of apprenticeship had taught her to read the wall before the patient.

Nurse Cydra Tavara gently nudged Terra's hand away from the necklace and unbuttoned the sleeve of her coverall to apply the blood pressure cuff.

"Last night," Terra said. "I was having dinner before my shift."

The display wall told Quinta that Terra was thirty-two, an atmospheric monitoring tech from sector one. She was running a fever of 38.8 degrees, and there was a fine sheen of sweat across her brow. Quinta had noticed it on her neck too, where the pendant stuck to her skin.

Terra hadn't taken her eyes off Quinta from the moment she'd walked into the room. People had looked at her that way since she was a child.

"That's when you began to feel feverish? Did it come on quickly or slowly?" Quinta prompted in her best professional tone. She had only six months left in her apprenticeship, but the baby face never helped. Sometimes Quinta wondered whether people trusted her expertise or were simply pleased to be treated by a Voss. Today was her first shift without either her father or the other sector one doctor, Liang, on duty, and Quinta had been speaking in a slightly lower octave than normal all morning.

"Slowly," Terra said. "I guess I woke up not feeling great, but I really started feeling sick at dinner. Normally I love cricket tacos but I couldn't stomach them."

Fever, sweating, lack of appetite – sounded like a garden-variety case of the ration crud. Quinta asked a few more questions, mentally ruling out dehydration and food poisoning. She was about to prescribe fluids and rest – including a three-day work release voucher – when she heard Cydra draw in a sharp breath behind her.

It instantly made Quinta's hairs stand on end. Cydra was in her sixties, the most senior nurse in the sector one clinic, and nothing fazed her. Quinta had memories of shadowing her father when she was younger and watching Nurse Tavara debride infections, prep the entire OR for emergency surgery, and expertly stitch gaping wounds without ever once looking out of breath.

"Dr. Voss." She sounded terrified.

Quinta turned around. Her eyes went immediately to Terra's

exposed forearm. Terra's skin was pale and blue-green veins stood out prominently.

Quinta's heart scrabbled up into her throat and her eyes widened.

"What?" Terra asked. When Quinta just swallowed, her free hand flew to her pendant and she demanded, *"What?"*

"I need my dad," Quinta squeaked out, instantly hating herself for saying it, and in such a child's voice too. She was nineteen years old, not quite a doctor, despite what people called her, and she was about thirty seconds away from peeing her pants.

Cydra shook her head. "No time."

"Dr. Liang?" Quinta cast about desperately.

Sector one's second-in-command had never kept it much of a secret that she was no fan of Quinta, but right now she wanted *anyone in the entire hab* who wasn't herself to run this protocol.

She'd done the drills a thousand times – as a citizen and again as a doctor's apprentice. She knew what to do. But she'd never done it without her father by her side. All the awful photos of Glass victims she'd seen in her training flashed behind her eyes.

She couldn't afford to let this get out of control.

She couldn't be the reason the colony had its third outbreak.

"Valence," she said, her voice surprisingly steady, "begin Glass quarantine protocols."

"Oh Voss," Terra cried, "I knew it."

Then the Glass drill alarm started to blare – three short bursts followed by a long, eardrum-piercing wail through the clinic speaker system. Quinta's vision was blotted out by a massive pop-up:

ALL-COLONY ALERT: Contamination protocol initiated. Begin quarantine procedures. This is NOT a drill.

The doors all over the hab would be locked down now, and they would stay that way until one of two things happened: one, Quinta verified that Terra did *not* have the most contagious, deadly infection humanity had ever encountered. Or two... everyone who'd come in contact with the patient was dead.

Quinta locked eyes with Terra. If she had it, it was certainly too late for her and Cydra. But that didn't mean they could ignore protocol.

"Biosuits," she said to Cydra, her training overtaking the adrenaline coursing through her veins. "And we need to seal off the treatment room."

"What about me?" Terra asked, eyes wide with panic.

"We don't know for sure you have it," Quinta said. "We're going to find out. Until then, try to take deep, slow breaths."

She'd never seen a Glass victim in the flesh. There was an old rumor about a survivor of the second outbreak living in sector four, still looking like a see-through anatomical model, but that was just hab lore. If you got Glass, you got a fever like Terra. You became delirious. The bacteria sucked all the oxygen out of your cells and left your skin a sickly, cyanotic blue and clouded your eyes.

And then it killed you, one hundred percent of the time.

Cydra pushed a button on the wall to deploy an inflatable decontamination chamber between the treatment room and the rest of the clinic, then pulled a pair of tightly folded biosuits out of a cabinet nearby. She handed one to Quinta.

"Have you ever done this before?" Quinta asked.

Cydra nodded. "Once or twice, always false alarms. We've both trained for this day – we've drilled it."

Quinta didn't feel prepared, but letting Cydra and Terra know she was moments away from a panic attack wasn't going to help anyone. As she flipped the hood of the suit up over her jet-black ponytail, she opened the messages in her overlay and used eye gestures to send one to her father.

Possible Glass case. Why today of all days?

She didn't expect an answer – he was teaching a specialized surgical technique to one of the doctors in sector three. But he'd be listening to the same alarms Quinta heard.

"Check my seal?" Cydra asked.

Quinta's overlay pinged with a message.

Take a minute to breathe first. Then do what we practiced. Trust your-self, sugar beet. You're prepared for this.

For half a second, she felt normal – relieved, even. But when she saw the nickname he'd used for her since she was a child, her throat tightened. He never used the name in the clinic, in front of colleagues. He'd even stopped calling her that at home since she became an adult.

She blinked the overlay closed and took a long, deep breath. Her hands weren't shaking as much when she told Cydra to turn around.

"Seal's good," Quinta told her as the alarms finally died down. "We've got this."

LIRA

YEAR: 2083

Lira Salonga was portioning carrot greens for the rabbits when the module door slid open behind her. "Hey, Dana, you're a few minutes early for your appoi–"

"Ada's sick."

It wasn't Dana's voice, and it short-circuited Lira's brain. For a few seconds, her hands just kept untangling voluminous carrot greens and separating them into piles.

It was Jamila, and if she sounded rattled, it was bad. Jamila was one of the colony's best botanists – poached from one of the most prestigious research organizations on Earth after she managed to wring record yields out of desert greenhouses. She was unflappable, but right now, she sounded panicked.

Lira spun on her heels. "What's wrong with her?"

"I don't know, exactly. There was some kind of malfunction at the excavation site, the whole dig crew is sick." Jamila's eyes were big and her ordinarily neat curls were wild around her face. "She's in med clinic two."

Lira was already shoving her way past Jamila in the narrow doorway, her heart pounding. She and Ada had arrived at the colony together five months ago and a small, carefully guarded part of her had been expecting news like this every single one of those hundred and fifty days. There was a night four months ago when Lira sat bolt-upright in bed, listening to a hab-wide alarm blare through the speaker in her ceiling, and just knew in her gut that it was for Ada.

She'd been right, but Ada had survived it.

They'd jailed her, then after her sentence, Valence assigned her to the dig crew expanding the hab.

Lira had actually started to convince herself in the ensuing months that things were going to be okay. Nothing had happened to Ada in all this time, she hadn't had any "mysterious accidents," or been stuck in the torture chamber people here called therapy. VossCorp knew who she was and why she was here and they let all this time pass... Lira thought they were going to subject Ada to hard labor and call it even.

But now...

"I'll watch the rabbits," Jamila called to Lira's back.

She'd had about ten of the growing warren out of their hutches, playing on the grass that grew across a good portion of the rabbit module's floor. With the door open, they'd be free to hop all over sector one, and at this moment, Lira didn't care if they binkied their way right out the nearest airlock.

"Great, thanks," she called over her shoulder, running breathless through the white prefab hallways that wound through the sector like their own sort of warren.

The hab was made of modular sections, most of them shipped in parts to Mars and assembled by robots before the first human colonists arrived. Each sector was arranged in identical spoke patterns, with the most commonly used resources at the center and fanning out to residences further out. The rabbit module, which pretty much everyone referred to as the rabbitat, was in sector one, about a twenty-minute jog from the sector two med clinic.

Ten minutes if Lira ran full-out, using the low gravity to push off the walls and propel herself forward.

She slammed into two people on her way there, and knocked the wind out of herself once.

"Hey, watch it!" a fabrication tech in sector one had complained, rubbing his shoulder after she rounded a corner and hit him full-force.

"I'm sorry," Lira had said, not slowing down. The second person she knocked into the wall didn't even get an apology.

Lira arrived at med clinic two out of breath, dizzy from the exertion, and sweating so hard one of the nurses looked up from the absolute chaos going on in the clinic to ask if she was okay.

The med clinics were all normally pristine and quiet, their white walls and floors gleaming and their waiting areas wide-open and calm. Right now, it looked like a regolith bomb had gone off in here, the fine red dust of the planet's surface coating everything, footsteps dragging through it in every direction.

There were patients in every treatment room, med staff clustered around them, and somewhere, Lira could hear someone retching violently. Two more people sat in the waiting area, and one of them was cradling his head, rocking and moaning. When he moved his hand, his face was beet-red.

Lira's stomach sank. This wasn't some bug, or food poisoning from the standard fare slop that was all Ada could afford.

She thought of the solar flare alert Valence had sent out this morning, warning everyone that the solar shields would be closed until further notice.

"Where's Ada Bello?" she demanded of the nearest med staff.

"Treatment room four," the nurse said, a sad look in her eyes that shot a fresh jolt of fear into Lira's heart. "But you can't go in. They're–"

"Ada!" Lira shouted, wading through the carnage before the nurse could stop her.

She reached the door just as Dr. Ethan Kalb was stepping out of it. Lira's jaw set and her nerves shot little jolts of electricity through her body as she looked over the shiny-domed doctor. Of course, *he* had to be Ada's treating physician.

"How is she? What happened?" Lira demanded.

"Radiation exposure," Dr. Kalb said, not deviating from his course toward the next treatment room. "From these symptoms, the solar flare must have been much worse than predicted. They shouldn't have been working."

The hairs on the back of Lira's neck stood on end. Radiation poisoning? This was bad.

Radiation on the surface of Mars was fifty times what it was on Earth, a constant threat if not for the expensive shielding technology that covered every window and skylight, and the regolith that the hab was mostly buried in. Lira always worried when Ada was doing a surface mission. The dig crew was so much more exposed than the rest of them, working in pressure suits in unfinished parts of the hab. It wasn't fair that Ada was forced to dig, while some of the others did it because it was their job.

Lira had tried to convince Ada to make an excuse, play sick to get out of work this morning.

"Valence says it's just a C-class flare," Ada had tried to reassure her, showing Lira the message. She was one of only two colonists without a retinal implant, so she had to lug a tablet around in her coverall pocket to get alerts. "If we stopped for every small flare, we'd never get sector five built."

Ada had been working on the dig crew for about three months, and the clock was ticking on the expansion. They had their first pregnant colonist and more would follow. They'd already expanded once, but the four existing sectors were at capacity.

Lira kept arguing that it was too dangerous, that Ada had already served her prison sentence and it wasn't fair to make her dig too. But Ada never complained. Lira thought she secretly believed the colony would finally forgive her if she did this.

"The robots are the ones doing all the hard work anyway," she'd tried to reassure Lira on multiple occasions. "I'm just sweeping up behind them."

Maybe it's not that bad, Lira thought now, even as she carefully avoided looking at the two guys with the reddened skin in the waiting room. She stepped into the doorframe of treatment room four and froze there.

Inside, her stubborn, brave, infuriating partner lay on a hospital bed, a nurse inserting an IV at her left side. Ada's dark complexion was somehow both dull and clammy, her features tense, but when she saw Lira, she smiled. "Hey, babe."

"Oh, thank God," Lira breathed, rushing to her bedside. "Are you okay?"

Hot tears streaked down Lira's face and she started to throw her arms around Ada when she lifted her hand to hold her back. "Don't."

Lira stopped. She looked down at Ada's arms, which she noticed were bandaged from the elbows down to her wrists. Her hands were raw and pink and blistered. "Oh honey... how bad is it?"

"Bad," Ada grimaced.

"What happened?"

"Radiation shield failed," Ada said as the nurse stepped out of the room. "We were working in a pressurized module with a skylight, doing the final prep to connect it to the new sector. Every-thing was normal all morning, but then people started feeling sick. Complaining they were hot, nauseous. I had my sleeves rolled up and my arms started feeling tingly and numb. I was having trouble holding the broom I was using. Torres had his whole coverall unbuttoned and wrapped around his waist cuz he was sweating. He wasn't even wearing a t-shirt underneath."

"Is he..." *The one who hasn't stopped retching since I got here?* Lira wondered, but she didn't want to interrupt Ada because it seemed like a struggle for her to talk. Ada got the implication, though, and she nodded. "Everyone got exposed?" Lira asked.

"Everyone working in the module," Ada said. "About ten of us, I think. Enough that they had to send us to two different clinics."

Lira had begged Ada to flat-out disregard her dig assignments and just come back to work in the rabbitat with her. It wasn't fair. Ada was being punished day after day, month after month, for a crime she'd already paid for.

But the colony AI only saw an able body without a permanent job assignment who was needed to build sector five.

"I knew this would happen," Lira sniffed.

Ada gingerly took Lira's hand. "No, you didn't. No one did. This was just a freak accident."

"That solar flare was supposed to be small," Lira shook her head. "How much radiation did you take?"

"Not sure yet. I wasn't wearing a dosimeter, but a couple of the others were. The number wouldn't mean anything to me even if I knew it."

Lira moved to layer her hand on top of Ada's, her skin was blistered and raw. She hesitated, then put her hand on Ada's shoulder. "You'll be okay."

"I'll be okay," Ada agreed. "Come here."

Lira perched on the side of the bed. "Sorry, I'm sweaty. I ran here."

Ada laughed. "I don't care." And she kissed Lira's salty lips, then nuzzled her forehead against Lira's cheek. Both of them were sticky with sweat for different reasons, but the touch was comforting nonetheless.

"Rest," Lira said, standing and pulling a chair over from one corner of the room. "I'm not going anywhere."

KELLAN

YEAR: 2179

Kellan Reilly's knuckles whitened as he gripped the wrench, straining against a rusted bolt that refused to budge. His ears rang with the noise from the ventilation fans whirring just centimeters from his head. This deafeningly close, he could hear the unsteady rhythm of them, threatening to give up on their century-old task.

"Come on," he grunted, putting all his weight into one last push.

The bolt sheared off with a metallic *ping* as its head ricocheted around the air shaft and Kellan tumbled forward, catching himself hard on his wrist.

"Ouch!"

"You okay?" Jace Windham called from further down the shaft, sounding only half concerned. They'd done enough of these jobs together that he knew the difference between *ouch, that hurt* and *ouch, I need medical attention.*

Besides, they'd been friends since school and Jace was far more likely to be the cause of an *ouch* than compassionate about one.

"Fine," Kellan called back, lifting away an access panel. "I'm in."

He wiped his arm across his brow, only noticing after the fact that he had grease on his forearm, and now his forehead was sticky with it. He tucked the wrench into his toolbelt and turned on his headlamp, aiming it at the air compressor in front of him.

"'Bout tank-dredging time," Jace called back, his voice echoing in the ductwork. "Pressure's dropping, we have to get the compressor back online *now*."

The sector four ventilation system had been limping along for weeks, the air cycling unevenly, the compressors' pressure regulators randomly misfiring. Today the whole system had finally given up all at once, three different compressors failing like dominoes and triggering automatic airlock activations in a couple of modules.

There were people trapped in the laundry module one over from them, and if Kellan and his crew didn't get the compressors fixed fast, they'd pass out as the pressure dropped and the CO_2 levels rose.

"Tell me what I'm looking at," Kellan said. He'd read the schematics before he crawled into the air shaft, but there hadn't been time for memorization. That was what Jace and their friend Echo were for at the other end of the ductwork.

"You need to find the pressure regulator," Jace said. "It'll look like a long metal canister with a gauge on the front. It should be off to the side of the main body of the air compressor."

"Got it," Kellan said.

Locating it wasn't difficult, but disconnecting it from the compressor without causing an explosion inside the ductwork was a different story. He checked the gauge – it should have been at point-seven atmospheres, and instead, it was flitting erratically at less than half that. He leaned in to direct his light on it and saw the problem: there were several hairline fractures running up to the threaded connector between the regulator and the compressor, and a bigger one running down the length of the canister that must have blown open when the whole damn thing went down.

"It's cracked," he reported back. "Deimos, I hope it's just the regulator and not the whole compressor. Hand me the new one."

They'd been lucky to have it. Everything in the hab was at least a hundred years old and there was only so much you could fabricate with the raw materials they had, which wasn't much.

The citizens in the other three sectors – the ones Kellan's people called Blinkers for the way they zoned out and blinked a lot when they were hooked up to Valence – took great joy in hoarding all the important things. Truly, it was a miracle the Non-participating Colonists – AKA sector four, the un-implanted, the uncredited, the unworthy – had any spare pressure regulators at all. Kellan wouldn't be surprised to learn someone had stolen or even bartered for the one Jace carefully handed up to him now.

If he messed up this install, that was it.

There was no back-up.

Kellan worked carefully, sweat and grease dripping down his forehead and plastering his chin-length hair to his skin. He released the remaining pressure and brought the air compressor fully offline, got out his wrench again to remove the old part and spent a long time inspecting the connector to make sure it wasn't damaged before he tried to install the new one.

"Compressor looks solid still," he called back. "We got damn lucky with that. Hand me a sealant gun, I want to make sure this connection stays tight."

"Laundry's losing pressure fast now," Echo warned.

"I know, I turned off the compressor." Kellan kept working steadily, his ears ringing from the noise. "Five minutes," he promised, although that was a wild guess, and maybe a stupidly optimistic one.

"CO_2 levels are rising and we've got ten people in the laundry module," Jace called.

"Not helpful," Kellan gritted out. He ran a bead of sealant all the way around the connector. It'd take at least thirty minutes to cure, but they couldn't wait that long to turn the compressor back on. He flipped the switch and winced at the high-pitched squeal of the motor. "Moment of truth."

He left the access panel off, holding his breath the whole time he watched the needle creep back up.

"Reading?" he called after about two minutes, which was as long as he could stand to wait.

There was a long pause and Kellan started to wonder if they could even hear him over the combined roar of the fans and the now fully functioning air compressor. Then Echo said, "What's the pressure gauge say?"

Kellan shined his light on it. "Point-five atmospheres and rising steadily. Why?"

"The pressure's not increasing in the module like it should," she said. "CO_2 is not rising anymore, but it's not dissipating either."

"Tank sludge," Kellan muttered. That meant something was still wrong. "Have the other crews reported problems besides the pressure regulator?"

There were two more teams working on the other broken compressors, and more people trapped in other modules. It was just a guess that the same thing had gone wrong on all of them, but an educated one.

"Not that we've heard," Jace said, then trailed off unhelpfully.

Kellan swiped his greasy arm across his forehead again. "Well? I'm blind in here, tell me what I'm supposed to be looking for!"

"Don't pop a seal," Jace said, testy. "We're looking at the schematics."

Several painfully long, loud minutes went by and all Kellan could do was crouch there, his calves cramping and his knees aching in the small space, staring at an air compressor he knew very little about. And then at last, Echo said, "The other two modules serviced by this compressor are showing normal pressure readings. It's got to be the junction box on the other side of it that feeds the air out."

"How am I supposed to reach that?" Kellan asked, beyond frustrated. "This vent ends at the compressor."

"You're going to have to come out."

"I bet the laundry module vent is jammed shut," Jace said. "Would explain why the fans have been cycling like hell. They can't push enough air."

Kellan backed out of the shaft and Jace and Echo helped him reposition the ladder so he could get to the next access point. Kellan wasn't confident Jace's shoulders would even fit in the shaft if he sent him, and Echo was better on the schematics, being Kellan's eyes. That left him as designated vent crawler.

Kellan looked down at his crew just before entering. "You confident the vent is the problem?"

Jace just shrugged and held up crossed fingers.

Kellan grunted and climbed up to the air shaft. Echo called after him, "Looks like the laundry module is junction three, the one on your far right."

His knees complained as he popped off the panel to see the manifold that exchanged air into different modules right after the compressor. "I'm here," he called, dismantling the top of the manifold to look inside. "Deimos, what's going on here?"

"What are you seeing?" Echo asked.

"There's way more than just three modules being fed by this thing. It must service other sectors too."

"Sludge," Jace cursed. "Well, don't touch anything that isn't ours."

"Which one again?"

"Far right," Echo said.

"The valves are stacked on top of each other," Kellan complained, craning his neck to try to get a good look. "There are three on the far right."

"That explains why our schematic was wrong, all we've got is a drone's eye view," Jace said.

"Well, is one of them stuck closed?" Echo asked.

"Let's find out," Kellan grumbled under his breath. He popped each duct off the manifold in turn, looking inside. First fine, second fine, and then, "Oh here, this one's jammed."

He jiggled the valve but it didn't give.

"Pressure's still dropping in the laundry," Echo warned him.

Kellan pulled the wrench out of his toolbelt and started hitting the valve with the handle end. After a few good whacks, it sprang open like it should have been. "There! I got it."

He reinstalled the duct and stayed in the air shaft while Echo and Jace monitored the laundry module. For what felt like an eternity, the pressure reading hovered at point-four, long enough to make him think it hadn't worked.

"Well?" he asked. What on Mars could have happened to–

"There!" Jace called. "Point-four-two atmospheres. It's rising, and the CO_2 is dissipating. Airlock should open soon."

"Thank Phobos," Kellan said. "I'm coming down."

Echo and Jace were glued to the tablet when he got back, not quite trusting the numbers to keep adjusting in the right direction. "We'll tell the overnight crew to keep an eye on it, just in case. I don't know why that valve was closed."

"Not just closed," Kellan said. "Totally jammed. I had to hit it with my wrench to punch it back open."

"Weird," Jace answered. "There wasn't any documentation about why it would be closed, was there? Like laundry was supposed to get rerouted to some other compressor?"

Echo shook her head. "Nothing I saw. I'll ask around, though."

QUINTA

YEAR: 2179

Terra had started to shiver despite the fever. Quinta ran through everything she knew about the Glass bacteria while she retrieved a blanket. Terra was wearing standard-issue coveralls, and the hab was kept at a constant, comfortable temperature. Chills weren't a Glass symptom.

That was a good sign.

But it mutates with every outbreak.

The thought arrived uninvited.

Quinta draped the blanket over Terra's shoulders, moving clumsily in the biosuit, while Cydra prepared blood-draw instruments in a row on a wheeled tray. Terra was still worrying the sharp point at the bottom of her necklace – the V for Voss, or Valence, depending on who you asked.

Quinta had wanted one when she was little – it had her initial on it, after all – until her mother explained who that symbol was for.

"I have it, don't I?" Terra asked, pulling the blanket tight around her. "How?"

"It's unlikely," Quinta said, to remind herself as much as Terra.

"You work in atmospheric monitoring. Do you ever come in contact with regolith?"

Terra shook her head.

"Have you been in contact with anyone who does?"

She shook her head again. "No. I don't know anyone in filtration. I almost never go to the maintenance garage. And of course, I have no business in sector four."

"Of course not," Cydra reassured her as she brought the tray bedside.

"We need to take some blood," Quinta said, willing her voice to be steady and confident.

"I'm just so cold," Terra apologized as she reluctantly opened the blanket and presented her forearm. The veins at her wrist were more visible than the ones in her forearm. Just like in the case photos Quinta had seen. The areas where the skin was thinner got affected the most severely.

She took a deep breath, the sound loud inside her hood. Cydra helped Terra pull her coverall down over her shoulder to expose her entire arm and tied a tourniquet around her bicep. Quinta picked up the needle.

Terra flinched when it punctured her skin, and out of the corner of her eye, Quinta saw Cydra do the same.

As the dark red blood began to fill the vial, Terra asked, her voice watery, "Am I going to die?"

Quinta looked at her. Her eyes were filled with tears and her hand clutched the Heart of Mars as if it were her only lifeline.

She wanted to say no. But the entire hab was locked down, awaiting the answer to that question, and Terra would know any reassurance was a lie.

So instead, she forced a smile and said, "Let's not get ahead of ourselves. Your symptoms are concerning, but the blood test will tell us what we're dealing with."

QUINTA

YEAR: 2179

Quinta was perched on a stool just on the med clinic side of the pass-through window into the microbiology lab, waiting impatiently, when her overlay flashed with a notification. She was surprised to see an incoming call from her dad.

"Hey," she answered, constrained to audio only because she was still in the hot, bulky biosuit. But her father's end connected with video, and she was surprised to see a nurse bent over a patient behind him, bright surgical lights shining above her. "Are you calling me from the OR?"

She could hear the tell-tale metallic clack of instruments being dropped on a tray and the beeping of monitors in the background.

"Taking five to hydrate while Dr. Nilsen closes," her father explained, then took a sip from a straw, the contents just out of view. Quinta's mouth watered and a quick wave of exhaustion washed over her.

ALERT: Hydration levels dropping, four percent of body weight lost.

Quinta blinked away the warning. She could see exhaustion in her father's features as well. His surgical cap kept his salt-and-pepper hair neatly tucked away, but his khaki scrubs were darkened with sweat around the collar. "How did it go?"

"It was a success, and now we have one more doctor trained on lung decortication. The patient had bronchospasm during intubation so I'm going to stay for a while to help with post-op monitoring." He glanced off-screen for a moment, checking what was going on on the table, then refocused on Quinta. "But I didn't call to tell you about my surgery. What's happening with your patient?"

"We're still waiting for labs," Quinta said.

"I'm working as fast as I can," Dr. Ito announced from the microbio lab, his tone undeniably irritated.

"Remember, the statistical probability it's Glass is extremely low," her father said. "There have only been two outbreaks in the last century."

Yeah, two outbreaks that killed off fifty percent of the population each time. And if Terra was patient zero for a new outbreak, every death that followed would be squarely on Quinta's shoulders. "You haven't seen her veins," she said. "They're so visible. And she's feverish and a little disoriented."

"I know it's scary," he said. "My first time doing the Glass protocol, I was a nervous wreck and even though it was a false alarm, I didn't want to go home to you and Mom afterward… you know, just in case the test was wrong."

"What did it end up being?"

"Perchlorate exposure from the hydroponic system," he said. "You know there are more conditions that present with fever and pallor than just Glass."

A voice behind him called, "Dr. Voss, we're ready to bring him out of sedation."

"I've got to go," he told Quinta. "You're doing all the right things. I'll buy you a cup of Candor dark when I get home and you can brief me on the case."

When the call ended, Quinta peeked back through the pass-through window and saw Dr. Ito and his assistant conferring in low voices. Quinta strained to hear. "Well?"

Dr. Ito came to the window. "It's not Glass. No trace of V. martialis, or any other bacterium."

"Could it have mutated again?" Quinta knew she sounded paranoid, but the consequences for being wrong were too dire.

"Not so much that we wouldn't recognize it."

Quinta nodded, suddenly feeling ten times hotter and thirstier in her biosuit. "Thank you." She opened her overlay again and sent a quick message to Cydra.

NOT GLASS. I think Dr. Ito was getting ready to kill me for camping in front of his window. Moving on to standard blood panels.

As she slid off her stool, she sent a second message, this one to her dad.

You were right. Not Glass. How could you be so confident?

His reply was simple: *Experience. You'll get there too, don't worry.*

LIRA

YEAR: 2083

Ada nodded in and out of sleep all afternoon, and Lira listened to the sounds of the clinic. Dr. Kalb finally gave that poor man next door an anti-emetic, and after a couple hours, the stereophonic sounds of agony gave way to an uneasy rhythm of medical noises.

The steady beep of monitors.

The shuffle of feet as the nurses made their rounds.

The occasional groan or whimper that made Lira imagine horrible things going on in the other rooms.

Once while Ada's nurse, Pema, was changing her fluid bag and Ada was sleeping fitfully, Lira whispered, "Are they going to be okay?"

"I hope so," Pema said with a grim expression. "Some of them took a lot of radiation."

But not Ada, Lira reassured herself. Ada only took a little on her arms. Ada wasn't as sick as the others.

When the nurse left, Lira double-blinked to activate her retinal display and asked softly, "How strong was the solar flare today? Respond via overlay until otherwise instructed."

She didn't want Valence to respond over the room speakers – Ada was tossing and turning, but she was mercifully asleep and Lira didn't want to risk waking her. Instead, she read:

Solar flare classification: X1.2

Peak emission: 1100 hours

Interior exposure averaged over elevated radiation window: 0.03 grays

---

Lira tried to remember what she'd learned during training all those months ago about units of radiation and the allowable exposure limits, but couldn't recall. She asked softly, "What are the safe limits for single-dose radiation exposure?"

An entry from the colony manual appeared.

Per colony medical standards, the following thresholds define maximum acceptable levels for single-dose ionizing radiation exposure in humans:

   <0.05 grays: No significant clinical effects expected
   0.05 to 0.25 grays: Low-dose exposure, no intervention required

---

Lira paused. "Wait, 0.03 grays is the dose I got indoors. What dose did the dig crew get?"

A section of the solar event report popped up.

Ten members of the sector five dig crew were exposed to an unshielded skylight during the solar flare for approximately three hours. None

*wore pressure suits, and several had shed layers due to rising temper-
atures inside the module, which had not yet been connected to air
conditioning units.*

Average exposure to unshielded extremities: 4.1 grays

Estimated core body exposure, with protective clothing: 2.7 grays

---

Lira was starting to feel sick herself. She switched back over to
the Radiation Exposure Limits document and scanned further
down the list.

---

*>2.0 grays: Acute radiation syndrome likely, requires medical treat-
ment; onset 1-6 hours*

*>4.0 grays: Severe radiation syndrome expected; morbidity probable
without intervention*

Now Lira was practically hyperventilating, and she double-
blinked to clear the screen. Ada was getting intervention. The dig
crew had come in as soon as they started showing symptoms, and
Nurse Pema was in here every half-hour checking Ada's vitals and
replacing her IV and keeping her medicated enough to sleep
through the worst of it.

She was being treated.

This didn't apply to her.

Lira put her head down on the edge of the bed, careful not to
bump Ada's arm. She'd watched Dr. Kalb change the bandages
earlier. The skin underneath had been angry and peeling away,
intolerably painful if it weren't for the meds.

LIRA

YEAR: 2083

t must have been dinnertime because a new nurse brought trays of food around for all the patients. She left one for Lira too, but both trays sat untouched on the table next to the bed. Ada's dark brown skin was becoming ashen in spite of the sheen of sweat that remained on her cheeks and brow no matter how often Lira gently mopped her face with a damp cloth.

"You should eat," Lira said when Ada's eyes fluttered open. "They brought soup. Don't move your arms, I can feed it to you."

"You first," Ada said. "Don't starve yourself on my account."

"Together," Lira compromised. She scooted her chair closer to the bedside and picked up a spoon. She swallowed a spoonful, then dipped it into the bowl again and held it up to Ada. "It's good. Cream of broccoli."

Ada dutifully took the spoon into her mouth, but Lira saw her lips curl and she grimaced as she swallowed. She turned her head away when Lira tried to offer her a second spoonful. "I can't right now, babe, I'm sorry."

Fear rippled through Lira as she thought about Torres next door.

He was way worse off than Ada. He'd gotten a much higher dose. The fear that Ada was just a few hours behind him on the radiation sickness train roared into the forefront of Lira's mind and she shoved it down just as fast.

"Are you feeling nauseous?" she asked.

Ada shook her head. "I'll eat in a few minutes, I promise. Eat yours before it gets cold."

But Lira pushed the tray table away. She reached for Ada's hand on instinct and stopped just in time. The blisters were getting worse, starting to peek out around the edges of the bandages. Lira put her hand on Ada's thigh instead and leaned close. She whispered, "Did they do this?"

Ada let her head fall back on her pillow. "I don't know. I don't think so."

"We hoped they were done with you, but it's only been three months since your trial. They let you out because they needed diggers, but they could have been–"

"It wasn't just me," Ada said, lifting her head to look toward the door. "There were ten of us in that module, and none of them did anything to deserve this."

"That we know of."

The thought that the entire dig crew could have been targeted never would have crossed Lira's mind before she met Ada. For the first few months, she'd thought Ada's theories were insane, delusional.

After all this time working for the company that ran this colony, Lira no longer thought Ada's theories were crazy.

Ada moved her arm, ever so carefully, and laid her blistered hand on top of Lira's. "There are easier ways to kill me than all this, we both know that." She gave Lira a thin, tense smile, her dimples making a brief appearance. "Face it, babe, you were right – construction is dangerous."

Lira smiled too, the first genuine one since she arrived in the med clinic, and put her other hand on top of Ada's. She grimaced, her whole body curling in toward the pain, and Lira pulled her hand away.

"I'm so sorry!"

"It's okay," Ada said. "I'm okay."

Lira nodded. "That's right, you are." She let out a chuckle that was more like a nervous expulsion of air. "Hey, you're not dying, so if this was a VossCorp assassination attempt, they failed."

Ada grinned again, a little easier this time. "Hey, what time is it?"

"It's a little after 1800 hours," Lira provided from the clock in her overlay.

"The rabbits will be wanting their dinner," Ada said. "You should go feed them."

Lira shook her head. "I'm not leaving your side."

"But they need to eat–"

"Jamila's taking care of them," Lira fibbed. Jamila was with them hours ago, but that didn't mean she'd stayed. She had duties of her own. And Ada was right – a rabbit's digestive tract was a sensitive thing that didn't tolerate emptiness well.

Just a little longer… until I get some food in her and she falls asleep again, Lira told herself. She reached for the damp cloth. She folded it until she found a new, cool area and dabbed it along Ada's hairline. Her short hair was damp with sweat and her lips were taking on a grayish-purple hue. Lira glanced toward the door, wondering if she'd just be scaring everybody if she called the nurse in here to check it out.

"How are your arms feeling?" she asked.

"Like I dipped them in twin hornets' nests."

"Any numbness or tingling?"

"No… I don't think so. Why?"

Lira was silently querying Valence for signs and symptoms of cyanosis in humans, and cross-referencing the progression of acute radiation syndrome. The lists didn't seem to match up, but then, Lira was a veterinarian, not a medical doctor.

"Never mind. Think you can have another spoonful of soup?"

"Maybe with some anti-nausea meds," Ada said. "I'm sorry."

Lira used her overlay to call the nurse, then asked, "What are you sorry for?"

"Being sick," Ada said. "Maybe worse than we thought."

LIRA

YEAR: 2083

ira got Ada to eat her soup after the meds kicked in, and Ada fell asleep pretty quickly after that. Lira didn't go back to the rabbitat like she'd promised she would. Instead, she slept in the chair, waking up often to check on Ada and try to find a more comfortable position.

Ada's skin just kept getting grayer, and her temperature was rising. The overnight nurse was keeping as close an eye on her as she could, but several times, Lira heard patients in other rooms calling for help, or their monitors sounding alarms that startled her out of sleep. Ada wasn't the top priority, and Lira was grateful for it.

It meant she wasn't as bad as them.

Ada's limbs twitched and her eyelids fluttered in her sleep. Dreaming, or struggling against the pain? Lira didn't know. She slept fitfully and infrequently herself, wondering if the rabbits were hungry, feeling guilty for not having the bandwidth to even reach out to Jamila and ask for help.

"Start chest compressions!"

That was what jolted Lira awake at 0130, the sound of frantic lifesaving measures in the room next door. She sat bolt upright, listening to a half-dozen monitors going off and the staff shouting urgent orders at each other.

She looked to the bed, where Ada was wide awake, propped on her elbows. "Torres?"

"I think so."

Lira reached for Ada, gripping her shoulder. She'd turned off the overhead lights around 1900 hours. Now, the treatment room was illuminated only by the crack at the bottom of the door and the glow of the wall display reporting all of Ada's vitals. The two of them sat in the dark and listened to the sounds of Torres coding and the medical team trying desperately to save him.

There was the elevated beep-beep-beep of Ada's heart rate.

And then the distinctive sound of a flatline next door.

"We're losing him!"

"Push atropine, one mil."

They waited. Lira barely breathed.

And then, almost too quiet to hear from one room over, the overnight doctor said, "Time of death, 0143 hours."

Lira watched the shadows of feet along the floor, the awful parade of them leaving Torres' room. Then someone knocked and opened Ada's door. It was the nurse who'd given Ada an anti-nausea med so she could eat her soup. She asked softly, "How are you feeling?"

"Torres died?" Ada asked, breathing a little too fast and rubbing her eyes.

"He was exposed to the largest dose of radiation," the nurse said, trying to be comforting. She stepped into the room. "Since you're awake, would you mind if I turn the light on to check your vitals?"

"Please," Lira answered for Ada. She didn't like how fast Ada's heart rate was, telling herself that was to be expected considering they'd just listened to Torres die.

The nurse dialed the light up slowly to keep from blinding

them. She was looking at Ada as the room lightened and she gasped, then quickly tried to school her face into blank professionalism.

Lira looked from the nurse to Ada.

She gasped too.

Ada was blinking rapidly, still rubbing her eyes. "My vision's blurry. What's going on?"

The nurse gently took Ada's wrists, lowering her hands from her eyes.

"Your eyes," Lira stuttered.

"What?" Ada asked, panic pinching her throat.

Where they used to be a deep, chocolate brown, Ada's pupils and irises were milky white, like the worst, longest neglected cases of cataracts that Lira used to see back home in her practice.

"Dr. Rollins?" the nurse called loudly. "Can you come in here, please?"

Anxiety jumped in Lira's chest again, and she grabbed for Ada's thigh. "What is it?"

"Am I blind?" Ada nearly shouted, her pallid face reflecting Lira's fear.

"We've begun seeing this in the others, too," the nurse told her, then called again, more urgently, "Dr. Rollins!"

QUINTA

YEAR: 2179

uinta moved down the dining hall line, peeking at what was on offer. The standard fare – a single portion of which was available to every citizen free of charge – was mushroom loaf in gravy. Quinta spied a lentil stew, which her overlay told her cost ten credits, and she could smell something sweet and rich for dessert.

Her stomach was roaring. She'd hardly eaten breakfast because she was nervous and excited about her first day alone in the clinic, and then she'd been too busy and scared to eat the cricket protein bar Cydra tried to give her while they were in lockdown.

"I'll have two portions of the mushroom loaf with a bowl of lentil stew, please," she said when it was her turn to order.

"Of course, Dr. Voss. Would you like a serving of root mash for ten credits?" the server asked. "It was just harvested this morning."

"Yes, please." Quinta watched him heap an extra-large portion onto her plate, then add a generous ladle of gravy over the mash and the mushroom loaf. In the top corner of her vision, she saw twenty credits being deducted from her Exchange account – even though the massive mound of root mash was more like one and a half servings. She glanced at the citizen waiting in line right behind her, and sure enough, his eyes were on her abundant portion sizes.

He said nothing as she took the tray and scurried away to her usual table.

It's Valence's job to make sure everything is fair, not yours, her mother would have reminded her if she was here. But the family dining table was empty and Quinta sat down alone.

She'd worked extra hard today. The job of making sure the hab didn't succumb to its third fatal Glass outbreak had fallen on her shoulders alone, and she'd handled it perfectly. That was why she got an extra-large helping of root mash – because she'd burned a lot of calories today in that biosuit.

She took a big mouthful of mushroom loaf, sighing with relief as her stomach finally stopped screaming at her, and looked around the dining hall. Her dad was still helping with post-op in sector three, of course, and the hab map said that her mother was in the central commons, the hub in the middle of the wheel shape that made up the habitat. That usually meant she was in a meeting with the other colony leaders, and she'd probably miss dinner entirely.

The dining hall was packed at the height of dinnertime. There were citizens standing around the perimeter, craning their necks to look for an empty spot, and others leaving with their trays, having given up on getting a seat. The din of conversation and cutlery filled the air, and the ceiling display was projecting a spectacular sunset full of reds and oranges and even purples. It was, apparently, what the sky used to be like on Earth, but Quinta always secretly suspected some artist had gotten creative when they were programming the display. How could a sky have so many brilliant colors? The earth had been destroyed close to a century ago – it wasn't like anyone could call out the lie if it was one.

"Quinta!"

She straightened, a smile coming to her lips as she spotted her best friend weaving his way through the crowd toward her table, tray in hand. Castor Marcellus was only a few months younger than her and they'd been all but inseparable ever since the nursery. He'd shot up almost ten centimeters in the last few years, and he sat down somewhat clumsily across from her, still not used to his own height.

"Heard you had quite a day," he said.

She nodded. "Did the lockdown mess up your day much?"

"Well, I got trapped in the server room for a few hours and it gets pretty hot in there," Castor said. "What happened?"

"Just a false alarm," Quinta said. "Hypersensitivity pneumonitis."

Castor shook his head. "Whatever that means."

"Basically, an allergic reaction," Quinta explained. "Hopefully to a contaminant and not something that's normally present in her work module, or else she'll have to apply for a reassignment."

"Must have been terrifying, thinking it was Glass," Castor said, shaking his head.

"I don't want to think about it while I eat. Tell me about your day."

Castor rolled his eyes. "Getting stuck in the server room was the highlight. You'd think I was still in my apprenticeship, the way my dad breathes down my neck."

"Still micromanaging you, huh?" Quinta returned her attention to her food, taking too-big bites to quell her hunger.

"When the lockdown finally ended, he made me reconfigure an entire data relay because I used a shortcut he didn't approve of," Castor grumbled.

He'd started apprenticing under his father in the computer systems lab at the same time Quinta began her own apprenticeship, but training as a computer engineer didn't take nearly as long as becoming a full-fledged doctor. He'd finished training last year, with the hope that would mean his dad would finally trust him with the colony's delicate programming. So far, Rio Marcellus hadn't shown any signs of noticing that his son had graduated.

"I can't talk about work anymore," Quinta said with a sigh,

taking a scoop from her root mash and plopping it onto his tray. As hungry as she was, she couldn't eat it all and she wasn't allowed to let it go to waste.

"Thanks."

"Did you see who we're scheduled to play next week?" she asked.

The two of them were on the same team in the adult Parallax league, and so far this season, they'd been systematically kicking all the other teams' butts.

"Dorm 2B," Castor said. "They have that new striker. I don't remember his name, but he's incredible at trick shots."

KELLAN

YEAR: 2179

Kellan was still studying the schematic, trying to discern whether there was any good reason for the valve into the laundry module to be like it was and who decided on such a stupid way to draw the manifold, when he heard footsteps squeaking over the resin-coated floors behind him. A short, stocky woman with a tool belt and bandana-wrapped hair appeared, followed by two younger men.

"Shift change," she announced. "You three have been on duty since what, 0500?"

"0430," Kellan corrected, not looking up from his tablet. "Jace, Echo, you go. I want to monitor the airflow for a little longer–"

"What, we're not up to the job?" The woman – Vallis, head of the night crew – crossed her arms. "Protocol says you clock out after eight hours. Bet you didn't even take lunch."

"Nope," Jace tattled.

"We found something weird," Kellan told her. "The airflow through the manifold was rerouted without documentation."

"Kellan fixed it," Echo added. "Everything should be functioning properly now."

"We'll monitor it," Vallis promised, and when she saw the hesitation still flickering in Kellan's eyes, she held out her hand. "Hand over the tablet. You're too much like your mom, Reilly – you think the system will fall apart if you don't personally oversee it."

"It's not that, it's just–"

"You don't trust it," Vallis filled in. "I get it. But burnout is more deadly than equipment failure. Go home."

Echo's hand brushed Kellan's sleeve. "She's right. Fresh eyes on this will be good anyway."

Reluctantly, Kellan handed over the tablet, pointing out the area in question on the schematics. "Watch this valve, in case it's malfunctioning and seals itself again."

"Got it," Vallis said, already absorbed in what was on the display.

Kellan, Jace and Echo made their way out of the maintenance tunnel toward a decontamination shower. They were strategically placed all around the sector, but here, there was only one so Echo took the first turn. Standing next to the regolith and resin wall, careful not to touch it, Kellan was acutely aware that his skin was sticky with sweat, and his normally curly hair was still plastered to his face and matted with grease.

His wrists and knees ached from crawling in the air shaft, and Jace didn't look much better. Before the compressor emergency, the three of them had been descaling the condenser coils in the water reclamation system, which was dirty, exhausting work. On top of that, they'd had to listen to the Blinkers' alarms wail about a Glass lockdown the whole time.

Long before Kellan was born, a team of NPCs – the Non-Participants, Valence liked to call them because they refused to play her games – had gone around and disconnected all the cameras and speakers they could find in sector four. That way they didn't have to listen to all-colony announcements and the tones that told the Blinkers it was time to go to breakfast or start their shifts or whatever other intrusive orders the AI liked to bark out.

But the safety alarms were tied into the life support systems. They couldn't be turned off, unless you didn't want oxygen anymore. So every few months, the NPCs had to listen to the Blinkers' Glass drills for a few hours.

This one was supposedly not a drill, which did make it harder to concentrate on the work at hand. But the NPCs had their own protocols for these things. Seal off the airlock into the central commons, let Valence handle the air exchange between the modules – she cut them all automatically for containment's sake – and hope for the best.

At least it was all over by the time the compressors failed. Having to do that critical task with a splitting headache and a paranoid heat creeping up his neck would not have been good.

Echo emerged from the decon shower, dressed in an oversized set of coveralls. "Hit the showers, Reilly," she said, hooking her thumb over her shoulder. "You smell like air shaft dust."

The decon shower was a cramped metal stall tucked into a nook in the regolith-brick hallway. Kellan pulled the door closed and undressed in the changing alcove, then stepped into the shower stall. The tile was already slick, and he took a wide stance, arms held out from his body as he punched a button on the wall. Lukewarm water rained down in a fine mist from the showerhead in the center of the ceiling, as well as out from two of the three walls.

Kellan turned in a slow circle, making sure the water-peroxide mix touched every part of his body. He scrubbed his hands over his face and down his arms, sluicing away the grease and sweat, and when he was clean, he pushed a second button. The water cut off and a jet of ozone replaced it. Kellan squeezed his eyes shut and tried not to breathe as he turned in it. It stung his nostrils and his throat, always his least favorite part of the process.

Once he was clean, Kellan headed for his apartment. As he walked, his eyes automatically scanned along the walls, checking for cracks in the resin. They usually formed in the seams between the wall and the floor, or around openings that had been cut into the regolith brick for things like access panels and everything added to the sector after it was first built a hundred years ago.

Most of the time, cracks formed due to dust storms that battered the hab and shook the walls. Rarely, it was because someone was being careless and damaged the delicate protective layer. Either way, it was a major emergency when one was found.

Kellan pushed open the door to the apartment – a two-bedroom unit that his family shared with another, the Matsudas. There were six of them in all and the apartment was relatively spacious, compared to some others which managed to house up to twelve.

"Kellan, that you?" his grandmother, Solenne, asked. She had her back to him, meticulously scrubbing the tabletop in the middle of the room.

"Yep, just me."

She lay down her cleaning rag, which was little more than a few strings held tentatively together. It had a few more washes in it, but then it'd need to be retired. "Runa just got home a minute ago, she's changing into a fresh coverall. You ready for dinner?"

Kellan's grandmother looked unlike any other living colonist. Her skin had the blue-gray sheen of cyanosis, and her veins traced visible patterns across her neck and up her cheeks, everywhere the skin was thinnest. Kellan had seen photos of her as a girl, when she had jade-green eyes just like his, but now her pupils were milky, obscuring most of her vision, although she compensated well and a lot of people forgot she was almost blind.

Solenne Reilly was the colony's only Glass survivor. In a hundred years and two outbreaks, everyone who contracted the disease had died from it... except for Solenne.

Most people shrank away from her when they saw her striking features. Even when they knew her, and knew she posed no threat, it was an automatic reaction for the breath to catch in the throat, the eyes to quickly avert themselves. To other people, she was a harbinger, a reminder of how perilously close to oblivion they always were.

To Kellan, she was just Grandma Sol.

"You should leave some of that cleaning to me and mom," he said. "You don't have to do all of it every day."

Solenne wagged the rag at him. "It's my way of contributing."

Their bedroom door opened behind her, and Kellan's mother emerged, pulling her hair up into a thick ponytail at the base of her neck. When she spotted Kellan, she asked, "How bad was it?"

"Word got around fast, huh?"

"Three modules locked down with the pressure dropping in each? Yeah, we heard."

"We fixed it," Kellan said. "But the airflow to the laundry module was all messed up with no documentation. It was weird."

"You know, the Blinkers have made changes to the filtration system without telling us before," Runa said as she led the way to the door.

"I think the valve just got jammed shut," Kellan said.

The three of them walked to the dining hall, an oblong room with long metal tables and benches bolted to the floor. Rows of LED light bars on the ceiling cast the whole room in a sterile, clinical glow, and the line for food stretched almost to the door. They'd made the mistake of arriving at peak dinnertime, and Kellan counted at least fifty people ahead of them. A few closest to them kept stealing glances at Solenne and then quickly looking back toward the front of the line.

"We're not getting a seat here tonight," she said, eyeing the crowd.

Runa nodded. "A rabbit's chance in a vacuum."

Kellan heard someone two back in the line whispering, and when he turned toward them, they abruptly stopped pointing at his grandmother, their cheeks coloring.

"We should eat in the apartment," he suggested. "I'll get the food and meet you there."

Solenne and Runa squeezed back through the doorway, careful to avoid brushing up against the regolith wall. Kellan crept forward in line, eventually receiving three plates – standard-ration protein paste formed into a loaf, plus hydroponically grown greens and a small portion of starch. Tonight, it took the form of turnip mash. No gravy. No frills. Not a single extra calorie for spending the afternoon hunched up in an air vent and saving ten lives.

That was okay, though. The greens and turnips had been grown by NPC hands. Everything they had in this sector was earned. And while Kellan would likely go to bed hungry tonight, he wouldn't starve.

LIRA

YEAR: 2083

I t was 0500 hours and this time, the shouting was coming from inside the room.

Lira awoke to Dr. Rollins and two nurses crowded around Ada's bedside, their movements frantic, bumping into Lira's knees as they squeezed past her in the small room. She heard monitors screaming and she saw a laryngoscope changing hands.

"Ada?" She tried to get out of her chair but with so many bodies crowded around the bed, Lira was practically pinned in place.

"I'm still not getting a pulse. Push one mil epinephrine," Dr. Rollins said.

"What's going on?" Lira demanded, crawling up the chair itself to stand on it and get a view over the doctor's shoulder. Ada lay prostrate, her eyes closed, her skin so oxygen-deprived that it was practically blue. Lira could actually see the bigger veins and arteries along her neck and in her cheeks.

Tears started flooding her own throat, practically choking her. "Please save her! She can't die. She didn't even get that much radiation!"

The doctor and nurses ignored her. One nurse working an

Ambu bag over Ada's nose and mouth squeezed rhythmically, and Lira watched the mechanical rise and fall of Ada's chest. She unconsciously timed her own breaths to match.

"Still flatlining. Push another mil of epi," Dr. Rollins ordered as he started chest compressions, his big hands pushing against Ada's sternum with frightening force. He was going to crack her chest right open but Lira didn't care, would help Ada through any amount of healing as long as he kept her heart pumping and kept her here.

"Ada, please," Lira whimpered, her throat constricting as she watched everything over the doctor's shoulder. Her legs felt like boneless rubber, but she kept herself upright on her perch atop the chair, unable to tear her eyes away.

The second nurse took over chest compressions. The first was relentless and methodical with the Ambu bag. They breathed for Ada and they beat her heart mechanically. Dr. Rollins pushed a third milligram of epinephrine and watched the vitals display but there was no rhythm. Not even a faint one.

His shoulders slumped after a while – a couple of seconds, a couple of hours, the time passing was unknowable to Lira. They'd been rotating positions for so long they all looked just as sweaty and sallow as Ada.

"How long has she been coding?" Rollins asked a nurse. The defeat in his posture was familiar. How many times had Lira been in his shoes, forced to surrender when one of her own patients was slipping away despite her pouring every ounce of her medical knowledge and her energy into saving them?

"Twenty-seven minutes," the one doing chest compressions said, and Lira's knees gave out. She fell hard down to the chair.

Twenty-seven minutes without perfusion meant brain death, even if they could keep her body going.

Dr. Rollins seemed to become aware of Lira for the first time since they entered the room. He turned to her with a regretful look on his deep-lined face. "I have to call it." There was a long pause in which Lira's own heart stopped beating. And then he turned back toward the bed and said, "Time of death, 0531."

The nurses stopped working. The Ambu bag was set aside. The display was turned off, the incessant screaming of the flatline alert going with it.

The nurses filed out, taking the crash cart with them, but Dr. Rollins stayed a moment longer. He turned to Lira. "I'm so sorry."

Lira felt like she was standing in an open airlock without a pressure suit. She could hardly hear the doctor's words, the phantom flatline alarm still ringing in her ears. She couldn't bring herself to look at Ada yet, so she blinked and looked up at the doctor. "How many others?" she asked.

The utter exhaustion and slackness in his face said it all, but still, Lira was not prepared to hear his answer. "Ms. Bello was the last. They've all succumbed."

Lira's stomach turned, broccoli soup threatening to repeat on her. "How is that possible?"

Dr. Rollins just shook his head. "I don't know. It shouldn't be. At least not this fast." He glanced at Ada. "Take all the time you need with her."

And then he left the room, closing the pocket door behind him, and Lira summoned the courage to look at her partner for the first time since the monitors were turned off. She lay perfectly motionless in the center of the bed, the sheets and pillow and the damp cloth Lira had been so diligent in keeping on Ada's forehead all cast to the floor when the team was working frantically to save her.

Her eyes were closed, her forehead smooth and peaceful. The dimples that Lira had fallen in love with were no more than subtle indentations in impossibly blue-gray skin.

"Ada..."

They hadn't quite known each other a year. Lira had always told Ada that she couldn't pin down one moment when she'd fallen for her, but that was a lie. The first time they touched, Lira had just gotten a video message from her mother, telling her the government was evacuating Manila and that she wasn't going to leave her home. Lira had been so overwhelmed with fear and frustration and if she'd been on Earth, she would have taken the first flight available and dragged her mother out of the flood area by her hair if she had to.

Lira had barely been holding it together and Ada had pulled her into a completely unexpected embrace, her strong arms tightening around Lira like a constrictor. Lira had melted into her then, and her walls had begun to crumble.

That was the moment.

Lately, she'd been thinking of ways to get the rabbits to help her propose. She'd been cocky, thinking the rest of their lives was a long time.

And now she would never be able to tell Ada she loved her again.

Why hadn't she said it in their last few hours?

God, why hadn't she said it?

Because you didn't think these were *her last few hours,* her rational brain reminded her, from deep down beneath the emotional storm in her head.

"I'm so sorry," Lira told Ada, taking her hand, no longer worried about hurting her. The blisters hadn't worsened, but as Lira examined Ada's skin more closely, she realized she could see every vein and artery on the back of her hand. This was so far beyond cyanosis. Lira had never seen anything like it before: Ada's dark complexion had turned hazy, tinted that low-oxygen blue, but it was more than that. If Lira wasn't touching her, she'd think she was looking at an anatomical model made of fogged-over glass.

Lira set Ada's hand down and retrieved a fresh wash cloth, dampening it. She carefully wiped away the perspiration on Ada's forehead, and along her hairline. Then she leaned forward to kiss her one last time.

QUINTA

YEAR: 2179

Quinta's whole body jolted and she stiffened, expecting to hit the hard floor.

She'd only fallen out of bed after a nightmare a couple of times in her life, but it always started with a jolt like that and ended with a painful thud. She couldn't remember what she'd been dreaming this time, but the thud didn't come.

Instead, she heard her mother's voice, much more shrill than normal. "Quinta! Wake up!"

She realized her mom was clutching her arm. *It really was Glass,* she thought, her eyes popping open as her heart began to race. "What's wrong?"

It was still pitch-dark in her room, too early for Valence to begin the dawn simulations. She could barely make out her mother standing, fully dressed, at the side of her bed, her normally tidy hair full of wisps and flyaways visible against the hallway light behind her.

"Your father is dead."

Quinta's heart went from racing to frozen, and it felt like she was sinking into her mattress, being pulled down by someone else's gravity. "No, that's not possible."

Her father was forty-one years old. He was the smartest doctor this colony had. He was practically immortal in her eyes, so he couldn't be dead.

"Honey."

Quinta shook her head so hard it made her dizzy. He hadn't come home in time for dinner yesterday, and he still wasn't home by the time Quinta turned in for bed. She'd been waiting for him, eager to tell him about her almost-Glass case, but she hadn't thought anything of his absence. There were dozens of times when she was growing up that both her parents had missed her Parallax games and family dinners and trips to the rabbitat, and it happened even more now that Quinta was grown.

Hadrian and Havana Voss had important jobs, and he'd been doing his yesterday late into the night.

"Valence told me not long ago," Havana said softly, sinking down onto the edge of the bed. Her eyes went distant for a moment as she turned the lights up, still dim but now Quinta could see her better. Her undereyes were puffy, like she was desperately holding back tears, and her fair skin was blotchy and uneven.

"No," Quinta insisted. "He can't be. I just talked to him."

She pulled up her messages and checked the timestamp of the last one, then looked at the time. It was nearly 0600, and it'd actually been close to twelve hours since the last message he sent, a voice memo: *Still stuck in post-op. I'm proud of you, Quinta. You did well today.*

A knot of emotion rose in her throat and she called up the colony map, using eye gestures to send a desperate command to locate Hadrian Voss.

Every colonist with a functioning implant showed up as a little red pin on the map. Quinta had looked for her father on it countless times, especially when she was a kid and he was supposed to come to a class presentation or credit ceremony or one of her games. If he wasn't where he promised to be, he was always in his clinic, or sometimes one of the other sectors' clinics helping out.

She scanned all four now – even the NPCs' clinic – but there was no Hadrian pin in any of them. Not in the dining halls, not in any of the medical labs, not making a housecall to one of the residences.

He wasn't on the map.

"Where is he?" she demanded.

"His implant went offline when his vital signs ceased," Havana said, guessing what Quinta was doing. That gravity pressing down on her ramped up a few notches, and Havana reached out and pulled her into a fierce hug, clutching Quinta to her chest so hard she could barely draw a breath.

"How?" she asked into her mother's shoulder. "What happened?"

"There was a malfunction," Havana said. "Valence is still working out why it happened, but something went wrong with the air ventilation system in the sector three clinic. It started dumping CO_2, and then the module went into automatic lockdown. Your father was trapped in there with his surgical patient and an overnight nurse. Really, it's lucky they were running a skeleton crew at that hour."

A wave of petty anger washed over Quinta as she sat upright. He could have come home and been with his family, who also needed him, but everyone in the colony believed Hadrian was so important that his work couldn't be delegated, and he'd started to believe it too. He stayed to monitor another doctor's patient, and it had killed him.

"All three of them…?"

Havana nodded, then added, "It wasn't just the clinic. One of the sector three dorms was affected, downstream of the same malfunctioning air compressor."

Quinta's hand went to her mouth. CO_2 pumping into the vents of a dormitory in the middle of the night, when most people were already asleep, could be very, *very* bad. "Why didn't Valence catch it?"

"She did," Havana said. "She dispatched maintenance crews. They got the vents sealed off until the compressor could be repaired and they broke the dorm airlock open to evacuate it. There are a number of people in critical condition, but no other deaths."

"But Dad…"

"The clinic was much closer to the source of the malfunction," Havana explained. "It received a much larger dose of CO_2 and by the time the crews got in… it was too late."

It felt like there was an invisible hand wrapped around Quinta's heart, squeezing with all its might. If she was Chosen, she might have imagined it was Valence's hand.

The two of them sat in silence for a few moments, Havana's hand rising like she was going to brush over Quinta's shoulder, or maybe pull her into another hug, but then it dropped limply in her lap. Quinta blinked numbly, imagining her father lying unconscious on the floor of someone else's clinic, waiting for him to wake up and tell her he was fine.

Then she moved to the edge of the bed, scooting past her mother to stand up. She went to her closet and retrieved a fresh coverall and her white coat.

"Where are you going?" Havana asked.

"If there are dozens of people in critical condition, sector three needs all the doctors it can get," she said.

It was what her father would have done.

QUINTA

YEAR: 2179

The half-hour walk to the sector three clinic had been the hardest part of the day. Quinta had been alone, trapped with her thoughts, trying not to imagine her father's final moments.

Whether he'd been in pain.

Whether he'd been scared.

Whether he'd thought about her while he took his final breaths.

The waiting area was packed with sick citizens from the dorm – at least two dozen of them holding their heads, looking nauseous, slumped in their chairs. She spotted Cydra weaving through the crowd. Either she'd had the same idea to come help, or Valence had reassigned her for the day based on patient volume.

That must have left Dr. Liang on her own in sector one.

Quinta would have to finish her apprenticeship under Liang. She hadn't thought of it until now. She only had six more months to do, but she couldn't picture training under anyone but her father. Dr. Liang had never even liked Quinta that much, for reasons she'd never been able to ferret out.

"She's just focused," her father had told Quinta one time when she complained about how harsh Liang was after Quinta took too long to intubate her patient. "She may not have a teacher's mind-set, but she's just as good a doctor as I am. You can learn a lot from her."

She wasn't here now, though, and these patients needed help. As Quinta buttoned up her white coat, she spotted the sector doctor across the waiting area, entering a treatment room. *You went home and let my dad die in here.* The thought raged to the surface, and Quinta forced it down.

Where did he die?

What room was he in?

Where was his body now?

More intrusive thoughts warred for dominance, and instead of listening to them, Quinta went over to Cydra, who was triaging the waiting citizens.

"Hey. Who's the head nurse here?"

"Quinta, I'm so sor–"

She shook her head tightly. "Not now. I need to work so I don't have to think. Head nurse?"

Cydra gave her a pitying look, but pointed to a woman coming up the hallway with her arms loaded with medical tubing and face masks. "Nurse Chen. You should really talk to the doctor if you're gonna help, though."

Quinta ignored that last comment. If she talked to the doctor who was responsible for her father being in this sun-forsaken module when it locked down, she wasn't sure she could keep up her professional tone, at the very least. She marched over to Nurse Chen and relieved her of some of the masks she was juggling, and together they passed them out to all the waiting patients and got them connected to portable oxygen tanks.

As the morning progressed, Quinta sank into her work. She didn't think about her dad, or the fact he was likely lying in the morgue just down the hall. She didn't think about what the colony would do without one of its most highly trained doctors. She didn't wonder why Valence couldn't find a way to save everyone. She monitored the oxygen levels of a teenage boy whose room had gotten an exceptionally high dose of CO_2. She administered antiemetics to an elderly woman. And she prescribed dose after dose of pain reliever for the headaches that virtually all of them suffered from.

Dr. Nilsen cornered her once at the nurses' station, sneaking up behind her and making Quinta jump when he said, "I'm so sorry about your father."

The words pierced through the careful numbness she'd been cultivating, and for an instant, that invisible hand was back around her heart. She turned, looking the tall doctor up and down. He was blond, with faint wrinkles at his temples, at least a decade younger than her father. There were dark circles beneath his eyes, and the collar of his coverall had a dried sweat line on it.

Looking into his eyes, the urge to attack him melted away and Quinta just nodded. "Thank you. He loved teaching. I'm sure he enjoyed spending his last day here with you."

"Dr. Nilsen?" Nurse Chen called. "The patient in room three is ready for you."

He stepped away, and Quinta turned back to the chart she was updating. She could feel the eyes of the patients still sitting in the waiting room. They all knew who she was, and what had happened. A few of them had tried to console her, but she had to rebuild that wall of numbness if she was going to get through the day.

"Dr. Voss, are you available?" Cydra asked from a treatment room doorway.

Quinta nodded, setting down her tablet. "What have you got?"

For just a moment, she was back in her own sector, before that filtration system broke and changed her whole damn life. For a split second, she thought Cydra was about to say, *Possible Glass case* and she'd get to run through the whole day over again, do it differently, insist her father come home so no one got stuck in this dust-damned clinic.

"Eight-year-old girl. Mild symptoms, mostly scared," Cydra said. "She and her mother have been waiting a while."

In the room, Quinta found a small girl with dark braids wearing an oxygen mask and clutching a worn rabbit-fur stuffie. The pelt was white with black spots and it made Quinta's stomach twist for a moment. She'd owned a rabbit with that coloring once – a real live one, not a doll – for just a few days, around her twelfth birthday.

She shook off the memory as she met the eyes of the child's mother standing beside her. "Hi, I'm Dr. Voss." She shook the mother's hand, then turned to the girl. "What's your name?"

"Callie," she mumbled through the large oxygen mask dominating her face. She tightened her grip on the stuffie. "My head hurts."

"I know, honey. Let's get you fixed up, okay?"

Quinta turned to the display wall, reading through Callie's vital signs, and her mom said quietly, "I can't believe you're here, Dr. Voss. After what happened... I can't imagine how difficult this must be. You're so generous to come give us your time."

Patients had been saying things like that all morning, mentioning her dad, offering condolences. A few of them fingered Heart of Mars pendants, and one had offered to pray to Valence for her. Quinta couldn't do much more than nod tightly and croak out a thank you or else she would lose control of that wall of numbness.

"Every hand for the colony," she said, then moved on to adjusting the flow of oxygen into the mask. She turned to Cydra. "Don't we have any kid-sized masks?"

"I'll see if one's available," she said, then left the room.

"The maintenance teams were amazing," Callie's mom continued. "They were at our airlock almost instantly after the alarms started to go off, and they ripped it open like it was nothing. If I hadn't had to carry Callie by myself, we would have gotten out faster. Valence sees what we cannot."

Another proverb. Quinta made a non-committal *hmm* sound and the woman didn't seem to notice how disengaged she was.

It wasn't true in this case, was it? Valence *hadn't* seen the problem until it was too late for Hadrian and two other souls.

"Did you hear how it happened?" the mother asked.

"I haven't had much time for details," Quinta said, curt enough she hoped the woman would take the hint. She softened her tone and bent to Callie's eye level. "Will you let me listen to your breathing, sugar beet?"

The little girl nodded and Quinta put her stethoscope in her ears. Even through the echo chamber of the earpieces and the rhythmic rise and fall of the girl's healthy lungs, she heard Callie's mother say, "People are saying the NPCs did something to the air filtration system."

Quinta's hand stilled. "What?"

"I overheard the maintenance supervisor talking when we were in the waiting room," the woman continued. "Apparently, the air routing was changed without authorization. They think sector four tampered with it."

"Why would they do that?" Quinta asked, pulling her stethoscope down to her neck.

"They've been complaining about their air quality for weeks," somebody in the waiting room said, and then he poked his head through the open door. "Instead of putting in a request the right way, they just decided to take some of ours."

Quinta stepped between the man and Callie. She wasn't doing anything particularly private, but it was the principle of it. "Sir, can you please step back into the hallway? I'm seeing a patient."

He ignored her, turning to Callie's mom. "My cousin works in central supply. Says they've been stealing resources for years."

"The whole sector should be locked down until Valence figures out who did it," Callie's mom said, and Quinta used her overlay to shut the door. The man from the waiting area had to jump back or get his nose clipped, and Callie's mom just looked puzzled. "Are you okay, doctor?"

"Fine," Quinta said. "Callie's oxygen levels are normal and her lungs sound good. I don't think she needs any more oxygen, but I'll have Nurse Tavara bring something for the headache, and once it starts to work, you can go."

"Where? The dormitory is still airing out, and it's not safe until the airlock is fixed," she said.

"Valence is making temporary assignments to other quarters," Quinta explained. "You'll find yours in the Exchange."

The hab was crowded as it was. People in this sector would be doubling and tripling up until the dorm could be made habitable again. Maybe the NPCs were used to being packed together like filter fibers, but the citizens weren't.

"You can stay here as long as you need to," she added before stepping out of the treatment room.

There were still close to a dozen people waiting to be seen, the portable oxygen tanks scattered around only adding to the visual chaos. The man who'd intruded on Callie's room was holding court, a handful of people listening to his diatribe against the Non-participating Colonists.

"I'm not saying they did it on purpose," he was ranting, "but the problem is they don't *care* if they hurt us."

"They only care about themselves. It's their whole *thing*!" someone else said, which got rumbles of agreement.

Quinta found Nurse Chen and Cydra both behind the desk. "The waiting area is getting rowdy. People are blaming the NPCs for what happened."

"They're not wrong, from what I hear," Nurse Chen said.

"Maybe not, but we can't have a riot in the clinic," Quinta said.

She'd seen it happen, elsewhere in the hab. A small idea sparks a panic, and soon it's all the Auditors can do to maintain order. These people had just been through a Glass scare only to be woken up in the middle of the night to alarms blaring for the second time in twenty-four hours. Half of them were sick from the gas inhalation, and the last thing any of them needed was to be carted off to the jail cells or the Emotional Equilibrium Module for a time-out.

"We need to clear as many of them out of here as possible. Anyone stable enough to leave should get their temporary room assignment from Valence and go, before they start feeding off each other's anger."

"Good idea," Chen nodded. "I'll start discharge paperwork for those with normal readings."

"Cydra, did you find a kids' mask?" Quinta asked.

Cydra shook her head. "They're all in use. I can send for one from another sector if you need it."

Quinta shook her head. "Can you just bring Callie something for her headache? She can be discharged after, she and her mother don't need to be sticking around here."

"I'll take care of it," Cydra promised, but instead of leaving the nurses' station, she narrowed her eyes on Quinta. "Have you eaten anything today? It's past lunch and I haven't seen you stop working since you got here."

Quinta waved away the concern. "I'm fine."

"Dr. Voss–"

"Really, I'm fine," Quinta insisted, cutting her off more sharply than she intended. She immediately regretted her tone and added, "I just need to keep moving right now, keep focusing on the patients. I don't want to stop."

Cydra didn't push further, but her expression made it clear she wasn't convinced. She opened a drawer at the back of the station and retrieved painkillers for Callie, then headed for the treatment room.

Quinta turned back to the waiting area. The loud man had pulled a tablet out from somewhere, and he was pointing to something on it, fervently explaining about vents and schematics. His little group of followers were nodding along, their brows all down-turned in anger.

Hadrian would have known exactly what to say to diffuse the situation. He would have done something to bridge the gap, to remind them that even though they lived separately and didn't follow the citizens' rules, the NPCs were human too, and they were just trying to survive like everyone was.

Quinta wasn't her father. She didn't know what to say, and there was something small but calcifying deep in her gut that kept whispering, *They're not human. They're not trying to survive. They killed your father!*

LIRA

YEAR: 2083

The clinic was a ghost town when Lira emerged from Ada's room, the staff shuffling from room to silent room, turning off lights and closing doors. Leaving Ada behind felt like a betrayal, like Lira was abandoning her, but what could she do? Not bring her home, that wouldn't bring her back.

Lira walked zombie-slow back to sector one, passing people who were just beginning their days, looking forward to a hearty breakfast of scrambled chickpeas and cricket chorizo, smiling at her as they passed. Completely clueless that the colony had just had the single largest fatality event in its history – by a wide margin.

Would Valence announce it soon? Send out an all-colony alert?

Or would it be swept under the rug, like a lot of things Lira had learned VossCorp would prefer to keep quiet?

"Hey," Yuri from the hydroponic gardens waved when he saw her coming up the hall. "How's Ada? Jamila told me she got hurt."

Lira didn't answer. She wasn't sure she could have if she'd wanted to, and she definitely did not want to.

"Lira?" the sun-weathered man called as she passed him

without so much as looking him in the eye. As Lira kept mechanically moving forward, she heard him mutter, "Rude."

Jamila. The name made Lira remember that she had responsibilities beyond crawling into her bed and rotting there. Jamila had made sure the rabbits didn't escape the rabbitat and go wandering the halls yesterday, but had anyone thought to give them dinner?

Maybe Valence had assigned the task to someone.

Lira pulled up the colony map in her overlay and saw no one in the rabbitat. The rabbits needed their breakfast after a long night. They could go into GI stasis if they didn't get their meals on time. Once their guts stopped moving, things got painful. They stopped wanting to eat, and worst-case scenario, they'd be dead within twenty-four hours.

Ada had died in eighteen.

What the hell happened back there?

Instead of taking a right toward her dorm, Lira turned left toward the rabbitat. It was still early, so there was little likelihood she'd run into anyone else, at least.

The rabbitat was in perfect order when Lira arrived. Jamila had loaded all the rabbits in the hutches and secured them all, and she'd even tidied up the toys Lira had left scattered across the grass. The autofeeder still had a few pellets from last time she'd filled it, but it wasn't enough for a full day. The rabbits' ears perked up when they heard her. Perhaps a Pavlovian response because she was the human who provided the carrot greens.

Or maybe they never got dinner last night.

Guilt and mourning warring in her chest, Lira went around to the hutches and opened all of them, and bunnies started flooding out. A few went and nibbled at the grass, and a couple of the friendlier ones came over and tried to take a nip out of Lira's shoes. Ordinarily, she would have tried to avoid that – all the rabbits she ever knew had a weird affinity for the texture of rubber, but once the soles were gone, there'd be no replacing them until the next resupply.

Right now?

The rabbits could eat her clothes off her back and she'd barely notice. You didn't need clothes or shoes to lie down and wallow, which was all she wanted to do as soon as the rabbits' needs were met.

She went over to the refrigerated bin where she stored about a day's worth of greens at a time. The supply was getting low. Making runs to hydroponics to restock had been one of Ada's regular tasks before she was imprisoned. These days, Jamila brought the greens to Lira most days to save her a trip.

Lira was sorely tempted to just dump the entire bin in one big pile in the grass – that was about as much energy as she had – but there were a number of bucks and does in heat right now. There would be fighting. So instead she forced herself to give enough of a crap to pull the greens out in handfuls, walking in a wide circle around the play area and dropping breakfast here and there.

The rabbits fanned out to pick their piles, and Lira dropped the empty bin at her feet.

If she went to her bed right now, she'd have to drag herself back here in twelve hours for dinnertime. Well, to hydroponics for a bin refill first, and then back here. And she didn't need to open her overlay to know there were a half-dozen daily tasks waiting for her in the Exchange. Valence would start popping up increasingly insistent alerts in her line of vision if she neglected them for too long. And if she let a whole day go by without recording breeding pair biometrics, the AI would start using the speaker system in the ceiling to nag Lira into action.

She knew that because she'd seen Valence do it one time when Ada left *Conduct karyotype analysis on breeding pairs* unfinished for close to a week because she had not the slightest clue how to do it. Lira had never studied genetics deeply enough to help, but Valence had been rather unpleasant until the two of them did enough research to finish the task.

Poorly, for sure, and possibly not accurately, but enough to appease Valence.

Lira sank down to her knees in the grass. The regolith beneath it gave pliantly, in an Earthy way that Lira had no idea she would miss until she got here. A lot of the floors in the prefab sectors were raised, with a network of cables and other life support systems running underneath them. Great for the maintenance crew, weirdly buoyant for Lira, even with the reduced gravity. She'd been here five months and still wasn't used to it. This dirt, though… it was red and much finer than anything you'd find on Earth, but sitting in the grass felt the same.

She put her hands on the soft, cool blades, then lowered herself down to it.

It prickled her cheek, and Valence must have run a rain cycle not long ago because Lira could feel her clothes dampening. She lay on her belly and closed her eyes, letting the wetness seep into her bones.

How could they all be dead? Ten people died from a solar flare that Valence had forecasted would be mild.

It wasn't an accident, Lira thought once again, but again pushed the thought away.

Ada was right, the AI's primary objective was to protect the colony. Even if it saw Ada as a major threat, its programming would prevent it from allowing nine innocents to die to remove her from the equation. Plus, she'd already been punished.

Lira felt long, sharp incisors sink into the toe of her shoe. She yanked it back, and a second later, there was a rabbit on her back.

It hopped up her spine and soon she felt more nibbling, this time on the ends of her hair.

"That's great, get my split ends for me," she murmured into the grass.

Ada would have laughed at that. Why go to the colony salon when you have rabbits at home?

LIRA

YEAR: 2083

Lira lost track of time pretty quickly, but the digital sky over the play area was much brighter now, so she assumed it was around noon. She'd been drifting in and out of consciousness, not quite sleeping but unwilling to be awake. She tried not to think at all, periodically earning a few seconds of distraction whenever a rabbit decided to use her as a platform or binkied dangerously close to her face.

She was alert now because someone was hailing her at the rabbitat door. From the increasing frequency and urgency of the pings, they'd been trying for a while.

Lira pulled up her overlay and found a handful of messages from Jamila.

Hey, are you okay?

I heard about Ada, I'm so sorry.

I know you're in there, I can see you on the hab map.

I have rabbit greens.

Lira could see Jamila on the hallway camera outside the rabbitat, but instead of opening the door, she messaged back, *Just leave them.* Then she got a hold of her manners and added, *Thanks.*

She waited, listening in the direction of the thin pocket door, to hear Jamila setting down her basket. Instead, Lira got another message.

No way. Open up, I'm not leaving.

Lira was sure Jamila was not joking. She must be on her lunch break right now if it was noon, but she'd take the credit hit for not returning in time for the rest of her hydroponics shift if she had to. Lira groaned and dragged herself to her feet.

She wouldn't put it past Jamila to make up some excuse to force Valence to open the door for her, or simply wrench the door open herself, and Jamila would never leave if she found Lira lying in a heap on the floor. She looked down. Her coveralls were stained a Christmas tie-dye of regolith red and grass green, and they were damp from the watering.

Jamila would just have to ignore the mess, because all Lira's clean coveralls were in her room.

"Come in," she called, simultaneously triggering the door open.

Jamila stepped inside and set her basket on the ground, then swallowed Lira up in a bear hug. It was so tight Lira thought she heard a rib crack, but she just surrendered to it. Her arms were pinned at her sides anyway.

"I'm so sorry," Jamila said into her hair. "I can't believe it."

"Me neither."

"Oh, Lira." She hugged tighter. "What the hell happened?"

She let go, and Lira noticed a couple rabbits heading for the open door, drawn by the basket of greens. She closed the door, then looked at Jamila. "I can't talk about it right now. I really can't."

If she opened her mouth to describe the first thing about what she'd seen in the med clinic... well, she wasn't sure what would come out, and she couldn't trust that. Jamila had always been their friend, even when the rest of the colony hated Ada, but she'd never come all the way over to Ada and Lira's side about what had happened.

No one had.

Jamila nodded. "I understand." When Lira looked away, Jamila took her by the shoulders, drawing her attention back. "Hey. I really do understand. It took me a long time to come to terms with what happened to Glory. You need to talk about this eventually or the grief is just going to fester – Dr. Lawrence told me that and it was true."

Lira averted her eyes again. Dr. Lawrence was one of the colony psychologists. She hadn't checked the Exchange yet, but she wouldn't be surprised if she had already been assigned a session with him.

That or time in the Emotional Equilibrium Module. An involuntary shiver worked its way up Lira's spine.

"But that day is not today," Jamila finished. "You talk when you're ready, but know that I'm here to listen, okay?"

Lira nodded. She was sure she'd never want to talk about the last twenty minutes of Ada's life, watching her spirit drain out of her ravaged body while three people worked frantically to stop it.

The way her veins stood out.

The cataracts in her eyes.

How suddenly it had all happened.

When it was clear Lira wasn't planning to speak, Jamila let her go at last and retrieved the basket. "I have greens for the day. I'll deliver them for however long you need, so don't worry about that, okay?" She found the empty bin abandoned on the grass and filled it up, then loaded it back into the refrigerator unit. "What about you? Have you eaten?"

"Some broccoli soup."

"How long ago?"

Lira shrugged. "Not sure."

"So you haven't eaten," Jamila said. Her eyes flicked up and to the right momentarily, checking her overlay, then she said, "It's 1300 hours. I can get you something hot from the dining hall if I hurry."

"I'm not hungry."

"I know you're not, but you have to eat. I'll be right back."

Lira sat in an actual chair this time instead of on the floor. She looked down at her coveralls, the material starting to stiffen over the stains as they dried. Jamila hadn't even commented on what a mess she was. It must have been so bad it didn't bear mentioning.

Lira started scanning her overlay to see if there was any information about the fatalities.

She found a report filed by Dr. Rollins in the colony news feed, but she only got a couple sentences in before she saw Ada's name and had to turn off her overlay.

KELLAN

YEAR: 2179

Kellan slouched in his seat, prodding his cricket wrap with disinterest. Ordinarily it was one of his favorite lunches, the iceberg lettuce providing a watery crunch that paired perfectly with the chewy, spicy cricket crumbles, but today he just couldn't get excited.

"You gonna eat that or torture it?" Jace asked, polishing off his own wrap. Cheeks full, he added, "I'll eat it if you don't."

"You know you don't have to say that at every meal, right? I know the offer stands." Poor Jace was a bottomless pit and no matter how many calories Valence allotted and the sector harvested, it was never enough to fill his belly. "Just thinking."

"About?"

Kellan took a bite and washed it down with a swig of Mars mud. It was piping hot, even if there wasn't much else to recommend it.

"If you're still obsessing about that air valve, I swear I'll throw this mug at you," Echo said. She sat across from Kellan and Jace, sketching something on her tablet. She had one of the few without any dents or cracks, and whenever anybody needed something graphic or artistic, they knew who to come to. Her dreadlocks were pulled back in a messy bun, exposing the sharp angles of her cheekbones and the stern downturn of her brows as she concentrated.

"I'm not," Kellan lied. "I checked the sensors this morning. Everything's normal."

He kept hearing strange little hiccups and pauses in the air exchanger whenever he listened to the vents, but it wasn't constant or even regular, and it hadn't just suddenly begun since they made their fixes. The systems were all old, limping along. All there was to do was monitor.

"Told you it was just an accident," Jace said, reaching for a carrot chip on Echo's plate. She swatted him away. "You worry too much."

"No such thing."

They were in the sector commons once again for lunch. The dining hall pretty much always filled up before they got done with their morning work, but the commons was one of the few places in their sector that had a ceiling window so it was nicer in here, anyway.

Granted, right now – and usually – the sky was orangey and overcast, but at least it was a view.

"Anyway," Kellan said, "about that hydro upgrade. I think we should plan out the irrigation channels first. Space is our most limited resource so we need to lay them out as efficiently as possible."

Echo looked up from her tablet. "We're working with limited materials too, though, and if the plants don't have good light it won't matter how many we can fit. The LED panels are so far beyond their prime it's ridiculous. They flicker all the time and they're barely enough to sustain the plants. If we can't figure out how to fix them, there's no point expanding the irrigation channels."

"You know we can fix the lights. We figure everything out eventu-"

"What the hell are you doing here?" someone shouted across

the room. Heads turned as more voices rose, a mix of confusion and anger. Kellan stood, and he had to crane his neck to see over the crowd that had already formed.

"What's going on?" Echo asked, pocketing her tablet. An uncracked one, she guarded it with her life.

"Don't know," Jace said, also rising. "Whoa, I see Blinkers."

"Seriously?" Echo climbed up on the bench to try to see. Kellan was a head and a half taller than her and could just barely make out a cluster of men in pristine coveralls standing at the mouth of the hallway that led into the Blinker sectors. "What are they doing here?"

The noise grew louder – sharp voices, the scrape of chairs, people standing and moving toward the disturbance.

"You two stay here," Kellan said. "I'll check it out."

Echo snorted and jumped down from the bench. "To Deimos with that. I'm coming too."

Jace was not about to be left behind and he started shouldering his way through the crowd ahead of Kellan. It thickened as they approached the hall entrance, NPCs pressing forward, Blinkers standing their ground, shoulder to shoulder with clenched fists. Kellan used his lean frame to his advantage, weaving through gaps and slipping past the broader backs blocking his way. Echo slipped her hand into his so as not to get left behind, and he pulled her through the crowd.

"–come in here throwing accusations!" he heard someone shout.

"We want answers!" a Blinker in clean khaki barked back, furious.

Kellan squeezed between two fabrication workers, finally reaching the front. Five Blinkers stood just inside the commons entrance, unmistakably interlopers with their woven coveralls and leather-soled shoes. One held what looked like a metal pipe at his side, and another clutched a kitchen knife.

"You have no right to be here," an older NPC woman was

saying, arms crossed. "Whatever happened in your sector is your problem."

"Typical," one of the Blinkers grumbled.

"Our problem?" The tallest one stepped forward, his face flushed with anger. "Three of our people are dead because of you! Dozens more are injured!"

Kellan's stomach dropped. Dead? He hadn't heard about any deaths, but then, Blinker news didn't often reach his sector. "Does this have something to do with the Glass alarm?" he wondered to Echo, who just shrugged and held up her hands. *Don't know.*

"We did nothing!" someone shouted at them. "Go back to your own sectors!"

"We know you messed with the air filtration system," another Blinker said, the one holding the pipe at his side. "Changes were logged in the NPC shaft that connects to our air supply!"

"It's our shaft, we have every right to be in it," Kellan heard Jace's voice somewhere behind him.

More voices joined in, overlapping in a chaotic defense:

"That's tank sludge!"

"We maintain our own systems, we don't touch yours!"

"You're blaming us for your system failure?"

But Kellan just kept thinking of what the tallest Blinker said. He tried to raise his voice above the crowd. "What happened? Who died?"

The Blinker in the center – older, with graying temples and mercifully no weapons in his hands – looked Kellan up and down with undisguised contempt. "Massive CO_2 leak in sector three yesterday," he said. "Affected the medical clinic and a dormitory full of people, both downstream of the shaft *you* were working in."

He meant *you* generally. There was no way he could have known he was talking to the man who actually made the change, but it hit Kellan like a metal pipe to the gut anyway.

"We lost Dr. Voss!" one of the Blinkers shouted.

Voss. The name hit Kellan like a second blow. He'd met the man years ago when his mother was sick. He'd been the only one in the whole damn Blinker clinic who treated Runa and Kellan like humans instead of crickets.

He'd also been the father of the girl with the rabbit Kellan had met on that trip.

"A doctor, a nurse and a mechanical engineer," the one with the knife said. "Three highly valuable citizens."

Unlike you, the implication was clear.

"And you think we had something to do with it?" somebody behind Kellan demanded. "Scrap that."

"We know you did," the Blinker with the pipe said, stepping forward. "You rerouted the air flow from the central hub and reversed the exhaust into our sector!"

"That's impossible," Kellan heard Echo's voice beside him. "We never touched the central systems… did we?"

Kellan felt dizzy as confusion and guilt warred inside him. The closed valve. It shouldn't have been like that, and at the time he'd thought it only affected the laundry module. But he hadn't studied the schematics himself, he'd relied on what Echo and Jace were telling him, and they hadn't had the full picture either. He'd spent a lot of time monitoring the system in the past twenty-four hours because something had gnawed at him, telling him it wasn't right.

It never would have occurred to him that what he did had changed something in a Blinker sector.

It shouldn't have been possible.

"You should give us one of your doctors to replace ours," the only female Blinker in the group growled.

"Their doctors couldn't save a cricket with a cracked shell," the pipe-wielder snarled.

The crowd surged forward at the insult, NPCs shouting back:

"You think you're so much better than us?"

"We didn't do anything to you. We never have and still you hate us!"

And then, "You want a fight? Fine, you got it."

Kellan stiffened, knowing what was about to happen. He tried to tuck Echo behind him as the crowd surged forward, pushing him along with them. The Blinkers retreated a step, brandishing their makeshift weapons.

"Back off!" the pipe-wielder shouted, swinging it in a wide arc that forced the front line of NPCs to contract.

But the crowd behind them kept pushing, angry voices rising to a fever pitch. Someone lunged for the pipe. The Blinker dodged and swung, catching a bystander across the shoulder.

"Stop!" Kellan yelled, but his voice was lost in the chaos.

The Blinker with the kitchen knife slashed at the air in front of him, trying to keep the advancing NPCs at bay. A woman next to Kellan grabbed a tray off a nearby table and hurled it at the Blinkers. One of them put his arms up in a cross to deflect it and it clattered to the ground.

"Go back where you came from!" an NPC shouted.

"You killed Dr. Voss!" the female Blinker screamed back, her face contorted with rage.

"We did not!" someone shouted back. "Liar!"

The whole room seemed to turn into a brawl at once, nothing but swinging fists and bodies crashing all around Kellan. It shouldn't have been a fair fight, five against dozens, but the weapons evened the battle, holding the NPCs off.

Echo's hand slipped out of Kellan's grasp and she was no longer beside him, but he could see Jace holding his own on the other side of the room. He'd spent their entire childhood raving about what would happen if he ever got a chance to take a swing at a Blinker, and he wasn't backing down now that it was happening.

"Echo!" Kellan called, spinning around, searching for her face in the churning mass of bodies.

She was gone, swallowed by the melee.

There was a glint of metal out of the corner of Kellan's eye and he turned just in time to see the pipe swinging directly at his head. He threw his arm up instinctively and the pipe connected with a sickening crack. White-hot pain shot through his forearm and he staggered back, gasping.

A welt the size of a meatball swelled instantly from his arm. His vision swam as he clutched it to his chest. Through the haze of pain, he saw the NPCs surging forward en masse, overwhelming the Blinkers. Someone nearby screamed and Kellan caught a glimpse of blood streaming from a man's shoulder where the knife had sliced through his patchwork coverall.

If this went any further, there would be four bodies instead of three… maybe even more.

"HEY! Listen!" Kellan shouted, pushing his way toward the center of the fight. People threw punches all around him, bumping into his throbbing arm and paying him no attention. "It was me!" he yelled at the top of his lungs. "I made the reroute. No one else here is at fault!"

"Kellan!" He just barely caught Echo shouting his name. She'd heard him, but no one else even paused.

His words were drowned out by the shouts and grunts of the brawl. The Blinkers were being pushed back toward the hallway, and the guy with the pipe had dropped it. Now he was throwing punches with both fists, and the one with the knife was backed up against the wall, slashing wildly at anyone who got pushed close to him.

"Stop! Listen to me!" Kellan tried again, his voice breaking with the strain. "I'm responsible!"

A nearby NPC glanced at him, startled, before being pulled back into the fray. No one else heard. Or maybe they just didn't care – maybe the chance to finally unleash years of resentment against each other was too tempting.

Kellan cradled his injured arm and was preparing to shout one more time when a piercing wail cut through the cacophony – a high, constant electronic shriek that started Kellan's ears ringing. The NPCs all looked around in confusion, but the Blinkers all immediately stiffened, and the one with the knife dropped his weapon and kicked it away.

"What is that?" someone near Kellan asked, hands clapped over her ears.

The alarm was coming from the hallway to the central commons. Was there a speaker somewhere in there still?

No, it was getting louder, coming closer.

And then there were more Blinkers at the end of the hall, one of them carrying a small airhorn high overhead. All three of them wore the bright red armbands of the Auditors – the Blinkers' idea of police. Kellan had never actually seen one before – they had no jurisdiction here – but he knew about the armbands.

The original five Blinkers visibly shrank back against the wall, and someone from the NPC side of the crowd shouted, "'Bout time! Take these savages back to your own sectors!"

The tallest Auditor stepped forward, the wail of the airhorn abruptly cutting off as he lowered it. His face was impassive as he slowly turned his head, surveying the scene. "What's going on here?" he demanded.

"Sir," the Blinker who'd hit Kellan in the arm stepped forward, his tone disgustingly obsequious, "we came to find whoever tampered with the air filtration system and killed our people."

"Was that task assigned to you by Valence?" the Auditor asked, his voice so chillingly steady it even sent a ripple of unease through Kellan's stomach. The Blinkers looked downright terrified and he wondered what punishment looked like to these people.

"No," the guy replied, head hung like a chastened child. "But they killed our best doctor. They have to pay!"

"Just because they're NPCs, they get away with literal murder–"

"Who says they aren't going to pay?" the tall Auditor demanded. He had silver, slicked-back hair and the pock marks of ancient acne scars across his cheeks.

"They never do!" the woman answered, too angry to be scared

of him, apparently. "They do whatever they want and they still get to drink our water and breathe our air and–"

That set off a firestorm of replies from the NPCs.

"We didn't murder anyone!"

"We're not responsible for mistakes in *your* sectors."

"You have no authority here!"

"Stop!" Kellan barked. He'd spent his whole sun-forsaken life listening to the hatred the Blinkers spewed at him – almost always second-hand, in rumors passed around by NPCs who'd experienced it themselves. He'd only met Blinkers one other time in his life, but the sooner he could get them out of his commons so he never had to see them again, the better. He stepped up on a nearby bench seat and shouted over the top of the crowd, "It was me!"

They all hushed, finally listening to him, and the tall Auditor's gaze locked onto him, calculating.

Kellan's mouth went dry as he realized every single eye in the commons was on him. He could barely even feel his arm throbbing anymore. "I changed the airflow. It wasn't malicious, we– *I* was just trying to repressurize our laundry module. We had people in trouble too."

Immediately, the NPCs formed a wall around him. Kellan knew some of them – maintenance workers, fabricators, kitchen staff. These were people he'd fixed flickering dormitory lights for, people he played Parallax with after a long day, kids he'd quizzed on filter maintenance protocols so they could pass their exams. Some he knew by name, others only by face, but they formed a solid wall of bodies in front of the Blinkers.

Jace materialized at Kellan's side, whispering up to him, "What on Deimos are you doing, dude?"

"They need someone to blame, let them blame me," Kellan said. "What can they do, anyway?"

Whoever had screamed it was right. The Blinkers had no authority here – not even the Auditors. NPCs governed themselves, and they fixed what they broke.

If someone was dead because of what Kellan did, he'd find a way to make it right... however he could.

"You're under arrest!" one of the Auditors yelled, trying to push his way through the crowd.

Kellan's heart momentarily stopped in his chest, and he could actually feel the line of NPCs tightening in front of him.

"Tank sludge," Jace shouted. "You can't do that!"

"We can and we are!" the tall one hissed. "Valence's protocols apply to every sector when citizen lives are lost!"

Kellan looked at Jace. "Is that true?"

Jace shook his head, his eyes wide. "I've never heard of it."

The Auditors produced batons from their belts, flicking them open. The ends sparked with electricity and NPCs pressed back so hard Kellan almost lost his balance on the bench.

Echo reappeared at his side.

"Go get Runa," she told Jace, shoving him away.

The NPCs were shoulder-to-shoulder, doing their best to fend off the Auditors, but Kellan watched the pockmarked leader jab his baton straight into the chest of one of them. The man's muscles all contracted at once, his whole body going stiff, his face turning into a rictus of pain, and then the baton was withdrawn and his legs immediately gave out. A few people around him were mercifully close enough to catch him before he fell to the ground.

"Who's next?" the Auditor sneered. "You still want to protect him? We've got all night and plenty of juice."

Another Auditor extended his baton toward the crowd, but Kellan shouted, "No, stop!"

He looked down at Echo, whose eyes had gone watery with fear.

"It's okay," he said, mostly for her benefit, then turned to the crowd. "I'll go. If I'm to blame, I want to make it right. No one else needs to be harmed."

He stepped off the bench, extending his wrists for the Auditors to cuff him. They were not gentle with his welted and throbbing forearm.

"Everyone else return to your quarters," the tall Auditor barked. "There will be a mandatory all-colony meeting tomorrow night at 1900 hours in the central commons to address this incident." He scanned the crowd, which refused to move despite the threats, and his eyes locked on the five Blinkers, looking smug as they watched the handcuffs being slapped onto Kellan's wrists. "Beginning immediately, any citizen found in this sector without authorization will have their Exchange account locked and will be placed on standard rations for a month."

They blanched.

"But sir–" the one who'd dropped his knife began, looking pale, like standard rations was the same as a death sentence.

"Return to your sectors. Now," the Auditor barked, and the Blinkers scurried like scared little rabbits up the hallway. He grabbed Kellan by the scruff of his neck and started dragging him up the hall toward the Blinker sectors.

"Kellan!" He heard his mother screech just before he rounded the bend in the hallway. He turned, but he couldn't see her in the crowd.

QUINTA

YEAR: 2179

Quinta stared at the dress hanging in her closet. Her fingers trailed over the smooth fabric – indigo blue with white trim, far more elegant than the standard-issue khaki coveralls.

Her father had given it to her as a gift on the morning her apprenticeship began three years ago. He'd spent an outrageous number of credits on it, and she'd tried it on and for once felt like the royalty that the most fanatical Chosen believed she was. He'd taken half a dozen photos and then she'd changed back into her coverall and white coat, because of course you couldn't wear something so nice to a clinic where people might be bleeding or vomiting or clutching your sleeve in pain.

Mostly, the dress hung protected and untouched in her closet. She'd worn it to Castor's graduation party, their Parallax team's championship celebration at the end of last season, a couple of administration dinners she'd attended with her mother.

Now she would wear it to her father's funeral.

Quinta pulled it from the hanger, the fabric cool and slippery between her fingers. She'd moved mechanically through her morning routine – shower, teeth, hair – all while trudging through a mental fog that made every step a chore.

Yesterday she'd thrown herself into work, using the sudden surge in sector three's patient volume to avoid thinking about anything.

But today there was no escaping it.

Her father was gone.

She stepped into the dress and pulled it up over her shoulders, struggling with the zipper at her back. Her mother was getting ready in her own bedroom. Quinta could have asked her. But the idea of going in there and seeing her father's side of the bed untouched, the pillow still dented from where his head should have lain… she just kept reaching and squirming until she managed to catch the delicate zipper pull between her fingers and draw it up.

Quinta walked soundlessly on bare feet to the bathroom, closing the door so she could use the mirror mounted on the back of it. The indigo blue made her skin look pale, almost sickly. Or maybe that was just the fact she'd barely slept all night. She'd always thought she looked more like her mother, with Havana's gently arched brows and the defined cupid's bow above her lip, but now she could see her father in the shape of her eyes, in the stubborn set of her jaw.

She didn't know what to expect today. In her nineteen years, she'd never attended a funeral. She knew from her studies that death on Mars was practical – bodies were processed efficiently, Returned to the colony's resource cycle. She could talk to a patient sensitively about the process, tell *them* what to expect… but standing there staring at her father's eyes on her face, it suddenly hit her that she had no tank-sludging idea what would actually happen today. She'd seen Returns during her apprenticeship, but she'd never been to a funeral, outside her grandparents' but she was too young to remember those.

Would she have to watch as they sealed her father in the sterile composting container? Would she witness his body being stripped of everything that made it Hadrian?

The thought made her stomach turn, and she actually took a step toward the toilet, fearing she might be sick, when there was a soft knock on the door.

"Honey? Are you okay?"

She took a long, slow breath and the nausea resided. "Fine, Mom."

"Are you almost ready?" Havana called. "I don't want to be late."

"Of course not." Quinta opened the pocket door.

Waiting just outside, her mother stood tall and composed as ever, wearing a deep green dress that Quinta had only seen her wear once before, at the last Day of Renewal dance. Her blonde hair was pulled back in an immaculate twist at the base of her neck, not a strand out of place. Her face was carefully made up, concealing any evidence of the tears Quinta had heard her shed through the wall last night.

This was the Havana that the colony knew – Resource Manager Voss, efficient and always fully in control. So different from the emotional woman who had burst into Quinta's room yesterday morning and shattered her world.

"Do I look alright?" Quinta asked, suddenly self-conscious about the dress. Maybe it was inappropriate, ostentatious. Maybe she should wear her white coat in tribute to her dad.

"You look beautiful," Havana said, reaching forward to tuck a loose strand of jet-black hair behind Quinta's ear. "There. Now you're perfect. Did you eat?"

It was past mealtime, and Quinta hadn't given a moment's thought to going to breakfast. The idea of getting in line and taking a tray and sitting there eating chickpea scramble knowing what lay ahead in the Exchange schedule for her made her wonder once again if she might be sick.

Quinta shook her head, and her mother gave her a sympathetic smile. "Me neither. I've got a couple cricket protein bars in my pocket if you need something later." She reached out, palm open. "Ready?"

Quinta put her hand in her mother's, breathing already ragged before they'd even stepped out of the apartment.

They weren't going far – just to the sector one commons – but it felt like they passed everyone in the sector. They'd timed it poorly. The halls were busy with people heading to their work assignments after breakfast, and Quinta kept her eyes on the floor so she didn't have to soak up all the pitying glances being directed her way. Havana smiled at all of them and accepted their condolences, slowly transforming more into her Resource Manager Voss persona with each one. At least a few of them had the decency to hurry past without saying anything.

When they got to the commons, Havana paused at the door and stood a little taller. She smoothed one palm down the front of her dress and then fluffed the bun at the base of her neck. "It'll be okay," she promised with absolutely no authority to do so, and for a moment, Quinta thought about making a break for it. The rabbitat was only a ten-minute walk from here, and she could certainly use the comfort of holding one.

But then the double sliding doors swished open and there were already row upon row of chairs set up, nearly every one filled with citizens in their best clothing. Where were all those people in the hall going, if everyone was already here?

Havana stepped into the room, immediately surrounded by her administration colleagues trying to console her. They swallowed her up and left Quinta standing there, still holding her hand from the outside of the circle, feeling like an unused appendage. She looked around, noticing all the changes to the room.

The memorial wall was alive with light and color in a way she'd never seen before.

Every digital tribute had been activated.

There were hundreds of names etched into it, dating back to the very first Glass outbreak in 2083, and each was surrounded by holographic flowers, notes, and personal mementos. Photos floated beside some names, short videos beside others. The collective effect was dazzling and disorienting, an entire wall exploding with memories and loss.

Quinta had seen individual tributes before. When she got her retinal implant at twelve, her parents had brought her here and showed her how to set her overlay so that her grandparents' memorials would be lit every time she walked into the room. Some families paid a premium in the Exchange to have their loved ones' memorials lit up for everyone on anniversaries. But she'd never seen all of them, the entire wall lit at once. The visual density was overwhelming – a century of grief represented in pixels glowing against the wall.

When she finally managed to tear her eyes away from it, her mother was still lost in hand-shaking mode, probably trying to escape the pain the same way Quinta had yesterday. She scanned the room and spotted Cydra sitting next to Dr. Liang, although both their backs were to her.

Then her eyes fell on the stage set up at the front of the room, and her breath caught in her throat all over again.

Three shrouded forms lay there, side by side.

Three bodies. Not one.

The realization hit her like a slap in the face. Of course there were three. Her father, the nurse working the overnight shift, and the post-op patient. She'd known this – had heard their names, had processed the information on some intellectual level – but all morning, she'd only been bracing herself to see her father's shroud up there.

She'd forgotten about the other two lives that were lost.

She'd spent the whole day yesterday treating people who'd been injured in the accident, listening to them rant about how the NPCs had killed her father with neglect or stupidity or both. And it hadn't once occurred to her that there were two other families in the hab consumed with just as much grief as the Vosses.

Her mother's hand tightened around hers, steadying her as she swayed slightly. Her entourage was gone and it was just the two of them again. "Let's take a seat."

"I didn't think…" Quinta started, unable to finish the sentence.

Havana just nodded like she understood and started to guide Quinta down the aisle toward the two seats reserved right up front for them. Along the way, Havana did her politician's smile, tight-lipped with an equally tight nod because a real smile wouldn't be appropriate, but she couldn't bring herself to ignore all these people who still needed her to be Resource Manager Voss, even on the worst day of her life.

Quinta passed a woman who was sobbing quietly into a hand-kerchief. Across the aisle, an elderly couple sat rigidly in their seats, their faces carved with grief as they stared at the shrouded forms. Everyone in this room had lost someone important to them, and it wasn't just Hadrian. The selfishness of forgetting that fact made Quinta's cheeks burn with shame.

As she and her mother passed each row, conversations had a way of dropping off and every eye in the room seemed to follow their progress – the Vosses, the colony's first family, now reduced by one.

Quinta felt those stares like physical pressure against her skin. Most were sympathetic, filled with the same pity she'd felt in the clinic yesterday. Others held the reverence she'd grown accustomed to receiving – that subtle awe that had followed her since child-hood, sometimes tinged with envy.

But today, there were other looks too.

A man in the third row leaned over to whisper something in the ear of his seatmate, all the while making unreadable eye contact with Quinta. A woman two seats down looked at Quinta, then quickly away, as if her gaze had sharp edges.

Her stomach clenched. Why were they looking at her like that?

A terrible thought crept into her mind: *They know.* They knew how little she'd thought about the other victims. They could see through her facade of composure to the self-absorption beneath – the part of her that had been consumed by her own loss while barely acknowledging that the colony had lost more than one person.

Of course they were disgusted. She was disgusted with herself.

Her mother's grip tightened on her hand, pulling her forward when she faltered. Havana seemed oblivious to the hostile stares. She nodded solemnly to people she recognized, her face a perfect mask of dignified grief.

As they approached the front row, Quinta passed Cydra and Dr. Liang. Their eyes met, and Quinta raised her hand in a small wave.

Cydra looked away, her gaze sliding past Quinta as if she hadn't seen her.

The snub was so unexpected that Quinta nearly stumbled. She and Cydra had worked together for three years. Cydra had been Hadrian's right hand for most of his career. What could possibly–

"Here we are," Havana murmured, guiding Quinta into her seat.

Quinta glanced back at Cydra, who was staring straight ahead now, her expression making it clear she was absorbed in her overlay. Quinta tried to make eye contact with Dr. Liang next, but then Administrator Weyland stepped up onto the stage and the room fell quiet.

QUINTA
YEAR: 2179

Elise Chandra. Owen Markovic. Hadrian Voss.

The names of the three deceased citizens, now etched forever into the memorial wall, their letters still faintly glowing from the heat of the task. As soon as the etching was complete, people began flooding the space with holographic flowers and stuffies and photos and notes. Quinta watched a child's drawing of a red-haired man pop up beside Owen Markovic's name, *Grandpa* scrawled beneath it.

Administrator Weyland had done a fine job of eulogizing the three of them, although Quinta thought he'd sounded too generic when he got to Hadrian. Maybe Elise and Owen's families thought he'd been too general with their eulogies.

Quinta couldn't decide what to leave on her father's memorial. She hadn't anticipated it, and nothing seemed quite good enough. Others were leaving photos from his medical training days, from his wedding, from colony celebrations. There were notes from his patients, and so many flowers she could hardly see his name through them.

The crowd was beginning to disperse. It felt like the whole thing was anticlimactic, three lives briefly eulogized then pinned on the wall and promptly forgotten. People filed past Quinta and Havana's chairs, murmuring their condolences. Quinta shook hands with them on autopilot, until one of them wouldn't let go.

"Miss Voss," she realized he was saying after the third or fourth repeat. He was a short man, older than her by a few decades but at least five centimeters smaller.

"Dr. Voss," she corrected him, and then her throat threatened to close up at the realization that she was the *only* Dr. Voss now.

"Yes, I was just saying it's time for the immediate families to accompany the deceased to the final Return ceremony."

Quinta let go of his hand, palm sticky with sweat. "Oh. Right." She noticed the patch on the breast pocket of his coveralls. He was a Return attendant.

"Are you okay?" her mother asked.

Quinta felt like a zombie stumbling through the day, but what could she say? She nodded and started to follow the short man, then paused. She turned back to the memorial wall and added the last voice memo her father had ever sent her.

I'm proud of you, kiddo.

The Return room was a long way from the public areas that Quinta was used to. The entire group of mourners – Elise's family, Owen's family, the little boy who must have left that drawing – walked in complete silence, each family pushing a shroud-covered gurney. At last, the attendant led them into a small room with padded chairs lining two walls. The room felt warm and cozy, with landscape art on the wall that reminded Quinta of a coffee table book of Earth landmarks she had in her room. There was the Grand Canyon, Mount Everest, the Great Barrier Reef.

The room was trying too hard to be calming.

"Each family will be invited in separately to say their goodbyes before their loved one is Returned to the colony," the man said. "I just need a few minutes to prepare."

He slid open a heavy steel door, and Quinta got a glimpse of the room where her father would soon be going. It was industrial, with several human-sized composters in the center. Two more attendants emerged from it, taking the gurneys away. Quinta looked away before the door closed.

An awkward silence descended on the room. Havana pulled Quinta down to sit in two chairs on one wall. The Markovics claimed the chairs across from them, Owen's widow cradling his grandson in her arms. Nurse Chandra's family circled up in the corner, their backs to the others, whispering among themselves.

"I'm so sorry for your loss," Havana said to the Markovics. "I wish I'd known Owen better. Elise, too."

One of the Chandras – a blue-eyed man old enough to be either Elise's brother or her husband – turned to look at her, his brows knit together. He opened his mouth as if to respond, then closed it, turning away again. One of the other relatives placed a hand on his arm and whispered something too low to hear.

Quinta looked at her mom in confusion, and Havana shook her head minutely. "Did I say something wrong?" she whispered.

Elise used to work in the sector one clinic years ago, before Quinta began her apprenticeship. Maybe that was the problem – sour grapes because the head doctor's wife had never taken an interest in his coworkers?

The big steel door opened again and Quinta carefully averted her eyes this time as the short attendant emerged, saying , "The Markovic family may come in now."

Five of them rose and followed him through the door, which closed with a soft hiss. The Chandras didn't sit. Minutes ticked by. Quinta could hear muffled voices – quiet weeping, murmured words. She tried not to listen, and when the Markovics emerged about ten minutes later, their faces were tear-streaked but composed. Owen's widow nodded briefly to Havana as they passed, and then the attendant called for the Chandras.

There were only three of them, and they were still whispering among themselves as they passed. Quinta was sure she saw the blue-eyed man look sideways at her, and she thought she heard the word *hoarding* pop out of their mumbled conversation.

"What?" Quinta asked, and her mom put a hand on her knee. "Shh."

As soon as the door closed and they were alone again, Quinta turned to her. "Did you hear that?"

"Hear what?" Havana looked completely wiped out from a morning of strained smiles and handshakes.

"He looked at me and said 'hoarding.'"

"Are you sure it wasn't something else? 'Hoarding' doesn't make sense."

No, she was right, it didn't. Hoarding was one of the worst things you could do in a colony as tight on resources as they were, punishable by corrective therapy in the EEM for a first offense. Sometimes it happened out of fear or a desire to protect your family, but rarely, it was to sell the goods on the black market to enrich one's Exchange account.

Quinta sat back in her seat, trying to keep her mind blank as the seconds ticked by and her turn approached.

"Did you notice people looking at us strangely today?" she asked after a while, unable to hold it in. "Like they're angry or something?"

"Probably just don't know where to direct their anger at what happened," Havana said. "It was a horrible, tragic accident." Quinta thought about that for a moment, and just as she was opening her mouth to say no, it felt personal, Havana changed the subject. "I know it's been a long, bad day, but you are planning to attend the all-colony meeting tonight, aren't you? We could walk together."

Valence hadn't announced exactly what was on the agenda, but with the timing, it had to be about the accident.

"I... I haven't thought about it," Quinta admitted. "You're going?"

Havana nodded. "Yes. I have to be there, I'm head of resource management. It's regarding your father. You should be there too."

"How do you know it's about Dad?"

"Administrator Weyland told me," Havana said. "It's an important meeting."

"Okay, I'll go."

The word hung in the air until at last the door opened again and the Chandras emerged. This time, all three of them kept their eyes straight ahead, Elise's mother weeping softly, the blue-eyed man's arm tight around her shoulders.

"The Voss family," the attendant said at last. "Please come with me."

Quinta rose on unsteady legs, her mother's hand finding hers once more as they entered the room. The air had a metallic scent she wasn't expecting, and... a burnt smell. Her father's shrouded form waited on a gurney in the center of the room.

"Take as long as you need to say your final goodbye," the attendant said. "When you're ready, I'll begin the disposition process. Or if you prefer, you may step outside."

"What exactly is the process?" Havana asked, and belatedly, Quinta realized she might be the only person in the room who didn't know. At least not in detail.

The attendant cleared his throat. "Thermophilic bioconversion," he said. "Your husband's body will be placed in a sealed chamber with a starter culture of bacteria–"

"Okay," Havana said sharply, holding up a hand. "That's quite enough detail, thank you." Her hand went to her hair, nervously fluffing it. "We'll step out before you begin."

KELLAN

YEAR: 2179

Kellan stood on the stage at the front of the teeming central commons, his wrists in handcuffs, a pair of Auditors flanking him. Beneath his shirt sleeve, there was a welt the size of a new potato, but no one had offered him medical attention in the past twenty-four hours.

It wasn't the most important thing on Kellan's mind, either.

The central commons was at capacity, with close to a thousand people crammed into every corner, some of them spilling into the halls branching off to all four sectors. There was a small contingent of NPCs, about thirty of them who were there to find out what fresh hell the Blinkers were dreaming up and report it back to the others. They weren't foolish enough to all show up just because an Auditor decreed it.

Kellan was dismayed to see that his mother was one of them. She'd waved at Kellan when she first walked in, tears already streaming down her face. The crowd was so thick she couldn't push her way closer to him, and he could see her trying to shout something, but it was too loud to hear. He saw Jace and Echo standing near her, and a few more familiar faces.

The only other person he recognized sat at the very front of the room, in one of only a few chairs. She had jet-black hair plaited over one shoulder, and she'd been working very hard to look anywhere but at Kellan from the moment she sat down.

Quinta Voss.

The girl with the rabbit, the one whose father he was accused of killing.

Where were the families of the other victims?

Kellan had no clue what the Blinkers had in store for him, but if it involved them all hurling rotten fruit and rabbit shit at him, he wouldn't be surprised.

Likely, this would be a trial of some sort. Presided over by their AI god?

The noise of the room changed quality, people settling down as a tall man with broad shoulders and a closely trimmed salt-and-pepper beard weaved through the crowd and stepped up on the stage. Administrator Adam Weyland. His skin was more leathery and wrinkled than in the pictures Kellan had seen.

He spared a brief but disgusted look at Kellan, then stepped up to a podium awaiting him. His deep voice boomed through the room's speakers. "Citizens of VossColony, we gather today to address a tragedy. As many of you know, we have lost three valued and worthy citizens."

He paused and the room was so completely silent, Kellan could hear the irregular rattling in the air vents.

"Dr. Hadrian Voss, Nurse Elise Chandra, and Engineer Owen Markovic." Weyland articulated each name carefully and slowly.

Kellan felt sick hearing their names again. He couldn't help looking at Quinta Voss. Her eyes flickered to his, a fire ignited in them, and then she looked back at Weyland, who was explaining what happened during the malfunction, according to Valence's official reports. It didn't seem possible that opening one stuck valve in sector four could have set off a cascade of failures all down the line like he was describing, but the Blinkers were all nodding along like it made perfect sense.

Like it had been malicious, even.

Kellan got a cold feeling in his gut, like someone just poured ice water down his throat. What was he really here for?

"We now know who was responsible for this horrific act," Weyland said, and swept his arm widely around to point at Kellan. "This Non-participating Colonist went into the air vents and changed the configuration of a delicate and non-redundant system without once thinking to consult Valence, which would have prevented the entire catastrophe."

"Make him pay!" someone shouted. A lot of heads turned toward the NPCs all clustered near their access hall, like they were all guilty by association. Their delegation of thirty seemed smaller and more defenseless by the moment.

"Murderer!"

"He should be Returned!"

Those who were standing surged forward, dozens of Blinkers pointing and screaming at Kellan. Would they kill him right here on the stage? Was he their entertainment for the night?

The Auditors on the edge of the crowd stepped forward.

"You can't punish him!" someone in the back shouted. It sounded like his mom, but he couldn't see her anymore, her small frame lost in the crowd. "You have no right!"

"We have every right!" Administrator Weyland's voice boomed through the speakers. It was so abrupt, so piercing that the room fell into another complete silence. Weyland slicked one hand over his hair, and Kellan thought he looked a bit sweaty.

"I'm afraid I haven't finished explaining the consequences the hab is facing from this NPC tampering," he said. "During her investigation into the incident, Valence discovered additional downstream damage to the pressurization system."

Kellan blinked in disbelief. Multiple system failures, from

changing the routing of one air vent? Now he was sure it was all tank sludge.

Weyland's eyes went distant, and the next time he spoke, his speech pattern was clipped, measured. "Corrective measures are required to restore system integrity. The responsible party must perform remedial operations in proportion to the harm inflicted."

The responsible party? Okay, so they were going to make him fix the system… it was fair, something he would have suggested anyway. Kellan breathed a little easier thinking this wouldn't be a public execution after all, in front of his mom and two best friends.

"The unit is functioning at seventy-five percent and dropping," Weyland continued, and Kellan realized he was reading something – no doubt something Valence was feeding him. "Furthermore, the unit cannot be repaired. A new system must be fabricated and installed, and at the current rate of deterioration, it must be completed by month's end or there will be wide-ranging system disruptions."

The entire room seemed to go silent, a collective held breath. Things broke all the time, but a primary unit – one the entire hab relied on – broken beyond repair? It had never happened before. It'd explain all the clanking and intermittent disruptions, though.

"The unit is outside," Weyland said, and his skin was unmistakably clammy now. "Replacing it will require digging."

Kellan froze, no longer feeling the tight cuffs around his wrist or the ache in his forearm. All he felt was the claustrophobic presence of the two beefy Auditors standing beside him, just waiting for him to make their job interesting by attempting to run.

Rule one of VossColony was you do not disturb the soil. Even NPCs knew that.

"As penance for the three citizen lives he took, Kellan Reilly will volunteer his own life to save the colony," Weyland said, and Kellan could no longer tell if he was reading or proclaiming. "Once the atmospheric unit is replaced, his debt to society will be considered paid in full."

There were cheers. Actual cheers at the idea of sending him onto the surface of the planet, where dust storms raged and the fine orange regolith had a way of infiltrating every crevice as if it had a mind of its own. The odds of getting Glass after a single exposure to it were fifty percent. What would they be if he went outside and dug around in it for a few days?

This was not paying a debt. It was a death sentence, and the completely silent, stunned cluster of NPCs at the back of the room knew it.

Kellan's legs turned to jelly, and it was all he could do not to collapse in front of all those angry Blinkers cheering for his death.

It was a public execution after all, in a sense.

Kellan caught sight of his mom again, being boosted by Jace, and there went his legs after all.

QUINTA

YEAR: 2179

The Auditors caught the NPC under his arms just as his legs gave out on him, and dragged him out of the room.

"Regretfully, this repair is not a one-man job," Weyland continued, sending a new jolt through Quinta's frayed nerves before she'd even had a chance to catch her breath. She looked to her mother, who put a soothing hand on her knee as if none of this was news.

Maybe it wasn't. If anyone other than Weyland had access to Valence's private reports, it would be the head of resource management.

"Valence has determined that nine additional participants will be required to replace the unit before it fails," Weyland went on.

"We can't dig!" someone shouted. "You can't ask us to commit suicide like that!"

Weyland cut through them, his tone sharp and amplified. "No citizen will be compelled. Those who volunteer will be recognized for their sacrifice, and they or their families will be compensated generously in the Exchange. Valence requests that all qualified applicants submit their names before the end of the week."

The silence that followed felt more tense than the interruption had.

The meeting ended shortly after, Weyland making his escape before too many questions could be asked. The NPCs had disappeared back to their sector before Quinta even stood and turned around. Most people were stunned into silence as they made their way out of the central commons, but there were quiet murmurs of anxiety. Quinta caught snippets as she and her mom were buffeted along by the crowd.

"No *way* am I volunteering."

"–should just make *every* prisoner dig."

"Or every NPC."

And then, one whisper that was unlike the others:

"–heard he was doing it to afford all those angora sweaters his wife and daughter wear."

Quinta's ears pricked up as she tried to find the source. Were they talking about her father? She thought of what she'd heard Elise Chandra's relative say earlier today.

Hoarding.

Even the thought turned her stomach. And she didn't even have that many sweaters – she had two to rotate through, and her dad replaced them for her only when they got threadbare. They must be talking about someone else. Quinta was just sensitive right now – that was all.

"It's a death sentence, plain and simple."

"–tibiotics, painkillers, even surgical equipment. There's a market for anything."

"Maybe for all of–"

"But what does he need it for? He's a Voss."

Quinta felt nauseous. There was no doubt left now, but who was saying these things, and two days after her father's death? How could they talk about the head doctor like this? She had her head on a swivel, trying to identify who was saying what, but the crowd was thick and the whispers were too hard to tease apart from each other.

Then her mother hooked a hand around the inside of her elbow, guiding her toward the sector one hallway. "How are you holding up?"

Quinta's whole body was shaking, and Havana must have noticed because she said, "It'll be okay. Valence has a plan to fix that unit, and I'm sure we'll have lots of brave volunteers."

"I didn't know Auditors could arrest an NPC."

"They can when they commit a crime that impacts the whole colony," Havana said, and then she stopped Quinta, turning her to face her. People brushed past them as Havana stared into her eyes, her brows stern. "That boy murdered your father and two other citizens. Don't feel bad for him, Quinta. Valence dispensed justice."

Quinta nodded and they started walking again. Part of her wanted to ask about those awful whispers. Had Havana heard them too? Did she already know what they meant, like she knew Valence's meeting agenda before Weyland unveiled it?

But another part of her didn't want to open that proverbial airlock. Havana had put on her meticulous makeup and tucked her hair into a meticulous bun and shook hands and smiled all day, but under that, she was hurting too.

She didn't need to hear about ugly rumors Quinta didn't even understand.

LIRA

YEAR: 2083

Lira didn't leave the rabbitat the whole first day. She didn't see much point – in anything, really. Jamila had brought her lunch and a clean set of coveralls because apparently she *had* noticed what a hot mess Lira was.

The new clothes went ignored, as did the food. Even the best Earth meal would have tasted like wet cardboard, and Lira couldn't force down more than a couple of bites at a time even while reminding herself that Jamila had bought those extra rations with her own Exchange points, and the coveralls too.

Valence started sending push notifications to Lira when her tasks started turning overdue, but Lira dismissed every warning without looking at it.

People kept coming to the rabbitat like it was a normal day. Lira turned a couple of them away and had gone into the Exchange to mark the rabbitat closed to visitors until further notice, but Valence had received complaints and overruled that after lunch. Lira did read that passive-aggressive warning message, which came in the form of an excerpt from the colony manual, section 11.1: *The rabbit program is, among other things, a comfort animal initiative intended to improve the mental health and morale of the colonists. It is available to all colonists with a medical referral, and to those with sufficient Exchange credits to book a non-prescription play session.*

"Yeah, well, my mental health and morale need it to be closed," Lira had grumbled and dismissed the notification, but she found she could no longer control the door lock. The rabbitat remained open and people kept coming in.

Most of them seemed blissfully unaware of what had happened to the dig crew. A few who had been keeping up to date with the news feed appeared to be here because they were feeling down about it. Lira mostly ignored them, sitting on her stool by the computer and pretending not to be catatonic with grief. No one expressed their condolences. Most of them still hated Ada, and thought she was a threat to the colony.

That was fine. Lira didn't want to speak to anyone, no matter what they thought of her partner.

She would have been content to stare at her computer screen all afternoon, ignoring the world, but about an hour before closing time, she got a visitor she recognized. His name was Hoyt Reilly and he was a chemical engineer. His girlfriend, Dana, made a *lot* of appointments for rabbitat time – as many as she could afford.

He walked in, gave Lira a sad wave, and immediately sank down to his knees in the grass, his shoulders slumped, his tall frame curling in on itself.

It was just the two of them, and Lira couldn't ignore his posture.

"Are you okay?" she asked, getting up from her stool.

"Better than you, I bet. I'm sorry about Ada," he said softly. His longish hair was greasy-looking, like he'd spent all day running his hands through it.

Lira sat on the grass beside him, and after a minute, Watson – one of the most outgoing rabbits in the warren – came over and hopped into her lap. She felt fresh tears welling behind her eyes, hot and unwelcome. She'd been sobbing off and on all day and she was so tired of crying that it hurt in her sinuses. She passed Watson to Hoyt, who cradled the cinnamon-coated rabbit in his arms.

"Dana's sick," he said. "Pneumonia, she's going to be fine," he hurried to add. "But she's been in the sector three med clinic since yesterday. I went to visit her. I just saw…"

Lira didn't need him to finish the sentence. Instantly, she was transported back to sector two, to all those beeping monitors, to the doctor working frantically just inches from her, pushing round after round of epinephrine to try to keep Ada's heart beating. To the monitors being turned off and the clinic descending into deadly silence.

"It was awful," Hoyt finished, in lieu of describing what he'd seen in sector three.

Lira just nodded. She thought of Dana to avoid thinking about Ada. The very first time Lira met her, Dana said she'd been so excited when she heard the rabbits were coming that she'd volunteered to spearhead the building of the rabbitat. She'd had rabbits as a kid back on Earth, and she'd done a great job fabricating all the right kinds of toys and tunnels for them.

"We met on the trip here," Hoyt said. "Did you know that?"

Lira shook her head.

"We've been here three years and I just got up the courage to ask her out a few months ago," he said with a smile. Then he looked at Lira, at the deep exhaustion written all over her face. "I'm sorry. Not that me worrying about her pneumonia is anything near what you've just been through. Dana's going to be fine. I just wish she didn't have to witness…"

He trailed off again, and Lira picked up his hand, placing it gently on Watson's back. It was what the rabbits were here for. To bring comfort. Hoyt started to stroke the soft fur, and Lira said, "Dana's a strong woman. She'll be okay."

He nodded. "Do you want to talk about Ada?"

Lira shook her head vehemently. "No." Hoyt stiffened beside

her, so she softened her tone and added, "But it's okay. We can just sit."

If it was anyone else – any stranger who'd wandered into the rabbitat wanting to act like it was a normal day – she would have kicked them out, colony manual and Valence's warnings be damned. But Hoyt had seen what it was like in the med clinics.

He understood better than anyone else in the hab, except the medical staff and poor Dana.

"Tell her to come by when she's feeling better," Lira said. "I'll make sure she gets an hour on the house. You too."

Hoyt nodded his thanks. Watson hopped out of his lap to graze on the greens Jamila had brought. A few other rabbits came near and Hoyt held out his hand, letting them sniff him. When they saw he had no treats, they wandered off. He and Lira sat amid all the toys and play structures that Dana had 3D printed, and Lira saw Ada's ghost in a thousand different places inside the rabbitat, filling up their water bottles, cleaning the litter trays without complaint, doing her best to make observations on the breeding pairs to keep Valence happy.

LIRA

YEAR: 2083

t was around 2000 hours that night when Lira's plan to sulk around the rabbitat indefinitely fell spectacularly to hell.

It was closed for the night but Lira couldn't summon the desire to make the trek home to her lonely dorm room. She was puttering around, refilling the rabbits' water dishes, when a video call alert popped up on her overlay, accompanied by Dr. Kalb's official colony headshot.

Lira's eyes rolled automatically. Dr. Kalb was well-respected by nearly every colonist, but he just so happened to be calling one of a very few who would rather bleed out in the hallway than let him treat her. Now, seeing his face was even worse because it reminded Lira of those first horrible moments in the clinic, looking for Ada.

"Decline call," she told Valence.

Overhead, the sky display abruptly darkened. It'd been overcast all day, which Lira found welcome because who wanted a bright, sunny summer day when their almost-fiancée had just died? The clouds gathered and lightning flashed, and the rabbits scattered just before "rain" started to fall from the ceiling sprinkler system to water the grass. It happened every few days, usually well after Lira had gone home for the night.

She wandered into the middle of it, figuring it was the only shower she was going to get in the near future and the rabbitat visitors might appreciate it if she stank ten percent less.

Another video call alert overtook her vision, and this time along with Dr. Kalb's smarmy face there was a flashing red icon blinking *Urgent.*

Lira growled and said, "Screw you," as she declined it again. She didn't want to debrief about Ada just so he could file his official report on the incident. He could either do it without her, or he could wait until she felt able to draw a full breath again.

What was he doing working so late, anyway? He was a day shift physician.

She tilted her head up to the rain. It was cool and refreshing, even if it did have a slightly metallic scent from traveling a few kilometers around the hab through zigzagging pipes.

A window opened on her overlay a third time, but instead of an alert she could dismiss, the call connected automatically and Dr. Kalb just started talking. Lira barely had a chance to be shocked that Valence would override her comms like that before her attention was on the doctor.

He looked like hell, with a sweat-dampened forehead and – she couldn't quite tell through the glare from his glasses, but were his pupils slightly cloudy?

"Dr. Salonga, I'm sorry to break in on you like this, but I must know if you're experiencing any symptoms of illness. Anything at all, but especially fever, chills, sweating, confusion, brain fog–"

Her heart seized in her chest. "Are you saying there's been secondary exposure? From the flare victims?"

She was no expert in radiation sickness, but she knew that was exceedingly rare. The paleness of Dr. Kalb's already fair skin told her all she needed to know, though. The closer she looked, she could see the veins crawling up his jaw.

"Do you have any symptoms?" he insisted, ignoring her question.

"I'm fine," Lira said even as a nagging voice in her head started to wonder what the difference was between the grief-fueled fugue state she'd been in all day and the brain fog Dr. Kalb was talking about. "You think I could have been irradiated just by being in the room with Ada?"

"You're sure you don't have any symptoms?" he pressed, once again dodging her question. "Difficulty with your vision, nausea–"

"I feel fine, what's going on?" Lira demanded.

"All the same, I think you should quarantine. Where are you?"

"In the rabbitat."

Dr. Kalb frowned. "Well, that's not ideal, but it's probably still better that you stay there than risk spreading the infection by traveling–"

"What are you talking about?" Lira practically shouted at him. "You can't seriously be worried about tertiary exposure from a solar flare. Secondary is unlikely enough."

Dr. Kalb put a cloth to his brow, trying to mop the sweat from his bald head before it dripped into his eyes. "What I'm about to tell you cannot go beyond the two of us. It could start a panic. I'm only telling you because you were in the clinic for a long time, and I need you to understand how important it is to quarantine until we're positive you're not contagious."

"I don't understand. Contagious?" Lira's stomach was suddenly full of stones and she was glad she hadn't managed more than a few bites of the lettuce wrap Jamila brought her for dinner.

"I don't believe this is just acute radiation syndrome like we initially assumed," he said. "I don't know what it is yet, but it doesn't act like radiation sickness. It never should have killed all ten of them that quickly, even at extreme doses, which not all of them received. And the physical changes... I've never seen anything like it."

"Me neither," Lira breathed, her distaste for Kalb getting pushed to the background as she absorbed what he was saying. She saw Ada's cloudy gaze behind her own eyelids every time she closed them. Seeing the same cataract effect forming over Dr. Kalb's eyes gave her chills. "How long have you been sick?"

"Eight hours," he said. "Dr. Salonga, nearly everyone who worked the day shift in my clinic yesterday has fallen ill, and I've gotten similar reports from med clinic three. We're monitoring the afternoon and night shifts, and reaching out to visitors and patients who were present when the dig crew arrived."

Lira's mind went to Hoyt and Dana. He'd thought the horror was having to watch the dig crew die one by one.

"How many patients and visitors are we talking about?" she asked.

Dr. Kalb's face went grim. "If you're truly asymptomatic, then you're one of three who were exposed early in the day and haven't yet acquired the… infection, for lack of a more specific term."

Yet hung in the air like a rain cloud.

"I'm working with the biologists now to find out what it is and how it's transmitted," Dr. Kalb went on. "My first assumption was an aerosol… or direct contact with broken skin, maybe… but the nurses tell me you were in that room with Ms. Bello for many hours, is that right?"

"Sixteen," Lira supplied. "I only left her side once, to use the restroom."

"And you're not sick. That means I don't know how this is spreading," Dr. Kalb said, shaking his head. "But I do know that the transmission rate is alarmingly high, I know it's more than radiation sickness, and that the first round of infections was one hundred percent fatal within sixteen hours."

Lira's heart felt like it'd calcified into a tiny, hard ball in her chest.

"My theory is that you aren't contagious if you're not showing symptoms – Lord, I hope I'm right about that," Dr. Kalb went on, "but I need you to quarantine until further notice. And submit health reports to Valence at regular intervals so we can track any symptoms."

"I understand," Lira said. "I'll do that."

Dr. Kalb wiped his brow again. He really didn't look good, and Lira started to imagine some unknown, deadly infection sweeping through the close quarters of the hab, with its recycled air and constantly reclaimed and recirculated water supply...

"But I can't just sit around filling out health questionnaires," Lira added, the will to live – to be a productive member of the colony – peeking out from its burrow for the first time since they turned Ada's monitors off. "How can I help? Do you need more hands at the clinic?"

"You can't come here."

"I'll mask up, and wear a full protective suit while I travel," Lira said. "I have one here in the rabbitat, and I know my way around triage and emergency medicine. My training is on animals, but I could still be helpful–"

"No," Dr. Kalb interrupted. "You could still get sick. I won't have you spreading the infection on your way here, and if you're not sick, I can't risk you receiving any more exposure. I appreciate the offer, Dr. Salonga, but you need to stay put."

Her heart fell, even as she struggled to reconcile her old negative opinion of him with this careful, proactive Dr. Kalb. Had she been wrong about him?

In any case, her idea had been half-baked, a desperate bid to avoid being alone and helpless. He was right to refuse it.

He surprised her by saying, "I could use your help, though."

"With what?"

"Contact tracing," he said. "Are you familiar with it?"

She nodded. "I've had to do it in my clinic back home." Tracking down and identifying everyone who'd been in the two affected med clinics, plus everyone they'd been in contact with, et cetera down the line, until she'd identified every possible exposure to whatever this was. "I can do that."

"Thank you. I'll request access to the clinic's visitor logs for you from Valence." Another swipe of the cloth over his damp brow. "Submit the names to me as you find them and I'll make sure they all quarantine too."

Dr. Kalb ended the call, and Lira just stood there for a moment, thinking about how many people had passed through the rabbitat today. If she was wrong, if she was sick, this could already be out of control. Her forehead felt wet and for an instant, terror shot down her spine.

Then she remembered she was standing in the rain.

QUINTA

YEAR: 2179

The morning after the all-colony, Dr. Liang called Quinta into her office.

Hadrian's old office.

Eden Liang was currently the only fully trained doctor in the sector, and she'd wasted no time moving into the biggest office. She'd brought her own chair and taken over Hadrian's tablet as well as her own, both set up on the desk side by side. She was tapping on both screens alternately, a deep furrow in her brow, ignoring Quinta completely as if she hadn't called her in here.

It was a power play. Liang had been trying to prove herself while working in the shadow of Dr. Voss for the last fifteen years, and now was her chance to eclipse him.

Quinta just sat patiently and waited. She wasn't about to let Liang know she was irritated.

She looked around and noticed a box of her father's stuff in one corner — a worn rabbit stuffie with patches of fur missing, a gift from a little girl he'd treated for leukemia right when Quinta began her apprenticeship. An antique vial of seeds commemorating the first hydroponic wheat harvest, another gift from a patient. There was a polished steel nameplate that Havana had given him when he got the head doctor position, and an old book Quinta had bought for him on the Day of Renewal one year when she was a kid. She'd saved up her credits for almost a year, knowing he loved Earth books no matter the subject.

This one was called *The Grapes of Wrath.*

About Earthlings who'd lived through something called the Dust Bowl, getting sick and dying from the soil the same as people did here. Quinta hadn't read it herself, but the ancient hardback was well-thumbed, its leather cover worn at the edges from a century of changing hands.

When she looked away from the box, she noticed Liang was now glaring at her like Quinta was the one wasting her time.

"I wanted to speak with you about the remainder of your apprenticeship," she said. "I assume you'd like to continue training under me?"

Quinta nodded, although reluctantly. Liang had always been chilly toward her, but Valence would have to approve a transfer to another clinic, and she wouldn't do it over mere personality clashes. Eden Liang had been trained by the best, and she was the best one to pick up where Hadrian had left off with Quinta.

"I realize you've only got six months left, but this is my clinic now and there will be changes," Liang said. "For one, I'll be implementing some efficiency improvements from Valence that Hadrian was putting off. I've already been testing them out on the night shift and they're excellent."

"Whatever you think is best."

"We'll be utilizing the EEM more often," she said.

That was, the Emotional Equilibrium Module, a virtual reality room that synced with patients' implants to deliver targeted mental health treatments. It was old technology running on software the engineers couldn't update, and while a lot of citizens requested it, there was only one device and for fairness' sake, Hadrian had defaulted to pointing them to talk therapy with the hab psychologists instead.

Quinta had had a few EEM sessions, purely out of curiosity, and they'd been just as good as cuddling a rabbit.

"I think the EEM can be useful," she said.

"We'll certainly be needing it more with all the anxiety about digging. I'd like to figure out a way to squeeze in more sessions – maybe overnight," Liang added. "And we'll be reducing the number of NPC patients we treat. Especially in light of what just happened to sector three. I trust you have no objections... considering."

Quinta bristled. "It's our duty to never turn away a patient who needs care."

"And we won't," Dr. Liang said quickly. "But that doesn't give them a free pass to use our facilities without contributing anything in return. They should submit a request through official channels just like everyone else, and if Valence says they need care, we certainly won't withhold it."

"Our NPC visits have already been trending down over the past few years," Quinta pointed out. "They're only coming for true emergencies and taking care of everything else themselves."

"Yes, and I wonder where they buy the supplies for that."

Quinta stiffened. "What's that supposed to mean?"

"Nothing. We just need to rebalance the–"

"No, what did you mean by that?" Quinta might not have been able to broach the subject with her mother, but she certainly was willing to challenge Dr. Liang if she was going to drop hints like that. "Are you talking about the rumors about my father?"

Liang's whole face tightened and she shifted in her seat. She glanced at her tablet screens for a moment, then adjusted her seat, sitting a little higher. "I have heard the whispers about your father's... conduct. That he was stealing medical supplies and selling them on the black market for his own personal gain."

Quinta blanched, to hear her say it so bluntly. "And you believe he… did that?"

She could hardly even bring herself to say the word. Hoarding was one of the worst things you could do in a colony already so overcrowded, so resource-scarce. Her father earned all the credits he could want just for performing his assigned tasks. Why would he do it?

"It doesn't matter what I believe," Liang said, fingers going instinctively to her tablet and then falling back to her lap. "Valence knows the truth. Now, I have a few charts to update. That will be all, Dr. Voss."

She turned back to her tablets, the conversation over.

Quinta snatched the box of her father's things off the floor on her way out, and promptly ran smack into Cydra in the hallway. For a second, Quinta's pulse fluttered, wondering if Cydra would speak to her at all, after the way she'd averted her eyes at the funeral.

"Hey. Crazy meeting last night, huh?" she tested the waters.

"Yeah," Cydra said. "We're about to have a storm of anxious people thinking they have Glass as soon as that digging starts."

A tiny ripple of relief worked its way up Quinta's spine. Maybe she was imagining the way Cydra had avoided her gaze at the funeral.

"Hey, these are some of my dad's things," she said, shuffling the contents of the box. "Anything in here you want to keep? Like, for sentimental reasons?"

"No, thanks." Cydra hardly even looked inside. She noticed Dr. Liang emerging from her office, and stepped around Quinta. "Dr. Liang, I have Mrs. Amato's labs."

Left standing by herself, Quinta let out a frustrated breath, then checked the waiting room queue. There was only one person in it – a follow-up for Dr. Liang – so Quinta ducked into the clinic's supply closet. It was large and neatly organized, with medical supplies on the shelves and medicines in a separate locked cabinet on one wall.

Quinta set the box down, then opened the clinic's inventory management system in her overlay. Like Phobos was she going to sit around listening to people ruin her father's good name. Her name. If he had been hoarding supplies, there would be evidence.

She scrolled through the clinic's inventory records, starting with controlled substances – the most obvious thing to steal if you were looking to earn credits on the black market. The records were meticulous, as she suspected they would be, every prescription accounted for in corresponding patient files, and the cabinet perfectly reflected what was in the records.

Not a dose missing.

She moved on to bandages, IV tubing, even basic items like reusable silicone gloves. Everything in the records matched what was on the shelves. She'd stocked them herself many times, since before her apprenticeship even began. The inventory was tightly controlled and always accurate. It wouldn't take Valence long to notice if there were discrepancies.

Quinta picked up the box and opened the door control in her overlay. She was about to step out when she paused.

Valence would notice discrepancies. That was so obvious, no one would ever just come in here and steal supplies off the shelf – it'd be discovered by the end of the day, if not moments later.

No, if you were going to try to steal something without getting caught, you'd have to make Valence think that you used it.

You'd have to forge a patient record.

That's how Quinta would do it. Wait until a patient needed the same medicine you want to pocket, mark them down for two doses and dispense only one.

Take the other for yourself.

That way, Valence wouldn't notice the missing dose.

She set the box back down and closed the door again for privacy. She switched from the inventory system to the patient records, filtering down to just Hadrian's patients in the week before he died. She started to skim through them.

They looked like his usual caseload – routine checkups, minor injuries, medication adjustments. An NPC who presented with a compound fracture that Hadrian had reset and splinted. All procedures Quinta had either assisted in or heard about.

She was starting to feel a lot better about her idea – it was scheming and anti-social, and her father *hadn't* been doing it.

Then she reached the records for the day of his death.

There shouldn't have been any, except the surgery in sector three.

And yet, there was a record for an exam that had taken place here in sector one early in the day. Thaddeus Griggs, a fabrication specialist who'd come in six months ago with a severed tendon in his hand. According to the record, he'd returned for a follow-up and Hadrian had prescribed him a course of broad-spectrum antibiotics.

It wasn't right. Hadrian had been in sector three all day. He'd have been scrubbing in for Owen Markovic's surgery at the time Griggs' visit was logged.

Just to be sure, Quinta pulled up Markovic's patient file and confirmed it – he went under sedation at 0815, and Griggs' appointment supposedly began at 0900. Her father certainly hadn't scrubbed back out and raced from sector three to here, just to do a routine follow-up Quinta could have handled.

The antibiotics were logged as dispensed, with her father's access code right beside the inventory update.

What on Deimos had her father been doing?

KELLAN
YEAR: 2179

Kellan's prison cell was a converted Blinker dormitory room. It had blank white walls that hurt his eyes and a speaker and camera built into the ceiling, right above the doorframe so that Auntie Valence could watch every move he made.

Not that there was anything to do but pace. The dimensions of the room were exactly three steps wide by four steps deep. If he pressed his face to the slot cut into the door for his meals (three times a day, an unrecognizable puddle of cricket slop that the Auditors called stew), he could see an endless hallway and a few other doors. Periodically, he'd hear the Auditors talking to each other, but never to him.

On his first day, they'd stationed an Auditor right outside his door – maybe they expected an NPC mob, or maybe they thought he'd try to Return himself. Couldn't have that, not now that the almighty Valence had dispensed justice.

Kellan had tried to talk to one of the guards early on. Ask him what was next, whether he could get painkillers for his arm, what the dig would entail, whether Valence actually had a plan to protect him from Glass or if this was all a glorified execution. The man had just stood there, hands folded in front of him, chin tilted slightly up, staring at Kellan's door.

But not quite *at* it. That had been the uncanny part.

He'd stood there for hours, not moving, eyes unfocused but moving periodically. It reminded Kellan of his grandmother's cloudy gaze, except hers still had a warmth to it that this man lacked. At first, Kellan had thought the Auditor was having some kind of seizure. He'd actually called through the slot for help, only for the man to snap back to awareness with an annoyed expression.

"What are you screaming about?"

"You were… Your eyes… Are you okay?"

He hated himself for caring, then hated the Auditor even more when he laughed. "What, you never seen someone use the overlay? You'll figure it out soon enough."

Then he went promptly back to zoning out. Whatever was in there, it held him rapt for the rest of his shift – or at the very least, it was better than staring at Kellan's door.

After the first day, they must have realized there was no way for him to hurt himself with the bed or the toilet, the only two items in that plain white room, because they stopped bothering to post a guard so close to his room.

When he got tired of pacing or needed a distraction from the ache of his arm, he'd sit by the slot and wait for the Auditors to talk to each other at shift change. It was rarely anything interesting – usually just what was on the menu in the Blinker dining hall or who was playing who in the next Parallax league match. Mind-numbing inanities, but better than silence.

On the third morning, while he was mindlessly swallowing cricket slop, err, stew, he heard a woman's voice at the end of the hall. Soft at first, the words indistinguishable. Auditors arguing back. And then, "I don't care what your protocols say, he's my son!"

Kellan immediately dropped his spoon and was at the door. "Mom?!"

He hadn't seen her since the all-colony meeting, hadn't spoken to her since breakfast the day before.

"Kellan!" He heard scuffling. "Let me through!" And then he heard the fleshy impact of a fist striking a doughy stomach.

"Fucking parasite–" the Auditor hissed, but then Runa was kneeling in front of the door slot.

"Bunny," she gasped. "Are you okay?"

"You shouldn't have come, they could arrest you too."

"They have no right. I've harmed no one. I had to see you."

He shoved his good arm as far through the slim food slot as he could, grabbing hold of his mom's hand. "I thought I'd never see you again."

"This isn't the end," she said, squeezing his hand so hard it ached. "They're right about the special circumstances, but they can't make you put yourself in danger. We're working on–"

And then she was ripped out of his grasp with a yelp.

"Don't hurt her!"

"Shut up, murderer," the Auditor snarled and Kellan could just see his mother being dragged to her feet. "Get out of here before we get Valence involved."

"That machine doesn't rule me," Runa said, trying to dig her heels in, but the Auditor was much bigger than her and easily muscled her away from Kellan's door.

"Maybe not, but I could have you in the cell next to him for assault," he said. "Want to see how Valence handles NPCs who attack Auditors? I'm curious myself."

"Mom, just go," Kellan called. "It's not worth it."

At this point, the rules seemed pretty meaningless. Who knew how far the Blinkers would bend them?

"I love you, bunny!" Her voice was already further away, and she'd been shoved beyond Kellan's range of visibility.

"I love you too! And Grandma!"

"We'll get you out of there, okay? Be strong!"

That was the last he heard from her. A door slammed somewhere far away, and Kellan's heart gave a little hitch at the possibility it was a cell door locking. Then his own door was yanked open without warning, startling him because he hadn't even heard anyone approach.

The tall Auditor with the acne scars stepped in and ate up all the light in the doorway. "Get up."

Kellan complied, hope and fear warring in his chest. "Where's my mother? Is she okay?"

"Turn around, hands behind your back."

"What's going on?"

"I said put your hands behind your back *now*."

Something in the guard's tone made Kellan's mouth go dry. He knew from his arrest this guy wouldn't hesitate to grab his injured arm if he didn't comply. He stood and turned, placing his hands carefully behind his back. "Where are you taking me?"

He received no response, but felt the cool metal cuffs tightening around his wrists, digging into the skin. The Auditor gripped his upper arm – the good one, at least – and steered him into the hallway.

Two more Auditors waited outside. Neither met his eyes as they flanked him.

"Is it time to dig?" he asked as the pockmarked Auditor gave him a mean-spirited shove to start him marching down the hallway.

Kellan looked at the slots in the cell doors they passed. Most were empty. A few Blinker eyes looked out at him. One was waiting with his face pressed up against his slot, a hateful glint in his eyes. "Terrorist," he said, then spat through the slot as Kellan passed.

"Hey," barked one of the Auditors, and slammed his palm against the door.

The man recoiled, then hissed at Kellan's back, "I hope Glass hurts like hell!"

"Turn here," the tall Auditor said, wrenching Kellan's arm and making him bite down on his lip to avoid crying out.

They were leaving the prison module, entering the sector proper. Immediately, Kellan's presence with his cuffed hands and patchwork clothes drew sneers and distrustful glances. A few Blinkers turned and went the other way when they saw his envoy coming. He started trying to steel himself for the airlock, for the dig, for his final few days.

And then the Auditor tugged on his cuffs, bringing him to a halt outside a metal pocket door in the middle of the sector. "We're here."

Kellan looked up at the pristine etched metal sign over the door. "Medical?"

Did they finally care about his arm?

He didn't trust it.

QUINTA

YEAR: 2179

Quinta arrived at work feeling hung over, despite the fact that she hadn't touched a drop of fruit wine since her last birthday. The stuff was far too expensive to waste on the deep depression she'd spent the last week falling into.

No, she'd hardly slept last night because she was too busy rooting through all of her father's patient files, cataloging every instance where she knew he couldn't be where his records said he was. She'd slogged through the past three months of records and found a dozen instances where she was sure there was a fabrication before she was brave enough to ask Valence to cross-check his Exchange schedule.

Fifty-three more discrepancies. That was what Valence found, and it had knocked the breath out of Quinta's lungs, harsher than being in an airlock without a pressure suit. And those were only the patient visits Hadrian had invented out of whole cloth. Who knew how many times he'd given a legitimate prescription but doctored the quantities?

She'd had two cups of Candor dark and nothing else at breakfast – she didn't think her stomach could handle solid food – and still she felt like composted shit when she walked into the clinic on autopilot. She was thinking about her indigo dress. All those sweaters and the non-prescription trips to the rabbitat over the years. The beautiful Earth jewelry her father bought for her mother whenever he found a piece at the market.

Was it all tainted?

Bought with black-market credits from stolen supplies?

Was that what her father thought his family cared about?

Was it what *he* cared about?

She was still swimming in those thoughts when she practically walked into Dr. Liang in front of the nurses' station. The older woman narrowed her eyes, looking Quinta up and down. "You look terrible."

"I had a rough night."

"You know, no one would think less of you if you took some time off," Liang said. "You're grieving. It would be perfectly under-standable if you spent a few weeks harvesting strawberries."

From anyone else, it would have sounded like sympathy, but Quinta knew Dr. Liang all too well. Time off would only translate – to her, to the rest of the med staff, to Valence herself – as weakness, and that kind of thing always got held against you later. When it was time to graduate, or get a promotion, or even in the amount of credits Valence assigned to your tasks.

"I'm fine," Quinta said, straightening her posture. "Just a bad night's sleep. It won't affect my work."

"If you're sure." Liang's skepticism dripped from her tone. "I've assigned you to rooms one through four this morning. Do you think you can handle that on your own, or should I observe?"

She was six months away from the end of her apprenticeship – she didn't need to be observed doing routine physicals. She clenched her jaw and forced a smile. "Nope, I've got it."

"Room one has already been waiting fifteen minutes."

Quinta turned away without comment, pulling up the patient

chart. It was Terra Levitt, the woman who'd sparked the Glass scare what now felt like an eternity ago. She was here for a follow-up. Quinta steeled herself. She wasn't sure how it would feel to see her and be reminded of that day.

She stepped into the room, closing the door behind her.

"Hi, Terra, do you remember me?"

"Dr. Voss," Terra said, and Quinta could practically see the stars in her eyes. "How are you holding up? I watched the funeral video. Such a beautiful service."

"I'm fine, thank you." Terra was sitting up today and a healthy color had returned to her skin. Quinta pulled up her vitals on the display wall. "How have you been feeling? Any lingering respiratory issues?"

"Nothing physical," Terra said, fingers finding her Heart of Mars pendant. "I've been praying for your father, you know. And thanking Valence for serving justice to that wretched NPC who killed him. She always balances the ledger."

Quinta faltered for a moment, forgetting what she was going to do next. She never knew what to say to Chosen babble. Then she tucked her stethoscope into her ears, moving to Terra's side. "Take a breath for me?"

She put the end to Terra's back and heard clear lung sounds.

"Again," she prompted, moving her stethoscope to the other side.

"Have you been following the chats about volunteers?" Terra asked, obscuring the sound as she inhaled. "At first I couldn't believe Valence was going to have regular citizens digging alongside that criminal, but actually, the more I think about it, it's actually beautiful."

Quinta couldn't help herself. "beautiful?"

"She's not just punishing him, she's allowing him to redeem himself through service to the colony," she said. Quinta gave up on trying to listen to her lungs and moved on to preparing a syringe so she could take another sample. Terra went on, "And after all that ugliness at the meeting, she's proving to us that she really doesn't play favorites. Our people will dig beside an NPC, a murderer, and when they fix the system together, something meaningful will have come out of a tragedy."

"My father's death was not some object lesson for the colony," Quinta said, forgetting her professional voice entirely.

Terra blinked. "Of course, Dr. Voss. I'm sorry."

Quinta had her roll up her sleeve for the jab, and left the room as quickly as she could manage after that. Fucking Chosen.

She stepped into the waiting room, but just as she was about to turn right toward the next treatment room, Dr. Liang emerged from a door further down the hall in that direction. Rather than have to meet her overly critical gaze once again, Quinta took a sharp left and ducked into the staff restroom. It wouldn't hurt to splash some cold water on her face, anyway.

She was letting the water air-dry, her hands braced against the sink, when the door slid open. Expecting Dr. Liang and another lecture, Quinta was relieved to see Cydra Tavara.

Cydra was not so happy to see Quinta.

She paused mid-step the minute their eyes locked in the mirror over the sink, and Quinta's jaw dropped when she saw her pivoting on her heels, about to flee. Apparently the modicum of camaraderie the other day had been a fluke.

"Wait," Quinta barked, with a commanding tone she didn't even know she possessed.

Cydra turned back to Quinta. Then she nodded toward the decon shower tucked into the corner. "I just saw a patient from waste management. I need to follow protocol," she said.

Quinta nodded, holding out one arm in a *be my guest* gesture.

Cydra entered the antechamber, pulling the flimsy aluminum door closed behind her so she could undress. Quinta knew Cydra would be able to hear her, and she'd never get a better chance to get to the bottom of this than while Cydra was trapped in there.

Quinta went up to the door. "Why have you been avoiding me?"

"I haven't," Cydra lied. "We've been busy, and the sector three CO_2 patients–"

"Have been following up with Dr. Nilsen in their own sector," Quinta finished for her. "You have too, ever since the funeral."

She heard the rattle of pipes and then the familiar hiss of the water-peroxide bath beginning. For a minute, she thought Cydra wouldn't answer. But then she said, "There've been rumors. I didn't know what to make of them."

"You could have *talked* to me about them. You were my father's right hand."

"Which made it all the more confusing and painful to hear about," Cydra snapped.

"So you're saying you didn't know?"

"What? Of course not!" There was a pause, and then she asked, "Are you saying you believe the rumors?"

Quinta let out a long sigh. "Valence found fifty-three discrepancies in my father's charting," she said. "You worked with him for most of your career. *All* of his career. And you knew nothing about what he was doing?"

"If I knew I would have told Valence!" she hissed, and the mist clicked off. Next in the cycle was about a minute of high-pressure ozone, and that was too loud to talk over. All Quinta could do was stand impatiently outside the chamber, trying to make all the puzzle pieces fit.

Her father was not a selfish man, nor was he starved for credits as one of the most skilled doctors in the hab. So why do it?

When Cydra finally stepped out of the chamber in a fresh set of coveralls, she looked dismayed to see Quinta still standing there, arms crossed over her chest. "Who told you?"

"What?"

"Where did you hear the rumors?" Quinta demanded. "Nobody

said a peep about any of this until the day after he died, and then suddenly everyone in the hab knew. Who told you?"

Cydra swallowed so hard Quinta could see her throat muscles move. "Eden."

Quinta's hands closed into fists at her sides. "I should have known. She always wanted to be head doctor. And what does she do the minute he dies? Starts changing everything around here, takes his office. She's trying to erase him."

"Do you know your father was once investigated by the medical board?" Cydra asked.

Quinta remembered it. She'd been about thirteen, and no one would tell her what it was about. All she knew was that both her parents had been tense and testy for weeks.

"It's nothing for you to worry yourself over," her mother had said.

"Just a little colony bureaucracy," her dad had tried to reassure her.

"Yes, I heard," Quinta confirmed.

"I didn't know what it was about at the time," Cydra said. "No one wanted to talk about it, and I wasn't going to risk my position by asking. Eden told me after he died that it was about theft. She said she was the one who went to the board with her suspicions, but nothing ever came of it. She was afraid to speak against him after that."

"If nothing came of it, then he must have been found innocent," Quinta said."

Cydra shook her head. "The record is sealed. Look it up, the file is locked. Do you know how rare it is for a medical board inquiry to be sealed?"

There were all kinds of logs that Valence restricted for a bunch of reasons – because they contained personal details about a colonist, or information that could be dangerous in the wrong hands, or simply because they were outdated and archived. But medical board records were typically open to everyone working in the department.

"Valence wouldn't let him just keep stealing for the last seven years."

"But why would the file be sealed if he was innocent?" Cydra asked. "I just keep wondering if he bribed the board to keep the whole incident quiet."

"He wouldn't do that," Quinta said, although even she heard the conviction leaking out of her voice.

"I was so blind–"

Quinta didn't hear the rest of it. She was already storming out of the restroom and down the hall, head whipping around as she hunted for Liang. The only bit of luck she had that day was finding her in her office instead of a treatment room. They didn't need an audience for this.

Quinta barged in and shut the door behind her.

Liang's eyes went wide as she looked up from her desk. "Can I help you?"

"Yeah, you can tell me why you sat there and pretended the rumors weren't coming from you!" Quinta was shaking with anger now. "You waited until he couldn't defend himself to ruin his reputation."

"I *tried* to say something when he was alive," Liang hissed. She stood, coming around her desk so there was nothing between them. It unnerved Quinta, like it was probably designed to. "Do you know how much courage it took to go to the board and accuse a *Voss* of one of the worst sins in the colony? And look what happened."

She smacked her hands together so angrily it made Quinta jump.

"Nothing," Liang said. "Do you know what kind of punishment Valence would have handed down if it had been *me*? But it was Hadrian Voss, so she sealed his record and people went right on worshipping him."

"That's not–" Quinta started to object, but she was old enough to notice all the extra helpings at dinner, the favors she never asked for… Sometimes she even suspected she got a few more credits for the same work as other people.

"The irony is that I actually assumed he stopped after that investigation," Liang said. "The supply inventory discrepancies stopped. But the fact that you're in here yelling at me about *when* I chose to speak up and not accusing me of spreading vicious lies tells me all I need to know." She turned her head sideways, narrowing her eyes. "Were you helping him?"

"What? No! I figured it out because of your rumors!" Quinta's face felt hot – it must have been beet-red by now, and tears were threatening in the back of her throat. "If you thought he stopped, why did you do it? It's over, he's dead!"

"It's not over!" Liang roared. "You think Valence was going to realize I've been the better physician all along and award me the head doctor job that I deserve? When she has a brand-new Dr. Voss six months away from graduation?" She huffed. "Not a chance, unless I could make the rest of the colony see what I already know – the Vosses are not perfect citizens, they're corruptible and selfish and weak, just like any of us can be. And you're just like your father, whether you know it yet or not."

Quinta couldn't speak. Couldn't argue. Because underneath the rage and grief, she knew Liang was right. Her father had stolen. The system had protected him. And she'd benefited from all of it – the respect, the training, the stupid angora sweaters.

She turned and left, leaving Liang's door open behind her.

Cydra was at the nurses' station. There were patients waiting in the treatment rooms for Quinta. She ignored all of it, letting the tears streak down her face and drench the front of her coveralls. She walked right out the clinic doors, stripping off her white coat as she went.

She'd worked with her father every day for three years, some days without leaving his side once. How had she missed all of it?

Not only the hoarding, the greed, but the self-importance? The belief that because they were Vosses, they deserved all the attention and extra rations and special treatment they got.

Quinta felt contaminated.

She opened her overlay and gave a voice command. "Valence, I wish to resign my medical apprenticeship. Requesting reassignment to another module." Her voice broke as she added, "Any other module."

There was an unusually long pause before Valence responded, two words big and red across Quinta's field of vision: *Request denied.*

QUINTA

YEAR: 2179

Quinta's feet carried her almost without conscious thought to the rabbit module. Of all the places you could spend a few credits to relax – the pleasure gardens, the Parallax court, the market – it was Quinta's favorite, and where most of her discretionary credits went.

Ada and Dana's Place. That was what the small 3D-printed plaque beside the door called the module, decorated in delicate flowers. Citizens from generations ago, and though Quinta didn't know their significance, the plaque always made her smile. Until a few days ago, she could have easily pictured a similar one appearing outside the med clinic doors with her father's name on it. Now, it seemed no one wanted to commemorate him, and Valence wouldn't allow her to ignore his crimes, either.

She could at least distract herself for an hour. She used her overlay to call the hutch supervisor, Mylo, and a moment later, the door slid open, the pungent, comforting smells of the rabbits and their hay and waste all hitting her full-force.

"Dr. Voss." Mylo looked up with a smile from where he was

refilling a water dispenser. "It's a bit early to be seeing you. No work today?"

Well, I tried to resign my post but Valence told me I was too far into my apprenticeship to waste all that training time, she thought angrily.

"I really need to hold a rabbit," she said instead. "Please."

"Of course. Anyone catch your eye?"

Quinta looked around the rabbitat. There were a few dozen hopping around the play area, a mix of sizes, colors and breeds. She spotted a white and black one with a line down its back like a racing stripe and her heart squeezed in her chest. She pointed to a tan lop instead. "That one looks calm."

"That's Pepper," Mylo said, lifting the rabbit into her arms. "She's good with people."

A notification pinged in Quinta's overlay. *Beginning one hour of non-prescription rabbit time, fifteen credits deducted.* She sat on the prickly artificial grass and cradled Pepper to her chest, feeling the rapid flutter of a tiny heart against her palm.

"I'll be over there if you need anything," Mylo said, gesturing toward his workstation.

Pepper's warmth seeped through Quinta's coverall, but the comfort she usually found here was elusive. Her father was dead and her new boss was gleefully dragging his name through the mud. Worse, what Liang said about him was true, and Quinta would have to walk into that clinic every single day knowing that everyone else there knew about it.

Her father was a hoarder.

Quinta still didn't know why, but one thing had to be true: he was selfish.

And what was worse, he'd lied to her for years, pretending to be a good man.

She sent her mother a message. *Are you free? I'm in the rabbitat.* It was time to ask those questions she'd been too scared to ask before. How much did Havana know? But the message went unanswered. The hab map showed her in the central commons, which usually meant she was in a meeting with the administration, and almost always meant she was too busy for her daughter.

Quinta stroked Pepper's soft fur, watching the other rabbits play. A recently shorn angora sniffed around Quinta's shoes. She ran a hand robotically over its oddly textured short fur and lost track of time. Mylo moved around her, doing his duties and racking up credits for them. An hour came and went, and Quinta extended her time.

"Are you doing okay, Dr. Voss?" Mylo asked, putting a hand gently on her shoulder.

She nodded, not quite trusting her voice.

"Your father was a great man," he said. "I'm sorry for your loss."

You must not have heard what he was doing, then.

"Thank you," she replied weakly.

Eventually, Pepper got tired of being held and Quinta had to let her go. Other rabbits sniffed around her and a jet-black one that looked small enough to be a juvenile hopped up on her lap. Every time Quinta thought she'd definitely overstayed her welcome and she should drag herself out of the rabbitat, another rabbit came over, curious head bobbing up and down as it crept closer, and her will to leave melted all over again.

If she left the rabbitat, she'd have to face reality. Figure out how she was going to look the clinic staff in the eyes in the morning. Wait for her mother to come home and have that difficult conversation.

"Are you staying open for me?" Quinta asked Mylo when she noticed it was past dinnertime. "I can leave."

"No, Dr. Voss, stay as long as you wish," he answered, although his smile looked tired.

"I'll donate extra credits to the rabbitat," Quinta offered, and then a knife of guilt stabbed her in the gut. Her parents had taught her that trick years ago – make donations, get what you want. Was that what her father had done to get that medical board record sealed? Made a charitable "donation"?

"No need," Mylo said. "I can tell you need the rabbits today. Please, stay."

She shook her head. "No, I should be going. Thank you for letting me stay as long as I did."

Overstaying her welcome. Getting special privileges because she was a Voss?

She transferred an extra hour's worth of credits to the rabbitat, then stepped into the hallway – and ran straight into Castor.

"Hey, I saw you were here on the hab map," he said, his brow furrowed. "I ran into Nurse Tavara in the dining hall and she told me you were having a bad day."

Quinta scoffed. "That's all she said? Just a bad day?"

"What's going on?" he asked. "And don't say 'nothing' because I've known you since we were infants. It's written all over your face."

The straightforward question broke something in her. The emotions she'd been pushing down all day surged forward and tears burst from her eyes. Before she could stop it, she was bawling right there in the hallway where anyone could see her, and she threw her arms around Castor, burying her face against his neck.

"Everything is ruined!" she sobbed.

Castor's hands tentatively found her back. He started rubbing circles on it. "It's… it'll be okay. I mean, I've never lost a parent, so I don't know–"

"It's not that," she said between gasps, struggling to get herself under control. She released him, wiping her eyes with the backs of her sleeves. "Have you heard what they've been saying about him?"

Castor's eyes darted away, then back to her. "Yeah. Vicious, despicable–"

"It's *true*," she said, fresh tears pushing at the backs of her eyelids, and Castor's jaw dropped.

"What? How can it be?"

For the first time since the tears came, Quinta was aware of her surroundings. Mylo could come out of the rabbitat at any moment. Anyone else could come up the hallway and overhear them. "Let's go to my room. I can't talk about this here."

Havana still wasn't home by the time they got there, but Quinta didn't need her walking in on this. She'd rather broach the subject with her mom delicately, and alone.

Quinta took Castor into her bedroom and closed the door. He sat at her desk and she told him everything, ending with Dr. Liang's declaration that the colony deserved to know who the Vosses really were and Valence's refusal to let Quinta resign to get away from her.

It was at that point that Castor's expression turned from horror to anger. "Wait, why would you let that ladder climber make you feel ashamed? Who does she think she is, talking to a Voss like that?"

Quinta grimaced. "That's kind of the whole point. Why should we get special privileges, especially if it turns out we've been abusing them all this time?"

Castor's face went deadly serious and he shook his head. "Quinta, your father was one of the finest physicians we've ever had. Your grandfather was the only reason we survived the second outbreak. We're all alive because your great-great-great grandfather knew we needed to get off Earth and he built this colony just in the nick of time. What did the Liangs do that was better?"

"Well, they didn't get credit-hungry and start stealing medical supplies to sell on the black market," Quinta said.

"There has to be some other explanation for what your father was doing," Castor said. "Maybe it only *looked* like hoarding. Phobos, maybe Liang set him up!"

Quinta flopped down on the bed across from him. "Valence found over fifty instances where he manipulated his patient files to cover what he was doing with the supplies."

Castor let out a sigh. "Even if he was stealing, what does it have to do with your career? All you ever wanted was to be a doctor. I can't believe you tried to resign."

"I just don't think I can show my face there again... or maybe anywhere."

Castor reached over and picked up her hand. She'd been wringing them, and he cupped her hand in his. They were firm and warm, and it was far more intimate a gesture than they usually shared. Quinta's heart skipped a beat.

"You can't just... what, hide in here forever? We'll figure out how to handle Liang together, okay?" he said. "Maybe we can report her to the board for bullying, get her reassigned to another sector."

Quinta shook her head. "It's not just her. They all know. I can't go back there."

The truth of it solidified in her chest as soon as it was out of her mouth. It had been coming to her slowly all afternoon, the determination that no matter what Valence said, she couldn't go back to work as a doctor. And there was only one thing Valence would let her do instead.

"You have to," Castor said gently. "Valence wouldn't let you resign."

Quinta looked into his cricket-colored eyes, dark with just a few speckles of lighter brown, and said what had been pushing at the back of her mind all afternoon. "I'm going to dig."

Castor froze. She watched his Adam's apple bob. "What did you just say?"

"It's the only job that has more value to the colony than me finishing my apprenticeship right now," she said. "And my family owes a huge debt to the colony after what my father did. I could start repaying it by volunteering."

"You're not serious." Castor's voice was flat with disbelief. "The regolith is riddled with Glass. You of all people know that – you're a doctor. If you touch it, you'll die."

"I have nothing left to lose."

"You have everything to lose!" Castor cried, his hands tightening over Quinta's. "You're brilliant, you're almost a doctor, you have your whole career ahead of you. You could be head doctor in a few years. And you know Valence will want you to start a family to continue the Voss line… The colony needs you alive, not desiccating in the Frozen Mounds… *I* need you."

His eyes were glossy with fear. "It'll be okay," she told him. "Valence's primary job is to keep us safe and healthy, so she wouldn't ask us to dig if she didn't have some plan to protect us."

"That's… a good point." Castor thought for a minute, then shook his head. "No, you can't do it. You'd have to dig alongside *him.*"

Kellan Reilly. The name popped into her head, unwelcome. The one who'd caused the malfunction that killed her father, Owen and Elise. It had occurred to her, she wasn't happy about it, but paying a debt to society shouldn't be a joy.

"Castor, I need this," she confessed. "Everywhere I turn, people look at me and see my father. That was true even before. But you should see the way they look at me now – especially Liang, but the others too. Cydra has known me my whole life and she can barely stand to be in the same room with me. I have to prove to them that I'm not like him, I wasn't in on it, or they'll never stop whispering behind my back. I'm doing it."

She opened her overlay, pulling up the task in her Exchange. She'd submit her application right here and now, before she lost her nerve.

"You're wrong. They might not know the full story, but they'll find out you did nothing wrong. They don't hate you – no one could," Castor said. There was a long pause where she figured he'd run out of arguments, but then he said, "I'm coming with you."

Quinta double-blinked the display closed. "What?"

"I won't let you put yourself in danger alone… especially with that NPC around," he said, and then suddenly, his lips were on hers. His hand released hers and hooked around the back of her head, and Quinta couldn't move.

Their first kiss.

His breath smelled like tonight's pasta dish, his lips slicking hers with too much saliva.

And then it was over.

He released her, too sheepish to make eye contact as he tucked his hands between his knees, a big grin on his face. "I'm sorry."

"It's… okay," she stuttered, because what else could you say to that? But her mind was racing. Was it okay? Was it long overdue or something she never wanted to happen again?

Oh Deimos, would he do it again?

"Umm, I'm submitting my application now," she said, blinking open her display again.

"Me too," he announced.

LIRA

YEAR: 2083

When Lira left med clinic two the morning Ada died, all she wanted was to be alone forever to wallow in her grief. After she talked to Dr. Kalb and learned that she was being quarantined in the rabbitat, not being alone became the singular goal her mind fixated on.

She had medical training, and she'd seen first-hand what happened in that clinic. She didn't want to be trapped here, helpless, but Valence was tracking her vitals constantly and even though they were normal, with no symptoms reported in the questionnaires, it refused to clear her to leave the rabbitat.

Lira focused on contact tracing and found nine people including herself who'd been in the two affected med clinics yesterday. Hoyt and Dana, of course, and one other person who'd come to visit a dig crew member after the accident. There were also six patients being treated for unrelated issues when the dig crew arrived, and a few who showed up after for medical attention and were turned away to one of the other clinics.

Lira had the complete list to Dr. Kalb by the next morning and kept messaging him periodically to check in on him and his staff, making pointless offers of assistance, as if she could do anything from a sector away.

It was amazing how quickly a dire prognosis could bury a hatchet.

His estimate of eight hours had been pessimistic, thank God, but there was no denying that whatever this was, it was highly infectious. Most of the overnight staff that had run so many codes and called so many times of death were now sick too, and it felt like there was a giant clock over Lira's head, audibly counting down to the inevitable.

Trapped with her thoughts, she did her best to avoid dwelling on it.

There were health reports to submit and rabbits to feed. Lira found a video that her mom had sent a few days ago, that had gotten buried in her messages. Her mom lived in Manila, in the middle of a flood plain that didn't exist just a few years ago, and Lira was perpetually worried that one day she'd wake up to terrible news that her childhood home had gotten swept away in a flash flood.

This video was a painfully quaint one, in which her mom asked whether she'd proposed to Ada yet, and wondered what exactly you use as an engagement ring when you're living on Mars without access to a jeweler.

"Can you have one forged, or shipped? Imagine the import duty on Mars! But I guess there must be markets there, you could find one second-hand," her mom was rambling, talking with her hands like she always did. "Well, it'd be sad if there was a second-hand ring there, though, because who wants to get divorced on Mars and then have to see their ex again and again in such a small space..."

The video was long and rambling, and it made Lira smile because her mom always talked like that, not waiting for an answer to her myriad questions, even when there wasn't a satellite delay preventing synchronous talk. She just wanted to ask and it didn't matter so much if she ever got an answer.

Lira started and stopped recording a response half a dozen times, trying to tell her mom what happened, but every time she started the sentence "Ada is..." her voice would crack or tears would threaten or anger would rise up so unexpectedly that she'd have to stop the recording. She wasn't ready to say those words out loud.

In any case, she wasn't confident VossCorp would let that information reach Earth at this stage in the crisis, so it'd be pointless to try.

Instead, Lira explained to her mom how various types of metal were forged on Mars, and that she'd been saving up her credits to bribe one of the fabricators to make her a ring. She'd brought a pair of sapphire earrings with her from Earth – a graduation gift from her mother, in fact – and she'd been planning to repurpose the stones.

"I hope you don't mind," she said, pretending there was still a proposal in her future.

She could save those earrings now, and have a few extra cups of Candor dark roast with all those credits. She ended the video before she could start crying again.

It would probably seem oddly emotional to her mom, but Lira didn't have it in her to record it again, so she sent it. Then, to keep herself occupied, she started monitoring the chattier side of her overlay.

Technically, gossiping via implant was discouraged – VossCorp still clung to the idea they were running a company that just so happened to be located on Mars, rather than a whole new iteration of human society with no expectation of a return trip. They wanted their employees professional at all times and their communications through company channels to be strictly on-topic. But it hadn't taken the colonists long to figure out how to use the overlay for less official purposes.

With ten people dead and more sick, there was no way the company culture could override the colonists' curiosity.

Within just a few hours of Lira's conversation with Dr. Kalb last night, it seemed like everyone knew. Every department's chat had some variation of the truth about what happened, some more fantastical than others, many just as panic-driven as the doctor had feared.

There's a Mars-born virus spreading thru in the hab and it's 100% fatal.

Some kind of mutant radiation sickness from the solar flare is killing everyone who had even a little exposure.

There's a deadly, infectious mold in the ventilation system and we're all breathing it.

Those were just a few of the theories floating around, and when Jamila came to the rabbitat that morning to deliver the daily greens, Lira learned things were even crazier out there than she'd read.

"There are people barricading their dorms," Jamila told her. They were talking through a video chat since Lira wasn't permitted to open the door until Jamila had left. "Trying to tape closed their air vents, thinking they can limit their exposure by not breathing anyone else's air."

"We don't even know how it spreads yet," Lira said. Dr. Kalb had said he didn't think it was aerosolized. "Wouldn't Valence have already sealed the vents if it would help?"

The hab was highly modular so that if any one sector became contaminated or any one redundant life support system failed, it could be isolated so as not to take down the entire colony. Valence was built to have complete autonomy in cases of mechanical failure, when human actions might be delayed or compromised.

"I'm no systems engineer but I think it has," Jamila said. "The hydroponic gardens are on recycled air right now. I think Valence *is* doing damage control."

"So people are duct taping their vents to make themselves feel better."

"Security theater," Jamila said. "They're barring a lot of the doors, too. It's chaos out here. You're kinda lucky to be in there."

In here with my thoughts, Lira filled in grimly.

"How are you doing?" she asked. "Are you scared?"

Jamila shrugged and swiped the back of her hand across her brow. "We're living in a human-sized rabbit warren, and we've been sharing our air, water, and food supply since before we knew this… infection, whatever it is… existed. If I'm gonna get sick, I'm not sure there's much I can do to stop it. Panicking isn't productive."

"Well, that's admirably level-headed."

"What about you?"

"I'm not sure I have the emotional range to panic right now." The immediate threat had done a good job of pushing thoughts of Ada from the forefront of her mind, but visions of her lying there, her skin glassy and damp, her eyes vacant, were never far. "I've made it this long without symptoms," she pointed out. "I'm probably fine. You came in here yesterday, though. If I exposed you–"

"If you weren't sick, I don't see how you could have made me sick," Jamila said. "Anyway, I'm going to leave so you can bring these greens inside now. It'd be a shame to let them wilt out here in the hall."

"Don't hang up," Lira blurted. "Please, keep talking to me. It's too quiet in here."

So Jamila took Lira back to hydroponics with her on the call. She had to switch to audio only, but she narrated for Lira, who wanted to know what it was like outside the rabbitat.

"There's no one in the halls," Jamila said. "I only passed one person on my way to you."

When she reconnected to video via one of the ceiling-mounted cameras in the gardens, Lira sucked in a relieved breath. The lush green towers and long, horizontal channels looked the same as they always did, filled with nutrient-rich, crunchy, delicious vegetables.

It felt normal, until Lira noticed the absence of other hydroponic techs moving up and down the rows.

"Is there anyone else working today?" she asked.

"Valence switched us to solo shifts of four hours each," Jamila explained. "Less chance of infecting each other. And of course, we have to undergo extensive health checks before we begin work. We can't risk the food supply by not showing up, but we also can't risk bringing disease into the module."

"Is everyone on your crew okay?"

"So far. I hope this is all blown out of proportion and we can laugh about those idiots barricading their dorms a few weeks from now."

"Well, you can laugh," Lira said. "Not sure I'll be up for it."

"Right. Sorry."

"Will you let me watch you work?" Lira asked, desperate not to end the call. "What are you doing?"

"Fertilizing the root vegetables," Jamila said. "I'll show you."

LIRA

YEAR: 2083

Jamila didn't bring the rabbits' greens the next day.

Lira got a sour stomach the moment she realized Jamila was late, and it took her another hour to get up the courage call her and find out why.

Jamila answered right away, and for half a second, relief washed over Lira so completely her legs threatened to give out beneath her. And then she noticed the veins creeping up Jamila's jaw, faint but undeniably present.

"Oh God," she breathed, her hand going to her mouth.

"It's okay," Jamila said, her voice weaker than yesterday. "I'm resting, I'm in quarantine and they started me on IV meds. I'm starting to feel better already."

But I'm not sick and you are, Lira's mind screamed. Jamila was a plant girl, not a medical one, so she didn't know how bad that was.

"How long ago did it start?" Lira asked, trying to stay calm. She was already doing the math in her head. It had been a little under forty-eight hours since she found Ada in the clinic, and pretty close to twenty-four since the first time she saw Jamila after and they hugged.

"I had a low fever when I woke up this morning," Jamila explained. "I reported it and Dr. Nilsen in med clinic one told me to stay home and keep sending health reports to Valence." She raised a hand to reveal an IV line taped to her cyanotic skin. "They sent a nurse with the meds. She was dressed like she was treating plague victims."

Jamila laughed, but Lira didn't.

The dig crew had gotten sick much faster, but Jamila's was the same timeframe Dr. Kalb had reported among the other secondary exposures. This thing, whatever it was, was exacting.

"You had to have been exposed through me," Lira said. "I'm so sorry."

"It could have been someone else," Jamila said. "I've been other places in the hab. The gardens have had four different people working in them, just not all at once. Don't blame yourself. It won't help anything."

"What are they giving you?" Lira asked.

"Antibiotics," Jamila said. "That's what they think it is, a bacteria."

Lira's brow furrowed. "No bacteria I've ever seen does this." No virus either, for that matter.

Jamila shook her head. "You might not have seen it before, but our microbiologists have. I got the scoop from my visiting plague nurse."

She paused to draw breath, getting winded in just this easy conversation. Concern gnawed at Lira's gut.

"I'd heard about it," she went on. "Kind of forgot until now because it had nothing to do with the hydroponics program."

"What?"

"The first colonists found a Martian bacterium in the permafrost when they were looking for water," Jamila explained. "They studied it extensively, of course, but it was dead when they found it. They concluded it must have gone extinct a long time ago."

"Right, I do remember that," Lira said, the memory surfacing.

She'd heard about it in news reports back on Earth, but it was around the time her vet clinic had gone literally under water so she hadn't paid much attention. "Sorin Voss put his name on it because that's what he does."

Jamila nodded. "Vossibacter martialis. It was a huge story at the time, the first native life ever found on another planet. It could have been life-altering, but then it turned out the bacteria was dead. I heard VossCorp never even sent any specimens back to Earth because they were afraid of losing exclusivity."

Did the scientists really screw this up so bad they mislabeled a living organism?

"It's alive?" Lira asked. "How?"

They were the best on Earth, hand-picked by Sorin Voss himself. They wouldn't have made that mistake.

"No clue," Jamila said. "Every microbiologist in the hab is working on answering that now." Her eyelids looked heavy, and she rested her head against the bedframe behind her. Lira's chest tightened, remembering how exhausted Ada had been once her symptoms began.

She said, "Get some rest, Jamila. I'll check in again later."

She ended the call and immediately placed a second one, this time to Dr. Kalb in clinic two. When he answered, it was as an audio call rather than the video he'd used yesterday. Suspicion rippled through Lira's veins, imagining what he might look like twenty-four hours into this disease. Ada hadn't made it past sixteen hours.

"Dr. Salonga?" His voice was huskier than yesterday, thicker, like his throat was full of mucus.

"How are you feeling, Dr. Kalb?"

"I'm doing all right, thank you for asking." She could hear him shuffling around. He must still be in the clinic – Valence would not authorize him to leave if he had symptoms – and Lira wondered if he was still well enough to treat the medical staff who'd fallen ill. "What can I do for you?"

"I just spoke to Jamila Jones," she said. "This is bad."

She didn't need to say more than that. Dr. Kalb said, "And the rumors are spreading as fast as the bacteria. We've had people lined up outside of our clinic all day demanding antibiotics. I couldn't open the door even if I wanted to."

"How much do you have on hand?" Lira held her breath, not sure she wanted to hear the answer. The hab operated lean in all regards – there were redundancies and backups and stockpiles, but the margins were always tight because they simply didn't have the raw materials or human resources to spare.

"This doesn't go beyond us," Dr. Kalb warned.

"Of course not."

"We keep two hundred one-week courses of broad-spectrum antibiotics on hand," he said. "And about fifty courses total of a few different specialized types. That's for the entire hab." There was a pause in which Lira heard him swallow, the sound sticky. "We've already started administering them to all medical personnel and the microbiologists, and the secondary exposures who are exhibiting symptoms."

Lira's heart dropped into her stomach. That was a lot of people. "How many are left?"

"A hundred and forty-five of the broad-spectrums," he said. "We're doing trial runs on the specialized antibiotics, just one patient each for now, so we have forty-six of those left."

"For the entire hab of a thousand people," Lira said, letting the numbers sink in. "Are we making more?"

"Of course," Dr. Kalb said. "But they take five days to synthesize, and we don't even know which ones are effective yet... if any."

Lira was thinking about the contact tracing she'd done, about how the med clinics were focusing on the original nine people – Lira included – who'd come in direct contact with the dig crew.

But all nine of those people had gone on to have contact with quite a few others before they knew that what happened to the dig crew was not isolated. Lira had had close to a dozen rabbitat visitors on that first day, including Jamila. Med clinics one and four had seen patients, who might have first gone to clinics two and three and been turned away, taking the bacteria with them. One of the original nine who'd watched his friend die in clinic three had gone to work after to keep his mind occupied… and his work was in a dining hall, handing trays to people, handling their food.

Now twenty-four hours had passed and Jamila was sick, someone who hadn't stepped foot in a med clinic while the dig crew was still alive.

All of it swam in Lira's head and she realized they were looking at a much larger number than they originally thought, a nearly uncontainable number. Containment was all but impossible now.

"What can I do?"

"I don't…" Dr. Kalb sighed, a sound of resignation. He drew a breath and came back stronger. "Help us keep people calm. Valence is sending us more health reports than we can handle, from the people you identified and from people self-reporting. Valence does a pretty good job of triaging and pointing us toward the ones who really need help, but there are a lot more who are panicking and demanding prophylactics. If I get you access to the clinic system, would you be willing to start calling people and calming them down? Is that something you'd be comfortable with?"

No, Lira thought immediately. None of her usual patients spoke and she was a heck of a lot more comfortable with non-verbal soothing, but she'd offered to help, and there wasn't much else she could do while locked in the rabbitat. "Yes, of course."

The relief in Dr. Kalb's voice was audible when he said, "Thank you, Dr. Salonga. I'll submit the request for access right now."

KELLAN

YEAR: 2179

Kellan squinted against the bright lights, bright walls, bright floors of the hallway. He'd never gotten used to how white everything was in the Blinker sectors, and his vision had been blurry and sensitive ever since they held him down and forced a retinal implant on him.

He still wore handcuffs, but they were in front of him today, and his arm was mostly healed by now. Small mercies, although Kellan wasn't in a particularly gracious mood toward them.

"Keep moving," the Auditor behind him said. "We're late."

It wasn't the pockmarked, silver-haired one he'd gotten used to. Not one of them had ever thought to give Kellan their name, but he'd gotten to know them by their attitudes. Some were openly hostile, sneering their hopes for him to die a slow death. Others seemed reluctant to have anything to do with him and wouldn't even make eye contact, but at least they weren't pushers.

Not like this one.

He jabbed something small and pointy between Kellan's shoulder blades, urging him onward. Kellan recoiled, and kept marching. He cradled a bulky pressure suit and helmet in his arms, the shiny new material mesmerizing and ostentatious all at the same time. It was the most expensive thing he'd ever touched, and he was going to wear it to go outside and dig in the regolith.

A notification flashed across his vision, along with a roll of nausea. *Atmospheric conversion unit replacement mission orientation in the sector three fabrication module begins in fifteen minutes, five credits.*

It had been happening for a few days now and he still wasn't used to the constant intrusions into his field of view. Alerts, messages, updates... they appeared without warning, and he couldn't figure out how to dismiss them so they lingered as semi-transparent overlays between him and the world that kept him in a state of constant low-level nausea.

The Blinkers wanted him hooked up to Valence, said it was necessary to avoid a Glass outbreak, but they hadn't bothered teaching him the gestures. Probably better for them if he never learned how to use the implant.

"How do I turn this thing off?" he muttered, mostly to himself, trying a series of different blink patterns, none of which dismissed the alert.

"You don't," the Auditor replied, not bothering to hide his amusement. "That's the point."

It made Kellan's skin crawl whenever he thought about how much of him was now being monitored, uploaded, analyzed. Everything from his physical location to his heartbeat was a part of Valence's data mines now.

The Auditor was leading him through a series of hallways he'd never seen before, and the modules they passed got increasingly more crowded as they walked. Blinkers lined the doorways, staring openly at him. Some pointed, others whispered behind their hands. A few shouted insults that the Auditor studiously ignored.

"Murderer!"

"Hope the dust eats you alive, NPC!"

Well, he wasn't an NPC anymore, was he? He'd stumbled upon the Exchange on his second day in recovery and found out he was being assigned tasks now. It was absurd, little rewards dangled in front of him for everything from eating his breakfast to allowing the nurse to administer a topical treatment to his arm, only every time he completed a task, he was credited and then his account was immediately debited. He wasn't allowed to earn credits while he was still being punished, apparently.

He wasn't sure how he got to the Exchange the first time and couldn't find it again if he tried, but the mere knowledge that they'd stolen that choice to participate from him made his skin crawl.

"Will my family know the dig is starting?" he asked, keeping his eyes averted from the gawking crowds. "Will I get to say goodbye to them?"

His mother had found a way to see him in the jail. Surely, she and Jace and Echo, maybe even Grandma Sol would be waiting for him before he had to go into this fabrication module, this orientation to a death sentence.

"No visitors," the Auditor snapped. "No time for it."

"How many others are there?" Kellan asked. "How many people volunteered?"

"Enough."

Kellan wasn't sure if he meant *enough people volunteered*, or *I've had enough of you*. Either way, they turned one last corner and Kellan's feet froze. The hallway opened up into a large atrium full of Blinkers – at least three dozen of them, all hugging each other and crying and carrying on. Among them, he saw a few carrying big, bulky pressure suits like his own – the volunteers. But others were clearly family members seeing them off.

The Auditor grabbed Kellan's wrist, yanking him around to face him. He unlocked Kellan's restraints. "Your sentence is complete when the mission is a success," he said, voice flat and emotionless. "You will be a free man when you leave that module so long as you carry out your commitment here."

Kellan rubbed his wrists, the pressure suit balancing on his forearms. They always loved to crank the restraints on tight, and this Auditor had taken extra joy in it. *Free to die with these fool volunteers,* he thought bitterly. Still, the absence of restraints was a relief.

"If you attempt to leave or fail to comply with instructions, you'll be returned to detention immediately," the Auditor said. "Understand?"

Kellan nodded, not trusting himself to speak without saying something that might earn him one final cuff upside the head.

The Auditor turned and began walking away, and before Kellan could turn to count the Blinkers he'd be digging with, he heard his name shouted across the tall, echoing ceiling.

His head snapped around. "Jace!"

There weren't just Blinkers here. He spotted a small cluster of NPCs in one corner. Jace was already running full-bore toward him, and threw his arms around Kellan in a fierce hug. It knocked the pressure suit from his arms and nearly sent Kellan to the floor, but he staggered to keep his balance.

"Thought I'd never see you again," he said, words muffled against his best friend's shoulder. "They said no visitors."

"For us, not for *them,*" Jace said, hooking a thumb toward the cluster of Blinkers. For each one holding a pressure suit, there were at least four others circling them, crying and hugging and reassuring. "Rules for me but not for thee, what else is new. Man, your mother's been going crazy. Auditors threatened to arrest her, we damn near had to lock her in her room to keep her safe."

"I saw her once," Kellan said. "They wouldn't let her stay." But things were clicking into place. He glanced back over at the cluster of NPCs. All of them were holding pressure suits, and there was an extra one lying in a heap on the ground. Kellan shoved Jace hard. "What the hell, you volunteered?!"

"Somebody's got to represent our interests," he said. "If we're not out there keeping them honest, maybe they don't even bother hooking us up to the new system."

"I would have made sure they didn't do that."

Jace threw an arm over Kellan's shoulder. "Yeah, well, we weren't going to let you be on your own with those credit pigs. Everyone who was willing drew straws."

"Is that Dr. Anya?" Kellan asked, squinting around all the pop-ups in his vision telling him orientation was starting soon. "What's she doing here? We can't afford to lose our best doctor."

"We can't afford to go mucking about in the regolith without an NPC doctor here," Jace argued back. "Come on, I'll introduce you to everyone." As they walked, he asked, "How was Blinker prison?"

"Lonely," Kellan said, blinking hard a few times in rapid succession, and to his surprise, a couple of the notifications disappeared. Okay, something he did there worked.

"What are you doing, man? You okay?"

"This fucking implant–"

Jace stopped dead in his tracks, just a few feet from the others. "Oh shit. They made you get one?"

Kellan blinked again, just once this time, in confusion. "You don't have one?"

Jace shook his head, horror written all over his face. "We all refused."

"They told me it was non-negotiable, that it was the only way to detect a Glass infection while we're digging," Kellan said. "And then they pinned me down and injected me with a sedative, so I guess for *me* it was non-negotiable."

Dr. Anya came over and pulled him into a hug that felt almost like the ones his mom gave. "Honey, I'm so sorry about how they treated you. They didn't have the right."

Kellan was discovering that the Blinkers took a lot more liberties than the NPCs believed they had a right to, and the consequences were not forthcoming.

"They just let you refuse?" he asked.

Jace nodded. "We told them no NPCs would dig, but we'd all

show up here and bar the dig crew's entry to the module if they tried to force us to get implants."

"They needed the bodies," Dr. Anya said. "I don't think they got as many volunteers as they expected from their ranks."

Kellan looked over to the veritable going-away party the Blinkers were having on the other side of the atrium. Indignation bubbled through his veins at the fact that Valence was inside his head, and yet he wasn't even allowed to hug his mother goodbye before he entered what very likely would be his tomb.

He felt Dr. Anya's hand on his back. "It's okay, honey, that thing doesn't change who you are. Come meet the others."

KELLAN

YEAR: 2179

A stocky man with onyx skin and graying temples extended a calloused hand to Kellan. "Dex Okafor," he said, his grip firm. "I run our water reclamation systems."

Kellan nodded. "I've read your reports a few times. You do good work."

"So do you," Dex said, releasing his hand. "Don't let the Blinker sludge tell you otherwise. That pressure fix you did saved those people in the laundry module. Happy to dig alongside you, son."

Kellan's chest felt tight, not sure what to do with praise for the action that had ultimately taken three lives, so he just turned to the next person in line. She was a woman about five years older than him and Jace, with sharp, intelligent eyes and short-cropped hair and the same dark complexion as Dex.

"Iska Okafor," she said, nodding to him. "His daughter, better hydro tech than him."

Dex laughed and put a hand on her shoulder. "It's not a competition."

"Only because you'd lose," she shot back.

"You both volunteered?" Kellan asked, blinking too many times and pulling up something that looked like a page out of the colony manual.

"I drew a long straw," Iska said. "He wouldn't let me go without him."

"And I'm Torrent," the final NPC volunteer stepped in, holding out his hand to Kellan. He was lean, tall, and Kellan recognized him.

"Mr. Hesp's partner," he said.

Ed Hesp had been Kellan and Jace's teacher all through school. They often saw him and Torrent eating lunch together, and once, Jace had swapped out their cricket-meat tacos for ones with live crickets in them. When Mr. Hesp took one bite and threw his taco across the room, Jace had howled so hard tears were coming down his eyes but then he and Kellan both got after-school clean-up duty.

The hazards of being best friends with the class prankster, guilt by association was a frequent occurrence.

"You volunteered?" Kellan asked.

"Drew a long straw," Torrent said. "Eddy drew a short straw and I told him not to do anything stupid like Dex over there. The kids need him, and I'll be back as soon as we're done here."

"That's right," Dr. Anya said. "We're going to take every precaution and get the hell out of here healthy."

"You really think that's possible?" Kellan asked. The Auditors had fed him all that tank sludge about how once he finished replacing the atmospheric conversion unit, his debt would be paid and he could go back to sector four, but he couldn't really bring himself to believe it. He'd spent the last week steeling himself to walk into that fabrication module and never come out again. He figured that was the whole plan.

"We'll do everything we can," Dr. Anya promised, not exactly a fully fleshed out strategy.

Kellan didn't respond, too busy fighting back the nausea as

another notification swam across his vision. *Mission orientation is commencing, five credits. All citizens not part of the dig crew, please depart now.*

Ping, five credits went into his account, and were deducted immediately back out. Kellan blinked twice, big and purposeful, trying to dismiss the notification, but only managed to make it bigger.

"What are you doing?" Jace asked.

"Nothing," Kellan lied.

"It's the implant, isn't it? Can you feel it in your eyeball?" Jace leaned in and tried to look at it, and Kellan gave him a shove. Jace staggered back a step, the window closed abruptly, and it left Kellan looking into the distance, where the Blinker volunteers were saying their final goodbyes to their families.

They all looked just as nervous as the NPCs – maybe even more. It was supremely unsettling. If anyone was going to feel reassured that they were protected and special and perfectly safe, it'd be them.

Kellan accidentally locked eyes with one of them, and his heart dropped into his stomach.

Her dark hair was pulled back in a shiny ponytail today. Her jaw was set with determination and her shoulders were squared with confidence. He'd seen that same defiant glint in her eyes before, seven years ago, in her father's med clinic when Kellan thought his mom was dying and she had tried to comfort him with a rabbit.

Quinta Voss.

"What on Deimos is she doing here?" Jace asked, following his gaze just as Kellan began desperately searching for something, anything else to look at. "That's the girl with the rabbit, isn't it?"

"That's a Voss," Dr. Anya said, astonished.

"She's not here to dig, is she?" Jace wondered.

"Can't be," Kellan said, eyes still sweeping around the atrium, looking anywhere other than at her. "Must be here to say a few inspiring words or some shit like that."

"She's holding a pressure suit," Iska pointed out.

Kellan risked a glance back at Quinta and sure enough, she clutched a shiny new pressure suit to her chest, and her eyes were still locked on him.

LIRA

YEAR: 2083

Lira spent the rest of the day alternating between messaging Jamila to check on her and calling people whose vitals were within normal range, who hadn't had any clear first- or second-level exposure, and who appeared from their requests for medical attention to be, well, freaking out a bit.

She stumbled through the first few calls on audio, not confident enough to have these conversations on video. People who were terrified, who only knew how to get angry when they were scared, who felt like they were being ranked and deemed not worthy of the small stash of antibiotics… those people were not easy to reason with. She tried explaining the locked down clinic from a medical perspective, which wasn't well received, and then from a statistical one – which went over far worse. She even tried pointing out that nobody even knew if the antibiotics would work yet, so those who hadn't gotten any weren't truly missing out on anything.

That didn't work, either. "You were exposed, you got your antibiotics," one woman hissed.

"Actually, I haven't received any antibiotics," Lira tried to explain, but the woman just grumbled, "Yeah, right," and hung up on her.

After about a half dozen of those calls, in which Lira was absolutely sure she'd done more harm than good, she finally got through to someone. The difference was that when he started ranting about how scared and frustrated everyone was, Lira was already worn out from the first six calls, so she just stayed silent and let him rant. After a while, he ran out of steam and calmed down, and Lira was able to talk honestly about the situation.

No, we don't know exactly what is going on, and we don't know the prognosis for sure.

The people who are sick now aren't progressing nearly as fast as the dig crew did, and that's good news.

Yes, we are testing all our antibiotics against the bacteria, and the microbio team is making more as we speak.

Things started to go a whole lot better after that. Lira started calling from her tablet so people could see her face, even if they didn't want to show theirs. She positioned the device on top of one of the rabbits' 3D-printed tunnels and pointed it into the grass, sitting in the middle of the play area so the people she called could see the rabbits hopping around in the background while they talked. She let them rant as long as they needed to, and she stopped taking it personally.

They weren't screaming at her. They were screaming at the terror of the situation, the fact that they were all trapped in a petri dish they once called home.

Some of them were screaming about the friends they'd lost already, and the ones who were sick now.

Lira could relate to that.

There were others who screamed because it seemed like Earth wasn't interested in helping the colony. Lira talked to a satellite operator named Marcus who said the replies from VossCorp had been sparse and unhelpful.

"They just keep telling us to stay calm and keep them updated," he said with a huff. "As if they're doing anything with the information we feed them about this. They're not even trying to help us look for a cure."

"My understanding is they've never received a sample of the bacteria," Lira said. That fact had baffled her when she heard it from Jamila. Was the CEO really so possessive he would stand in the way of scientific progress? He'd built an entire Mars colony full of scientists!

"They never wanted a sample," Marcus said. "You know what I think? They were afraid to have it. They must have known something we didn't." He rolled his eyes. "And considering how this is turning out, they were smart to be."

"They don't have the bacteria, but they're helping our microbiologists do research, sending relevant studies, things like that. Aren't they?" Lira had heard rumors to that effect.

"I don't think so," he said. "The last communication I saw just said *stay tuned, we're working on it.*"

That conversation stuck with Lira for a whole day after it ended. Partly because she didn't think she'd helped Marcus feel better, and partly because if what he said was true, VossCorp wasn't working very hard to stop the outbreak. Why? This was their colony, something Sorin Voss had poured billions upon billions of dollars into.

And now he was just going to let come what may?

Lira got a clue about why that might be in her first call the next day. A hydro tech told her about a message she'd gotten from an uncle in Sarajevo.

"It's forty-seven degrees Celsius every day there now. He can't go outdoors during the day at all anymore," the tech, Lys, said. "The Miljacka is so low kids walk across it, and the water is sludge thanks to all the pollution."

She told Lira about the potato barrel her uncle had on his balcony, extra calories just in case, but Lira was thinking of her mother a continent away in Manila.

She hadn't heard back after her message about the ring. It

always took a long time for a message to get to Earth and a reply to come back, especially with VossCorp first running all the colonist communications through Valence's filters to make sure they complied with company policy. Those filters had become even more strict after Ada was jailed, and they were certainly working overtime right now.

Mention of a deadly bacterial outbreak would get a message sent to quarantine. Lira knew better, but how many other colonists had attempted to reach out to their loved ones with the news in the past few days?

If Sarajevo was so hot, how was Manila faring, thirty lines of latitude closer to the equator? Was the flooding getting worse? Would her mom ever let go of that house and move to higher ground or would it take a rescue team to come get her in a boat while she sat on her roof?

Could she even climb to the roof with her knees?

That could be a reason why VossCorp wasn't helping. They were based in Houston, just fifteen meters above sea level. The daily briefings from mission control often reported that humidity there was nearly one hundred percent all the time now, coupled with rising temperatures and rolling blackouts. Houston was on the verge of existential crisis, like many places on Earth. Were they too busy fighting for their lives to help the colonists fight for theirs?

"Has your uncle ever grown potatoes before?" Lira asked, trying to put her attention back on the conversation.

"No, but he's obsessed with them now," Lys said. "He brings it inside at the hottest part of the day and mists the soil with whatever he can spare from his water rations. He didn't have any children, but he has potatoes now."

Lira let her talk until the potato topic ran dry, then shifted the focus to the rabbits hopping around near her. She told Lys their names, a little about their personalities, and promised to introduce her in person as soon as the quarantine ended.

"If you don't have the credits, I'll spot you," she said.

By the time the call was over, it felt like she'd actually moved the needle a little bit, unlike with Marcus the day before. Unlike a lot of them, who needed to vent but stayed on edge, on the verge of panic, no matter what Lira tried.

Plus, she had the rumors emanating from the microbiology lab to contend with.

It seemed like on every other call, there were new reports from the microbiologists: They confirmed it was V. martialis, however, it had mutated. They thought the radiation exposure had worsened the illness in the dig crew. They reported that those who'd received broad-spectrum antibiotics showed a slowed progression – they were all still alive sixteen hours after the onset of symptoms.

Good news, but it caused a new set of problems. New demands for prophylactics flooded the system, but the doses weren't available.

And when it somehow leaked that there were only a hundred and fifty courses left in the entire colony, people got desperate.

When the first person with second-level exposure died on day four, that was the match lit next to an oxygen tank.

LIRA
YEAR: 2083

"Dr. Ethan Kalb's biometrics are offline."

The warm female voice that VossCorp had assigned to Valence was jarringly ill-suited to the message it had just delivered through the rabbitat speakers. Lira had been trying to contact Dr. Kalb with no luck, and then she'd thought to search for him on the hab map.

She couldn't find him. Anywhere.

She'd asked Valence for help and those six words were all she got, stated as plainly as could be. When she asked for clarification, all Valence did was repeat the six words in her calm, unconcerned voice. "Dr. Ethan Kalb's biometrics are offline."

Lira had to call clinic two to confirm what she suspected it meant, and it was exactly what she'd feared. Kalb was dead.

"So it's fatal," she said, her voice gone flat with shock. "Even for people who didn't get the extreme dose of radiation."

"I'm afraid so," Nurse Pema said. She was one of the few healthy nurses, but Lira wondered for how long. "Dr. Kalb isn't the first that we've lost today."

"Shit."

There was a pause, and then the nurse said, "Don't tell anyone, all right? We can't afford a panic."

"Of course."

Lira hung up in a daze, her mind going immediately to Jamila quarantined in her quarters. Was there a countdown hanging over her head? How long had it been for Dr. Kalb? When had his first symptoms begun?

She didn't know the answers to those questions, but as she sat there trying to count backward to figure them out, her mind crept beyond just Jamila. According to the clinic's interface, nearly a quarter of the colony had symptoms now. Those crucial first few hours, when no one knew they were in danger, had allowed the bacteria to spread like wildfire through the contained atmosphere of the hab.

It wasn't only in the med clinics that people were dying. That meant that no matter how much Nurse Pema and the microbiologists hoped to suppress a panic, it would only take a few people dying in their beds. Then everyone would know.

This was no trivial pathogen, no common cold.

This thing was alive, it had mutated into something deadly, and they were all trapped in here with it.

Lira called Jamila, terrified she wouldn't answer at all. Instead, after a few rings, Jamila answered on audio. She clearly wanted to hide her appearance, but it was no use – Lira could hear how much weaker her voice was since the last time they spoke.

"How are you feeling? Are you getting your meals and fluids?"

"I'm okay," Jamila sighed, not at all convincing. "I've been getting my meal drop-offs."

Valence had been assigning the healthy to make food drop-offs to the doors of everyone who was quarantining. Lira watched hers on the hall camera every time, and saw the delivery people were suited up so well they looked ready for a surface mission.

"Why aren't you on video?"

"I haven't showered in two days," Jamila said. "I look like hell."

"You saw me the day after Ada died," Lira reminded her. "I was a mess."

She'd finally gotten around to changing into the coveralls Jamila had bought her yesterday, and she'd used the emergency decontamination shower in the rabbitat to clean up. She was trying to reassure the people she was calling. Being disheveled and filthy while saying everything would be okay would have only sewn more unease.

"Are you blue?" Lira asked at last.

There was a long silence, and then Jamila choked on her reply, a single word: "Yes."

It'll be okay was on the tip of Lira's tongue. She wanted nothing more than to reassure Jamila, to save Jamila after she'd been so helpless with Ada.

But that would be a lie, and Jamila was smart enough to know it.

They had no clue what it would be, but okay was clearly off the table.

"What can I do?" Lira asked. "What do you need?"

Jamila's voice wavered again, tripping over tears. "I don't want to die alone."

"This isn't a death sentence," Lira said. "They're giving you antibiotics. They're working for people. It's slower for people who don't have radiation exposure. You have time. You're going to survive this."

She said it even though it was a promise she couldn't make. She couldn't help it, and Jamila seemed to know it was a platitude. She ignored it completely. "Promise you'll keep checking in with me?"

Tears formed a firm knot in Lira's throat and she was instantly back on that chair in the treatment room, looking over the doctor's shoulder while he fought in vain to save Ada's life.

"Of course," Lira managed. "So often you'll get sick of me. I'm here anytime you need me."

Which, again, was an empty promise considering she was

locked in the rabbitat while Jamila was locked in her quarters, a sector away.

Jamila seemed tired, so they hung up a few minutes later with plans to talk again after she napped. Lira glanced at the backlog of clinic requests and considered calling more people, but she didn't have the heart for it just then. How could she tell them they were anxious over nothing when she was one of the few people who knew it was definitely not nothing?

So instead, she listened.

She opened her overlay and scrolled through the conversations. There were department-based group chats that had shifted entirely away from work to who was sick and who'd been in contact with them. Audio chats that were going on right now. Video conferences between people who were terrified and confused and, above all, lonely in quarantine.

Some sick, some healthy.

Even in the chats, the sick isolated themselves from the not-sick-yet.

And things were not going well. The longer Lira scrolled, the more desperation she saw.

The bacteria had reached three of the four sectors. They still didn't know how it was transmitted, but they knew it was very good at being transmitted. And they knew there were fatalities beyond the dig crew now.

The colony administrator, a bureaucrat who happened to be Sorin Voss's son Dmitri, had yet to make a colony-wide announcement. Some official guidance would have gone a long way toward calming people down, even if it was just to say, "We don't know much, but we're working on it." Maybe Dmitri was sick too. Maybe he knew far more than Lira did and it was so horrible, it was better to be silent. Either way, he said nothing and Lira's overlay was filled with rumors and misinformation and demands for leadership support.

Lira chimed into a few different chats, telling people that she'd spent most of a day at Ada's side after she'd gotten sick, and she was still healthy.

Death isn't inevitable, she wrote. *We don't know how it's transmitted or who's susceptible, but not all of us are.*

She was trying to be helpful, showing people they weren't doomed.

Instead, she got all the fear and anger the colony had no other outlet for.

I watched my boyfriend die this morning. Don't tell me it's not inevitable.

How can you know you're not sick?

You probably spread it to the rest of us when you left that clinic.

It was just like those first few angry, unsuccessful calls to clinic patients. They didn't want reasoning and logic. They wanted an outlet for their out-of-control emotions, and Lira was only making herself a target.

Besides, they were right. The fear that she'd brought this disease out of the clinic with her, that she'd made Jamila sick when she accepted that hug, gnawed at her constantly.

So Lira stayed quiet and listened some more.

She heard that the med clinics in sectors one and four had been looted. People had pried the doors open looking for antibiotics, and when they didn't find them – the antibiotics were stored in central supply, which was far more secure – they'd ransacked the modules and taken everything even remotely useful with them.

They didn't dare go into the med clinics in two and three, the ones where the dig crew had been taken. (Lira wondered what had happened to the bodies. Surely, Ada must have been moved to the morgue with the other dig crew members. But Dr. Kalb? His staff? Were they lying wherever they drew their last breath? Who would risk exposure to preserve their bodies?) Instead, they raided each sector's supply module, building hoards in their quarters.

It didn't even seem to matter what they took. Protein bars, batteries, extra blankets, bandages – they took whatever they could get their hands on as if they could use it all to build a wall around themselves that would keep the bacteria out.

Valence assigned extra security to central supply, granting anyone who would take the job access to stun batons and tear gas… and antibiotics. There were plenty of volunteers.

And there were self-imposed lockdowns.

First, it was the people who'd had the bright idea to duct tape their vents. All of Dorm 1B, which just so happened to be Lira's dorm, had gone into a full militaristic lockdown. There was tape over every vent and a person in a pressure suit standing guard at every entrance, threatening anyone who so much as sweated in their direction.

It was scary that the colony was breaking into factions like that, and even though Lira was locked in the rabbitat, a bit unsettling to know she couldn't go home even if she was allowed out.

Jamila thought they were idiots, that Valence could more effectively isolate their dorm from the hab's shared life support systems than they ever could, and the fact that it hadn't done so was proof that it wasn't necessary.

And then all of sector three locked down.

They closed their airlocks and manually overrode any system that was shared with the rest of the hab. Their air, water, waste reclamation – it was all sealed off and they would be self-sufficient for as long as they could last without the rest of the colony.

Assuming, hoping, praying that they'd sealed themselves off from the bacteria instead of sealing it inside with them.

It was Dmitri Voss's sector. He'd finally broken his silence to do something, and instead of trying to reassure the thousand people he was responsible for, he was sealing himself away from as many of them as he could.

His wife was pregnant. The first colonist allowed to attempt reproduction, after Lira reported half a dozen successful litters among the rabbit population with no birth defects or other complications from the Martian atmosphere. Well, this bacteria would certainly be a complication for Una, and part of Lira didn't blame Dmitri for wanting to do everything he could to protect his wife and unborn child.

Another part of her believed the rumors she'd heard that for days, he'd been ruthlessly evicting everyone who so much as sneezed in his sector.

There are no doctors left in that sector, someone said in a group chat that had once been for a garden diversity committee. *He damned that baby by sealing it off from the two functioning med clinics.*

You think he and his wife don't have all the antibiotics they can stuff in their gobs? someone else said. *They'll be fine.*

Still, the colony's first baby…

Never stood a chance.

Lira closed the chat, disgusted.

There were other conversations speculating on how many antibiotic courses were left now. By the time the med clinic staff and the microbiologists and people like Dmitri and Una got them, not to mention all the experimental doses given to those who were already sick… two hundred courses didn't go far.

That was one fifth of the colony that got even a chance for survival.

The other four fifths just had to quarantine and pray they got a mild case.

Lira tried asking Valence how many courses were left.

"That information is restricted," it said.

"Why?" she challenged. "I'm working with med clinic two. I need to know."

It was worth a shot, anyway.

Valence replied only, "Releasing the exact number of antibiotic courses remaining carries a sixty-seven percent chance of increasing anxiety among the colonists."

Lira tried Nurse Pema next, who didn't seem eager to share that information, either. She didn't know any of the microbiologists to ask them. Meanwhile in the overlay, the conspiracy theories abounded, along with a plot to take the remaining doses by force.

One dose for everyone in sectors one, two and four. Sector three chose their fate, and we don't have enough for them, anyway, someone suggested.

Again, Lira was tempted to reply. She wanted to explain that a single dose would do no good, and it could even result in an antibiotic-resistant strain of the bacteria, which had already proven itself eager to mutate. But they didn't want to listen. They didn't want facts and logic. They wanted to take action, no matter how reckless or wrong that action was. Lira sympathized. The last thing she wanted to do was sit on her butt and wait.

And then, they came for the rabbitat.

LIRA

YEAR: 2083

ira was in a black hole of rumors and conspiracies and pessimism, about fifteen minutes overdue to call Jamila and oblivious to what the rabbits were doing around her. There came an insistent pounding on the rabbitat door.

It took her a few seconds to register because apart from her meal deliveries, she hadn't seen evidence of another human being in two days, and it wasn't mealtime.

The pounding came again and a muffled voice called, "Dr. Salonga, we need to seal the rabbit module."

Alarm jolted through her. "What?" she called, standing up from the grass.

"We're told there's a large quantity of regolith inside," a man shouted through the door. "V. martialis comes from the dust and we can't take any chances."

Lira looked at the play area. They were right. Beneath the grass, there was close to a meter of red Martian soil. The rabbits sometimes dug burrows into it, and Lira had always thought it was charming when their fur became rusty with the stuff and she had to wash them off.

It wasn't the first time her mind had gone to the regolith in the room since quarantine, but what could she do about it?

Lira did some quick navigating in her overlay, identifying the man outside the door – and a silent companion. She initiated a video chat with them. The hab map identified the one who'd spoken as Moses Walker. It said he was from maintenance, and she'd never interacted with him before. His silent partner was named Yusuf Hasan, a metalsmith. Both men wore head-to-toe protective gear, including masks over their faces.

They could see her face, though, and she'd learned quite recently how important that was.

"You can't seal the rabbitat," she told Moses. "There's nowhere else in the hab suitable for the rabbits to live in."

"The rabbits will not leave the module," he said. She thought his voice cracked a little, like he was afraid to be here. "They're contaminated."

"They are not," Lira objected. "Not a single one of them has shown the slightest sign of disease since the outbreak began."

"All due respect, ma'am, we can't know how the disease manifests in rabbits. We barely know what happens in humans," the other, Yusuf, said.

From Dr. Salonga to ma'am in four exchanges, she thought and resisted the urge to scowl on video. "We *can* know because I'm a veterinarian," she said. "I've been monitoring them and recording their vitals every day. They're healthy."

"Sorry, we just do what the Exchange assigns us," Yusuf said. He seemed brusk, not scared as much as annoyed at having to do this task. "If you have a problem with it, you can submit a complaint to Valence, *after* we do our job."

"What about me?" Lira demanded. "I've been sitting on the regolith for four days. Are you sealing me in here too?"

"We have a protective suit for you," Moses said. "You'll need to put it on and vacate the area."

Lira got an alert as a new task appeared on her Exchange dashboard. *Proceed to temporary quarters in Dorm 1A, room 32. Continue to isolate there, five credits.* Lira rolled her eyes, which accidentally closed the dashboard. Five credits for what? Leaving the rabbits to die?

"I won't leave the rabbits alone in here," she told the men. "They need to be fed and watered regularly. They can't tolerate their stomachs being empty–"

"Not our problem," Yusuf said. "We were assigned to seal off the rabbit module, and that's what we're going to do. Your choice if you're still in it when we do."

"Well," Lira heard Moses say, quieter, "we can't just–"

"Listen, lady," Yusuf interrupted. "We're all scared."

Oh, so it was *lady* now. That was even worse than *ma'am*. Lira bristled.

"None of us wants to be out in the halls right now, getting exposed to God knows what," he continued. "I sure as hell don't want to be standing here when you open that door and let out all the spores that must be flying around in there. It's a miracle you ain't dead, but you're gonna be if we seal you up with the rabbits. There won't be food for you or them then, so there's no point in you staying."

He was right about that part. Didn't have to be such a jerk, though.

"Decline the task," Lira said. "Just go home and protect yourselves, leave us alone."

"Can't," Yusuf said. "We're already here."

"Here's what we're going to do," Moses interjected, still sounding nervous. "My colleague and I are going to leave this protective suit on the ground right outside the door. We're going to go to the commons and get a protein bar, and you're going to do whatever you need to do to get the rabbits situated in there. We'll be back in fifteen minutes and then we're going to have to seal the door. Don't be here when we get back, do you understand?"

"Or you're gonna have to eat them bunnies to survive," Yusuf added. Lira thought she could detect a small laugh.

Sicko.

"You can't do this."

"We're doing it," Yusuf said. "Count yourself lucky my friend's a bleeding heart. A lot of people want to kill the bunnies and get it over with, little disease-carrying resource hogs."

Lira's mouth fell open to retort, but there didn't seem to be much point with this guy. She just cut the video call, wondering how many credits Valence was offering them to seal the door. Must be a lot if they were willing to risk the exposure.

"Fifteen minutes!" Moses shouted through the door.

She looked around her. At least two dozen bunnies were out on the grass, eating it, digging in the regolith, their paws stained orange. The warren was up to over a hundred, more than twice what they started with, and she'd been telling the truth when she said there was nowhere else in the hab that she could take all of them. She couldn't transport more than ten or fifteen at a time, even if there was.

"Crap."

All they want to do is seal the module off, she tried to reassure herself. *You can appeal this later.* Fifteen minutes wasn't enough time to do it now, and those guys meant business – especially Yusuf. What did *seal it off* even mean?

Lira couldn't afford to be in the rabbitat when she found out, so she sprang into motion. She filled up the autofeeder that she used on her days off, setting it to its maximum interval. Then she started filling every container she could find with water, setting them on the floor in various places around the room to minimize the possibility of fighting over resources. Then she went to the produce bin and emptied what little was left all over the grass – no point holding any back now.

Finally, she went to the pellet storage bins and emptied those out too. Whatever wouldn't fit in the autofeeder got scattered in the grass. On Earth, rabbit pellets were made of dehydrated timothy hay. Here, plant waste found an additional use before heading to the compost machines, and the rabbits didn't like these pellets as much. That would work in Lira's favor now – it'd take them longer to eat, and give her more time to get back in here.

She was waiting in the hallway when the two men returned, wearing the full-length bodysuit and mask they'd left her. They were in even heavier-duty gear, thick plastic suits with hoods and plastic shields over their faces, and they carried tool bags.

"What are you still doing here?" the one she assumed was Yusuf demanded, his eyes small and dark behind the shield. He stopped ten feet away from her, refusing to get any closer. "You need to leave."

"I'm going to watch you," Lira told him. "To make sure you only do what you told me you've been assigned to do."

"What else do you think we're going to do?" Moses asked. Without the muffling effect of the door between them, Lira could hear the clipped vowels and formal cadence of his accent, absent the vitriol she felt coming off Yusuf.

"You said people want to kill the rabbits," she said.

"I don't want to," Moses said. "I promise."

"Well, I just wanna get this damn job done so I can go take a decon shower," Yusuf said. "Move away now, lady, or I will kill the little fuckers."

Lira stood her ground. "How will you seal it?"

Moses set his tool bag on the ground, kneeling to open it. He pulled out a large canister and held it up. "All we've been asked to do is apply this bioseal foam around the edges of the door. Valence will reroute the airflow inside the module when we're done, and create positive pressure out here in the hall."

"Will they still get fresh air?"

"The module will be turned into a closed-loop system," Moses explained. "The air will be filtered and recirculated." When Lira still didn't budge, he added, "We're just maintenance, Dr. Salonga. We're not exterminators."

"Plus, Valence voted against the 'kill the bunnies' idea," Yusuf added. "Too much stress on the waste reclamation system."

So they were holding votes she was unaware of? That didn't sit well, but it was another problem for later. Lira stepped back to give the men room to work, never taking her eyes off them, their canisters, or their hands as they completed the task.

QUINTA

YEAR: 2179

uinta had seen him at the all-colony, had spent most of the meeting staring daggers at him. Why it'd taken until right this minute to remember that Kellan Reilly was the boy she'd tried to share her rabbit with…

Well, it must have been a heroic amount of compartmentalization that allowed her to forget it.

The memories hit Quinta like a gust of chilled air from the morgue – Kellan's guarded expression in the clinic all those years ago, the raw hostility in his eyes when she'd tried to offer him her rabbit. He hadn't understood, had been too dumb or too stubborn to accept the comfort. And then that word, spat at her like a slur: Blinker.

Eyes locked with his now, anger flared hot beneath her ribs, hotter even than when she heard Elise Chandra's relative hiss the word *hoarder* about her father.

"I'm sure it's not too late," Quinta's mom was saying to her and Castor. "Valence must have backup volunteers for both of you. You have important jobs you should be doing, not this."

Havana had spent the past few days talking to everyone from

Administrator Weyland to her therapist, trying to find strings to pull to get Quinta off the dig crew, but Valence had rules. If Quinta herself did not withdraw her application, she would dig.

And Quinta didn't want to withdraw.

She'd finally asked her mother about the rumors and the medical board. She said she knew about the board meeting at the time, but it had all been vicious rumors.

She was still convinced what people were saying was nothing but jealousy and lies, even after Quinta showed her the doctored records she'd found.

"There must be a logical explanation for it," Havana had insisted almost dismissively. "Your father wouldn't do a thing like that. And we hardly need the credits."

She'd been walking around with her head held high, a grieving widow whose child had been so shattered by her father's death that she'd volunteered to dig to escape the pain of mourning. And she deserved to walk the hab without people casting suspicious, disdainful looks her way.

Quinta couldn't keep following in her father's footsteps, knowing where they led, but she could rehabilitate the family name. She could do something good for the colony to try to offset what Hadrian had done.

"We're proud of you both," Rio Marcellus said. Both Castor's parents were wrapped so tight around him Quinta thought she saw his eyes bulging. "We think you've lost your minds, but we're proud of you."

"Valence will watch over you," Castor's mom Nita said, smoothing his hair. "Valence will protect you. She always has."

He gently reached up and took his mom's hand out of his hair, and his cheeks reddened when he noticed Quinta watching the whole exchange. Things had been off between them since that night in her room, although it was hard to say whether it was because of the kiss or because they'd both volunteered to dig that night.

He hadn't tried to kiss her again.

She wasn't sure if she wanted him to or not. They'd been attached at the hip since they were kids so everyone assumed the two of them would end up together. A part of Quinta expected it too. But she never felt how she thought she should if she was in love with him. People talked about fluttering in their stomachs and giddiness and their hearts racing.

Quinta felt all that stuff when she played a great round of Parallax. She felt it when she knew she'd helped a patient in a meaningful way. She felt it when she watched the colony production of *A Midsummer Night's Dream* last month.

Maybe she had to surrender to the kiss more to feel the fluttering.

In any case, there wasn't much point in repeating the experiment, or even really talking about it, before they knew whether they'd survive the next few days. And so they endured awkward silences and tripped over their tongues to avoid bringing up the kiss.

Quinta's overlay alerted her that orientation was about to begin, and her mom latched onto her so hard she couldn't breathe for a minute. "Do not take any unnecessary risks in there," she hissed into Quinta's ear. "Let the NPCs do the dangerous work, you hear me? That's what they're on the crew for."

"We'll be okay," Quinta promised, the words hollow.

Finally, Havana wrenched herself away and Rio pulled Nita off Castor. The other citizens all said their goodbyes and the families filed out, and the atrium was eerily quiet with only the ten of them remaining. Four citizens, six NPCs. An airlock looming between them.

Quinta heard footsteps in the hall and turned to see an Auditor striding toward them.

Her heart caught in her throat. It was rare to see Auditors with their blood-red armbands, but between this and the all-colony meeting, she'd seen a lot of them this week.

This one had salt-and-pepper hair slicked back neatly, and the craggy cheeks of someone who'd struggled with acne once upon a time. He came to a stop exactly halfway between the two groups and tucked his hands behind his back.

"Listen up," he barked, as if he were snapping orders to a bunch of trainees. "I am Auditor Mercer. I'm here to orient you to your mission. The module behind you will be your residence, your dining hall, your restroom and your work area until the new atmospheric unit is operational and Valence is satisfied all quarantine protocols have been completed."

He triggered the airlock, which popped open with a hiss of air. He walked through it, not waiting for the two groups to figure out they should follow him.

The citizens went first. There was an older man and a thirty-something woman, plus Quinta and Castor. She didn't recognize either of the others. The NPCs followed at a slight distance.

The module was spacious and quite clearly had been repurposed for the mission. There was fabrication machinery on one wall, along with the raw materials and tools they would need to get the job done. There were a couple assistive robots that looked built for hauling and lifting – some of a very few that remained of the original fleet, the ones that had been lucky enough to be inside the hab at the time of the first outbreak. Anything left out in the elements was long dead.

There was another airlock, this one leading outdoors. A decontamination chamber similar to the pop-up one Quinta and Cydra had used for Terra was attached to it, only this one was much larger. The whole setup looked ominous, and Quinta turned her attention to the other side of the module, which was at least more familiar-looking.

There was a row of tables and a shelf full of prepackaged meals – a makeshift dining hall.

Two doorways appeared to lead to sleeping quarters, and a third must be the restroom.

"Leave your things on the shelves and take a seat," Mercer instructed, gesturing to the tables.

Quinta set her pressure suit in a heap on the shelf, along with the unwieldy helmet. Castor had brought a small bag, and so had some of the others. Quinta hadn't bothered with much – she just wanted to focus on the mission and leave everything else behind.

The two groups automatically segregated themselves, citizens at one table, NPCs at the other. Castor slid into the seat next to Quinta.

"I'll be guiding you through the steps of the mission today," Mercer said. "But first, you should know who's on your crew. They're the people you'll be trusting your lives with."

He went around the tables, pointing and providing names and job titles, beginning with the citizens.

"This is Ronan Solomon, systems integration specialist," he said. The man he pointed to looked a bit older than Quinta's father, with white temples and dark hair and kind eyes. He nodded to the group, and then Mercer moved on.

"Aris Thorne," he said, pointing to the woman sitting next to Ronan. "Fabrication lead, so she'll know her way around this module." Aris, who had dark braids pulled back tight against her head, sat with her arms crossed, watching the NPC table.

"Castor Marcellus," Mercer said. "Computer engineer. Quinta Voss, apprentice doctor."

Former, Quinta thought, although technically she had never resigned.

How many of them actually expected to survive this mission?

Mercer introduced each of the NPCs next, rattling off their names and roles quickly. Dex and Iska Okafor, Torrent Hesp, and when he got to a middle-aged woman with curly white-blonde hair arranged messily around her face, he said, "Anya Raymond, medic."

"Doctor," the woman corrected with a sharp look. "I've had just as much training as any Blinker doctor, and I'm twice as resourceful."

Mercer ignored the commentary as if she hadn't spoken. "Jace Windham, maintenance. And finally, Kellan Reilly, maintenance."

"Killer," Castor grumbled, just loud enough that Kellan stiffened.

Mercer opened his mouth to go on, but Kellan said, "Yes."

The room went deadly silent and everyone turned to look at him.

"It was a horrible accident," he said, "but I take responsibility, and I'm here to repay my debt to the colony. I'll work just as hard as the rest of you–" He glanced Quinta's way. "Harder."

She frowned. What was that supposed to mean?

Once again, Mercer ignored the tension, plowing ahead. "Your mission is straightforward but critical. The primary atmospheric conversion unit has deteriorated beyond repair, and over the years it has been buried by about three meters of regolith. You will excavate the site, build the new unit beside the old one, then swap out the connections."

"And we have *no* robots remaining that can do this work and spare us the exposure?" Aris asked.

Mercer shook his head tightly. "You will have access to assistive units to decrease the physical load." He gestured to the ones Quinta had already noticed along the wall. "The surface diggers are all beyond repair, exposed to the planet's weather conditions for too long."

He pulled up a schematic of the new atmo unit on a display wall behind him, explaining the process in more detail. Castor leaned forward, studying the diagram with intense focus. Quinta tried to follow along, but the technical details were pretty far removed from her medical training.

"The excavation will be done in rotating shifts," Mercer explained. "Half of you outside doing the labor, the other half monitoring from inside the hab. You'll rotate positions mid-day to minimize exposure."

"Any amount of exposure to Glass is potentially lethal," Quinta said. "What precautions are being taken?"

"You will be quarantined here for the duration of the mission, plus three days after. You will complete thorough decontamination protocols every time you go outside," Mercer said, "and Valence will be continually monitoring your vital signs via the retinal implants."

The NPC doctor raised her hand. "Five of us don't have implants," she pointed out.

"You will be asked to complete health questionnaires twice a day," Mercer said. "Please log any and all symptoms there."

There were murmurs of discontent.

"A questionnaire," the doctor huffed. "They made no real accommodations for us."

"It's tank sludge," the one named Jace muttered.

Mercer's eyes hardened in a way that sent a chill down Quinta's spine, even though the look wasn't directed at her. "You had the opportunity to receive implants which would allow Valence to closely monitor your physical health. You chose not to."

"We had the *opportunity* to bend to your rules because you think they should apply to everyone," Dr. Anya said, then turned to the NPCs. "I will conduct real health assessments." She looked over at the citizen table and added, "for anyone who wants them."

"Whole lot of good a stethoscope is going to do against a disease that spreads as fast as Glass," Ronan, the systems specialist, said. "By the time you've got symptoms, you're already dead."

"They should be on a dig team of their own," Ronan said. "Citizens take the morning shift, NPCs on afternoons. We segregate as much as possible inside the module to limit exposure."

"We can take the one with the implant," Aris, the fabricator, said. "It'll even up the teams."

"And I bet you'll leave all the dangerous tasks and hard labor for us too," Dex said, folding his thick arms over his chest. "No way, we mix the teams evenly, Blinkers and NPCs together. It's the only way we can trust each other."

"Like we trusted you to maintain your own systems?" Ronan shot back. "Now three people are dead–"

"It doesn't matter!" Quinta shouted, her voice echoing off the tall ceiling. It had the desired effect, though. Everyone in the module was staring at her, and you could have heard a cricket chirp in the corner. "If any one of us gets sick, we're all dead within seventy-two hours. There's no way we could isolate enough in this module to protect ourselves."

"She's right," a new voice came from the open airlock, making heads turn. A woman in citizen coveralls stood in the door to the atrium, a pressure suit under her arm. For half a second, Quinta thought her mom had found a way to send in a replacement for her after all.

Then Mercer said, "Ah, Ms. Helena Sato, decontamination specialist. Just in time."

KELLAN

YEAR: 2179

"**G**lass doesn't care if you're a citizen or an NPC," Dr. Sato said, crossing the room to stand beside the Auditor. "It doesn't care if you have an implant or which team you're digging on. It sleeps in the dust and it waits for any opportunity you give it to infiltrate your defenses."

She gestured to the helmet tucked under her elbow.

"That's why I'm here, to teach you how to use your pressure suits and the decontamination protocols. Those are the only things that stand between you and Glass. And don't get it wrong – it's not just the ten of you taking this risk. If Glass penetrates these hab walls, the entire colony is threatened."

Kellan's body felt jittery the way they always did when he heard a Glass lecture. No one knew how his grandmother had survived the last outbreak, but there was no guarantee that just because she did, he could do it too.

The whole rest of her family had perished, and she'd had to watch them die.

"Please retrieve your pressure suits," Dr. Sato said, "and meet me at the decon chamber."

The two groups remained segregated as they followed orders. Kellan caught a few suspicious glances from the Blinkers, and Mercer strode over to the decon chamber, his hands folded behind his back like he was still standing guard. Quinta Voss didn't look at the NPCs at all, but Kellan noticed her taking something small, rectangular and brown out of the folds of her pressure suit. She tucked it away on a shelf before joining the others.

"Watch me, and then I want you each to practice putting on your suits," Helena instructed.

She set her helmet down and stepped carefully into the body of her suit, pulling the bulky thing up over her and slipping her arms into it. The one in Kellan's arms was made of such thick, flawless material he could hardly believe it was real. It couldn't have been remade like the Blinkers' coveralls, or patched together like the clothes Kellan was used to. It was virgin fabric, and the only thing that would stand between him and V. martialis out there on the surface of the planet.

"You'll need a partner to help you zip the back and check all of your seals," Dr. Sato said, turning around so Mercer could zip her up. Then he handed her the helmet. She put it on, and the next time she spoke, Kellan watched her mouth move through the heavy-duty shield, but instead of hearing her with his ears, her voice was in his head. "You'll use the overlay to communicate with each other," she explained.

It gave Kellan the willies, someone else's voice uninvited inside his skull. He juddered, then looked over at Jace, who shrugged his shoulders. "What'd she say?"

Kellan raised his hand. "There are five who don't have over-lays." His voice came out testier than he'd intended, although he didn't exactly regret it. This Blinker-planned mission was getting ridiculous. How many times did they need to be reminded?

Dr. Sato tapped Mercer's arm, signaling for him to help her remove her helmet. "I'm sorry, what?"

"We don't *have* overlays," Dex said, and he definitely was not attempting to disguise the irritation in his voice.

"Oh, right." Helena blinked a couple times, then pointed to a shelf near the decon chamber. "There are microphone packs available for you, I forgot. Begin putting on your suits. I'll show you how to sync the microphones to the tablets and the other team members' overlays."

They all spread out, making room to don the unwieldy suits. The material even smelled brand-new, with a subtle chemical odor that kept wafting at Kellan as he maneuvered into his.

While Dr. Sato stepped out of her own suit and came around to the NPCs with microphones, Kellan observed the members of his new crew. He'd worked on a three-person team with Jace and Echo all year, and he'd known both of them since they were kids. Being dropped into a new crew with a mission none of them was familiar with, and almost half of them thinking he was a murderer… well, it wouldn't have the easy vibes of the maintenance crew, that was for sure.

The Blinkers had buddied up. Ronan was zipping Aris's suit up. Quinta was struggling with the seal on her helmet and Castor had his own suit down around his waist, trying to help her.

That guy never seemed to be more than five steps from her.

Were they dating?

Childhood sweethearts?

The idea made Kellan's stomach roll, although it mostly had to do with how big a tool Castor was. The first time they met in the Blinker clinic, they'd almost come to blows. Now, eight years later, Kellan was still a head taller, although Castor had filled out from the scrawny kid he'd been.

Just stay away from me and we'll be fine, Kellan thought as he pulled on his helmet and Jace tested the seal for him. Dr. Sato came around and showed Kellan where to go in the overlay to turn on his mic.

"Okay, looks like everyone's suited up," she said, her voice once again floating eerily through Kellan's mind. "Can you all hear me?"

Thumbs went up all around, NPCs included.

"Can someone with an external mic say something?" she asked. "Let's make sure they're working."

"Dust my vents," Jace said, and Kellan could hear the grin without even looking at him.

Dr. Sato gave a little cough. "Okay… they seem to be working. Now let's come over to the decontamination chamber and I'll walk you through the next part of the process."

Kellan lumbered over to the chamber with the rest of the crew. Digging was going to be a chore in this suit, and he couldn't even imagine attempting fine motor processes.

The chamber was a large structure big enough for all ten of them, or five and a couple assistive robots, built onto the airlock that led outside. Dr. Sato put her own helmet back on, then opened the door and they all filed inside – all except Mercer, who stood guard outside like there was somewhere for them to run to.

"You will do this in both directions, going out and coming back in," Dr. Sato explained as she pulled the heavy door closed behind them. "Going out, it's to make sure that your suits are properly sealed, so the process is abbreviated, just three minutes."

The chamber filled with the hiss of pressurizing air, not unlike the drying cycle of a decon shower.

"On the way back in, the process takes fourteen minutes," she said. "It's automated and the door will not open until it's complete. This is an extremely effective and thoroughly tested protocol that you can be confident in. Chemical wash first, then UV bombardment, followed by a hydrogen peroxide drying cycle."

Yeah, so the decon shower, with a few more bells and whistles. A fine mist began spraying from nozzles built into the chamber walls and ceiling. One big improvement was the helmet – Kellan didn't have to worry about breathing in the chemical spray, or getting it in his mouth.

"Be sure to lift your arms, spread your legs, turn around – you want the chemical wash to get into every little crevice and nook of your suit," Dr. Sato said, demonstrating. The liquid beaded and rolled off the slick material.

"Effective procedure my ass," Jace muttered through his mic. Kellan heard him clearly, and so did everyone else.

"I'm sorry?" Dr. Sato asked.

Kellan elbowed Jace, but with how padded these suits were, he might not have even felt it. Jace said, "We've been doing this protocol in sector four for years. This ain't exactly groundbreaking science."

"My team has done extensive testing on a variety of different chemicals and gasses–"

"Tested how?" Iska demanded. "The last time anyone disturbed regolith on the scale we're being asked to, half the colony died."

The chemical mist cut off and the UV lights kicked on, bathing everything in an unsettling reddish-pink.

"I understand your concerns," Dr. Sato said, still holding her arms out and turning slowly like her life depended on it. "But you need to remember this is not the same situation as the last outbreak, and it's certainly not the same as the first one. The first time Glass swept through the hab, no one saw it coming. They died because they didn't know what they were dealing with, and they had no safety protocols. The second outbreak happened because the survivors thought they'd eradicated the bacteria. They dug recklessly, assuming the danger had passed."

She came around to face everyone again, and finally realized they were all glaring at her, not swallowing her assurances. She dropped her arms to her sides.

"This time is different. We know Glass is out there. We know it's dangerous. We know we have to dig, but we're taking every precaution we can."

"We," Jace snarked, and Dr. Sato shot him a fiery look Kellan hadn't thought her capable of.

The UV lights shut off, and the last cycle began – high-pressure air jets that blew away any remaining dirt and chemical residue. Even through the suits, the noise made conversation impossible.

When the jets finally stopped, Castor was the first to speak. "So you're saying we have more safety protocols than ever."

"I'm saying you have a better chance than anyone who's attempted to dig before," Dr. Sato replied. "But only if you follow every protocol exactly as I showed you. No shortcuts, no matter what happens out there."

QUINTA

YEAR: 2179

After Auditor Mercer and Dr. Sato left, the module was sealed off and the mission officially began. At first, the two groups were completely fractured. Castor wanted to go scope out a couple of beds before everyone else claimed the good ones. The NPCs were fidgeting with the tablets left for them. Ronan was taking stock of the materials lined up against the wall.

It was Aris, the fabrication lead who wore her hair pulled back in a tight braid, who stepped onto a chair in the dining area and called, "Everyone, come over here. We should eat dinner and strategize how we're going to split up the teams."

Leadership abhorred a vacuum, so everyone trickled back over to the tables – even the NPCs.

Dinner turned out to be pre-packaged, shelf-stable meals. It was the kind of stuff you'd find in a quarantine emergency kit – technically edible, but nothing to get excited about. Quinta schooled her features as she took hers, trying not to show her disappointment.

She'd volunteered to dig as her own sort of penance. She shouldn't have expected a premium meal plan.

She sat down next to Castor, who was reading the side of the box. "Stew. I like stew."

He shrugged and opened it, and the self-heating container began to do its thing. A minute later, the not entirely unpleasant smell of cooked carrots and savory sauce emanated from it. Quinta figured it was safe to start heating her own dinner.

While she waited, she noticed that they were once again split into two groups, along sector lines. All the NPCs were at one table, digging right into their meals. It was probably fresher than anything they got back home, and hot. That had to beat cricket protein bar base rations any day.

"I think we should choose permanent teams and stick with them," Aris said, attempting once again to bridge the divide across both tables. "That way we get to know our teams, figure out how to work together, and limit exposure in case of a breach."

That won't work unless the exposed team drags themselves directly to the Frozen Mounds, Quinta thought, poking a lump of what she guessed was cricket meatball with her spoon.

"I've been reviewing the schematics," Ronan said. "The hardest part will be the excavation. Three meters doesn't sound like much, but there will be rocks if we're lucky, boulders if we're not, and digging in those pressure suits won't be easy."

"We should be monitoring vital signs for each person while they're outside the airlock," Dr. Anya said. "Not just for Glass – like you said, it will be strenuous, dangerous work. We don't need any heart attacks along with everything else."

"That's what the implants are for," Castor pointed out. "Valence will send an alert if anyone's in trouble."

"Yeah, well, *we* don't have them," Jace reminded him.

"And what a smart decision that was," Castor shot back.

"Enough," Aris barked, staring daggers at both of them. "This infighting has to stop right now. I don't care if you all hate each other's guts out there." She pointed to the airlock that led to the rest of the hab. "In here, we are one crew. We're doing something incredibly important, and being at each other's throats the whole time will only make it more dangerous. We can't afford to fail this mission. You hear me? The whole colony is counting on us, so no more fighting starting now. Valence doesn't assign missions like this lightly – her whole purpose is to keep us alive and healthy, so if she's calculated this risk is worth taking, we can't ruin it by sabotaging ourselves."

Castor looked cowed, taking a bite of his stew and avoiding Jace's gaze. The NPCs looked defiant, but they stayed quiet.

"Agreed?" Aris insisted.

"Yes," Dr. Anya said, and after her, the rest of them agreed too.

"Yes," Quinta said along with Castor and Ronan.

"Good," Aris said. "We split up the teams evenly. Two citizens, three NPCs on each. That way we always have someone's overlay data available and nobody can accuse anyone else of being unfair." She looked around, waiting for any more challenges, but everyone just nodded in agreement. "Okay, that's settled. Do we have any salt? Deimos, is this stew bland."

Things didn't feel settled, but true to their word, everyone was cordial through dinner. Afterward, they studied the documentation that Mercer had left them to work from. Quinta found the schematics in a new folder in her overlay, and the NPCs got them on the tablets. All except for Kellan, who was struggling with his overlay.

Quinta watched him out of the corner of her eye. He wore a stern expression, his thick brows furrowed, and his eyes kept going in and out of focus like he couldn't figure out how to stay in the interface.

"You seeing that?" Castor whispered.

"Yeah." Had anyone taught him how to use his implant?

"What is he doing?" Castor snickered.

Quinta was just about to stand when Aris walked over to Kellan.

"You look like you're fighting with it," she said, tapping her right temple. "Need help?"

Kellan let out a frustrated huff. "I can't make the old windows go away, and new ones just keep popping up."

"Double-blink to close a window."

Kellan did an exaggerated long blink… long blink… as if he thought he could brute-force his way through the interface. Aris and Castor both laughed, and Quinta felt one bubbling up her throat as well.

"No, faster. Smoother," Aris said, demonstrating the gesture Quinta had had memorized since she was twelve. "Like you have something in your eye and you're trying to blink it out."

"I *do* have something in my eye."

Quinta should have been reviewing the atmospheric unit schematics – they were like gibberish to her at this point – but she couldn't stop watching Kellan. He did the gesture, much less forceful this time, and relief washed over his face. "Oh thank Phobos, it worked."

Aris chuckled. "You'll get the hang of it. Ask Valence to walk you through the other gestures when you have some downtime."

"Ask Valence? No thanks."

Aris gave him a *your loss* look and a shrug. "There are a lot of gestures and they're helpful. Since you already have that thing, you might as well use it. Anyway, your files will pop up if you look up to your right then down diagonally. The mission documentation will be in there."

She was already walking away when he did the gesture she explained,and his face lit up. "It worked!"

He accidentally made eye contact with Quinta across the tables, eyes still sparkling with excitement. They both quickly looked away.

"It says the new unit has already been built by the fabrication team," Castor was reading from the notes.

"Yours truly," Aris said. "My crew spent the entire last week fabricating and assembling. That's why I volunteered – I had to make sure you all get the install right, after all that labor."

"Nah, she had to make sure she didn't screw anything up with the assembly," Ronan teased. He pushed his coverall sleeves up to his elbows, leaning them against the table, and Quinta spotted a Heart of Mars tattoo up high on his forearm. He caught her looking and smiled.

"The most dangerous part is going to be unplugging the old unit and hooking up the new one, right?" Castor asked.

Ronan nodded. "CO_2 levels will start to rise in the modules closest to the unit the minute we disconnect the old one. It'll be a slow process, but if anything goes wrong and we can't get the new unit installed, that's where the rabbit shit will hit the fan."

Everyone kept throwing out technical terms and pulling up schematics on the display wall. The NPCs were following along on their tablets, identifying possible bottlenecks in the process. Quinta tried to follow along, but she hadn't felt so lost since the early days of her apprenticeship, when it seemed like every word her dad taught her was in a foreign language.

They all seemed to have some skill they were bringing to the crew. Aris built the damn unit. Castor knew how to troubleshoot if Valence had trouble syncing up with it. Even Kellan had experience working on the system.

What was Quinta's role here?

They even had a doctor on the crew, a fully trained one.

Quinta was only here to prove something to herself – not the others, no matter what she told herself – and she'd been vain enough to think that because of who she was, she'd have something to contribute. Her mother was right. She hadn't thought this through and she shouldn't be here.

LIRA

YEAR: 2083

Once the rabbitat was sealed off, a big, brightly colored quarantine notice digitally imposed across the door, Lira realized she was a refugee.

Her dorm was a quasi-military zone. There was apparently a room waiting for her in another dorm in the sector, but just because Valence said it was hers, there was no guarantee the other residents would allow her to enter. Everyone knew she'd been in clinic two when the dig crew died. They knew she'd spent sixteen hours at Ada's bedside. Some of them probably also realized she'd spent the last four days sitting on a mountain of regolith with the rabbits.

On top of whether they wanted to let her in, Lira wasn't sure she wanted to go. For one thing, she didn't know if she was still capable of transmitting the disease.

For another, nothing of hers was waiting for her in that new room. The worn copy of *The Grapes of Wrath* that Ada had finally convinced her to read, sitting on her nightstand. The blue knit sweater she'd purchased from the Exchange shortly after she arrived. The pillow with Ada's scent on it, which Lira always breathed deeply into, even when she knew Ada was coming to lie down beside her. She didn't want a new, empty room.

There was a published list of the dead now. It was getting longer by the day. Ada's name was near the top of it, the ninth person to die. Dr. Kalb was number twenty-one. Lira had found Dana Perez's name at number thirty-four.

The list had only existed for a day, and already it was so long it was starting to feel meaningless. Inevitable. Infinite.

Jamila kept telling Lira she would be on it soon. Lira had become more and more hesitant to call, afraid she was bothering Jamila when she should be resting… afraid of the day she wouldn't answer. But she'd promised Jamila that she wouldn't leave her alone.

She'd been negligent in that promise, one of the few she actually had the power to keep.

She knew where she had to go now.

Jamila lived in Dorm 2A. When Lira arrived, there wasn't anyone in the common area, no games of HoloPong taking place, or movies up on the display that dominated one wall. The dorm wasn't locked down, but there wasn't a single resident out of their quarters. Lira made her way down the warren of halls toward Jamila's room. She passed several doors that bore the same type of bold-type, large-print warning that Yusuf and Moses had digitally pinned to the rabbitat door: *QUARANTINE ZONE – Unauthorized Entry Prohibited.*

It was too late. V. martialis was spreading, no matter how many doors the maintenance crew and Valence sealed off.

When she got to Jamila's room, Lira knocked and her heart climbed into her throat in the silence that followed.

Finally, she heard a faint "Yeah?" and slouched with relief.

"Jamila, it's me," she called. "Lira."

"You can't be here," Jamila rasped, barely sounding like herself. "I'm sick. We all are."

Fear jolted through Lira. We all are? That couldn't be true. And how would Jamila know, tucked away in her room? *We all are.* The words bounced around inside her head. Visions of being the final survivor came unwanted into her mind, wandering a still, body-strewn hab, wondering *why her*?

"That's why I'm here," she called back to silence those thoughts. "You need somebody to take care of you, and I don't know why, but I'm still not sick."

She'd had more exposure than almost anyone in the hab, and here she was five days later, perfectly, terribly healthy while even the people who'd been exposed after her were dying or dead. Some small part of her felt like she was betraying Ada by being alive right now. But for whatever reason… she was here.

"Open up," she called. "I'm not going away."

After a few long seconds, in which she wondered if Valence would even allow Jamila to unlock her door, Lira heard the release of the pocket door's lock.

Apparently the AI agreed – Lira was immune.

She pushed the door open and the smell of sickness, damp and sweet, hit her. The windowless room was dark, with only a dim running light illuminating the edges of the floor. She could make out Jamila in her bed, an empty IV bag and an untouched food tray at her bedside.

It was just dark enough she couldn't make out any of Jamila's features, and Lira's heart sped up when she asked, "Okay if I turn up the light a little?"

"Slowly. My eyes are sensitive," Jamila said. "Be warned, it's not pretty."

Lira was thinking of Ada and those opaque pupils when she found the control panel on the wall by the door, slowly increasing the brightness of the overhead light. She at least had the where-withal not to gasp at what she saw.

Lying in the bed, a dry washcloth draped over her forehead and the sheets thrown off in, Jamila looked limp. Sweat-drenched. Her eyes weren't quite as bad as Ada's had been – there were little pinpoints of milky whiteness over the pupils like new cataracts, not the massive, blinding orbs that Ada had had.

But her complexion was much lighter than Ada's had been and the effect on her skin was even more jarring. Lira had only gotten a glimpse of it on their last video call. In person, Jamila's skin was damn near transparent in places. Lira could see every vein and artery in her face, and the hands she clutched to the sheets at her chest looked more like anatomical models than living human hands.

And her eyelids… no wonder the light hurt, they'd gone nearly transparent, only a spiderweb of fine veins still visible.

"Oh, honey." Lira dialed the light down a few notches.

"I'm disgusting." Jamila turned her face toward the wall.

"You're not, you're just sick." Lira closed the door. She took off the mask and pushed back her hood, and Jamila tried to object, but Lira reminded her she'd already been practically bathed in the bacteria for the past four days. She knelt on the floor at her side. "I did this to you. I am so freaking sorry."

"I kept working, went places around the hab," Jamila said. "I could have gotten it from any number of people."

She let out a jagged sigh and Lira looked closer at the bedside table.

"Do you want me to get you some water? A fresh meal?"

Jamila shook her head. "How is it out there? I haven't checked the feeds in a while."

"They sealed off the rabbitat because of the regolith," Lira told her. She thought of the vote about whether to kill the rabbits, but couldn't bring herself to talk about it. "People are freaking out. Most of them are quarantining."

That, or they were already dead. Lira hadn't passed a single person on her way here. She picked up the washcloth and dribbled some water from one of the bottles into it, then carefully folded it into a long rectangle and laid it back over Jamila's forehead.

"How are you feeling?"

"Like hell. Most people don't make it past day four," she said. "I got that much from the group chats."

"Well, you're not most people," Lira said. "You're the best darn botanist on Earth *and* Mars. You figured out how to grow wheat on a barren planet. You stood by me and Ada even when everyone hated her. You are not most people, Jamila, and you're going to survive this."

That got a thin smile, and Jamila reached out and put her glassy hand on top of Lira's. "Thank you for coming."

LIRA

YEAR: 2083

Jamila went the same way Ada had, only without the crash team surrounding her and shouting orders. Lira did what she could, which wasn't much. She'd retrieved water and kept a cool washcloth on her forehead, and stayed by her side all day. Even if she'd had an MD instead of a DVM degree, there wouldn't have been anything she could do when Jamila's heart abruptly stopped beating. It didn't matter how long she kept up compressions or how loudly she begged Jamila to keep fighting.

Her name was added to the list of the dead the next morning. Lira was afraid to look at what number she was.

Lira shrouded her friend as best she could. There was no one left to come around with fresh bedsheets, and Lira couldn't force herself to go into one of the other rooms to steal a clean set, so she made do with Jamila's sweat-damp sheets, trying to find a clean corner to place over her face. Then she submitted a request to Valence to replace the notice on Jamila's door. It was already updated by the time she stepped into the hallway.

BIOHAZARD CONTAINMENT – Deceased Occupant. Entry Prohibited Pending Retrieval.

Retrieval. When would that be? Who was there to assign the task? Lira hadn't bothered to check her own Exchange dashboard since she got kicked out of the rabbitat, and for once, Valence wasn't pestering her with overdue task alerts.

She stood there in the hallway, her mask and hood up just in case she came across another person. She realized she was a refugee again already, and that there was nowhere she wanted to be. Her impulse was to go to the rabbits, to be of some use to them if she could help no one else, but Valence had rejected her appeal. The door was sealed shut and there was nothing Lira could do.

She ended up walking to the microbiology lab in sector two, where the four remaining microbiologists had been working. Maybe they could take samples and find out why she was still walking around perfectly fine while the entire colony was dying around her.

It took close to an hour to get there. Ordinarily it would have been thirty minutes, but the airlocks between the modules had been activated and it took time to pass through them all. She saw two people the whole way there, and both of them turned and went another direction rather than pass her. It was eerie. Normally, the hab felt like a sardine can, full of a thousand people all moving and breathing and sweating in each other's space.

Now, Lira yearned to have to turn sideways in a narrow hall to pass someone. To get to the dining hall just as they were running out of dessert. To wrinkle her nose as a whiff of someone else's body odor wafted through her air vent while she was going to sleep at night.

How many of them remained?

She could have checked the dead list, or consulted the hab map. But she was afraid of what she would find.

The microbio lab was tucked away in a branching hallway around the back of the med clinic. A bright red warning popped up over the door the moment she turned the corner, and her stomach turned to stone.

BIOHAZARD CONTAINMENT – Deceased Occupant. Entry Prohibited Pending Retrieval.

"No, no, no! What the fuck!"

Anger burst up her throat and she slammed the heel of her hand into the door. There was absolutely no give in the sheet metal and she felt the resistance all the way into her shoulder.

"Hello?!" she shouted at the door. "Anybody in there?"

They couldn't all be dead. There were four of them. At least one of them must still be working on making antibiotics or looking for a cure. Lira checked the hab map, but there was no one inside the lab – at least no one living.

"Valence, locate the microbio team," she demanded. Maybe one of them had died in the lab, as evidenced by the big red warning on the door, so the others had moved to another lab to continue their research.

Valence dropped a single location pin on the hab map. Just one. Out of four. Reg Simpson, who was currently in med clinic one. Lira's heart leaped into her throat in spite of every attempt the bacteria had made in the last few days to kill her hope.

Med clinic one wasn't a completely unreasonable place for a microbiologist to continue his research, if he had to evacuate his lab. Right?

"Is he healthy?" Lira asked. "Is he working?"

"It is against Colony Manual Section 1.4.3 to disclose the private medical information of one colonist to another," Valence said through the hall speakers.

Lira growled in frustration and used the pin Valence dropped to initiate an audio call with Simpson. She'd just have to find out for herself.

The call rang for what felt like ages. Lira occupied herself with mental images of Simpson frantically working, trying to manage the workloads of his three dead colleagues while a deadly contagion swept through the hab. Of course he didn't have time for calls from people he'd never met.

Then he answered. His voice was weak like Jamila's. The video blinked on and Lira saw his eyes were clouded over and his dark skin looked dull and gray. He lay in a hospital bed, not working in sector one but being treated there.

Lira's heart dropped from her throat into her shoes as she cast about for something to say, some reason for having initiated this call other than *I hoped you weren't dying, but clearly you are.*

"Hi," she settled on.

"Who are you?" Simpson asked. His overcast eyes weren't focusing on the screen and she realized the disease had stolen his vision, just like it had Ada and then Jamila, near the end.

"I just…" *I'm a freak. I'm immune. I hoped you could use me to find a cure.* All of it felt so pointless now, she let out a weak sigh and said, "Wrong contact, I'm sorry. But I can see you're sick. Do you need anything?"

The man smiled faintly and shook his head. "I'm being cared for well here. Are you okay?"

"Fine," she said meekly, and ended the call.

She slapped the door again, then kicked it for good measure. Her toes screamed through her thin canvas slip-ons, but the pain was the first thing she'd felt in days that cleared her head. She kept assaulting the sheet metal door like she could beat some kind of solution out of it.

Her partner was dead.

Her best friend was dead.

For all she knew, her mom was dead in Manila.

The rabbits would be dead as soon as their food and water ran out.

More names were being added to the dead list by the minute, and here Lira was, without so much as a headache.

She screamed at the top of her lungs and slammed her fist into the door. Something inside her hand gave. Her knuckles went numb instantly, then tingles shot up to her elbow.

You just broke your stupid hand, the veterinarian part of her brain said.

LIRA
YEAR: 2083

ira wandered aimlessly. Her body and mind had gone numb in the aftermath of all that adrenaline, but as it slowly leeched back out of her bloodstream, her hand started to hurt like hell.

It swelled and reddened, and with all that pressure just beneath the skin, she could feel her pulse throbbing across her knuckles.

It was definitely broken, but all the med clinics were locked down thanks to the one-two punch of the dead staff and the looters. There were medical supplies in the rabbitat but she couldn't get to those either. She held her hand up over her heart as she walked to dull the throbbing. The gesture made her feel like someone ought to be singing the national anthem.

She let her mind meander down paths like that – safe, mundane ones – while she walked the halls with no particular destination in mind. She pulled her mask down to her chin because she hadn't come within ten meters of another person since Jamila died. She passed at least a dozen more doors with BIOHAZARD CONTAIN-MENT overlays, and knew there would be many more in the residential modules.

Some of them had digital renderings pinned around the notices. Flowers and stuffed animals and virtual trinkets hovering around the doors. And then Lira noticed the notes and the photos. Some notes were open for everyone to read, full of love and grief and memories. Others were locked files, just between the author and the deceased.

Shrines.

People were erecting shrines within the overlay to honor the dead.

Lira started contributing a cluster of jasmine to each decorated door she passed. She'd left digital bouquets of them on Ada's bedside table a half-dozen times since they started dating, delicate white blossoms with cheery yellow centers that reminded her of home. She should have done it more often. She should have done it every single day.

But she was saving her credits for a ring, and she thought she'd have the rest of her life to surprise Ada with flowers.

When she reached the long hallway leading from sector two into the central commons, the hub that connected all the sectors like spokes on a wheel, she heard voices. A lot of them.

She started walking faster, curious.

The central commons was a large space, used formally as a meeting place for the administrative staff, as well as for all-colony meetings whenever there were hab-wide issues to discuss. It was also used informally as a coffee shop, a bar, a theater… a chameleon of a room that served whatever purpose the colony required. The last time Lira had been to a meeting here, Ada had been on trial.

Lira's body was tense with the memories when she stepped into the room. There were at least three dozen people gathered in chairs spaced generously apart from each other. A lot of them wore masks, but no one was in a full-body suit like Lira's.

She sat down in the nearest empty chair, hoping not to draw attention to herself. She let her injured hand settle delicately in her lap. Was this the group that had voted on whether to kill her rabbits? A few people turned to look at her, and the closest one narrowed his eyes distrustfully. Lira bristled and turned away from him.

There was a heated debate going on between two people she recognized. The first, Pavel Orlov, was standing at a podium on the small stage in one corner of the room. He looked uncomfortable to be there. He was a systems admin, great at his job but not the public speaking type, and he was second in command after Dmitri Voss. Since Dmitri was holed up in sector three, did that make Orlov the acting administrator?

The second person arguing was from the cohort that had arrived on Mars with Lira and Ada – Tim Robinette. He was a robotics engineer and he'd been rubbing Lira the wrong way since their first day in the shuttle. He was a typical cocky American, with a thick neck and a crew cut, always thinking the world revolved around him, and right now he was arguing for an antibiotic lottery.

"So what if I'm not a doctor or a sys admin?" he was saying, the only other person in the room who was standing. "I was important enough to ship here, so I should be important enough to get life-saving antibiotics."

"I heard the med staff have already taken more than half the doses themselves," someone in the crowd said. "It isn't fair."

Tim nodded. "I've heard that too. We all deserve an equal chance at the remaining doses. If anyone is in urgent need, Valence will prioritize resources for them, that's the whole point of the AI. But out of what's left, there should be a lottery. We should all have the same odds of survival."

Poor Pavel looked miserable up on the podium, his eyes shifting back and forth between Tim and the angry faces in the crowd. Lira wondered if he knew when he took his job that he'd end up in a position like this. It was clear from his hunched posture and the way he was white-knuckling the podium that he wasn't comfortable with taking control and making decisions for everyone.

"The antibiotics only slow the disease, they don't cure it," he said, and that was the wrong thing. It caused an uproar of people shouting, "I want those extra days!" and, "I'd have taken a few more hours with my wife!"

Lira considered speaking up, telling them what she'd just learned about the state of microbio. Maybe they wouldn't be fighting each other if they knew how few doses were left, that there would never be any more.

Then again, maybe that information would start an all-out war. Valence certainly wanted to keep it under wraps.

Tim more or less commandeered the meeting from there. Pavel kept his position of authority at the podium, but Tim turned to his audience and started walking them through exactly how he thought the antibiotic lottery should work.

"It's pretty simple," he said. "We need the remaining med staff to tell us honestly how many doses are left, and we need them to promise not to give any more out before the lottery can be conducted."

So much for those 'in special need,' Lira thought with a subtle roll of her eyes.

Everyone was nodding along, desperate for any leader to emerge. And Lira knew Tim had just that kind of opportunistic personality. He'd started strategizing ways to game the Exchange the minute their shuttle took off from Earth.

"Then all we do is divide the total doses by how many of us are still alive and let Valence run a randomizer to pick names–"

"Courses," Lira said, loud enough for her mask-muffled voice to carry across the room. A few people turned to her. "You need to raffle off courses, not doses," she clarified. "A single dose is worse than useless."

"Tell that to people who haven't had any," somebody in the crowd said.

"Who are you to tell us what we need to do?" someone else asked.

Lira started to say her name, list her credentials, but her response was drowned out by Tim's booming voice.

"I'd rather everybody have a little bit of the cure and we all take our chances with it," he said. "What's the alternative? A handful of people survive, surrounded by an entire hab full of dead, half-transparent people?"

"I'm not gonna be one of them," the man in the chair next to Lira said, arms crossed. "The med staff wants me to start turning to freaking glass before they'll say I deserve antibiotics."

"Equal distribution to as many of us as possible is the only fair way," Tim said.

Lira shook her head. "No, it's not fair, it's dangerous… and it's not a cure, either. Like Pavel said, it *might* extend your life by a few hours. But if you're going to do this lottery, it can't be single doses. All that will get you is a drug-resistant strain of the bacteria."

"She's right," someone spoke up, and Lira was surprised to see Nurse Pema in the crowd. "The winners have to get full courses. I've already had mine, so I've got no dog in this fight. I'm just telling you how it is."

"Okay, full courses," Tim said. "That's going to drastically reduce the size of the lottery but if that's the only way–"

"It is," Lira insisted, annoyed that it had taken confirmation from Pema before he would listen.

"Why are you wearing that suit, anyway?" he demanded. "You're not infected, are you?"

"No." Lira nearly said *I'm immune*, but caught the words on the tip of her tongue. What would this crowd do to her if they knew? Hell, what would they do if they knew she was wearing this because she'd been dust-bathing in regolith like a chinchilla? "It's just a precaution," she said. "Call me a hypochondriac."

"Where do I get one?" somebody asked.

"Central supply, I bet," someone else chimed in. "But it's guarded."

"So how'd she get one?"

"Were you exposed?" Tim demanded, his voice punching across the high ceiling with its gloomy orange view of the Martian sky.

"We've all been exposed," Lira said.

"But were *you* exposed?" His eyes bore down on her like they could ignite the thin protective suit everyone was so fixated on. Every eye in the room had turned to Lira. Pavel was standing still on the stage, hands clutching the podium, aware that he had completely lost control of the meeting.

Perhaps of the hab, if he was supposed to be acting administrator.

Lira lowered her mask to show everyone her face. "I was with Ada Bello when she died," she said. "I watched her 'turn to glass,' as you put it. I heard the rest of the dig crew die in the rooms around us. That was six days ago. I haven't heard of a single case where someone got sick and lived past day four. So yeah, I *have* been exposed, but I guess I'm just lucky or something."

She was sneering by the time she finished talking. She looked around the crowd, and instead of relief at the fact that she was at least two days past what should have been her expiration date, all she saw was terror. *I have been exposed.* That was all any of them heard.

"Make her leave!" someone shouted to Tim.

"Get out!"

"You'll kill us all!"

"They should put all of you into one sector and seal it off away from us!"

"That's not a bad idea," Tim said.

The fury of the crowd was so immediate and so strong that Lira stumbled to her feet, genuinely afraid they might hurt her. Her hand started to throb again but she couldn't think about that now. She looked to Pavel, who had fear in his own eyes, and it seemed like the podium was no longer just propping him up – it was a shield, a physical barrier between him and the crowd he was meant to be guiding.

She looked at Nurse Pema, who gave her a helpless look. Lira didn't blame her. What was one person supposed to do in the middle of an angry mob? Just lift up her feet and go with the flow, hoping not to get pulled under.

Then Lira looked at Tim. His square jaw was set, his eyes like hard little marbles.

"Leave," he said. And then, he turned it into a chant. "Leave! Leave!"

"Leave!" they all droned along with him. Lira looked around the commons. All she saw was a sea of tired and fearful faces, streaked through with a heaping dose of anger at something they couldn't possibly understand. All that energy had to go somewhere.

With tears welling in her eyes – of sadness or frustration, she wasn't sure – she turned and walked out of the commons. If they'd had pitchforks and torches, they would have chased her out of the room. All sense had fled that room long before Lira arrived.

QUINTA

YEAR: 2179

There was no gradual night-cycle lighting inside the fabrication module. Instead, there was a switch on the wall. When everyone was ready for it to be night, somebody toggled the overhead lights and boom, it was pitch-dark.

That was just one of the many reasons this place felt alien, and why Quinta was second-guessing her motives for being here.

"This mattress is a nightmare," Castor grumbled, shifting uncomfortably on the bed beside hers.

Quinta squinted into the dark at the other figure in the bed across the aisle. There had been no discussion about a women's dorm and a men's one – they'd all silently agreed to divide themselves the way they were always divided. Citizens in one room, NPCs in the other. It'd been pure luck that there were four beds in one room and six in the other, the same breakdown between men and women, citizens and non-participants.

"I don't think comfort was high on their priority list," Quinta said, shifting onto her back. The ceiling was plain white hab fabric, no skylight, no display panel.

"Comfort is for the worthy," Ronan said. "We'll earn it when we dig. G'night, you two."

"Night," Castor said.

The fourth citizen, Aris, was still out in the common area, pouring over the instruction sheet and triple-checking the unit she'd built. Quinta could see her light under the door, and she could hear the NPCs having conversations through the thin, quickly constructed wall that separated the two dorms. She couldn't hear their words, but their tone mirrored her own gut feeling: apprehensive, uncertain… afraid to say anything too critical of the mission lest it poison the mood of the crew.

The citizen dorm was quiet for a few minutes. Across the aisle, Ronan's breathing had already dropped into the steady rise and fall of sleep. Quinta could tell Castor was still awake, and her own mind wouldn't stop turning over everything that had happened in the past week, and everything about to happen.

She tossed and turned a couple times.

She checked her messages and sent a text to her mother letting her know she was settling in okay. She also told her that Dr. Sato had a souped-up decontamination protocol for them to go through. She wasn't sure she believed it was anything special, but it'd make her mom feel better.

She turned again, facing Castor's bed.

The kiss came to mind again.

Castor had tried to bring it up a time or two since it happened, but Quinta kept coming up with more important things to talk about. *Who do you think will be digging with us? What's your dad going to do without you in the computer lab? I'll bet you five credits it's stirfry for dinner tonight.*

She still didn't know how she felt about it. After almost twenty years of being best friends, she should know, right?

"They outnumber us," Castor said out of nowhere, making Quinta jump.

"What?"

"Four of us, six of them," he said. The NPCs were still talking in the other room. "And it's their fault the unit is broken in the first place. I don't care what Aris says, they should do the dirty work."

"All the digging?"

"The risky stuff," Castor said. "You know they'll try to weasel out of doing their fair share. It's what they do."

"We've already got our teams," Quinta pointed out. "They're evenly split."

That was one thing they'd all accomplished after dinner. Quinta and Castor would be digging with Dr. Anya, Dex and Torrent. She was just glad nobody suggested she dig with Kellan.

"We'll make them pull their weight—"

"Guys," Ronan's voice came from the dark. Quinta could make out his silhouette and see he was propped up on his elbows.

"Sorry," Castor said.

"I can't sleep." Quinta swung her feet out of the bed. "I'm going to see what Aris is up to."

"Want company?" Castor asked.

"No, you rest."

She shuffled out of the room before he could change his mind, squinting at the full brightness of the common area. Aris was sitting on the floor near the new atmo unit, an access panel pulled off it to reveal a rabbit warren of wires. Her vision alternated rapidly between the up-close wires and the middle distance of her overlay, and Quinta approached tentatively.

"What are you doing?" she asked softly.

"Quadruple-checking," Aris said. "If any of these junctions aren't right and we don't find out until the unit is installed…"

She trailed off, her vision going hazy again.

Clearly, entrenched in her work. Quinta would be no help to her. If she tried, she'd only be a distraction since she had not the first clue what she was looking at. So she wandered over to the little impromptu kitchen and found a mug and a jar of tea leaves.

She made herself a cup – chamomile, just what she needed – then wandered over to the table to sip it.

She thought about scanning through the mission documentation again. It felt like everyone else understood it better than she did. But the warm tea was finally starting to slow her thoughts down, and she didn't want to load even more technical details into her brain.

Instead, she went over to the shelf where she'd tucked away the only personal item she'd brought with her. Her father's well-worn copy of *The Grapes of Wrath,* which she thought she might read during the mission if she had the time.

She opened it and the spine cracked softly. The book smelled like nothing she'd ever experienced before – rich like the compost that came from the rabbitat, slightly mossy like when the hydroponic troughs needed cleaning, and oddly comforting. The binding was coming loose so she held it carefully and turned to the first page.

My sweet Lira,

    This book is about all the evil in the world, but I love it because it's a reminder that there will always be good people fighting back and supporting each other, even when they have nothing left to give.

    You remind me of that every day too.

    Love you!

The inscription was Quinta's favorite thing about the book. She didn't know it was there when she chose it as a gift, but she'd been thrilled to find it when she was wrapping the book. She could count on one hand the number of hand-written notes she'd seen, and even though she didn't know who Lira was or the identity of the writer, it felt like peeking into their lives.

She ran her fingers over the blue ink now, not pressing too hard for fear of rubbing it away. The book was well over a hundred years old, and likely so was the inscription.

She started to turn the page, then a smile broke over her lips and she turned back.

She'd left an inscription of her own for her father when she gave him the book. She'd forgotten all about it until now, and had no clue what it said, but she knew child-Quinta had wanted to leave her mark like Uchenna had.

She double-blinked to open her overlay. The note appeared, a big *Congratulations on your new role* embellished with digital jasmine flowers that she'd always been partial to, but Quinta barely even looked at it, because there was a second note on the page.

It was tiny. She had to pinch and zoom to read it.

Sugar beet,

If you're reading this, something has happened to me. Don't believe what they'll say. I wasn't hoarding, I was balancing the scales. There's more at stake than medical supplies. I'm so sorry I kept you in the dark about all this… I was trying to protect you. Find EC or AR if you're in trouble.

Dad

teebragus134.binPTQJV

She didn't understand the postscript – it had her initials in it, Quinta Jasmine Voss, but what was the rest? She checked the meta-data of the note to see if maybe it was just some strange artefact, and found that it was created just a week before Hadrian's death.

"Oh, Phobos." Quinta closed the book, her stomach roiling.

"Hmm?" Aris looked up from her work.

"Nothing," Quinta said, standing and tucking the book protectively under her arm. "I'm going to bed."

KELLAN

YEAR: 2179

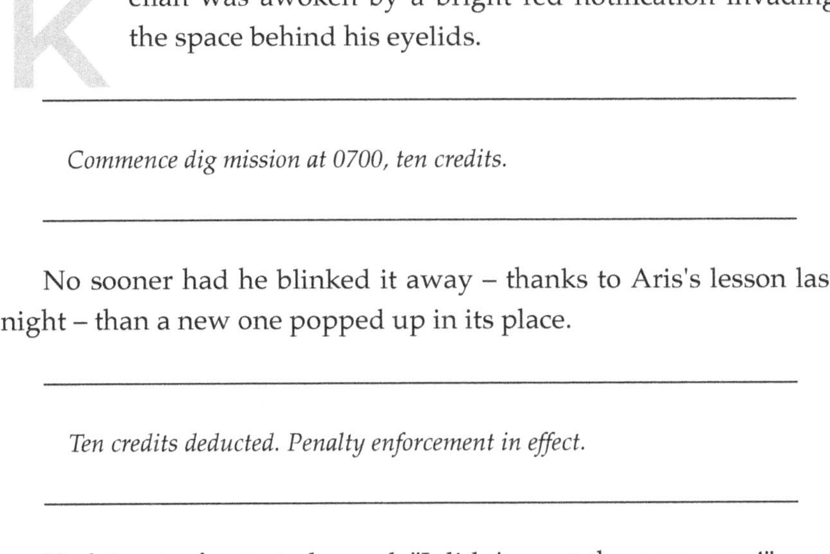

Kellan was awoken by a bright red notification invading the space behind his eyelids.

Commence dig mission at 0700, ten credits.

No sooner had he blinked it away – thanks to Aris's lesson last night – than a new one popped up in its place.

Ten credits deducted. Penalty enforcement in effect.

He let out a frustrated growl. "I didn't want them anyway!"

"Dude, you okay?" Jace asked, throwing one arm over his face to block the overhead light when Dr. Anya flipped it on.

"Swell."

"Breakfast in ten," Dr. Anya announced. "Up and at 'em."

Kellan climbed out of bed and grabbed a fresh coverall from a stack of them at the foot of his bed. They would all be in Blinker uniform for the duration of the dig. Kellan had gotten used to it during the week he was their prisoner, but for most of them, this was their first time stepping into the crisp khakis.

"I can't believe they wear these all the time," Iska said while everyone turned their backs to change. "They're like dried algae sheets."

"I'm chafing already," Jace complained.

"Say what you will about how our patches look, at least they're soft," Torrent agreed.

"I like the patches," Dex said. "Our clothes have personality, history. This…" He looked down at his coverall in disgust. "Well, at least it's only until we all get Glass and die."

He looked around the room, where no one was laughing.

"Too soon? My bad."

Nobody had slept well, judging by the dark circles under everyone's eyes at breakfast. Even the Blinkers looked rough, and no one did more than mechanically swallow their meals. This morning, it was cricket mash with peppers and onions, along with the finest synthetic Blinker coffee.

Which actually did taste pretty damn good.

While they ate, the Blinkers all zoned out, probably getting their morning dopamine hit from the machine. Creeped Kellan the hell out.

At the NPC table, Torrent swallowed his breakfast in a few efficient bites. Jace was on his third cup of Candor dark. Dex stretched his back with a series of pops and cracks that Iska scolded him for.

"You're going to pop a tendon or tear a muscle or something."

"Been doing it forty years, I'll be fine."

"Dr. Anya, will you tell him?"

The doctor just raised her hands and laughed. "Happy to help with solicited medical advice, but it's my policy not to get in the middle of family rows."

Kellan sat at a spot on the end, his own overlay open, trying to figure out how to get to the messages. There had to be a way to send one to Echo's tablet, so she could let everyone else know how the crew was doing. He'd gotten a lot better at the basic gestures already, but he couldn't find half of what Aris told him was there, and he'd be sun-forsaken if he asked Valence for help.

"You ready for this?" Jace asked, startling Kellan out of the overlay.

"It's not me who needs to be ready right now." He and Jace were both on the afternoon dig shift. This morning, all they would do was monitor.

He looked back at the Blinker table. Quinta was the only one not zoning out. She looked pale, with a permanent crease between her brow. Probably watching the clock tick down to 0700 and realizing there was no one was coming to rescue her from this.

"She's really going to dig, huh?" Kellan muttered. "A Voss… going into the regolith."

"Bet you my favorite screwdriver she doesn't even suit up," Jace said. "She'll find an excuse, or else the Chosen one will save her the embarrassment and tell her she can't go. She's too valuable, the great founder's progeny. Whatever would we do without her?"

It was the first thing Kellan thought when he saw her standing in the group of volunteers yesterday. There was a zero percent chance the girl who thought rabbits were Valence's special gift to her would be trudging through the Glass-infected soil with the rest of them.

Kellan was here for redemption.

The other NPCs were all here to protect their sector's interests.

Aris was here because the new atmo unit was her baby.

He didn't know Ronan's story, but he was pretty sure Castor was only here because he was surgically attached to Quinta's backside.

So what was she doing here? Whatever it was, they'd find some excuse to stick her on monitoring duty, keep her inside the module, or Valence would come up with some last-minute excuse about why it was more important to go back to her old job.

She wouldn't dig.

"First shift," Dr. Anya said after a while, loud enough for everyone to hear. "We start in fifteen minutes, so finish your breakfast, hydrate… vomit those nerves out if you have to because you don't want to do it in your suit. Get ready however you need to and then meet me at the decon chamber."

Kellan watched Quinta's reaction. A slight stiffening of her shoulders, a flash of fear in her pretty brown eyes, but that was all. Castor put his hand on her lower back, and they rose together and picked up their breakfast trays.

"The rest of us are monitoring their video feeds and comms," Aris said. "We'll work from the tables so let's get this area cleaned up."

Kellan's breakfast sat heavy in his stomach and he felt jittery from a single cup of coffee. Jace seemed fine for now, but it was even odds he'd be bouncing off the ceiling in half an hour. He had to be a fool to caffeinate like that fifteen minutes before the colony made contact with the regolith for the first time in five decades.

He watched the morning shift shuffle anxiously over to the decon chamber and start stepping into their pressure suits like they were lining up to be executed. There was very little chatter, except for Dr. Anya reminding them, "Check each other's seals. Be meticulous."

"My team, let's all sit together," Aris said, waving the NPCs over to the Blinker table.

"Her team?" Iska asked under her breath. "I don't remember electing her Fearless Leader."

"Somebody's got to step up," her dad said, patting her on the back. "It'll be okay." He was the last of the morning dig shift to head to the decon chamber and Iska grabbed his hand just before he left.

"Please be careful."

"Obnoxiously cautious," Dex promised.

Kellan sat down between Iska and Jace, Aris and Ronan sitting across from them.

"Here, everybody take a tablet whether you have an implant or not," Aris said, handing them around. "More data is always better."

Kellan accepted one and it immediately synced with his implant, flooding his vision with multiple video feeds from the other shift's helmets, plus vital signs he didn't know how to read and environmental data he could make no sense of. It was over-whelming and he blinked rapidly, trying to clear some of the clutter. "How can we track all of this?"

"We share," Aris said. "We'll all take a couple inputs to monitor, and make sure there are redundancies in case one of us needs a bathroom break or gets distracted."

"I won't get distracted," Ronan said, his hand going automatically to his forearm to touch the tattoo Kellan knew was tucked up under his sleeve. "My people are counting on me to keep them safe."

"They're our people too," Iska said. "More of ours than yours, in fact."

"And we're each going to pay equal attention to all of them," Aris interrupted before the spat could get very far.

"There they go," Kellan said, and four heads turned to watch the morning shift lumbering into the decontamination chamber.

Kellan couldn't tell which one was Quinta anymore – not from the back, when everyone looked like a human-sized puffball mush-room in those suits. But there were five of them. She was actually doing it, despite all his reservations.

Despite everything he knew about Blinkers and the Voss family. She was going to dig.

Or at the very least, she was going to go outside.

"They've only got a few minutes in there to pressure-test their suits and then the mission begins," Aris said. "Let's get organized. Test your comms, verify all life support readings are online. Iska, take Dr. Anya. Jace, take Torrent..."

She rattled off assignments, giving Castor to Kellan, because of course he wanted to spend the whole day staring at the helmet camera of a guy with the world's most punchable face.

The vitals were easier to read than he expected. Kellan had a much better time navigating with the tablet and he found Castor's in the cluster of windows. They were green across the board, and the suit seemed to be in perfect order.

It took longer to figure out how to talk to Castor... or maybe just an extra few minutes to convince himself he wanted to. "Hey... can you hear me?" he finally asked through the overlay.

A few seconds went by and he started wondering if he'd done it wrong when Castor said, "Yeah?"

The annoyance was audible. Great, this was going to be a lovely first shift.

"Just checking the comms," Kellan said, then muted his end before Castor had a chance to come up with another shitty reply.

Anyway, he had a lot more interesting things to look at now because he'd just found the external cameras. He'd never actually seen the surface of the planet before – only the orange sky visible from a small number of skylights in his sector and in the central commons.

Red dust stretched to the horizon, rippled from wind and pock-marked from quakes, broken only by a few scattered boulders and the rusted, hunched skeletons of the robots that had built the colony a hundred years ago.

They were sort of beautiful, in a tragic way.

And somewhere out there, three meters down, lay the old atmo unit dragging in its final, ragged breaths. Buried in the same soil where V. martialis hibernated, waiting for some fool to come along and disturb it.

"Decontamination cycle's complete," he heard Dr. Anya announce through Iska's tablet. "We're proceeding to the airlock."

KELLAN

YEAR: 2179

or the first twenty minutes, no one at the table even breathed.

They were all transfixed by the video feeds of the first shift stepping out onto the surface. Kicking up red-orange dust with every step. Venturing across the ground that had been untouched by anything but wind for fifty years.

It covered their helmets in a thin film within minutes, tinting all the camera views orange.

All their pulses were elevated, every last one of them, as adrenaline coursed through their veins, and then because the trek to the dig site was long. The atmo unit was tucked up against a module about two hundred meters from their airlock, and the team trudged along in their suits, a little assistive robot trundling beside them, hauling their supplies.

"Is everyone feeling okay?" Aris asked after a few tense minutes.

"Hot in this suit," Dex said.

"The dust is everywhere," Castor added, and Kellan watched him lift his arm in front of his camera. The white suit was already discolored and coated with fine regolith. "That decon chamber better be up to the task."

"Long as it stays on the outside, it doesn't bother me," Torrent said with a hint of bravado evident even through the slightly degraded audio of the comms.

"It's incredible out here," Quinta said. "I can see *so far*."

"I think we're here," Dr. Anya said after a few more minutes. "Let's get to work."

They dug for two hours. It was the amount of time they'd previously agreed on, the most they thought they could tolerate in the hot, tight confines of the pressure suits. Kellan went from sitting on the edge of his seat, all his senses hyperalert for the first signs of illness on Castor's monitors, to somewhat bored and too aware of the aching of his bladder.

No one was feverish, although they were all sweating profusely from the exertion, according to their hydration levels.

No one got disoriented or confused.

They were all just breathing hard into their microphones, huffing and shoveling and damning the assistive robot for not being capable of much more than schlepping the loosened dirt away from the dig site.

Not a single hint of Glass… yet.

When the two hours were up and the first shift was debating whether to leave the robot and the tools at the site or bring them back, Kellan's bladder gave another, more urgent complaint.

Damn Blinker coffee. Somehow, Jace – who'd had three times as much – seemed perfectly comfortable.

Kellan checked Castor's vitals for the fiftieth time. Heart rate still slightly elevated around one-ten, hydration levels still dropping because he'd been refusing to drink the reclaimed water his suit was equipped to filter and deliver back to him.

None of the NPCs had been that proud, but Quinta had spent the first hour resisting it too. Finally, she'd caved, and told Castor it was just room-temperature and ever so slightly salinated, but not that bad.

"I think I'll survive two hours and wait for decent water," he'd answered.

"Hate to tell you this, but the stuff you drink in here's been reclaimed a hell of a lot more times than what your suit's offering," Kellan had been unable to keep from chiming in.

Castor had muted his comms for a while after that, and still didn't drink.

He was doing fine now, and the dig was over for the morning. Kellan had about five minutes while they walked back to the airlock. He stood up.

"I'm gonna take a piss," he announced. "I'll keep monitoring Marcellus from my overlay."

It took him a moment of blinking, but he got the vitals and the camera feed ported over.

"Getting used to it after all, huh?" Aris said. "Told you it's convenient."

"Sure is convenient looking at Marcellus's ugly mug while I go to the bathroom."

Two hours wasn't that long on any ordinary day – Kellan had lost himself in tasks for well over two hours on many occasions, looking up only to realize he'd worked through lunch and was halfway to dinner. Today, though, being forced to watch from the other side of a camera lens as small winds kicked up regolith all around the digging crew, they'd been the longest two hours of Kellan's life.

Even longer than any of the hours he'd spent alone in his jail cell, or in a treatment room after they forced the implant on him.

As he made his way to the restrooms at the far side of the module near the dorms, Kellan listened to the crew through the comms. Sometime in those two hours, something in the group had loosened. They were still NPCs and Blinkers, still sitting on opposite sides of the table. But now it was painfully clear that if one of them got sick, they would all go, one by one. No matter who they were.

And they had no chance at all if they didn't work together.

"How deep did you get?" Aris was asking.

"Only about twelve centimeters," Dr. Anya answered. "We spent a lot of our time marking off the area and making sure we had the location right, but the soil composition is exactly what we expected – mostly fine regolith with some larger rock fragments. Your shift should make a lot more progress."

Three meters didn't sound like much. When Kellan first heard the details of the dig, he figured it would take them a day, tops, to uncover the old unit, another day to clear a space for the new one. Place the new unit, test it thoroughly, four or five days max and he'd be back in his sector, free of all Blinker obligations.

But watching the first shift dig, he could tell he'd underestimated the job. It was backbreaking labor, even with the assistive robot to do the hauling. The pressure suits made every movement clumsy and slow. Simple tasks like lifting a shovel full of regolith took twice as long and three times the effort as they would have inside the hab.

Kellan was just returning to the table when he heard the door between the airlock and the decon chamber hiss open, and his heart skipped a beat.

"Beginning decontamination now," Dr. Anya said through Iska's tablet. "Monitor us closely. Make sure we're a hundred percent clean because we can't see much with these helmets."

"Trust me, we will," Aris said.

And suddenly, things weren't boring anymore. All five of Kellan's team sat motionless, glued to their video feeds once again, making sure every member of the morning shift lifted their arms and rotated and let the decontaminating chemicals touch every crevice in their suits.

If they got this wrong, they were all done for.

"Don't forget the soles of your shoes," Aris said. "Clean them good, they must be caked."

When the team finally emerged, the tension that they'd started the mission with slammed back down on the module like an airlock door, only now, it wasn't NPCs and Blinkers. It was those who'd been in the regolith and those who hadn't.

"Everyone, hang up your suits and then clean up and change into a fresh coverall," Dr. Anya instructed as she pulled off her helmet, pointing to a row of hooks on the wall next to a row of decon shower stalls.

Kellan watched Quinta remove her own helmet, her dark hair plastered to her temples.

She'd dug.

A Voss, out there digging around in Glass-infected soil.

He'd underestimated her too.

QUINTA

YEAR: 2179

Quinta still felt dirty, even though she'd had a decon shower and a regular one and it'd been hours since she went outside.

She was sitting on her bunk after dinner, *The Grapes of Wrath* opened in her lap, but she hadn't gotten past "To the red country and part of the gray country of Oklahoma," the very first line. She had been fooling herself that the intention was to read the story. All she really wanted was to reread her father's note, and try to puzzle out who EC and AR were and what teebragus134.binPTQJV meant.

She'd already pulled up the hab roster and painstakingly scrolled through it to find every single EC and AR. It would have taken a second if she'd just asked Valence, but her father was leaving her cryptic notes from beyond the grave. It seemed like the kind of thing she should keep to herself until she understood it.

There were three ECs, one of whom was Elise Chandra. Quinta didn't know the other two, but one was a child in sector two and the other was a sector one cook.

There had been zero ARs in the roster.

"Hey."

Castor appeared at her side as if out of thin air and Quinta startled and slammed the book closed.

"Sorry, I thought you were reading."

"Just... researching," Quinta said.

"The mission?"

Quinta pressed her lips together, wondering just how much trouble her father had been in. Then she swung her legs over the side of the bed and told Castor to sit. "Close the door first," she added.

He crossed the dorm to close the door, and when he sat down next to her, he left only a few centimeters between their thighs. "What's going on?"

She put the book in his lap and opened it to the cover page. "Look at the digital note – the one right over the T."

She waited an eternity while Castor zoomed in and read, then turned to her. "What in Deimos is that supposed to mean?"

"That's what I'm trying to figure out. I think EC might be the nurse who died with my dad."

"Quinta..."

Castor was giving her the *I don't think you should be doing this* voice that he so often invoked when they were kids and she wanted to bend a rule. She took the book back, leaving it open in her lap this time. "You said yourself, there has to be another explanation for what my dad was doing. Well, here it is, and it's in freaking code. Whatever he was up to, he was terrified."

"Maybe you shouldn't be digging into it, then, if it's that dangerous."

She laughed. "Castor, look where we are. It doesn't get much more dangerous than this." Before he had a chance to object again, she asked, "Does that last line mean anything to you? It looks like programming code."

Castor sighed and reached for the book to pull up the note again. After a moment, he said, "It looks like a bin file."

"What's that?"

"Dot B-I-N," he spelled out, "it's a generic file for raw data. I don't know what the stuff after it is, though, PTQJV. That's not part of the file extension. But I really think you should leave whatever this is alone. I mean, if you think this is connected to your father's death—"

"Patient!" Quinta practically yelled, and this time Castor jumped.

"What?"

"QJV is my initials, I already noticed that," she said, opening the sector one medical system. "PT means patient, we use that abbreviation all the time. He must have been referring to my file. Good thing Valence didn't let me resign, I still have full access to the system."

"But..."

Quinta was hardly even listening to him. She pulled up her medical records and started scanning through them for anything that didn't look right. There was documentation of the time she slipped on condensation in the hydroponic module and her teacher brought her to the clinic worried she had a concussion. Her retinal implant surgery at age twelve. The second-degree burn she'd gotten on her forearm early in her apprenticeship when the cauterizer slipped from her hand.

And then a "visit" from just a few weeks ago, around the same time Hadrian left the note in *The Grapes of Wrath*. Supposedly she'd suffered a migraine headache and Hadrian had dispensed painkillers.

Probably dispensed them straight into his pocket.

She opened the visit note and scrolled for a moment. "Aha!"

"You found something?" Castor sounded excited despite himself.

"Yes." There it was, a file labeled *teebragus134.bin*. Sugar beet, spelled backward, she realized as she opened it – only to be met with a pop-up asking for a password. "Deimos."

"What?"

"Password protected." She tried a few easy ones. Sugar beet again. Her middle name. Her mother's name. Anniversaries, birthdays. None of it worked. "I'm going to send this to you. Think you can hack it?"

She transferred the file to Castor's overlay, and he gave it a look. "Not without more computing power than I have on me," he said. "You could keep brute-forcing it and hope there's no attempt limit."

Quinta swallowed. "If there is?"

"It could be locked forever."

She deflated, suddenly aware of just how close Castor was sitting on her bed. She turned to face him, putting the book between them. "This is something though, right? There's no way he was just hoarding to pad his own Exchange account."

"I don't know," Castor said. "But I don't think we're going to get any further with that file without the password. Do you wanna hang up your sleuth cap for tonight?"

"I kinda wanted to keep trying," Quinta said.

"Please," Castor added, and she realized that he had something tucked up against his leg on the other side of the bed. "I brought something."

"What?" she asked, curiosity getting the better of her.

He produced a pair of HoloPong paddles, a sly grin curling the corners of his mouth. "Wanna play, like when we were kids?"

Quinta had been staring at that note for at least an hour before Castor came in, and despite the breakthrough, she'd hit another brick wall pretty quickly.

Tomorrow, she'd have to dig again. There was no guarantee they'd get lucky out there twice. Tonight, she'd need to find a way to get some sleep, and she was completely wired right now. A little exercise would probably do the trick. Plus, Castor looked pretty desperate for a distraction himself.

He stood, holding a paddle out to her. "Come on. I'd rather not spend the rest of the night pissing myself every time somebody clears their throat."

"Yeah, okay." She got up, taking the paddle. "I'm gonna kick your butt, though."

Castor's expression warmed. "You always do."

Outside the dorm, people had broken into little groups. Dex had brought an ancient deck of cards, so old that if a Blinker owned that relic, it would be for display purposes only, but he and Iska were in the middle of a game of euchre. Quinta had never played with real cards before… seemed like it'd make cheating a lot easier.

Torrent was sitting with them, watching the game and sipping a mug of tea.

At the second table, Jace, Kellan and Dr. Anya were huddled around a tablet, which Kellan was tapping around on.

Over by the display wall, Aris and Ronan stood side by side, taking turns pointing things out on a diagram they had up on the wall. Knowing Aris's work ethic, it had to do with tomorrow's digging.

Quinta and Castor found an open area to play in. It was unpleasantly close to the decon chamber, but it was the only space with no furniture or machinery to get in the way. They both pulled up the game interface in their overlays and a shimmering ball of blue light appeared between them, hovering at chest height.

Just seeing it calmed something in Quinta. How many times had they played this game since Castor got paddles for his thirteenth birthday? Hundreds, at least.

The first few volleys were tentative, both of them self-conscious to play in front of the others. But then they found their rhythm, forgot they had an audience, and all the stress of the day started to melt. Not completely… just enough to make it easier to breathe.

The holographic ball moved much faster than a real one bound by Mars' weak gravity, making the gameplay far more rapid than a typical Parallax parlay. What HoloPong lacked in trick shots and acrobatic wall runs, it made up for with the sheer athleticism required to constantly lunge and change direction to meet the ball's sharp, fast trajectory.

"Remember before we started our apprenticeships, we would play for hours after class," Castor said, grunting as he lunged to return Quinta's serve with a just-in-time backhand.

"We were so good," Quinta said, rushing to where she thought he was aiming. "Too bad there's no HoloPong league."

Castor laughed. "You always were competitive. That one time we were tied for like ten games in a row and then finally I won. You threw your paddle so hard it cracked my living room wall display."

"I didn't throw it, it slipped," Quinta said, repeating the well-worn fib. "And my parents paid to have your screen repaired the next day."

She returned the ball hard, trying to put some spin on it so Castor couldn't guess its trajectory. This was the most normal she'd felt since the morning her mom woke her up to tell her that her father was dead, and for a few minutes, she wasn't locked in a module with six NPCs and an invisible pathogen.

She wasn't avoiding sitting too close to Castor lest he get the wrong idea about their kiss.

She wasn't waiting to die on this mission, or desperately reaching for any hope that her father wasn't as bad as everyone said he was.

She was just a girl playing a game with her best friend… and kicking his butt as promised.

She winged another one past him for the win. Castor held his paddle up in surrender, breathing hard as he said, "I need a water break."

"Good idea." Quinta brought a hand up to mop her brow, and it was only then that she remembered she and Castor were making a spectacle of themselves. They had drawn the eyes of most of the crew while they were huffing and puffing and lunging all over the place.

Probably getting that sweaty sheen the Glass victims had in their first hours of symptoms, too.

Quinta looked over at the tables and accidentally locked eyes with Kellan, his green eyes fixing on her.

He didn't look away, and heat started to creep up Quinta's neck. Not the same kind as the hot anger when she first saw him in the atrium yesterday. Something new—

Jace let out a laugh so sharp it echoed off the ceiling. "You two look ridiculous. Most pointless game I've ever seen."

"It's HoloPong," Castor said. "The ball is holographic."

As the two of them threaded between the tables to get water, Quinta saw the corner of Kellan's mouth twitch up. "He's right, though… you're both out of breath from furiously beating the air for ten minutes."

"There's haptic feedback," Quinta said, holding up her paddle, not quite sure why she needed to explain herself to him. "It feels real, and there's skill involved in how you hit the ball. It's not just about making contact."

"Contact with what?" Jace rolled his eyes.

"Be nice," Dr. Anya said under her breath.

And before she even knew she was going to do it, Quinta asked Kellan, "Do you want to try it for yourself?" She held out her paddle. "You've got an implant now. You can play."

It felt like the whole module went quiet, and Castor stiffened beside her.

"I only brought two paddles," he objected.

"He can play you," Quinta suggested, not really sure why she was doubling down besides the fact that those green eyes just kept boring into her and her skin was was on fire at being just a few paces away from the boy who killed her father. She shoved the paddle into Kellan's hand before he could refuse it. "Use the search bar in your overlay to find HoloPong. Once you activate the game, you'll see the ball."

Kellan stood, and something dark flickered across Castor's face – surprise, mistrust… hurt? But he recovered quickly, handing his own paddle to Quinta. "You play. I need a break."

He stalked off toward the water drum, and Quinta turned to Kellan. She hadn't been this close to him or spoken this many words to him since they were children, and her heart was pounding. Good thing they weren't still monitoring each other's vitals or everyone would know.

"See the ball?" she asked.

His eyes went distant for a moment, darting around as he searched, and then the blue ball of light appeared between their chests, just an arm's length apart.

Quinta cleared her throat, then pointed Kellan to Castor's place in the open area. "Stand over there. Do you want me to run down the rules for you?"

"I'm sure I can figure it out," Kellan answered, then gave the ball a smack with his paddle – hard, like how you'd want to hit a Parallax ball if you were going for a point. It went flying high over Quinta's head and out of bounds.

"Penalty," Castor announced from the kitchen area.

The ball reset itself, this time in front of Quinta for her serve. She sent an easy one Kellan's way, and he wasn't even close to fast enough to reach it in time.

"Point to Quinta," Castor said, his voice laced with mean-spirited amusement. Quinta shot him a *stop it* glare, but he just took a sip of water and folded his arms over his chest.

"This is basically the opposite of Parallax," Quinta said. She knew the NPCs played it – she'd seen kids organizing a game the one time she went to sector four. "The ball moves fast, so there's no time for fancy footwork or trick shots. HoloPong is all about speed and economy of movement."

She served again, making it a little bit harder this time. Kellan lunged with abandon, nearly landing on the floor, but he made contact with the ball. It went off in a wild direction and out of bounds again, but at least he'd hit it.

"There, you're getting it."

"Getting embarrassed," Jace said with another chuckle. "I wish you could see how stupid you look."

"Same as you look every day in the mirror," Kellan shot back with a grin, paying so much attention to his heckler that he nearly missed the next serve Quinta sent his way. He got there, though, and even returned the ball at an angle Quinta could actually volley back to him.

He caught on quickly, and soon whatever Jace and Castor were saying from the sidelines didn't even register. He got deeply focused, determined to keep their volleys going as long as possible, and she noticed he had a tendency to wet his lips when he was concentrating. Before every shot she made, his tongue would dart out and swipe across his lower lip, and then he'd be off, lunging or racing for wherever she'd aimed the ball.

Quinta won handily, but Kellan scored a couple points and they were both breathing hard and sweating by the time the digital ball blinked out of existence once again.

Kellan crossed the distance between them, holding out his paddle handle-first. "Thanks for the game. You're right, it's a lot more challenging than it looks."

Quinta accepted the paddle, tucking both under her arm, and turned back to the table. Jace and Dr. Anya had turned back to the tablet now that the entertainment was done. Dex and Iska were still deep in their euchre game. Castor was nowhere to be seen.

"Your boyfriend took off," Kellan said.

"Not my boyfriend," Quinta answered. "He probably went to bed." She hesitated for a moment, thinking she probably ought to return Castor's paddles to him – and maybe apologize for cutting him out of the game he'd suggested in the first place – but instead, she added, "I'm sorry he's been a dick to you. He acts tough, but really, he's just fiercely loyal."

"To you?" Kellan asked. "Or Valence?"

"Both."

She figured he'd walk away now. There was nothing keeping

either of them standing in the empty space by the decon chamber. Instead, he asked, "Why did you play with me?"

Something tightened in Quinta's chest, something like a whispered accusation that she shouldn't have. She shrugged. "You have an overlay. Why not?"

"Because of..." *What I did to your father,* she imagined him finishing the sentence, but he never did. He just asked, "Don't you hate me?"

She just stared at him for a moment, giving herself permission not to feel embarrassed by it, to just look him dead in those brilliant green eyes and see what was in them. At last, she said on an exhale, "I probably should. Castor certainly thinks so." She thought of the book, the note, all those patient files that were nothing more than lies. "A lot has happened in the past week. I don't know what I feel anymore."

"I would never do anything like that on purpose," Kellan started to say, but Quinta held up her hand, emotion suddenly squeezing her throat.

"Don't–"

"Please." He just blinked at her, and what she saw in his eyes was a deep pain. "I'm sorry."

She nodded, not trusting her voice with words. "Good night, Kellan."

She couldn't stay out here with him any longer. She walked past him, willing herself not to cry, and he said to her back, "Good night, Quinta."

LIRA

YEAR: 2083

ira had retreated back into sector two, but there was
nowhere to go except back to Jamila's dorm. She wanted to
get somewhere private soon. The idea of a mob forming
kept niggling in the back of her mind.

So she headed back toward Dorm 2A. While she walked, arm
still cradled to her chest, she scrolled through the chats in her overlay, hoping that group in the central commons hadn't broken
containment and started spreading their awful ideas.

No such luck.

The third video chat she popped into turned out to be a feed
from one of the cameras in the central commons, broadcasting the
meeting to anyone who cared to tune in. And there were a lot of
viewers.

Lira didn't really want to keep watching Tim whip all those
scared people into a froth, but it seemed like a good idea to at least
keep an eye on what he was saying. If he was telling them to storm
the central supply, or hunt Lira down in the halls like prey, she had
to know.

"I propose we seal all the sectors," he was saying. "As far as we can tell, Administrator Voss was able to seal his sector before the contagion breached it. That ship has sailed for the other sectors, but we need to create a hermetic seal around the construction area and the existing regolith-built sector. Then those of us who are healthy can move to sectors one and two."

Oh great, he was eyeing the sector Lira had retreated to. On top of that, what he said wasn't even remotely true. Dmitri Voss was hiding out in sector three like a scared little baby instead of leading the colony, and that was the sector that half the dig crew had died in!

Nowhere in the hab was safe anymore. The bacteria had spread to every corner before anyone even knew what was happening. Not even Valence had seen the danger before it was too late.

"Why can't we go to sector three?" someone in the audience asked. "If that's the only safe sector—"

"We can't ask them to unseal their airlock now," Tim explained. "It'd risk contaminating it. And besides, Una's pregnant. We have to protect her and the baby at all costs. They're the future here."

"Yeah, Una has probably had a round of every sort of antibiotic in the hab," Lira said. "If any of them help, she's covered."

Her hand was starting to throb again with the movement, and having a one-sided conversation with the video feed was at least a distraction.

"We've heard nothing from Earth in close to a week," Pavel finally chimed in. "We've likely lost contact with them, and our satellite operators are… unavailable to look into repairs."

"Unavailable. Dead or soon to be," Lira said grimly, remembering Marcus. Was he dead now?

"It doesn't matter," Tim wrested control back from Pavel. "Whatever happened, we're on our own and close to a third of our population is sick or dead. This bacteria is extremely contagious and highly fatal. We can't wait around until all of us are sick. Clearly the quarantine isn't working – the sick aren't abiding by it.

They can't be trusted to self-isolate, so we need to segregate them forcibly."

"You're disgusting," Lira snarled at the feed.

"Why should there be one healthy sector and three with contagious people running around mingling with us? There should be one sick sector and all the rest should be safe. Sector four is no good to us with its regolith walls. I say we move all the sick into it and seal it off."

"The bodies too," someone in the crowd said, softly, like at least they were ashamed to say it. "We don't know if they're contagious."

"I'm not touching a Glass body," somebody else objected.

"None of us should," Tim agreed. "It's too risky."

"So how are you going to make the sick move to sector four?" Pavel asked.

"We'll ask them nicely first," Tim said. "Surely there are still some good citizens among them, and they'll understand it's for the good of the colony. If they're well enough to walk, they can go on their own."

"And if they're too sick?" someone asked.

"Or too selfish?"

Lira thought of Jamila in her final hours. She'd barely had the energy to lift her head to look at Lira. She hadn't eaten in several days, her appetite abandoning her when the nausea came, and she hadn't gotten anti-nausea meds like Ada. There was no way she would have been able to walk across an entire sector.

"For those who can't, or who refuse," Tim said, "we'll convene a volunteer group to put on pressure suits and drag them there."

People were clapping and nodding along, and Lira's stomach rolled.

"Valence, can I patch into the speaker system in the central commons?" she asked. "I want to speak to the group."

They didn't want to hear from her, they'd already proven that quite vehemently. It was unlikely anything she said would be met with open minds. But she couldn't live with herself if she didn't try, didn't at least voice her objections.

A moment later, she had an open line of audio into the central commons.

"Wait," she said, and watched on the video as several people jumped in their chairs, heads swiveling up toward the ceiling like she was the voice of God – or Valence.

"Who's that?" Tim demanded.

"Dr. Lira Salonga."

"We told you to leave," Tim barked.

"You can't segregate the sick," she said, ignoring him. She wouldn't have long before they figured out how to override her audio connection and cut her off. "Half of them are too sick to be moved. All of them really should be getting more care than they are. We have access to enough pressure suits for all of us healthy people to be administering fluids and pain relievers–"

"They're already dead," Tim declared. "Valence says they should be quarantined, that it's too dangerous to be near them. Valence uses data, not emotion, which you are clearly overcome with."

"–will we even know if the progression could be slower if we just–" Lira kept talking even though Tim was doing his darnedest to shout over her.

"We're human. We're terrified. We make mistakes even on our good days. If there's a question, I say we put the problem to Valence, let it figure out what we should do for the best odds of survival."

"–just an algorithm!" Lira was desperately trying to be heard, but she could see all those eyes turned toward Tim, pinning their hopes on him just because he'd been willing to stand up and take control. "We don't need *odds*, we need to hold onto our humanity!"

"We need to survive," Tim said, and there was more clapping and even a few cheers, enough to drown Lira out. "I say we start with sector four. Get all the healthy people out, if there are any foolish enough to have stayed there. Seal it up. Let Valence run its calculations and see if it improves our chances."

Lira disconnected from the speaker, then turned off the video in disgust. They hadn't heard a single thing she said. She knew that was the likely outcome, but the fact that they didn't care about the suffering of the sick, even though those sick people were their friends, their coworkers, their loved ones... How had they lost their compassion in such a short period of time? Was fear alone enough to devour their empathy?

There had been a couple dozen people in the central commons. Many more tuned into the video feed.

How far were Tim's ideas spreading?

Well, whatever they did, Lira wasn't going down without a fight.

"Valence, bring up the hab map in my overlay and mark the location of every sick colonist."

LIRA

YEAR: 2083

There were forty single-room quarters in Dorm 2B, and Valence had dropped a glowing red digital pin on thirteen of them. It was more than Lira had been expecting, even after what she'd seen in the sector two med clinic. And the microbiology lab. And Jamila's quarters.

There were a few less pins in sectors one and four, and five glowing red pins in sector three. So much for Administrator Voss's idea that he was safe. How long would it be before he became one of those markers?

Lira changed course to Dorm 2B. It was the dorm with the most people in need.

As Lira approached, she asked Valence, "Are there any healthy people here other than me? Mark them on the map, please."

Green pins appeared over three rooms, and a cluster of them lit up the living room – four people were gathered there. Not from Tim's group, hopefully. Lira decided to start there.

What she found was a familiar face – Natalia Rostov, a pretty brunette geologist who'd been in Lira's travel cohort. Natalia had been no fan of Tim's on the Exodus, and hopefully she hadn't changed her mind since then.

She sat on a couch with three others gathered around her. A white-haired man Lira didn't recognize had his arm around Natalia's shoulders. Two more sat in arm chairs flanking the couch. All four of them had the look of soldiers after a battle, with distant stares that were similar to people absorbed in their overlays, but haunted, more hollow. They were debating about who should go on a supply run, but when Lira stepped into the room and lowered her mask, Natalia immediately recognized her and jumped off the couch.

"Lira!" Natalia threw her arms around her before she could object. She grimaced as Natalia crushed her swollen hand between them. "I'm so sorry about Ada."

Tears threatened in Lira's throat. *Don't think about her. Not yet. Not while there's work to do.*

Lira stepped back. "My hand."

It really was throbbing again, but it was more of an excuse to shift the conversation to something safe.

"Oh, I'm sorry," Natalia said in her throaty Russian accent. "What happened?"

"Punched a door."

Lira didn't offer an elaboration, and Natalia gave her a warm, sympathetic look. Lira took a deep breath for the first time since she left the microbio lab, then Natalia gestured to the group, who were all openly staring at Lira. "We're all geologists, but Henry's trained in first aid. He could look at your hand for you if you want."

Henry was the one who'd had his arm around Natalia. He was the oldest of the group, probably in his late fifties, although his pure white hair and thick beard made him look even older. He'd stood and subtly positioned himself between Lira and the other two still sitting in the armchairs.

"Don't worry, I'm not sick," Lira said, gesturing to her protective

suit. "They had me put this on when I left the rabbitat. But I think…
I'm immune."

It was the first time she'd dared say it out loud. She still wasn't
sure how she felt about it – about living when so many others had
died, about leaving Ada behind in that med clinic, about the utter
uselessness of having some sort of immunity when all the microbiologists in the hab were dead.

Henry's shoulders settled and he said, "We're guessing we are
too."

"Come sit down," Natalia said, taking Lira by her good hand
and leading her to the couch. "Henry, go get the first aid kit."

"I'm fine," Lira tried to object.

"It looks broken," Henry said. Lira looked down at her hand for
the first time in a while. It was swollen to at least twice its normal
size, the skin an angry red. "At the very least, let's get a cold pack
on it," he suggested, and Lira nodded assent.

She sat where Natalia pointed her in the center of the couch,
and Natalia introduced the other two. "That's Gaurav, and that's
Tamika. They live in sector three."

"Not anymore, huh?" Gaurav said. "Fucking Dmitri."

"Did he kick you out?" Lira asked.

"I was in the geology lab here when he sealed off the sector,"
Tamika said. "That was back when we still thought we might be
able to get some work done."

"We were working in shifts, trying to verify whether the
mutated form of the bacteria was localized to the sector five dig
site," Gaurav added. "I'd just finished working, stopped in a sector
two dining hall on my way home."

Henry returned with a big plastic tote full of first-aid supplies.

"This is how Voss repays us for our dedication to our work,"
Gaurav finished. "By exiling us."

"Have you tried getting new room assignments from Valence?"
Lira asked.

Tamika nodded. "Yeah, we have rooms here. We quarantined in

them at first, but by our estimation, all of us have had multiple exposures. If we were going to get sick, we would have by now. So why not weather this together?"

"What about you?" Natalia asked, perching on the arm of the couch while Henry sat on the coffee table in front of Lira. "Do you live in this dorm? I haven't seen you here before."

Lira shook her head, then hissed when Henry pulled her hand toward him.

"Sorry. Can you move your fingers?" he asked.

She tried to flex them and pain shot up the back of her hand, written all over her face. Henry reached into the kit and pulled out a packet of painkillers.

"Take these." She dry swallowed them and he handed her a cold pack, saying, "I want to get a splint on that hand but we'll give the meds a few minutes first."

"Thank you."

"So?" Natalia asked. "Where's your dorm?"

"1A, normally," Lira said.

"The barricaded dorm," Gaurav said. "You're a refugee too."

"I think everyone who's left is," Lira said. "Did you catch any of the video feed from the meeting going on in the central commons just now?"

They all shook their heads, oblivious.

"Tim Robinette wants to round up the sick and seal them all off in sector four. And that's not the only bad idea he has."

"That fucking guy," Natalia snarled, folding her hands in front of her stomach. "People aren't backing him, are they?"

"Seemed like it," Lira said. "He's got them thinking Valence and the data are on his side, even though there is no real data – not yet. But they're scared, looking for a leader since Administrator Voss is missing in action. I don't know why, but Tim decided he was the man for the job."

"Because he thinks he's God's gift." Natalia rolled her eyes.

"That's why I came here," Lira went on. "Most of the sick in this sector are quarantining in this dorm."

"What about 2A?" Tamika asked.

Lira just shook her head, thinking of Jamila in her makeshift shroud. How long before she began to decompose in there? Valence could turn the air conditioning down to cool the room, but if it did that times half the population of the hab, the energy requirements… It wasn't sustainable.

At least Ada was in a morgue. Lira had to believe she was because the alternative wasn't something she could think about right now.

"Mostly gone," she said, her voice clipped. "I can't get sick, and I can't get into the rabbitat, so I thought at least I could help the sick people here. And when Tim and his mob come and try to take them to sector four, they'll have to go through me first."

"That's brave," Gaurav said.

"It's a distraction," Lira said. "I'm just glad there are still people on this planet with some human decency. I was getting pretty worried for a while there."

"Can I try again?" Henry asked, gesturing at her hand.

The cold pack resting on the back of her hand had left it pleasantly numb, and when she removed it and tried to make a fist, her range of motion was still significantly diminished but her hand didn't throb and scream like before. She nodded.

While Henry carefully straightened her fingers and splinted them with the materials in the first aid kit, Gaurav and Tamika started debating whether, with this new information about Tim and his people, it was still safe to go to the dining hall.

"We have to eat," Tamika was saying.

"I don't have an appetite these days, do you?"

"No, but that's not the point…"

Lira tuned in and out of their conversation as the ice wore off and her hand began to ache before Henry was finished bandaging it.

She watched Natalia watching Henry. It was clear from the moment Lira walked into the room that they were a couple. But there was something new about Natalia, something that had changed…

Lira's eyes widened as she noticed the way Natalia cupped one hand against her lower stomach, the ever-so-slight swelling that hadn't been there on the Exodus. "Wait a minute. Are you…"

It seemed impossible, but Lira knew that protective gesture – she recognized it.

"Are you pregnant?"

Natalia looked at her belly, and then laughed.

It was genuine, a shocking sound that felt jarringly out of place. "Ten weeks. We just found out last week, right before all this started." She looked lovingly at Henry, who was beaming right back at her and her belly. "You know what that means, right?"

Lira gave a confused half smile and shook her head.

"If we did the math right, I'm two weeks further along than Una Voss."

And now Lira saw the humor in it. Una and Dmitri were supposed to be the first family on Mars. It was the whole reason Una had agreed to come here, and she'd come to the rabbitat almost every day for months asking Lira how the rabbit breeding program was going, whether there were any birth defects or complications, asking to hold the kits. It was all she ever talked about in the weekly Administrator's Wife messages she'd taken it upon herself to start sending out to the entire hab.

They had all been on baby watch for months after the rabbit trials were complete and she got the green light to start trying. When she'd finally conceived, there had been a hab-wide celebration. The halls were strewn with digital pink and blue bunting, the dining halls served themed meals, and there was an app added to the Exchange where you could add a countdown to her due date running constantly in the corner of your overlay. Administrator Voss had said there'd been nearly a one hundred percent claim rate, but Lira didn't know anyone who'd actually downloaded it.

"Does she know?"

Natalia laughed again, this one tinged with nerves. "No way. We're keeping it a secret for as long as possible. Can you imagine how pissed she'll be if I give birth before her?"

"I hope you do," Tamika said. "It's not your fault you snagged yourself a silver fox and her husband is a bridge troll."

"We have to see a doctor as soon as... all this is over," Henry said, his tone telling Lira he and Natalia had had this discussion before. "Our baby deserves vitamins and ultrasounds and whatever else an OB would do for them."

"How'd it even happen?" Lira asked.

Natalia just shrugged. "How does it happen on Earth? Birth control fails all the time, apparently even when you get it automatically in your food."

"Maybe you shouldn't be out here after all," Lira said, suddenly feeling less sure about her immune status. She hadn't worn her mask since she came in.

"I can't stay holed up by myself," Natalia said. "We have no clue how long all this is going to last. Am I going to sit in a room alone, getting my food shoved through a slot in the door, until I give birth?"

"It's what Una is doing," Gaurav pointed out. "It would suck, but if it's best for the baby..."

"And what happens after we give birth?" Natalia asked. "Are the babies just magically safe then? Will all the bacteria have been swept through the airlocks by then and there'll be no more threat to them and their brand-new immune systems?"

She was scared. Despite the laughing and the bragging, Lira could see now that Natalia was terrified of what could happen.

"A lot can change in seven months," Henry said, reaching over to rest his hand on Natalia's knee. "We might find a cure."

Lira thought about the sealed off microbio lab. How many people in this hab aside from her knew that all the microbiologists were either sick or dead? Did they know how screwed they really were?

Part of her wanted to tell them. Secrets wouldn't help anyone. But she decided to keep it to herself a little bit longer. They didn't need more bad news right now. They needed hope – like the wildly unlikely fact that in the face of a life-threatening epidemic, they had created not one but two new lives on a planet that humans had only just become self-sufficient on.

If they could find a way to survive the existential threat, maybe something good was waiting for them on the other side.

"Henry's right," Lira said. "We'll figure something out. Your priority right now should be staying healthy, even if that means quarantining." She stood, her newly splinted hand a little easier to lower to her side now without all the throbbing. She turned to Tamika and Gaurav. "I can't just sit here any longer. Why don't we team up and do that food run together?"

"Do you think you can carry stuff with that hand?" Gaurav asked.

"That's what backpacks are for," Lira said. "I'll go find one and then we can head out."

LIRA

YEAR: 2083

There was no one making fresh food in the dining hall anymore, and Valence had locked down the freezers and pantry to discourage looting. The only option still available was the ready-made food in the vending machines that colonists used in between mealtimes. What came out looked and felt stale, but Lira's stomach rumbled the minute the nutty aroma of cricket protein bars hit her nose. She'd missed several meals and hadn't even noticed until now.

She stuffed a big bite of one into her cheek while Gaurav bought some mushroom jerky and carrot chips. The standard fare was free at mealtimes, but if you wanted to snack from the vending machines, you had to pay, so the three of them took turns so no one's Exchange account got wiped out completely.

"Why are we even still using credits?" Tamika asked as she tapped electrolyte water over and over again on the second vending machine and collected the bottles in a laundry bag. "Half the colony is gone. It's not like we need to ration."

"For now," Gaurav said. "Soon, there's going to be a different type of shortage, and it's gonna be bad. For a while people were still tending the hydroponic gardens and feeding the crickets. I don't think there are enough of us to keep it up anymore."

"No one tending the rabbits, either," Lira added. Not that they were a significant food source – their meat was exclusively paid access, and the quantities were limited. But at least to her, they provided a whole lot more than just protein. She'd been trying not to think about them.

The list of topics she was actively avoiding was growing by the day.

"There might be," Gaurav said. "Have you checked your Exchange dashboard lately?"

"No point," Lira said. "I was quarantined in the rabbit up until a few hours ago."

"I bet you have some volunteer jobs available now," Tamika said. "Valence took my long-term research studies off my dashboard when quarantine began, but when I didn't get sick, it started adding essential tasks to the volunteer board. Hydroponic maintenance, delivery runs, restocking these vending machines." She gave the side of hers a knock with her knuckles, then her gaze shifted to the middle distance as she checked her overlay. "Right now, it says I could get fifty credits for changing out the air filter in Hallway 2F."

"And yet you're here with us," Gaurav said with a smirk.

"That's a lot of credits," Lira added.

"I'm guessing nobody wants to do that one," Tamika said. "It'll keep going up until somebody's willing to take the risk."

"You want it?" Gaurav asked.

Lira shook her head. "I'd rather guard the sick from Tim. Is that on the volunteer board?"

She was joking, but Tamika shook her head. "I think the protocol is containment only now."

The three of them carried their bounty back to the dorm. Natalia insisted that Lira sit down and eat and have a bottle of water, and when she didn't let Lira get away with the cricket bar she'd stuffed into her mouth earlier, Lira told her she was well on her way to being a good mom. After she had some berries that had seen better days and a packet of veggie chips, Lira repacked her backpack with an assortment of supplies: painkillers, fresh wash cloths, bottles of water.

As she prepared to leave the living room, Tamika and Natalia both stood and joined her.

"What are you doing?" Lira asked as Gaurav and Henry got up too.

"We can't let you do that work alone," Natalia explained. "If you're going, so are we."

A lump of emotion formed in Lira's throat, and she led the way. The five of them started working their way methodically through the halls, using the hab map with its pins to find people who might need them.

In the first room Lira chose, she found a man she didn't know lying in his bed. The overhead lights were on but his eyes were closed. His eyelids so transparent she could see the milky cataract effect on his pupils. He wasn't breathing, but he must have stopped just seconds ago because Valence hadn't gotten around to removing his pin from the map. He looked like he'd gone peacefully, at least.

The map said his name was Daniel Hascomb and that he'd worked in the fabrication lab.

Lira covered him with his sheet, damp from the fever that tormented all of them before they died. By the time she stepped into the hallway, Valence had logged his absent vital signs and changed the sign on his door from QUARANTINE ZONE to BIOHAZARD CONTAINMENT.

Lira went into two more rooms that night. In each, she found a dying person desperate not to be alone. She didn't know either of them before she stepped into their rooms, but neither of them sent her away. One still had enough strength to raise his hand and snag the pocket of her coverall to make her to stay. The other whispered weakly, "Please. Don't leave me."

She sat with them both. She dribbled water into their mouths and mopped their brows. She said the comforting words she wished she'd said to Ada, if she'd known it was the last time they would speak.

They all died the same way. When their bodies simply couldn't take the feverish, oxygen-stealing, relentless assault of the bacteria for another moment, their hearts gave out. Their muscles went stiff. They writhed and cried. Despite what it looked like when she found Daniel Hascomb in his bed, this was not a peaceful way to die.

After witnessing her third death of the night, Lira slumped against a wall in the hallway, trying to find the willpower to go into the next room on the map. She took a few long, deep breaths, trying to find some kind of emotional regulation. What she found was her mother.

You did something kind. Even if it hurts, it matters.

Althea Salonga's words surfaced without warning, dragging a gut-punch of a memory with them. Lira had been five or six years old. The cat her mom had owned since before Lira was born – her best friend from the moment she could lift a hand to pet him – was dying. It was old age, nothing they could do for him, but Muning was struggling. Blind, arthritic, not even tempted by the special wet food they bought for him.

"I think it's time," her mother had said one morning while Muning lay in Lira's lap, changing positions often and letting out pitiful little yowls of discomfort.

They took him to a clinic, even though it was more than her mother could afford. Lira was allowed to hold him after the veterinarian administered the injection. They'd wanted to keep Muning after it was over, but she'd refused. She'd wanted to bring him home and bury him in a corner of the garden. Those words – *even if it hurts, it matters* – were what Lira's mother said to her after they patted the dirt down on top of his grave, when it felt like the tears were never going to stop racking her body.

She couldn't cry now. She couldn't afford to let one slide down her cheek, because they might never stop coming.

Lira needed her mother.

She opened her overlay, surprised that the clock said it was early morning already. She navigated to her messages, hoping against hope despite what she'd heard about the satellites.

There was nothing new from her mother, no mission briefs from Houston, nothing from Earth at all. Had they even been able to send Lira's last message?

She recorded another one. In the last video, she'd been extremely careful to say nothing that would worry her mom, nothing that would risk her message getting stuck in VossCorp's filters.

This time, she had no hope it would actually reach its destination. It was possible even Valence would ignore it and it'd just go in some backlog of files somewhere for when – if – the satellites were ever working again. And so this time, she told her mother everything.

That Ada was dead, and so was half the hab. How terrified she was. How much she missed her and wondered if she'd made the biggest mistake of her life leaving her. It wasn't a mistake to come here because if she hadn't accepted the job, she never would have met Ada. But she shouldn't have allowed VossCorp to separate her from her only living family member. They could have found something for Althea to do. She was a great cook – she could have found creative uses for cricket protein with a Filipino flare.

Lira realized she was rambling after a while and ended the video with a watery *I love you*. She sent it to the great holding bin in the ether, stood up and went to the living room. Her body was sending hunger signals that she'd been ignoring for hours, and even more desperately, she needed one of those electrolyte water bottles Tamika bought.

The room was empty and the water bottles were waiting on a table. She retrieved another dose of painkillers from the first aid kit, then chugged an entire water bottle in a single go and dropped it into a recycle bin. Would anyone ever collect it again?

That had to be so far down the priority list it wasn't even visible to Valence.

"Lira."

She turned to find Natalia in the doorway. Natalia's expression turned from neutral to concerned the minute their eyes locked. For one quick second, panic streaked through Lira's body as she wondered what Natalia was seeing. Clear, clammy skin? Opaque whiteness creeping across her eyes? Had her vision started to blur and she hadn't even noticed it?

But all Natalia said was, "You look exhausted. I haven't seen you in hours. Where have you been?"

"Daniel Hascomb. Ophelia Brown. Derrick Tanner," she recited their names. "They all died tonight."

Natalia nodded, reaching for a water bottle of her own. "The hab map says we're down to five people still sick in this dorm."

Lira's eyes widened. Five! Just a few hours ago it had been twelve. More than half the sick had succumbed in the night. She knew they were dying – she hadn't heard of anyone making a recovery yet – but she didn't expect it to happen so fast. She sank backward, and luckily there was a chair there to catch her. "I know it moves fast, but... Jesus."

"I've never watched anyone die before," Natalia said, trailing off.

"Tim's camp is calling it Glass," Lira said. "It's pretty apt."

"It's awful." Natalia leaned against the table, taking a long draught from the bottle. "Wish this was booze."

Lira nodded. She wasn't much of a drinker back on Earth, and the options here were crude imitations of what you could get back home so they didn't usually tempt her. But after the night she'd had... the past five days that she'd had... Natalia was onto something. "Bet there's plenty of it in the pantry, if we could get access."

"That place is sealed up tighter than a Siberian prison," Natalia said. "Who am I kidding? I can't drink now."

Her hand went to her belly and it was on the tip of Lira's tongue to ask her if she was scared. Instead, she decided to change the subject. "If we did manage to get in, I'd be much more interested in a hot meal."

"Oh man, cricket meat tacos sound amazing right now," Natalia agreed. "That's not even a pregnancy craving, I'm just so sick of this stale vending machine crap. Oh, what about that mushroom pasta they serve whenever the mushroom crop is ripe? Or cauliflower-rice stir fry with fresh veggies, God, I'd inhale that. Oh! Rabbit stew–" Her eyes cut to Lira. "Shit. Sorry."

"It's okay." The two of them sat in silence for a moment. Lira grabbed a second water bottle and sipped a bit slower this time. Then she asked, "Where's Henry?"

"Sleeping. I forced him to. I don't think he's shut his eyes in twenty-four hours, fussing over me."

"Are Tamika and Gaurav with… patients?" For lack of a better word.

"I think so."

"Any Tim sightings?"

Natalia shook her head. "Not around here. He must have someone better to harass."

"When's the last time you slept?"

"I took a nap around midnight." Natalia smirked. "Henry made me."

"Let's go to the dining hall. If there are volunteer jobs restocking the vending machines, we can get into the pantry and scrounge some fresh food for breakfast. We'll bring it back here for the others."

"That's a good idea. We all deserve some real food after the night we had." Natalia pushed off the table and her hand went automatically to her belly. With a tell like that, it wouldn't be long before more people knew.

Not that there were many of them left to find out.

KELLAN

YEAR: 2179

Digging wasn't so bad. Kellan felt claustrophobic in his suit, with its recycled, humid air and puffball-esque shape, but in his first shift, he'd figured out a pretty good rhythm for driving his shovel into the ground, using his body for torque to lift it back out, then twisting and depositing the hard-packed soil into the robot to be carried away from the excavation site.

Every morning there was a lengthy health questionnaire, and Kellan filled one out in solidarity with the other NPCs even though Valence now had access to everything from his eye movements to the last time he moved his bowels.

Have you experienced any hot flashes in the past twenty-four hours? Have you noticed any changes in your vision? On a scale of one to ten, how optimistic do you feel about your mission?

He submitted his answers, Valence awarded him ten credits for his compliance, and then swiftly deducted them right back into its coffers to remind him that he was still being punished. And then he let Dr. Anya give him a real exam.

Everyone was fastidious about the decon process and hitting the showers right after they came in from digging, but some became more fixated than others. Kellan noticed that Quinta always showered twice before she settled down – once in the decon shower and then a second, regular one. He caught Ronan in a strange ritual one morning when he went to the bathroom to brush his teeth. Ronan was standing in front of the mirror, his coverall pulled down around his waist, turning over his forearms, carefully inspecting the thin skin under his eyes, looking for veins in all the places they would pop out first, while he mumbled some invocation to Valence beneath his breath.

"You're clear, man," Kellan had tried to assure him. "You look healthy."

He'd still been in there praying and inspecting when Kellan was finished brushing.

Psychologically, the mission was purgatory, but the digging itself was almost painfully mundane work. The same motion over and over again for two hours, until you thought your arm would fall off inside your pressure suit and your muscles screamed for you to stop. They were making steady progress, though, and after two full days of it, they could see the top of the old atmo unit.

Unfortunately, Kellan's team had also unearthed a large boulder that happened to be leaning right up against the unit – maybe part of the reason it was losing function.

It was a smooth chunk of volcanic rock, almost half as tall as Kellan, which had settled there who knew how many decades ago and been steadily covered by the wind and regolith ever since. Kellan's crew had tried to move it by hand and Phobos and Deimos both laughed right in their faces for even trying.

The thing must have weighed two tons.

They'd let the second assistive robot – the one meant for lifting –

have a go at it, and the sad little thing had strained its bucket lifter to the max, then tipped over into the excavation site. Lucky it hadn't been damaged in the attempt.

They couldn't go around the boulder, and couldn't access the connections without moving it, so Dex proposed explosives. Mercer had explained that they were available in the mission supplies, but it'd take a trip back inside the hab and some careful planning to break the boulder into liftable pieces. They'd spent most of that night arguing about where to place the charges to avoid damaging the atmo unit.

"If we blow the unit up, our whole timetable goes out the window," Aris warned. "Then we're in a race to finish the dig and place the new unit before everyone in the hab's breathing pure CO_2."

"So we don't blow it up," Dex said. "Look, it's the only option we have."

"What's the worst-case scenario?" Quinta asked. "If we damage the old unit, how long do we have?"

"About..." Aris's eyes went hazy as she calculated, then came back to them. "Six hours for the modules closest to the unit. Longer the further away you get."

"Okay, so we'll stay in close communication with Valence through the whole thing," Castor said. "That way she'll be able to start evacuating those modules right away if anything goes wrong."

"Why do you all call it *she*?" Jace interrupted. He looked at Ronan. "I mean, I understand why he does, he worships the thing."

Ronan stiffened, and his mouth closed into a thin line.

Kellan nudged Jace. "Man... read the room. Not now."

"It's been bothering me," Jace insisted. "The rest of you do know it's just a bunch of code bossing you around, right?"

"She... *the AI* uses a female voice," Aris explained, drawing on more patience than most of them bothered to summon for Jace, NPC and Blinker alike. "It has to have some voice, right? It's just shorthand."

"It's weird."

"Can we move on?" Ronan asked. Jace swept his hand out in front of him, a *by all means* gesture. Ronan turned his whole body away from Jace. "*Anyway,* that's a good idea, Castor..."

Predictably, the Blinkers had wanted to ask Valence where the best locations for the charges were, and the NPCs had wanted to do the math for themselves. That had started a second round of arguments, although the two groups had come up with more or less the same answers in the end, so it hadn't mattered.

Now, twelve hours later, the morning shift was outside again, carefully placing the charges exactly where they'd all agreed on. Suddenly, the mission wasn't boring anymore, and Kellan was once again on the edge of his seat watching through Castor's helmet camera.

"The sanitation module has been evacuated," Aris reported about the module that the old atmo unit was nestled up against. "Valence has activated the airlock so if it blows, nothing else goes with it."

"Try not to blow it, though," Ronan said. "That's sanitation for the entire sector."

"Heard," Dr. Anya said through comms. "We're almost ready here."

"Get well away from the area," Aris instructed.

"Don't have to remind us of that," Castor answered.

A few minutes of held breaths later, Kellan was looking at not much of anything through Castor's camera – just a view of the side of the storage module they were hiding against – when there was a loud, deep boom and Castor's camera shook. His heart rate shot up and he instinctively brought his hands to his ears, blocked by the wide helmet. Then his view was obscured by a sudden dust storm.

"Everyone okay?" Aris asked.

"Yeah." Kellan heard Quinta first, through Jace's tablet.

"All good," Dr. Anya said. "Let's see what we did."

It took a few minutes for them to feel their way back to the excavation site, the dust kicked up by the explosion so thick Kellan couldn't see a thing. And then slowly, it started to thin. Castor dropped down into the hole, and finally the visual cleared.

One huge boulder, cleaved into about six chunks of varying size, lying open like a cricket cracked out of its exoskeleton.

"You did it!" Jace whooped.

"How's the atmo unit?" Aris asked.

Castor angled himself around the broken pieces, his camera giving a pretty good view of the dulled metal casing. "Looks no worse for the wear."

They celebrated at lunch that day, indulging in extra cups of Candor dark and digging into that night's dessert in advance – double-carob cake with rich frosting that made Kellan's teeth ache. It had been their first big challenge: fuck this up and you might as well forget the whole mission. But more than that, it felt like they'd accomplished it together, the first thing that they could all be equally proud of, as a team and not just as two groups of people who quietly wished the other weren't here.

"We did the fun part with the explosion," Dex joked as he stuffed a huge bite of cake into his cheek. "Now you get to go out there and move the pieces."

"Yeah, that's how it's been going," Kellan said. "You take your time with the prep work, then we go do all the gruntwork."

"It's because you're so good at it, kid."

"We've got the robot," Aris reminded them. "It'll do most of the lifting. We just need to tether the pieces."

"The luxury," Jace said. "You know what I would give to have one of those things in sector four, doing my heavy lifting for me?"

"You know what you gotta do for it," Ronan said, tapping his temple, and for the first time, it felt like friendly ribbing without the undertone of judgment and subtle threat.

"Well, if I can play HoloPong," Jace snarked, "maybe it won't be so bad."

"Regardless of our status, all ten of us are here," Aris pointed out. "We've all volunteered to stick our necks out for the greater good–"

"Every hand for the colony," Ronan said.

"–so we're equals in that way," she finished.

"Except him," Castor said, looking right at Kellan and cutting the genial tone of the conversation as if with a knife. "He didn't volunteer."

For a few seconds, no one spoke. A few of the NPCs looked at Kellan. Aris and Ronan seemed determined to look anywhere else. Quinta's eyes were on him.

And then he said, "That's true. I'm here because Valence decided I should be, but you know what? If I'd been given the choice, I would have volunteered. NPCs fix what we break. I want to make it right."

"But you didn't–" Jace started to say, and this time it was Dr. Anya who cut him off, loudly asking the Blinkers, "What is it that motivated you all to volunteer?"

There was another beat of silence, the group trying to decide if they were going to go back to friendly chatter, then Aris said, "You all know my story. I built the new unit, I want to see it properly installed."

"I became a grandfather last month," Ronan said. "I hated to leave my family, but I couldn't stand by and risk a hab-wide failure when the future generation needs something I could provide."

"Quinta and I volunteered together," Castor said. "It was the right thing to do."

"My father was a hoarder," Quinta spoke last, her tone cold and flat, daring any one of them to challenge her. Kellan saw Dr. Anya's eyes go wide, and Aris and Ronan were once again extremely interested in the floor, the wall, anything but the person speaking. Quinta went on, "I don't know why he did it, but I couldn't keep being Dr. Voss knowing what people think when they hear that name. I thought digging to save the colony could… redeem me, my family." She looked directly across the table at Kellan and gave a little huff of a laugh that blew her hair up out of her eyes. "Pretty stupid, right?"

He didn't know what to say. He just returned her gaze until Dr. Anya said, "It's brave no matter what your reason. What we're doing is not a trivial risk, for us individually or for the colony."

Castor's hand went to Quinta's shoulder, and a little seed of something hot started to burn in Kellan's stomach.

"What about you all?" Ronan asked. "Why did you volunteer?"

"We didn't," Iska explained. "At least not individually. Everyone willing drew straws."

Quinta blinked in surprise. "You drew straws? For who would risk their lives?"

"It was the fairest way," Iska said.

"We take care of each other," Dr. Anya said. "When something threatens all of us, we all share the risk."

Quinta's brow furrowed abruptly and she asked, "How come you go by Dr. Anya? Instead of... what did you say your last name is?"

"Raymond," she said. "No reason in particular. Other NPC doctors use their last names, I just always felt more comfortable as Anya." There was a twinkle of mischief in her eye as she asked, "Why, are you thinking of switching to Dr. Quinta?"

Quinta looked down into her coffee mug. "No reason. Just wondering."

"Well, that boulder won't move itself," Aris said, slapping her thighs and standing. "Afternoon team, you ready to get out there?"

QUINTA

YEAR: 2179

R. Anya Raymond. She wouldn't have showed up on the hab roster because only those with implants did.

Quinta had no knowledge of her father ever working with Dr. Anya or mentioning her… but he'd been stealing medical supplies and she was a doctor in dire need of them. The NPCs were always allocated a much smaller portion of the inventory and told if they wanted more, they'd have to request it through the Exchange. The point was to encourage them to go to citizen clinics, where more tracking and diagnostic data could be collected.

Quinta found herself stealing furtive glances at Dr. Anya all through the afternoon shift, when her attention should have been on the video feeds in her overlay. What did she know? How could Quinta ask?

The afternoon team had been outside for an hour and a half, slowly and methodically strapping little chunks of boulder to the lifter robot and raising them up out of the excavation site. They were down to the last one, which happened to be the largest piece, and it was leaning right up against the atmo unit. They were working carefully to avoid damaging it and frankly, it was pretty boring to watch.

"We need more tension in the straps," Ronan was saying through comms.

"The weight distribution isn't right yet," Iska answered. "If we lift it now, it'll shift left."

"Kellan, adjust your strap higher," Aris suggested.

There was nothing for Quinta or the rest of the indoor team to do except monitor their vitals. Everyone was sweating and their heart rates were elevated from the acrobatic work required to put the straps in place, but otherwise normal.

On Quinta's video feed, which was coming courtesy of Aris's helmet, she saw Kellan's puffy, dusty suit lumber into view and attempt to get a foothold on the boulder so he could adjust the strap. The piece of boulder had broken in an awkward shape, almost like a teardrop, that was difficult to get a grip on.

"How much higher?" he asked, voice slightly distorted from the muffling effect of his helmet.

"About a handspan up from where it is now," Aris said.

He worked for a few minutes – a task you could do in a second inside the hab took at least ten times longer in the clumsy suits with the wind battering you and dust obscuring your vision. Jace stepped into view, bracing Kellan's back while he adjusted the strap then dropped back down to the ground. "Got it."

"Okay, we're ready to try again," Ronan said. "Aris, take the lifter controls. Kellan and Jace, help me hold the boulder steady once it starts to rise. We can't have it swinging like a pendulum and wrecking the atmo unit."

This was their second attempt at moving this piece. The first time, its shape made all the straps just slide right off when the lifter activated, so they'd added more.

"Be careful, you guys," Dr. Anya said over the comms, then everyone hushed to let them concentrate.

Aris stepped back, Quinta's view zooming out until she could see Iska at the top of the hole, next to the lifter, and Ronan, Jace and Kellan standing on three sides of the boulder, ready to guide it.

If they didn't get it on this attempt, Quinta's team would have to try again in the morning, or maybe bring out more explosives to blast it into smaller chunks. She really didn't want to do that. The first time had been scary enough. One little piece of shrapnel slicing someone's suit… it'd be all over.

On screen, the straps all went taut and the massive rock started to straighten.

"That's it," Aris called out. "It's working. Slow and steady!"

The boulder lifted a few centimeters off the ground. Ronan, Jace and Kellan closed in on it, their gloved hands up, ready to stabilize it if it began to swing.

"Looks like the old unit's not in too bad shape," Dex said across from Quinta. "Coulda been a lot worse with a boulder lying on it."

Achingly slowly, the lifter reeled it higher, revealing the slightly dented outer shell of the atmo unit. So slowly that Quinta's mind began to wander again, trying to figure out the best time to get Dr. Anya alone so she could ask about the note.

But if she wasn't AR and she was offended that Quinta had asked, they'd be stuck here for another few days–

"Oh, Deimos!" somebody outside yelled.

Everyone inside froze, Quinta's heart ceasing to beat as her attention snapped back to Aris's cam just in time to see the boulder slide once again out of the right strap.

"Move!" Aris screamed to no one and everyone, but it all happened too fast. The rock crashed back down to the ground and an ear-splitting howl of pain tore through the comms.

"Who's hurt?" Quinta demanded. A dust plume had kicked up where the boulder fell and she could only see a couple shadowy figures.

"Jace!" she heard Kellan shout. "Oh, fuck!"

"What's going on?" Dr. Anya demanded. "We can't see anything."

"He's pinned," Kellan said. "His left foot."

Quinta looked to Dr. Anya, who was already staring back at her, complexion pale as a Glass victim's last hours. This was bad.

"Is he conscious?" she asked.

"Yes," Jace answered, and Quinta could hear that he was clenching his jaw. "Wish I fucking wasn't!"

"Can you feel your foot?"

"I can feel the pulp that used to be my foot!"

"What about his suit integrity?" Aris cut in. "What do you see on the monitors?"

Torrent was the one monitoring Jace. "Pressure's holding steady, I think it's okay."

"That might change once they lift the boulder," Castor said.

"He's right," Quinta added. "You have to be ready to seal any breaches the moment you lift that rock."

"I've got the patch kit," Iska said, and the dust had settled enough for Quinta to see her tossing it down to Aris. She could also see Kellan crouching next to Jace and Ronan frantically trying to readjust the straps.

"Whose stupid idea was it to put both doctors on the same team?" Kellan demanded.

"Mine," Aris said. "But nobody can do anything for him until we lift that rock away. Forget lifting it out of the hole. Just move it off him."

"Ready?" Iska asked.

Ronan lifted his arm in what was probably an attempt at a thumbs-up. "Do it."

KELLAN

YEAR: 2179

Carrying Jace back to the hab while he screamed in pain had been the worst thing Kellan had ever experienced – even worse than taking his mother to a Blinker clinic when he thought she was dying. Jace just kept sobbing and wailing and Kellan prayed for him to pass out for everyone's sake, but he never did.

The wait in the decon chamber was even worse.

By the time they got inside, the morning team had set up a cot right next to the chamber and Dr. Anya and Quinta were ready with medical supplies. Kellan and Ronan deposited Jace on the cot, pressure suit and all, and stepped back to let them work.

The next few minutes were a blur of medical terms Kellan didn't understand. Crush injury. Rhabdo. Compartment syndrome.

"He's going into shock," Quinta had said. "We need to get him out of that suit and start an IV."

"Get me some scissors," Dr. Anya had demanded. "No point saving the suit—he won't be going outside any more after this."

Kellan hadn't even remembered he was still wearing his own suit. He'd just stood there sweating and watching his best friend fight for his life until finally Iska came over and unzipped it for him and he'd suddenly realized how hot he was.

Fever's the first symptom of Glass, his mind helpfully reminded him, but even that couldn't get his attention when he was watching two doctors bent over Jace, running needles into his arms and unwrapping the blood-soaked mess that was his foot.

Quinta took the lead. Dr. Anya had never treated a crush injury. They actually debated operating, and Kellan's blood boiled while he listened to them. Quinta wanted to amputate his friend's foot rather than take the time to fix him! Ultimately, they decided it was too dangerous to operate in a non-sterile environment and neither of them had done that type of surgery, anyway.

Jace ended up in his bed in the NPC dorm, his leg splinted and elevated on two rolled-up blankets. His skin was gray and clammy, an IV rigged up to the bedframe steadily dripping fluids and painkillers into him. He'd finally fallen asleep after Quinta gave him a sedative.

Kellan stood halfway between the dorm and the tables where the rest of the crew were gathered, unwilling to be too far in case Jace woke up.

Quinta explained to everyone what they'd done.

"He's got multiple fractures of the small bones in his foot and ankle, and we did our best to reset the larger bones," she said. "Luckily, the pressure suit boot was solid and took the brunt of the damage, but if he doesn't get surgery, he could end up with a permanent limp or range of motion loss."

"What? No," Kellan said. "That's unacceptable. If you can't do it, they have to let him out of here so someone else can."

"We're not done with our mission," Dr. Anya said gently. "We're in quarantine."

"We're not sick," Kellan argued. "We've been following all the decon protocols. They can sterilize him again on the way out, but they have to come get him."

They'd been trying to estimate how long the mission would

take, and they'd already had one big setback with the boulder existing. Now they were down a man, and they still had to decide what
to do with the last piece of rock. Kellan couldn't fathom letting his
best friend lie on that bed for days in agony when there was only
one airlock standing between him and a surgical suite.

"He volunteered to do this for the good of the colony," he said.
"The colony should care just as much about his wellbeing."

"I already submitted a request to Valence," Quinta said,
sympathy written all over her face as she added, "It was denied."

"The quarantine is to keep everyone safe," Aris piped up from
the table, and Kellan shot her a glare she didn't exactly deserve. It
didn't stop her, though. "Just because we're not symptomatic
doesn't mean we can abandon our protocols."

"He volunteered," Ronan added. "He accepted the risk that came
along with the mission. We all did."

Kellan shook his head. "That's tank sludge. You're telling me if
you needed surgery to save your foot, Valence wouldn't calculate
the risk differently? Or Quinta. If a Voss wanted out of this room,
do you think it would say no?"

"Yes," Aris insisted. "It's not about who we are, it's about
following the safety protocols for the good of the entire colony.
Your people included."

Kellan rolled his eyes. "*My people* are expendable. We didn't
need Jace to get hurt to figure that out."

"That's not true," Quinta said, taking a few steps closer to him,
but Kellan closed his arms over his chest. "Jace is stable. The treatment we've provided is adequate for now."

"Adequate. For now," Kellan sneered. "What happens if his foot
gets infected while he's in here? You said yourself this isn't a sterile
environment."

Now Dr. Anya was coming at him, and he actually allowed her
to put her hand on his shoulder. "We'll go through that airlock
when we come to it. We're monitoring him closely, and we'll get
him the care he needs as soon as the mission is complete. The best

thing we can do for him now is figure out our next step with the dig."

"Okay, then let's get back out there right now," Kellan said. "Let's start doing double shifts. Get done faster so he doesn't have to lie there in agony."

"I can't allow that," Aris said. "It's too dangerous. Two hours out there is exhausting as it is. If we're tired and working faster, there'll be more mistakes. More chance for injury or infection. I say we rearrange the teams – one doctor inside at all times in case Jace needs them – and then keep going as planned."

"This is tank sludge," Kellan repeated, jaw clenched.

LIRA
YEAR: 2083

amika and Gaurav had both found their way back to the living room by the time Lira and Natalia returned, weighed down by a coffee carafe and the cricket scramble they'd made with bell peppers that were just on the right side of rotten. Henry was still napping.

Gaurav peeled himself out of the armchair and came to sit at the table. He had a day's worth of stubble on his chin, black against his tan skin tone, and bags under his eyes. Tamika's hair was frazzled and she stayed sprawled on the couch, reaching her hand out pathetically and making tired grabbing motions until Natalia delivered her breakfast to her. Tamika propped the plate on her stomach and started picking at it.

"You shouldn't eat lying down," Natalia said. "Choking hazard."

Tamika just shrugged. "Used to do it all the time on Earth and I never did. Gravity's lower here, even less risk."

Lira huffed a weak laugh. "Great logic."

Tamika kept dropping bits of pepper into her mouth. "Leave me alone, last night was shit."

Gaurav nodded. "It was."

Nobody was in a particularly chatty mood – they'd all had identically awful nights. They ate mechanically and in silence, nothing but the ever-whirring air exchanger providing background noise from the vents. Lira stared into space, her eyes not focusing on anything in particular, while she chewed, wondering if she'd ever be able to sleep normally after all this. Or would their faces dance behind her eyelids every time she closed them?

Ada. Jamila. Daniel, Ophelia, Derrick. Dr. Kalb.

Countless other friends and acquaintances she didn't even know were gone yet, whose names were even now being added to that long, long list of the dead.

The rabbits.

God, she didn't even want to think about them trapped in the rabbitat, breathing stale air, their food dwindling. She should have fought harder when those two goons showed up to seal the–

"Oh hell," Natalia said. Cold fear flooded Lira's chest. It was becoming her default reaction.

"What?" Gaurav asked.

"Open your messages. See if you got one from Tim."

"What's he want?" Lira asked as she opened her overlay.

Still nothing from Earth – she couldn't help checking even though it'd only been an hour or two. But nothing from Tim either. "I got nothing."

"I did," Gaurav said. "I'll forward you mine."

"I got one," Tamika said from the couch. "Who is this guy?"

"An asshole," Natalia growled as the forwarded message popped up in Lira's overlay. She opened it.

My fellow colonists,

She had to stop there and roll her eyes. "My fellow colonists? Does he think he's a diplomat now?"

She kept reading.

We may not have met yet. If now isn't the time for introductions, I don't know when is. My name is Tim Robinette. I'm an engineer, so it's in my nature to be thinking about how to problem-solve, even in this crisis.

We've all been isolated and scared and alone so far, and yet the bacteria has killed nearly half of our population, and it shows no signs of stopping. Our leadership is isolating out of necessity to ensure the future of our colony, but I believe it's time for the rest of us to band together and adopt practical, fair solutions.

The first is an antibiotic lottery. There are 252 doses left and they are the best shot for all of us who are still healthy. We must do a randomized drawing with everyone given the same odds – an equal chance at survival.

Valence will help us manage this fairly, and we must move fast. If you're with me, let me know.

Lira almost stopped reading several times before she got through it, tamping down the urge to scream in frustration. When she finished, she closed her overlay with a huff. "I told him yesterday a single dose is going to do more harm than good, and so did Nurse Pema!"

"He's an idiot," Natalia tried to comfort her, but idiots could do a lot of damage.

"He's gaining traction," Lira said. "Did he send this to everyone but me?"

"I don't even know him," Gaurav said.

"Me neither," Tamika added, propped up on her elbows.

"He deliberately left me out because he knew I'd be against it," Lira fumed. She pulled up her overlay again. "I'm responding."

"Is that wise?" Natalia asked. "Doesn't sound like you've had much luck with him before."

"He's fear-mongering," Lira said. "Promising people a solution that will be ineffective *at best*, trying to make a power grab in the middle of a pandemic!"

And the worst part was that they really did need leadership right now. Dmitri Voss had always been a blunt, inelegant leader, but he was at least someone the colony could look to for authority. Right now there was a vacuum that Tim seemed determined to fill.

Lira fired off a reply.

Tim, stop this now. You're playing off of people's fear and offering a solution that I already told you won't work. If you want to round up the sick and dead and put them in sector four, fine. It's inhumane but a quarantine is at least scientifically backed. I'll volunteer to go in there with them so they get some kind of care. But this lottery idea could cost additional lives.

She read it out loud and got nods, the three of them telling her it was okay.

"He'll probably just delete it and move on with his campaign to... become Administrator of the Outbreak, or whatever he's doing," Natalia said.

She was right, but Lira hit send, then shrugged. "At least I said it."

"I hope he listens," Gaurav said. He reached for his cup and refilled it from the carafe of Candor dark they'd brought back from the cafeteria. The only good thing that had happened since the day Ada got sick – Lira and Natalia had found the store of premium synthetic coffee and made a strong batch, free of charge.

Lira was raising her own cup to her lips when an alert popped up in the top corner of her vision.

Message from Tim Robinette.

"He wrote back already," she said, stunned.

"Read it to us," Natalia said.

Lira opened the message and read: "*Do you really think you can take the moral high ground after you helped Ada fake her iden—*"

Lira trailed off and her cheeks got hot. She glanced quickly around the room, trying to gauge how much these almost-strangers were judging her. Of course, they'd all been to the trial, or at least heard all about it. A few people had surprised Lira afterward, quietly letting her know they sided with Ada. Jamila had been one of them. But a lot of people were still holding grudges, and Tim had a point.

Lira had lied for Ada.

Willingly.

For months before she got caught.

"It's okay," Natalia said. "Ancient history."

"Says more about his character than yours that he would bring that up right now," Gaurav added.

Still, Lira scanned the rest of the message to herself.

Perhaps you should just focus on your own responsibilities rather than presuming you know what's best for the colony... Oh, wait. The rabbit module's been sealed so you don't even have any responsibilities. Is that why you've been harassing me? What do you think the rabbits are doing right now? Consuming precious resources, that's what I think they're doing, and slowly starving to death anyway. It's not right. When you think about it, it would be a mercy killing if Valence gassed the whole module right now. I could submit the work order if it's too difficult for you. Just say the word, Lira.

"Well?" Natalia prompted when Lira didn't keep reading aloud. "What else did he say?"

Lira shook her head. Her throat was dry when she croaked out, "Nothing. Just petty crap."

But unease twisted in her gut, upsetting her breakfast, and she wondered just how far Tim was willing to go to cement his new role.

LIRA

YEAR: 2083

he last patient in Dorm 2B turned to glass and went still forever on day nine.

His name was Mateo Ruiz.

Lira wasn't with him when he passed. Tamika had been, dribbling water onto his lips whenever he opened his mouth to signal for it. The others knew he was close to the end and they all huddled in the hallway outside his door, quiet so he didn't feel like a spectacle.

Lira hadn't responded to Tim's message, nor had he sent any more veiled threats her way. He continued his mass-mailing campaign to everyone in the hab but her, and Natalia and the others forwarded the messages to her. He went ahead with the antibiotic lottery on day seven. Lord only knew how he got his hands on the remaining supply, but by day eight, every last dose had been raffled off to strengthen his popularity. Lira feigned surprise when she wasn't chosen. Tamika was, but declined her single dose of broad-spectrum antibiotics, which was then raffled off again.

Lira had finally gotten up the courage to check on the rabbits late in the evening while they were keeping vigil for Mateo. She'd accessed the rabbitat's video feeds with Natalia sitting next to her, clutching her hand for support. Lira had been terrified of what she might find.

The rabbits were still alive.

They'd eaten every scrap of the greens she'd scattered – no surprise there – so they weren't receiving optimal nutrition anymore, but the autofeeders were still dispensing pellets as programmed, and they had the water dishes. They looked fine. While Lira watched, they dozed, groomed themselves. One of the kits from the most recent litter thumped once and darted across the play area. They didn't seem to miss Lira.

That shouldn't have hurt as much as it did.

Mateo's door opened and pulled Lira out of her thoughts. Tamika stood there, a grim look on her face. The all-too-familiar BIOHAZARD CONTAINMENT notice appeared across the door in digital ink.

All five of them stood silently in the hallway for a few moments. Lira put a little cluster of Arabian jasmine on the door, just below the notice, and the others followed suit with items of their own, making a digital shrine for their final patient.

At last, Henry said, "That's a one hundred percent fatality rate. The pins in all the other dorms have been slowly disappearing too. What chance do we have to survive this long-term?"

Natalia wrapped her arms around his waist. "Immunity. We have immunity."

He put his hand on her belly, on the tiny bump you could see if her coverall lay against her skin just so. Did they *all* have immunity?

QUINTA

YEAR: 2179

Aris spent most of the evening sitting with the schematics and documentation, trying to figure out how to get the job done faster without making it more dangerous. Most of the others took turns reviewing the documents with her, trying to see something she hadn't.

Quinta didn't bother – the schematics were still gibberish to her and she knew she'd have nothing to contribute.

Kellan only left Aris's side to go check on Jace.

They'd pulled back on the sedatives and let him wake up a bit after dinner, but the pain had been so intense he'd begged to be put back under. He was still asleep now, and when Quinta poked her head through the door, she saw Dr. Anya carefully unwrapping his bandage.

The bleeding had slowed considerably, but it had soaked through in the hours since they first applied it.

Quinta softly knocked on the doorframe. "Need some help?"

"Sure, you can keep his foot stable while I apply antiseptic." She said it without looking up.

Quinta stepped inside and closed the door behind her, then

padded over to the bedside. Jace's unbandaged foot – purple and swollen in places, the skin broken open across the front of the ankle – was in complete opposition to the chemically induced calm of his expression. "Wound looks good so far. No infection."

"It's only been six hours," Dr. Anya reminded her. "But he's got two doctors in here with him. That's a point in his favor."

An NPC medic and an almost-doctor. That's what Dr. Liang would have said. She never let anyone forget their place, least of all an NPC. But Dr. Anya was putting them both on the same level.

An olive branch.

"Hand me the antiseptic?" Dr. Anya asked.

Quinta reached for a spray bottle on the tray of supplies Anya had laid out. Then she looked over her shoulder. The door was still closed and she could hear the muffled conversation of the other crew members in the common area. Everyone was occupied by the dig plan. This might be her best and only chance.

It wasn't easy psyching herself up to ask, though.

She spent several minutes watching Dr. Anya work, wondering what the best words were, until finally as she passed a fresh cloth bandage to her, she blurted it out before she could lose her nerve. "Was my father selling medical supplies to your sector before he died?"

Dr. Anya's hands stilled around the end of the rolled bandage. She turned to Quinta, blinking in surprise.

For a second, Quinta was sure she'd made a terrible mistake – crossed a line, revealed something dangerous, completely misjudged the situation.

But then Dr. Anya said simply, "He didn't sell them." Her hands began working again, unrolling the bandage and carefully wrapping Jace's foot. Quinta lifted it for her on autopilot. "He gave them to us."

Some small degree of relief washed over Quinta. Dr. Anya wasn't denying it.

"People are saying he sold them on the black market," Quinta said. "For his own gain. For angora sweaters and bribes."

"They're wrong," Dr. Anya said. "There was no exchange of credits. We wouldn't have had any to give. He was balancing the scales, giving us what was our due."

Balancing the scales. That was what his note had said.

"Our clinical stats have been showing steadily dropping NPC visit rates in every citizen sector for years," Quinta said. "Hardly any of you come for the basics anymore – wound care, antibiotics, first aid. We all just assumed you'd come up with more naturopathic treatments." And a lot of the citizen doctors were all too happy to treat fewer NPCs. Dr. Liang had made it a goal. "It's because my father was funneling supplies to you so you could take care of people yourself."

Dr. Anya finally looked up from her work, her ice-blue eyes meeting Quinta's. "I imagine those stats will begin to change again now that the supply chain has dried up."

"Why was he doing it? Why not just keep seeing the NPCs? I know he didn't mind like some other doctors."

"Your father was a good man," Dr. Anya said. "When he saw an injustice, he tried to make it right. Why should my sector have a disproportionately small share of the medical supplies if it actually put more strain on the other three sectors?"

"I don't know," Quinta shook her head. She watched Dr. Anya tuck the end of the bandage into place and settled Jace's foot back in its elevated nest of blankets. "Was there someone else my father was working with? EC?"

Dr. Anya's eyes flickered with recognition. "Elise, I think her name was."

"Elise Chandra," Quinta filled in.

"I only met her once," Dr. Anya said. "For that matter, I only saw your father in person a couple of times. He was helping us out, but it wasn't like we'd all go down to the dining hall for a Mars mud afterward."

"What about Owen Markovic?" Quinta asked. If Elise was part of it, was Owen connected too?

Dr. Anya shook her head. "Doesn't ring a bell. It was just your father and Elise, as far as I know."

"What about a password, or a code word? Did you have one?"

Dr. Anya shook her head. "Your father mostly left dead drops for us. I imagine that spycam in his eye had something to do with it."

Something like guilt mixed with mourning mixed in Quinta's chest. She'd never truly believed that he was selfish, that what he was doing was for his own benefit, and here Dr. Anya was giving her an honorable explanation for his actions. But she still had so many more questions than answers.

Dr. Anya started to pack up the supplies she'd brought in, and Quinta asked, "How did it start?"

The older doctor turned to her again, looking for something in Quinta's eyes. Whether she found it or not, she pursed her lips a moment, then said, "You should ask Kellan about that."

"Kellan?" Quinta blinked in surprise. "What does he have to do with it?"

"He started it."

QUINTA

YEAR: 2179

Quinta had been staring at Kellan all day.

Her hand had shot straight up in the air when Aris asked which one of the two doctors wanted to switch teams, figuring it would be the easiest way to get close enough to him to ask what he had to do with the smuggling.

It had earned her a suspicious glare from Kellan himself, and Castor had tried to put up a fight. He'd wanted to switch teams too, but Aris had overruled him, saying the teams needed to stay as even as possible.

Castor and the morning team had gone out and finished nudging the last piece of boulder far enough to the edge of the excavation area that it wouldn't be in the way. Quinta had stepped away from the table a few times to check on Jace, who finally had the right mix of painkillers in his system so that they could ease back on the sedatives. Kellan had started to enter the dorm once and Quinta thought it might be her chance, but then he'd spotted her fiddling with Jace's IV and vanished.

Now, it was after lunch and time for her first trip out with her new team.

Quinta's algae curry was sitting like a brick in her stomach as the whole crew lifted the new atmo unit up onto the hauler robot and carefully maneuvered it into the decon chamber.

Then Quinta wormed her way into her pressure suit. The thing was crunchy after multiple days of digging and decontaminating, rinse and repeat, and the inside had layers of recycled air and stale sweat emanating from it. Quinta couldn't wait to step out of it for the last time and send it straight to the incinerator.

The NPCs on the morning shift had been good teammates. Quinta had learned to put her trust in Dr. Anya, Dex and Torrent.

Would Iska, and especially Kellan, have her back out there?

It was time to find out.

She zipped up and waddled over to where Kellan was donning his helmet. He hadn't spoken to her since their argument about Jace the previous afternoon, and as badly as Quinta wanted to ask him what Dr. Anya had meant, it was more important to make sure there was no bad blood between them before they got out there on the surface.

"Could you check my seals?" she asked directly from her comms into his. She turned so he could inspect the back of her suit.

"You sure you trust me to do that?" he asked.

She kept her back to him. "That's what I'm here to find out."

She felt his gloved hands running over the seams of her suit. There was a surprising gentleness to his touch, and he was doing a thorough job.

"I know you'd never risk the entire dig team by letting me get Glass," she said to fill the silence. "Whatever else is between us, you're not that kind of person." Kellan's hands kept roaming over her suit, meticulously checking the seals of her helmet and gloves, so she kept talking. "Jace is doing better this afternoon. I checked on him after lunch and he says he was able to eat a bit."

"I know. I'm the one who brought him the food," Kellan replied. "I'm done. Now you check mine."

She nodded, turning around to see him already facing away

from her, ready for inspection. She began, just as careful as he'd been. She worked silently, trying to think of a good way to transition to asking what she really wanted to ask, when Kellan came out with a question of his own.

"Will he be able to walk normally?"

"I… don't know," Quinta answered, trying not to hesitate too much. "It depends on how his foot heals. Dr. Anya and I used a portable X-ray and we did our best to realign the bones, but it'd be best if he can get surgery when we're out of here."

"And it won't be too late?"

"I hope not," she said. "Done." She thought he might just walk off toward the decon chamber, but instead he turned to face her. Seizing the opportunity, she quickly added, "I want you to know I really did give Valence my best argument when I requested he be evacuated to a clinic. She would have rejected it no matter who it was."

"Even you?"

Quinta nodded. "Glass doesn't know our names, or our family trees."

She saw a flicker of softness in his green eyes, the first one all day. She glanced behind him to where Iska, Aris and Ronan still had their helmets off, apparently going over the documentation for the new unit one more time. It was now or never. Quinta looked back to Kellan.

"Do you know what I'm doing here, on the dig?"

"You said you had to rehab your family name," Kellan said. "From where I'm standing, it's unnecessary. You could shove Weyland himself out of an airlock and no one would bat an eye."

Quinta shook her head. "That's not true. You should have seen how fast they turned on my father after he died and the hoarding rumors began. Turns out, they weren't rumors, but it wasn't just for his own benefit. He was doing it for Dr. Anya."

Kellan's brow rose. "Really?"

"You didn't know that?"

"How would I?"

"Dr. Anya said you would," Quinta told him. "She said you started it."

Kellan's eyes went wide, almost comical. "I don't think so."

"You had nothing to do with it?"

He shook his head and Quinta deflated. Another dead end.

Then Kellan asked, "How many years?"

"I don't know exactly," Quinta said. "There was a medical board investigation seven years ago, so at least that many."

Kellan thought for a minute, and then a small smile curled his lips. "Maybe I did help. Though not intentionally."

"What do you—"

"Hey, chatterboxes, are you ready?" Aris cut in, and Quinta whipped her head around to see that the rest of the crew now had their helmets on and were standing around looking impatient.

No! she wanted to scream, but Kellan said, "I'll tell you about it when we get back in." And then he was shuffling over to the decon chamber and Quinta had to hurry to follow him.

KELLAN

YEAR: 2179

ust getting the new atmospheric conversion unit to the excavation site had taken almost the entire two hours of their shift. It weighed over a ton and was at least three times the size of the little hauler robot, so the five of them had had to stand evenly spaced around it, holding it steady as the robot bumped over the uneven surface of the planet.

If it'd tipped, there was no way any one of them could have caught it. Probably would have wound up with a second compression injury to deal with – another person who might have permanent disfigurement all because the colony AI didn't think them valuable enough to break quarantine for.

It didn't tip, and eventually, they arrived at the excavation site. Kellan drew his first full breath since the airlock door slid open, and then they had to get it hooked up to the lifter robot to carefully lower into the hole they'd dug.

"Is there going to be enough room?" Ronan worried. "If it can't sit level, it won't run efficiently."

"We've measured twice, but let's measure a third time," Aris answered, dropping down into the pit.

Kellan went down with her to help, mostly because he wanted nothing to do with the job of attaching the straps to the new unit. It hadn't been his that slipped when Jace got hurt, but he had enough blood on his hands as it was. If he could pass that job on to someone else, he would.

In the end, they stayed out for an extra half hour and got the unit lowered down into the hole, just about a meter from the old one, not a scratch on either.

"Good work, everyone," Dr. Anya said over comms. "One step closer to completing this mission."

One step closer to getting Jace whatever care he needed.

By the time they hit the decon showers, Kellan was exhausted from the extra-long stint in the sweaty, bulky suit and he'd been tense with worry the entire time. He'd forgotten all about what Quinta asked him right before they went out, so he nearly jumped out of his skin when he stepped under the shower spray and she said right into his head, *"Well?"*

"Deimos, are the comms still on?" he asked, bracing himself against the wall.

"Just ours," Quinta said. "We never closed the channel from earlier."

"Maybe we should, I'm... kinda busy here," Kellan said, looking down at his naked body dripping with the chemical spray.

"Please," Quinta said. "I didn't say a word while we were out there because I didn't want to be distracting."

"You're distracting me now."

"Kellan–"

"Five minutes," he said. He didn't want to have this conversation without clothes on. "Meet me by the tables."

"No, I don't want everyone hearing this," she said. "Meet me in your dorm. I'll be there checking on Jace."

So that was where Kellan found her exactly five minutes later. Her hair was still wet, wrung out and pulled back in a twist but dampening the back of her fresh coverall. She was taking Jace's pulse, but the moment she heard Kellan enter, she turned.

"Close the door," she ordered, then went back to her work. Kellan did, then sat on his bed, waiting.

"Seventy-four, that's normal, just like your temperature," she said. "No sign of infection yet." And then, in the same breath, she spun around to face Kellan. "Now tell me everything you know."

"Deimos," he cursed.

Jace laughed. His complexion was still gray, but if he was entertained by this, he must be feeling better. "Tell you what?"

"How he was involved with the medical supply smuggling," Quinta said. "From my sector to yours."

"Oh, this is some tank sludge–" Jace started, trying to push up on his elbows.

"Calm down, she's not accusing," Kellan said. "Lie down before you hurt yourself." He turned to Quinta. "I wasn't involved. Best I can figure, I might have given your dad the idea."

"Explain," she demanded.

"That time my mother was sick and we had to keep coming to the Blinker, err, your dad's clinic," he said. "That evil nurse who worked for him said my mother could only have a week's worth of antibiotics at a time."

"Cydra," Quinta said.

"No, that wasn't–"

"Nurse Tavara," she said. "That's her last name."

"Nurse Terrible," Jace cut in.

"Yeah, that's it," Kellan affirmed. "Well, she left the bottle out on the counter, so I swiped some. Enough for my mom, and some left over to give to Dr. Anya. I never heard anything else about it. So I figured they didn't notice."

"They definitely noticed," Quinta said. "That has to be what the medical board report was about. The timing is right."

"What report?" Kellan asked.

"I don't know the contents, the record was sealed, but my dad was investigated by the board shortly after your mom got sick. I remember it now, we met on my twelfth birthday and the board thing happened just a few weeks later. I think they wanted to know where the pills went."

"Are you saying he covered for me?" Kellan asked.

"Maybe…" Quinta trailed off, then asked, "Did you ever speak to a citizen named Elise Chandra? She was a nurse."

Kellan stiffened. "She's one of the ones who died."

Quinta nodded.

"No. I never did."

She was still zoning out, doing something in her overlay, and she mumbled, "I just can't figure out why he would do it. Why take the risk?" She came back to the room. "No offense, it's just that he doesn't have any special connection to the NPCs, that I know of. He knew what he was doing was dangerous."

"Maybe he was just, you know, *a decent person*," Jace suggested. "Does he need more of a reason?"

"Yes," Quinta said flatly. She paused again, and this time Kellan got the impression that she wasn't distracted by her overlay, she was simply struggling with her words. "I'm afraid it got him killed," she said, so softly he barely caught it.

"No, we know that… it was my fault," Kellan said. He'd never said it to her face before – not quite so bluntly. "I changed the air manifold configuration, rerouted the vents. It was my mistake. Your father's death was an accident."

"There are just an awful lot of coincidences piling up," she said, then took a deep breath. "I need to take a shower – a real one. Thanks for telling me about the antibiotics."

Kellan just nodded.

"When do I get my next dose of painkillers?" Jace asked.

"I'll have Dr. Anya bring them now," Quinta promised. She went to the door, but paused halfway through it, turning back to Kellan. "What was the name of the antibiotic you stole? Do you remember?"

"Umm…"

"That was seven years ago," Jace pointed out.

"Sorry," Kellan said. "Why?"

"It's probably nothing," she said, and then she was gone.

"What was that about?" Jace asked.

Kellan opened his mouth to answer, but someone in the door demanded, "What's going on in here?"

They both turned to see Castor poking his smug face into the room.

"What business is it of yours?" Jace asked.

Castor stepped into the room, visibly puffing out his chest and standing a little taller. He was still a few centimeters shorter than Kellan, but he had long, lean muscles and Kellan had learned ages ago not to expect a guy like him to fight fair, if it came to one.

"I saw you come in here after Quinta," he said.

"This is my dorm," Kellan said.

"And you thought it was appropriate to close the door with her in here?" Castor's beady little eyes got squintier.

Kellan shot a glance at Jace that said, *Can I just hit him already?* The guy had been needling him since the day they got sealed up in here. Jace gave him a minute nod, but Kellan already knew as good as it would feel to realign the jaw of Quinta's attack animal, it'd only make the rest of the mission harder.

And of course, Castor would be the innocent victim in it all, assaulted by a vicious, savage NPC.

"Why don't you go ask her yourself if anything happened?" he suggested. "Or better yet, let her handle her own business and decide who she wants to be in a room with."

"Keep your distance from her," Castor snarled. "She's stuck on your team, there's nothing I can do about that, but that doesn't mean she should have to deal with you during the rest of the day too, murderer."

Kellan couldn't help noticing he'd only made it a few steps into the room. Talking tough, but afraid to come any closer? With Jace at his side – fit to fight or not – he was feeling cocky so he said, "She asked me to close the door."

He even gave Castor a little smile. *Do with that what you will.*

"Hey!" Castor snapped. "It's not enough for you that you killed her father? You have to toy with her on top of it? Don't let me catch you in a room alone with her again."

"What am I, cricketmeal?" Jace asked.

Castor ignored him, directing all his ire at Kellan. "Don't play HoloPong with her. Don't check her seams. Don't fucking talk to her. She's a Voss. You're rabbit shit."

Kellan took a step forward, willing to accept the consequences of swinging on this asshole, but then Castor spun on his heels and stormed out of the room. Kellan looked at Jace. "What on Phobos was that?"

"Somebody's jealous," Jace said, the undisguised amusement on his face, overtaking the pain for the first time all day.

LIRA

YEAR: 2083

"That's the last of them," Gaurav said, his voice flat with exhaustion.

The five of them had all entered Mateo's room and shrouded him in his bedsheets, a final ritual to complete a task they had no clue would be over so quickly. Now they were back in the hall, wondering what to do with themselves next.

Tamika nodded, her usual energy subdued. "Dorm 2B is officially Glass-free."

"For now," Henry added grimly, his arm wrapped protectively around Natalia's shoulders.

"What do we do next?" she asked.

"There are some volunteer tasks in the Exchange," Gaurav said. His eyes lost focus for a moment while he opened his overlay. "Looks like sector three hydroponics has a squash crop that needs harvesting."

Natalia checked her own overlay and said, "I got that assignment too."

"I think it's a good idea for you," Lira told her. "Hydroponics has its own air and water filtration systems. That's one of the safest places for you to be right now."

"I can't protect the baby forever," Natalia said, a hand on her belly.

"But you can reduce your risk," Henry pointed out. "Come on, we can both take the assignment."

Natalia nodded, then looked to Gaurav and Tamika. "What about you?"

"I have filter maintenance on my volunteer board," Tamika said. "I'm not saying I'm *scared* to do that job–"

"I am," Gaurav cut in.

"–but it's not where I'd be most useful," Tamika went on. "We haven't talked to the microbiologists in days. I want to touch base with them and see if there's anything else geology lab to help."

"There are none," Lira said.

Tamika furrowed an eyebrow, and Gaurav narrowed his eyes. "What?"

"I went to the microbio lab before I came here," Lira explained. "Three of them were dead and the fourth was in med clinic one. I haven't checked, but I'm guessing he's... gone too."

That news settled around the five of them, and then Natalia said simply, "Shit."

"Yeah," Lira agreed.

It wasn't exactly a surprise when people died anymore. The shock had worn off pretty early on, but this particular fact – that there was no one left on the entire planet who was working on a cure – was one Lira had been dreading sharing.

After a minute, Tamika said, "Well, that's all the more reason for me to go back to the geo lab and not risk my health changing some stupid filter."

"What are you going to do?" Henry asked.

"Try to find a cure," Tamika said with a shrug, like she was telling them what was for dinner. "I'm no biologist but somebody's got to think about what's causing this and how to stop it."

"I'll come with you," Gaurav said. "Two heads are better than one."

Tamika nodded, then looked at Lira. "What about you? What are you doing?"

Lira's dashboard wanted her to go to the sector clinic and inventory the remaining medical supplies. It seemed only marginally important (who cared how many bandages they had left when half the hab was dead?) but she had something else in mind. The idea had been incubating all night.

"The bodies need to be properly stored until we can figure out how to inter them. They deserve more dignity than getting rolled up in a sheet and left to rot in their rooms, and I'm not going to let Tim take over disposal. He won't do it respectfully."

"Are you sure you want to do that?" Natalia asked, concern etched across her brow.

"We could stay and help," Henry suggested, but Lira shook her head.

"No, the squash will go to waste if you don't harvest it, and Gaurav and Tamika are right, somebody's got to be looking for a cure," she said. "This is how I can help. I want to do it."

What she left unspoken was the gnawing reminder that Ada lay in a med clinic. Alone. Hopefully refrigerated, but Lira had to go and find out, make sure she was taken care of.

"By yourself?" Natalia frowned.

"I'll be fine," Lira reassured her. "I'm used to doing things alone."

The five of them went their separate ways, planning to check in with each other via messages. Tamika and Gaurav left first, then Natalia hugged Lira and left with Henry, and then Lira was alone again. The air vents hummed their usual background song. She went to the living room and drank another bottle of electrolyte water and took another painkiller. This would be difficult with a broken hand, but she'd figure it out.

She pulled up the hab map and asked Valence to pin every room in Dorm 2B with a deceased person in it.

They fluttered across her vision like a tiny swarm of fire ants. She counted twenty-two red pins for the dead. When she got here just yesterday, there had been twelve pins marking the sick, and now every single one of them was gone, not even twenty-four hours later.

Her knees buckled and she reached for the wall to steady herself. For just a second, her mind screamed, *I CAN'T DO THIS!*

"Yes, you can," she reminded herself as she let go of the wall.

Ada. Jamila. Daniel, Ophelia, Derrick. Dr. Kalb. Mateo. There were so many of them, and most weren't even in cold storage. They'd start to decompose soon, and Lira could not go inventory bandages while that happened to people she'd called friend. Lover. Enemy, even.

She went to the med clinic first. The doors slid open easily for her – perhaps Valence thought she was here for the ten credits her Exchange dashboard was offering.

"Maybe if there's time," Lira grumbled to the AI, which she always assumed was listening through the speakers mounted in every room.

She'd come for a gurney, and as many body bags as she could find. But first, she'd make sure Ada was taken care of. It had been two weeks since she died. The thought of what she might find made Lira's stomach clench, but she had to see.

The last time she'd walked in here, the clinic had been chaotic – medical staff rushing between rooms, monitors beeping, the desperate sounds of dying in every room. Now it was eerily quiet but for the sound of medical alarms going unanswered in the distance. Lira only made it a few steps in when a sickly sweet odor constricted her throat. It overpowered the usual antiseptic smell, and she only needed to enter the first treatment room to find its source.

A patient lay in the bed, monitors on the display wall the source of the high-pitched whine, a flatline that had started days ago if the stench was any indication.

"Oh God, please no…" Lira stepped forward and looked into the bed. A middle-aged man lay there in a pair of scrubs, stubble on his cheeks standing out prominently against the telltale blue hue of his skin. His eyelids had gone translucent so that even though they were closed, his cloudy gray eyes stared up at Lira.

His jaw hung slack, like he'd died calling for help.

Lira looked at the name on the wall. Aksel Gunnarsson. She didn't know him, but she knew he wasn't on the dig crew. Part of the medical staff, maybe? It gave Lira hope that they'd been well enough long enough to move their first patients into the morgue and start trying to treat themselves before they all succumbed.

She turned off the steadily crying heart monitor only to hear a second flatline coming from one of the other treatment rooms.

"I'll come back for you in a minute, Aksel," she promised.

Lira found two more people in scrubs and Dr. Kalb himself dead in the other treatment rooms, and she found a nurse slumped over the desk in the waiting room, her head resting in her arms like she'd doubled over in exhaustion and never moved again. She turned off the monitors as she went until the whole clinic was silent.

Finally, she found a thick metal door at the end of a narrow hallway marked "Cold Storage." She pulled the door open and shivered instantly at the sight of six body-shaped mounds in thick black bags, stacked on metal shelves against the wall.

That was all the room there was in the morgue – six bays, already filled. Lira had counted five people in the clinic alone, and twenty-two more in Dorm 2B. How many waited for her in 2A? And in the other modules around the sector? Even if she put the bodies on the floor, they wouldn't all fit in here.

"A problem for later," she reminded herself, then stepped up to the rack. She had to find Ada. She took a deep breath and unzipped the body bag on the lowest shelf.

It was one of the dig crew members she remembered seeing in the waiting area on the day Ada got sick, the one whose face had been burned by the radiation. Lira closed the bag and moved to the next shelf up. Another stranger.

The third contained a severely radiation-burned body with the distinctive Glass symptoms entwined with the burns – a bizarre visual effect of mottled red and blue and raw skin that made Lira's stomach turn. She closed it quickly.

With trembling hands, she pulled open the fourth body bag, just above her eye level.

Ada lay there, her features peaceful despite the unnatural blue-gray cast to her skin. Her eyelids weren't quite as see-through as Aksel's, which Lira was grateful for, and someone had arranged her hands over her chest. They'd cared for her, even if only a little, even while the whole hab was melting down around them.

A sob tore from Lira's throat, raw and painful. "I came back for you," she said, tears streaming down her face. "I'm sorry it took me so long."

She brushed Ada's cheek with her fingers, right over the place where her dimple popped out every time she smiled. Her cold skin somehow even felt like glass now. Lira stroked her hair, short and tightly curled, one thing that was still *Ada* even in death.

Then she pulled up her overlay and, with a few eye movements, began constructing a digital shrine over Ada's shelf. Arabian jasmine blossoms materialized in the air – delicate white flowers with bright yellow centers cascading in a waterfall over the cold metal shelf. The same pixelated flowers Lira had left on Ada's bedside table when she was alive, the ones she'd been leaving in Ada's memory at every memorial she found around the hab. She could practically smell them, sweet and homey.

"I should have given you more of these," Lira said, watching the digital petals flutter in an artificial breeze. "Every single day."

She kept making more of them until they positively over-whelmed the shelf Ada lay on, until Lira could hardly even see past them to the midnight-black body bag. And then she threw more of them out around the rest of the rack for the other five bodies, for the loved ones who would want them to be remembered – if they themselves were still alive.

Then Lira put her palm to the side of Ada's face, trying to imagine her skin warm and soft and full of life. Full of dimpled smiles aimed right at Lira. Looking at this version of her, Lira could hardly remember how she looked just a few weeks ago.

Those memories would come back, she knew that from losing Muning. From losing her grandparents. From saying goodbye to her mother.

Right now, she couldn't picture it, a world without Ada, but one day, she would.

"I don't know why I'm still here," Lira told her through tears. "Sometimes I wish I wasn't. But I am, so I just have to keep going. I'm leaving you again now because there are some things I need to do... but I'll be back, okay? This is not where your story ends. I'll figure out a better place for you, one you'd have liked. I love you, Ada."

She took a deep, shuddering breath and zipped the body bag closed. Then she squared her shoulders and wiped her eyes. There was a lot to do, a lot more bodies, and Lira didn't have the first idea where she was going to put them all.

She turned toward the door, and at least one of her problems was solved. Tucked into the corner of the morgue was a small scissor lift with a stainless-steel person-sized tray balanced atop it. She found a toggle on the side of the lift and flipped it down. It went smoothly almost to the floor. She reversed the toggle and it rose up to her chest height. The whole thing was on wheels, and with a little help from Valence, she found a remote control program in her overlay, tucked in among the systems Dr. Kalb had given her access to days ago.

At least she had a way to move the bodies with her broken hand now.

LIRA

YEAR: 2083

t didn't take long for Lira to come up with a system for labeling and relocating the bodies. She started with the clinic medical staff, arranging them as respectfully as possible on the floor of the morgue, then moved on to Dorm 2B. Moving them from their beds to the scissor lift was the hardest part, but she used some of the lifting techniques she'd been taught in her large animal medicine classes and figured it out.

While she worked, she scanned the chats in her overlay to see what the hab was talking about. The central commons' video feed showed it empty, and no one had forwarded her any more all-colony-except-Lira communications from Tim. The chats were filled with what was quickly becoming 'the usual' scared and paranoid chatter, although it seemed like the lottery had actually lowered the temperature of the colony a bit.

"Now he's going to think he was right," Lira grumbled to herself.

She wondered what he was doing now. If he'd begun his plan to relocate the sick to sector four, he'd started somewhere other than sector two. Lira hadn't seen a sign of anyone since she split up from her group in the living room.

She wondered what he'd think if he knew she was moving the bodies.

Then she wondered what Dmitri Voss thought of Tim taking over.

Whatever he thought, it wasn't enough to tempt him out of the sanctuary of his barricaded sector. With a morbid curiosity she couldn't suppress, Lira pulled up the hab map again and asked Valence to drop a pin on all the sick people in sector three.

It'd been five last time she looked.

The pins dropped all across the map and Lira's heart skipped a beat.

There were eleven now.

Whatever good Dmitri thought he was doing by isolating himself and his wife in that sector, it was no match for V. martialis. All they'd done was buy themselves a little extra time.

Valence let her into every room she requested access to, provided she put on a full complement of protective gear first. After five hours, Lira had only managed to move four bodies from Dorm 2B to the clinic and even with the scissor lift, her hand was throbbing, the latest dose of painkillers long gone.

She'd run out of room in the morgue and begun using the Emotional Equilibrium Module with its temperature turned down. It was the only one in the entire hab, and the only room with a solid metal door like the morgue that could retain cold. Lira shuddered the first time she stepped foot inside it – it was the reason Ada had wound up in jail – but it was surprisingly suitable as a makeshift morgue. It was about the same size, with blank display screens for walls and only a single chair in the center to work around.

Valence hadn't had a problem adjusting the temperature for her.

As Lira went into the next room on the map, a notification popped up from Natalia. At first, Lira assumed she was just checking in, but it was a new video from Tim. Lira hit *play*, minimizing the video in the corner of her vision while she started positioning the scissor lift beside the bed.

"I know it's hard, but we're doing important work, restoring order and making sure those of us who remain are safe," he said. He'd been sending videos about once a day, patting himself on the back for the success of the antibiotic lottery and acting like he was the administrator. Lira zoned in and out of his latest rant until she heard him say the word *rabbits* and had to rewind the video. "They've always been luxuries, and I'm sorry to say it but we can't afford luxuries right now."

"They're vital research animals," Lira corrected, grinding her teeth. "And I happen to know for a fact you spend credits on rabbit ragu."

"They're consuming critical food and water that could go to colonists in need," Tim was saying, "and their environment is toxic. We can't ever let them out of that module, so it's a mercy to end the rabbit program now, before they starve to death."

"Asshole," Lira hissed, then closed the video. Did he actually care about how many resources the rabbits were taking up, or did he just know it would get under her skin if he said so? They ate waste materials from the hydro gardens and right now, their water was fully recycled within their module – nothing they had was something the rest of the colony needed. She thought about sending him another message telling him that, but he probably wouldn't read it. Even if he did, Lira found his reading comprehension questionable.

She raised the scissor lift and guided it on the long journey back to the med clinic. One more trip, and then she'd take a break, get some more painkillers. Maybe eat something.

When she stepped into the waiting area, there was a man already there. Lira froze in the doorway. His back was to her and he appeared to be rummaging in the drawers behind the nurse's station. Was he one of Tim's?

"Hello?" she called.

The man spun around, eyes wide, an apology on his lips until he realized she wasn't part of the medical staff. And relief melted down Lira's spine.

"Hoyt?"

She hadn't seen him since the day he visited the rabbitat, a wreck because Dana was sick. His eyes shifted from Lira to the scissor lift and he asked, "What are you doing? Are you… moving the bodies?"

It was an accusation laced with fear.

"I am," she said cautiously. "They need to be preserved until we can deal with them properly."

"Valence asked you to do that?" he asked, incredulous.

Lira shook her head. "No, but it okayed it. A dead body presents no more risk of Glass exposure than a live one – less, actually, if the bacteria is aerosolized. But bodies decomposing all around the hab is going to be a problem so I'm fixing it. What are you doing here?"

"Looking for bandages and antiseptic," he said. "My friend cut his hand trying to replace an air filter."

Somebody had finally taken that job. Lira wondered how many credits it had been worth.

"There's a supply closet down the hall," she said. "It's ransacked, but you should be able to find what you need. I'll show you."

She led him down the hall and together they sorted through the mess. Hoyt gestured to Lira's bandaged hand. "What happened there?"

"I was an idiot," Lira said, hoping he wouldn't make her rehash the whole thing.

Instead, as they went back to the waiting area, bandages acquired, he looked again at the scissor lift and asked, "Do you have many more to move?"

Lira laughed, a dry, hollow sound that echoed a bit in the empty room. "I've barely scratched the surface. There are sixteen more bodies in Dorm 2B alone. I want to get to 2A next – I have a friend there. And there are three other sectors, although I'm not sure which ones I can still get to."

"Dana's in sector three," Hoyt said. "No one's getting in there."

Lira nodded. "Maybe someone in three is doing this too." *If they're not all busy dying,* she thought. Did Hoyt know there was Glass in sector three? Did anyone?

"I should get back to my friend with this stuff," Hoyt said. "But… I could come help you tomorrow if you want."

Lira blinked in surprise. "You'd do that? Why?"

"You're right, it needs to be done," he said. "Plus, I think Dana would make me if she was here," he added with a grin. "She loved your rabbits. I know she woulda wanted to give back."

"You don't have to," Lira said. "But I'll be in 2B if you still want to help tomorrow morning."

QUINTA

YEAR: 2179

"Eat up, everyone," Aris said as she slid prepackaged meals across the table. "We'll finish the install tomorrow, if everything goes according to plan. Then it's just three more days of quarantine and you'll never eat another shelf-stable boxed dinner."

It was lasagna tonight, and Quinta absentmindedly opened hers, beginning the chemical reaction that would heat it up. She was barely paying attention to the food, or to the conversation going on around her, busy searching the medical archives for a seven-year-old file.

"Am I the only one who's absolutely stunned that we're not all dead right now?" Dex asked. They were all still sitting at their segregated tables, but they'd started talking to each other here and there, instead of pretending there was an invisible wall between them.

"No kidding," Torrent said. "I put on a brave face for Eddy, but inside I was preparing to never see him again."

"Valence wouldn't send us on a suicide mission," Ronan said.

"At the very least, she knew we'd be able to fix the unit for the sake of the colony, or we wouldn't be here right now at all."

"Yeah, yeah, every hand, right?" Dex said, parroting the citizen saying with a bit too much snark.

"Your lasagna's getting cold," someone said at Quinta's shoulder, and she looked up just as Castor slid into the seat next to hers.

"I'm looking something up..." She trailed off.

"I can see that," he chuckled. "What?"

"The name of the antibiotic Kellan's mom took..." She nibbled her lower lip while she searched. She couldn't remember the woman's first name – wasn't sure she'd ever known it – and she'd only ever heard Kellan's last name spoken, so she was having to try different spellings. She'd just ask, except he hadn't come out of the dorm since their conversation.

"Why?" Castor asked. When Quinta didn't answer him, he opened his own lasagna and blew the steam off it before he started eating. "Was that murderer bothering you earlier? I saw him follow you into the NPC dorm earlier."

"I was checking on Jace's foot," Quinta said, distracted. "It's Kellan's dorm too."

Reilly! She hit on the correct spelling at last and a handful of records came up. Most had to do with someone named Solenne, and they were much too old. Finally, she found the one dated on her twelfth birthday.

"Can you believe we're almost out of here?" Castor asked. "What's the first thing you're ordering from the dining hall? Me, I think I'm gonna need a double-helping of ice cream with fresh berries–"

"Castor, please."

"What are you doing?"

"Heliomycin!" she said, then looked up from her overlay. "I've tried every password I can think of to open that file. If it's not the antibiotic that started it all, I'm out of guesses."

"We can always try to hack it once I get back to the computer lab," Castor said.

"Just cross your fingers it's this," Quinta told him, then switched over to the file. *teebragus134.bin.* She opened it and got prompted for the password. "Here goes."

She entered *heliomycin* and held her breath as she submitted it.

A file popped up.

"I'm in!" She shouted it so loud everyone at both tables turned to look at her.

"Everything okay?" Aris asked.

"Umm, just checking on some clinic work," she lied. "Sorry."

"I'm just saying that no matter how Valence rewards you all for the dig, the rest of us are going back to sector four with nothing more to show for it than a new atmo unit," Dex said.

"Are you saying you want a credit reward?" Ronan asked. "Because say the word and Valence can arrange that."

"I'm saying we're the ones that get called lazy and selfish, but the Blinkers are the only ones who need material reinforcement for doing what needs done around here."

"Let's go to the dorm," Quinta said, grabbing Castor's elbow. "I can't make sense of this file and it's too loud out here."

She got up, her lasagna untouched. It'd be stone-cold by the time she returned to it, but either she'd eat it or someone else here would. It couldn't be wasted.

Right now, though, she only had eyes for the confusing block of letters and numbers and symbols that had appeared as soon as the bin file opened. She sent it to Castor even as they walked. "What do you make of this? Is it code?"

"No..." Now Castor was the one trailing off. "Give me a minute."

They went into the dorm and Castor sat down on his bed while Quinta paced the floor. *Please don't let it be meaningless, or a corrupted file, or–*

"It's the medical board report," Castor said.

"What? How do you know?" At once, Quinta was at Castor's side on his bed.

"A bin file is just a bunch of data in a small, efficient file," Castor explained. "It's meaningless if you don't have the right program to open it." A satisfied smirk spread across his face as he looked to Quinta. "Lucky for you, your best friend's a computer engineer who has access to a lot of different programs. Here, I'm sending it back to you in a format you can read."

A notification popped up, a new file incoming, and Quinta popped up from the bed and started pacing again as she read it.

Medical Board Internal Review Meeting Minutes

Sol 194, Standard Year 2172

Subject: Findings On Inventory Irregularities In Sector One Medical Clinic

---

Quinta scanned, hungry to read the entire document as fast as she could, but it was long, including several excerpts from interviews the board had conducted. She spotted Dr. Liang's name.

...reported discrepancies in inventory logs, including missing broadspectrum antibiotics, sterile bandages, wound-care kits...

There were several pages of inventory records with highlights and notations all over them, and then finally, the board's interview with her father. Quinta stopped in her tracks.

"What is it?" Castor asked.

"Listen to this," Quinta said, reading aloud. "'Dr. Hadrian Voss acknowledges diverting supplies to Non-participating Colonists in sector four, claiming to address an emergent care gap. He has submitted a dataset of twenty case studies comparing patient recovery rates when NPCs are treated in their own sector versus in a citizen clinic. He argues a statistically significant improvement in both infection rates and healing time for all colonists when NPCs are provided with a larger portion of the medical supply inventory.'"

Quinta looked at Castor, then slumped down on the nearest bed, her legs feeling wobbly.

"He's saying NPCs would take care of more of their own crap if they had more bandages and antibiotics," Castor said with a shrug. "So what? That doesn't mean they've earned the right to take ours."

"No, he was is saying the *citizen* outcomes improved as well," Quinta said, going back to scanning. She was looking at the excerpts from the case files now. "My dad was arguing that equipping NPC doctors to handle their own medical emergencies gave citizen doctors more time with their own patients too, and better outcomes for everyone."

Another line caught her eye.

When asked why redistribution was not requested through official channels, Dr. Voss stated these channels were "non-responsive" and that multiple prior requests "failed to generate any corrective action."

"He tried to tell Valence and she just… ignored it."

"That's not possible," Castor said.

"Look at the board findings, at the bottom," she said. "'Board requests review of supply allocation by Valence.'"

And right after that, *Dr. Voss to complete mandatory compliance reeducation for appropriate use of medical supplies and treatment of Non-participating Colonists.*

"Okay, so she reviewed it," Castor said. "Does it say whether any tweaks were made?"

"It doesn't actually say she reviewed it," Quinta argued. "It says the board requested it." She closed the window. "Can we check?"

A smirk came involuntarily to Castor's lips. "Can we check what Valence's internal systems did seven years ago? Quinta, you know even the engineers don't have access to those kinds of logs."

"Well, shouldn't you?" Quinta argued back. "My dad was saying there was a better way to do something that would improve health outcomes for everyone in the hab. This file got sealed, and then he continued to steal supplies and give them to the NPCs for six more years. My father may have died over this, Castor. And it doesn't sound like Valence ever changed the allocations."

If this was true, Valence was acting in opposition to her primary objective. She was degrading the quality of care for every NPC in the hab… knowingly.

Quinta didn't dare say that out loud.

"You don't know this is why he died," Castor said, the smirk long gone.

"Come on," Quinta said, throwing her hands up. "How much more evidence do you need?" A thought occurred to her. "Can you see the metadata for the bin file? Who sealed the record?"

"This is your dad's copy, not the official one," Castor said, his vision going distant to check. "All I can see is that he's the one who password-protected it, but we already knew that."

"What about Valence's review, if she did one? Could you pull that up?"

"Quinta, I don't think you should be digging into this stuff–"

"*Why not?*" she practically yelled, clamping down on the volume just enough to keep from alerting everyone else in the module. She came and sat next to Castor again, whispering now. "My father is dead. This file says Valence *chose* to ignore data that would have improved the survival odds of this colony… unless you can prove to me that she looked at my dad's data and determined it was flawed. Can you?"

Castor's face went grim and he shook his head. "I wish I could, I really do. But if she ever did a review, the data has been archived for almost a decade. It's been encrypted and archived and even the computer engineers couldn't access it now."

"Why?"

"It's just so much data," he said. "Think about it. Every day, the hab itself, all the sensors and cameras and systems, and every implant create exabytes of data. Valence keeps it all, but the server room would be the size of the planet itself if she didn't compress it constantly. It's usable to her, but we can't just pull it up – even if we found the data, it'd be as meaningless to us as that bin file before I found the right program to view it."

"We can't find a program for her compressed data?"

Castor shook his head. "It's not just one compressed file. She has her own classification system, her own taxonomy… and we don't speak her language."

"So it's gone."

"Yeah. I'm sorry. All we have is your father's version of the report."

"Great, another dead end." Quinta dropped her head into her hands, the tears rising behind her eyes again.

KELLAN

YEAR: 2179

After dinner, Jace convinced Kellan that he was feeling well enough to go out and join the others for the evening.

Well, really what he'd said was, "I'm going stir-crazy staring at these ugly white walls. You can't expect me to stay in here alone all the time. It's cruel and unusual."

"Yeah, I guess I'm the only one with a prison sentence around here," Kellan agreed.

Unfortunately, there were no wheelchairs in the module and Dr. Anya didn't want Jace moving his leg, so that meant Kellan, Torrent, Dex and Ronan all taking one corner of Jace's bed and hauling his ass out to the common area. He bit his lower lip and gripped the bedframe every time they accidentally jostled it, and Dr. Anya went for more painkillers the moment they set him down.

"Thanks for the lift, boys," Jace managed through gritted teeth.

While he was carefully adjusting the blankets beneath Jace's foot, Kellan caught movement out of the corner of his eye and spotted Quinta and her little sycophant creeping out of the Blinker dorms, her face flush with emotion. Kellan caught Castor's eye and he grinned wolfishly.

"What do you think those two were up to?" Jace asked. Kellan looked at him and he wiggled his brows, watching Quinta and Castor rejoin the Blinker table.

Of course he noticed, too.

"Who cares?" Kellan said as Dr. Anya returned with a needle full of liquid painkillers to push into Jace's IV. "You wanna play cards?"

Jace laughed, loud enough to draw attention. "Sure, you don't care. I can see that written all over your face, bud."

"I don't," Kellan insisted.

"You need anything else?" Dr. Anya asked. "Another blanket under your foot, an ice pack?"

Jace shook his head, the movement slowing as the drugs hit his system. "Nah, I can't even feel my toes right now." His expression darkened briefly. "Hope that's the meds and not nerve damage."

"Don't joke about that sludge, man," Kellan said, smacking his arm.

Dex, Torrent and Iska came back over, bringing chairs with them. Torrent set one down in front of Kellan. "Euchre?" he asked.

"Yeah, I wouldn't mind beating all of you," Jace said. "Deal 'em."

"We don't have even numbers," Kellan pointed out. "I'll just watch–"

"Yo, Ronan," Dex called. "You Blinkers know what euchre is?"

"Do I know?" Ronan asked. "I'm the champ."

"Well, pull up a chair, Chosen one," Torrent said. They'd all seen the tattoo and heard Ronan praying before trips outside, but he'd never gotten too preachy about it and he took the nickname in stride now. He dragged a chair over and joined the NPCs.

"I am Chosen," he said, reaching for the deck. "Chosen to win every trick we play tonight."

"We'll see," Dex said, turning to Iska. "Just make sure he doesn't look at our cards with that implant or something."

"That's not how it works," Ronan said. He gave his best attempt at a shuffle, and the cards went everywhere. For a moment, everyone just looked at them scattered all over the floor, and then

Ronan laughed. "See? You've got the upper hand with these physical cards."

Torrent and Iska stooped to scoop them all up, and then Torrent started to shuffle, putting a little extra flourish into it just for Ronan. "Nothing to it."

They settled on teams – Kellan was with Jace, just like every game they ever played back home – and Torrent dealt the first hand. While they played, they talked about the steps for connecting the new atmo unit tomorrow, and how boring it'd be sitting around for three more days in quarantine, and who they most wanted to see when they got home. They'd gone from waiting to die to annoyed at the inconvenience of quarantine.

"I've sent Echo's tablet a few messages," Kellan said. "Maybe it's not set up to interface with an implant because I haven't heard back from her. Hope she's getting them."

"She's usually glued to that thing," Jace said. "If they went through, she got them. Wait, what are you saying to her?"

"Just letting her know everybody's doing okay, nobody's got Glass–"

"You didn't tell her about my foot, did you?"

"Of course."

"Deimos, man, my parents are going to be freaking out."

"This is hardly the first bone you've broken," Kellan pointed out. "At least this one was a heroic injury."

"Every hand for the colony," Dex mocked.

"More like every foot," Kellan said. He laid a club, the wrong suit but he had nothing, then looked around the common area. Aris was sitting at the other table, her back to the group, eyes on the schematics up on the display wall as always.

Quinta and Castor were playing a pretty low-energy round of HoloPong. Kellan didn't bother activating his overlay to see the ball, so it really did look like they were batting at nothing.

Quinta's eyes flashed to him and he looked away. Jace was giving him a *really, man?* look about the card he'd played.

"So what's going to happen when you get out of here?" Dex asked Ronan. "Valence gonna crown you royalty for your service to the colony?"

"That's right, you're looking at the next King of Mars," Ronan teased, then laid down a heart. "And that trick is ours. Nice work, Torrent."

That night, after they hefted Jace's bed back into the dorm and Dr. Anya administered a final round of painkillers before bed, Jace reached out and tugged Kellan's sleeve before he could leave.

"Heyyy." He was slurring – whether with fatigue or from the drugs or both, Kellan didn't know.

"Yeah?"

"You suck at euchre."

"Thanks. You sucked tonight, too."

"You were distracted."

"I had bad cards."

"Right," Jace said, his eyelids heavy as he grinned up at Kellan. "It had nothing to do with you staring at the princess all night."

"The princess?" Kellan asked, but his cheeks were already heating.

"Princess Voss," Jace said. "Your eyes follow her like she's the last water ration in the hab."

"They do not." Kellan shoved Jace's hand away from his sleeve. "That's ridiculous. Go to sleep, you're loopy."

He retrieved his toothbrush from the shelf by his bed and was most of the way out of the room before Jace added, "Echo's gonna be disappointed."

Kellan turned to him. "I'm not dating Echo."

"No, but she wishes you were."

Kellan shook his head, narrowing his eyes. "Echo and I are just friends. And Quinta and I… we're not even that. We're dig team members."

Jace laughed, another one of those too-loud ones. "Yeah, and I'm gonna win a Parallax tournament tomorrow."

LIRA

YEAR: 2083

oyt was true to his word. Lira found him waiting for her in the living room early the next morning, and he wasn't alone. Two other engineers – a woman named Ellis and a man named Chen – had joined him. All three wore protective gear: surgical masks, gloves, and coveralls they'd scrounged from medical storage. Chen had a couple adhesive bandages crisscrossed over the back of his left hand.

"I figured you wouldn't object to some extra help," Hoyt said after he introduced them. "They both lost people too."

Lira nodded gratefully, not trusting her voice. She hadn't expected this kind of support. She'd spent the night sleeping fitfully on a borrowed bunk, glassy faces and maps with far too many pins on them invading every dream. Plus, she was exhausted and her hand was throbbing from yesterday's efforts.

The four of them got to work. Hoyt and Chen were a lot stronger than Lira, even with the scissor lift to help her. They made lifting the bodies look effortless. Ellis, who'd been a paramedic for a few years on Earth before going to school for environmental engineering, knew how to position the body bags for the easiest transfer, and she retrieved a gurney from the clinic so they could transfer twice as many bodies at a time. By early afternoon, they'd moved ten of them. Lira's muscles burned, but her hand wasn't killing her like yesterday.

"Lunch break, everyone," Hoyt announced when they returned to the dorm after their fifth trip. Lira handed out bottles of electrolyte water left over from when she raided the vending machines with Gaurav and Tamika, and Hoyt pulled cricket protein bars from a backpack he'd brought with him.

"They're stale, but it's protein," he said as he passed the bars around.

"I'm so hungry I'd eat the crickets plain right now," Ellis said, which elicited a disgusted sound from Chen. She just shrugged. "I've had them chocolate-covered. Not bad. Imagine a peanut M&M but crunchier."

"Stop," Chen complained, "you're gonna ruin my appetite."

Lira half-listened to them, mechanically biting and chewing while she scanned through her overlay. Chats, video feeds… then she noticed the Exchange had updated her task list to include *Relocate deceased colonists from Dorm 2B to the medical clinic for temporary storage, ten credits per body.* So apparently Valence did find what she was doing useful.

Ten credits per body, though? Was that all a human being was worth?

"That's it, you've ruined it for me," Chen said, dramatically folding the wax cloth wrapper over his protein bar. "I'm done."

"I'll eat the rest if you're not gonna," Ellis said. She'd been listing all her favorite bug-based meals, and the list had been getting increasingly ridiculous.

Lira went to her messages, expecting to find either nothing or some forwarded piece of fear mongering from Tim. Instead, there was a system alert from the rabbitat.

WARNING: Rabbit module food supply at 10% capacity. Autofeeder pellet reservoir critical.

Ages ago, in a different life, a message like that would have been a final failsafe meant to warn her that something was going catastrophically wrong in the rabbitat. Lira went there every day to check on them, even on her days off, and Jamila used to bring them fresh greens every day too. There had been no shortage of fresh and dried foods, and little likelihood of Lira ever encountering a message like this.

But no human had set foot in that module for close to a week. The rabbits hadn't had anything fresh in far too long, and Lira hadn't thought they would eat their way through the dry goods nearly this fast.

"Hey," Hoyt said, nudging Lira's arm. "What's wrong?"

Was it written all over her face? "The rabbits," she explained. "The autofeeder's almost empty. It won't last another day."

"Can't you go refill it?" Chen asked.

Lira shook her head. "The rabbitat's been sealed off because there's regolith beneath the grass in the play area."

"I remember Dana hauling it there so the rabbits could dig," Hoyt said. "She was so excited to make the room a little more natural for them. If only we knew then what we know now."

"I've been running through possible solutions in the back of my mind ever since I got kicked out," Lira said. "How I could dig the regolith out, or where I could move the rabbits to. I've suggested a few things to Valence but containment is the only answer it will accept. Anyway, I can't actually do anything because the door's been sealed shut."

"What happens when the food runs out?" Ellis asked.

"Best case, Valence will cull the warren," Lira said. "As much as I hate to think about it, it'd be better than letting them slowly starve to death."

"Tim Robinette keeps saying it's necessary," Chen said. "He seems obsessed."

"He seems deranged," Hoyt added, and Lira felt something loosen in her chest, making it a little bit easier to breathe. Tim might have followers out there, but not everyone left in the hab was buying his story.

"He's telling everybody his lottery was a hit," Chen said. "No new Glass cases in the last two days."

Ellis snorted. "Of course there aren't any new cases. Everyone who was susceptible has already gotten sick."

"You think anyone's recovered?" Hoyt asked. Lira thought of Dana again. They knew she was dead because she was no longer listed on the hab map, but to know it intellectually was totally different from being able to see her and come to terms with it. Hoyt couldn't do that until Dmitri Voss crawled out of his hole and started letting people into sector three.

"I haven't heard of a single case," Ellis answered.

Chen agreed. "Everyone I knew who was sick has died."

The words hung in the air for a minute, jarring and stark.

No one had survived Glass. Not a single person in a colony of a thousand.

If you got sick, you died.

Lira's mind drifted back to Ada lying stiff in that cold room. To Jamila's last hours. To the three faces she'd shrouded in sweaty sheets on that terrible night in Dorm 2B.

The rabbits would be next, slowly starving in their sealed habitat. Then what? How long before the hydroponics failed without proper maintenance? How long before a critical system broke down and they found out the skilled workers who knew how to fix it were all dead?

"Has anyone heard from their family on Earth since the outbreak began?" she asked quietly.

Hoyt shook his head. "I was trying to reach my sister in Chicago before they announced the satellites are down. Never heard back."

"My parents are in Shanghai," Chen added. "I sent three messages last week. Didn't get a delivery confirmation."

Ellis stared at her water bottle. "My dad's in Austin. Same story."

"Do you think the satellite is really down?" Lira asked. She didn't know where she got the courage to say it out loud – people in this colony had been silenced for less. But who was left to police her? "If I was Sorin Voss, I wouldn't want to have to explain this outbreak to my shareholders. Just look at how secretive he was about V. martialis in the beginning, before it turned into a killer."

"They've got plenty of their own problems, too," Ellis said. "The methane hydrate releases are intensifying. I read that in the last daily brief they sent."

Again, silence settled on the group as they contemplated just how screwed they were. It hadn't occurred to Lira until that moment that things could always get worse. What if the satellites *never* worked again?

They'd have to send someone to rescue the colonists. Wouldn't they?

Or would they leave the satellites down, pretend they didn't know anything?

Would they want to risk bringing Glass back with them?

"Let's get back to work," Lira said, standing. "I can't sit around here thinking about this or I'll go insane."

"Right," Ellis said, capping her water. "Lugging around dead bodies that are starting to smell is so much better."

LIRA

YEAR: 2083

That evening, they camped out in the 2B living room. It was like deja vu with all the faces swapped out, but Lira was too bone-tired to even mention it. Chen and Hoyt had gone to the dining hall and found a frozen mushroom loaf they brought back for dinner, and Ellis asked Lira to put the rabbitat's video feed up on the display wall.

Lira had been hesitant, afraid of what she might see, but the autofeeder was at three percent now. They weren't starving yet. They would be soon, but not yet. Now might be their last chance to watch the rabbits acting normally, blissfully ignorant of what was about to happen.

So Lira queued it up, and her throat instantly tightened at the sight of them. The camera showed several bunnies huddled together near one of the feeders. Others were stretched out on the grass. Flash, a white angora male, hopped enthusiastically across the play area.

They all looked fine. Healthy and happy.

How would Valence do it? Was there some gas already filling the pipes above the play area, just waiting to be deployed?

"Why can't we transport them?" Ellis asked as she accepted a generous helping of mushroom loaf and a ketchup bottle from Chen. "Assuming we could jimmy the door open, why can't we use the gurneys and scissor lift to move the cages?"

"We could move them, but where?" Lira answered. "The rabbitat was purpose-built with environmental controls, grass, hiding places – everything the rabbits needed. They would survive if we put them in a dorm room or something, but without that ceiling, the rain, the sun, they wouldn't thrive. The rabbitat is the perfect place for them."

"If it wasn't for that damn regolith," Ellis added, thoughtful.

Lira positioned her body away from the rabbitat feed. It felt cowardly, but she couldn't watch them while she ate.

The conversation drifted to the rapid climate change happening on Earth. Ellis said her dad was planning to sell his house to move further north to escape the heat. Chen described how quickly his body had started to scream for hydration at the mere mention of water rationing going into effect when he was in Shanghai with his family. Lira's thoughts went to her mother, hoping against hope that she'd relocated like Lira had been begging her to do for months.

Hoyt sat silently, picking at his mushroom loaf, crumbling it across his plate. Lira figured he was thinking about his sister when suddenly, his fork clattered against the table.

"What about a resin sealant?" he asked.

"For the methane hydrates…?" Ellis asked, skeptical.

"For the rabbits," he answered, turning to Lira. "The problem is that we can't move the regolith out of the rabbitat, and the rabbits can't live anywhere else, right? We could make a resin and layer it on top of the regolith, seal it up and make it inert. The rabbits wouldn't be able to dig anymore, but if we can remove the threat of Glass, they'll get to keep their habitat. Man, I can't believe I didn't think of it earlier."

Lira felt her pulse quicken. "Will that really work?"

Hoyt turned to the other two engineers for backup. Ellis looked thoughtful. "Theoretically, yes, but it'll be tricky. We'll need to formulate something that will harden quickly but not release toxic fumes, and it'll have to form a complete, nonporous seal."

"We'll need to do a test run first," Chen added. "This bacteria is like nothing we've ever dealt with before. We need to be sure it'll be enough."

"I have some compounds in mind already," Hoyt said. "I just need to get my hands on some regolith to start testing."

For the first time in weeks, Lira felt a flicker of hope. "There's regolith in the geology lab. And they'll have a fume hood you can use while you're testing." She thought of that three percent warning sitting in her inbox. "How soon could you start?"

"Well, we're not finished here–"

"The rabbits are down to their last hours of food," Lira said. "If you think this will work, we need to switch gears."

Hoyt nodded. "Then let's start testing now."

KELLAN

YEAR: 2179

"Last time out there, if all goes well," Iska said, dropping into the seat next to Kellan and passing him a lunch container.

"You mean this could be my last..." Kellan glanced at the label before he opened the box. "Protein mash and root vegetable stew?"

"They're not actually that bad," Iska said, starting to heat hers. "Although I did overhear Aris saying this is probably the best food we've ever had. As if we don't have a hydroponic garden of our own."

"Better than prison," Kellan said. "Cricket protein, three squares a day. And I do mean squares."

Iska wrinkled her nose, then nodded toward Quinta, who was sitting with her back to them, Castor at her side as always. They were using the wall display and he was walking her through the final steps to connect the new atmo unit. "Bet those two practically have to choke down this food. What do you think they normally eat?"

"Rabbit stew, braised rabbit, fried rabbit..."

Quinta tucked a strand of hair behind her ear, leaning in to concentrate on the screen. Jace's words recurred to Kellan. *Your eyes follow her like she's the last water ration in the hab.* He rolled his own eyes and turned his attention back to Iska.

"You ready for this?" she was asking.

They'd watched the morning crew level the new atmo unit and carefully brush away all the regolith that had accumulated on the old unit since the dig began. No dust storms during the mission, thankfully, but the stuff was fine and light and had a way of coating everything within seconds. Now both units were prepped, and before she would let them eat lunch, Aris had gathered the afternoon team to review the exact steps they'd need to take to transfer power and airflow to the new unit.

That was what Quinta and Castor were studying now.

It wouldn't be terribly difficult, but everything had to be done precisely and in a specific order or they risked contaminating the hab's ductwork with regolith. And if that happened, the endless minutes the crew had spent standing in the decon chamber while chemicals misted over them would be pointless.

"Not exactly," Kellan answered.

Aris had assigned him the task of connecting up the new ductwork and flushing it out before the power transfer. Every fiber of his being had wanted to beg her for a less important task – he just kept seeing the names of the three people he'd killed scrolling through his mind.

Hadrian Voss.

Elise Chandra.

Owen Markovic.

If he screwed up again, it'd be a hell of a lot more than three names this time.

If the team had been all NPCs, he probably could have found an excuse for why he didn't want to do this – or he could just tell them, *I messed up once, somebody else needs to take the lead here and I'll be the one who pushes the button when it's all done.* Something simple that couldn't possibly lead to fatalities.

Besides, it wasn't like there were unimportant tasks. While Kellan hooked up the new ductwork, Aris would be powering down the old one, which had to be timed right so the modules nearest the atmo unit didn't begin to fill with CO_2. Iska would unplug all the old stuff. Quinta was responsible for monitoring the air pressure in both units. And finally Ronan would connect the power to the new one.

There was, unfortunately, no designated power button presser.

This morning, Kellan had quietly tried to convince Dex or Torrent to switch shifts with him, but Aris had shut that idea down as soon as she heard it. "The teams work as they are," she'd said. "We already had one shake-up, we don't need another one at the last minute."

He wasn't even sure why they wanted "the murderer" on the team doing the final swap. Maybe so they had an easy scapegoat if things went wrong?

He pushed his stew around with his fork, already going cold. *Hadrian Voss, Elise Chandra, Owen Markovic.*

"Hey," Iska said. "This won't be a repeat of the air vents. This time, we have the latest documentation straight from the machine itself and you won't be alone out there. We all want to make sure we get this right."

He gave her a weak smile. "Thanks."

"Plus, you'll be done first," she added. "You know Aris and Ronan picked the most important jobs so they can claim most of the credit for themselves."

"Praise be to Voss," Kellan said, mimicking a Chosen saying he'd heard Ronan say a few times. At the other table, Quinta's ears pricked up – subtle, but Kellan just happened to be looking at her exactly when they twitched.

KELLAN

YEAR: 2179

"Disconnect the air intake valve at port C," Quinta read over comms. Aris had asked her to keep the documentation pulled up in her overlay and read out the steps to make sure everything was executed perfectly.

"Got it," Iska confirmed.

Kellan was hunched over the new unit, a coil of heavily insulated ductwork curled around him. It was nothing like the ducts he was used to working on inside the hab, thick and heavy and difficult to maneuver. He'd been meticulously attaching it to the new unit for close to half an hour now, and everything – himself included – was tinged red. It was impossible to prevent regolith from getting into everything, so the flush would have to do a damn good job.

He tested his seal, closing off the end of the duct that connected to the hab and injecting air into the new ductwork from a canister the hauler robot brought. It pushed the regolith into every crevice of the new unit. Just the thought of it made him queasy, but they couldn't flush if they didn't have a good seal.

"Pressure reading?" he asked into his comms.

"Steady," Dex reported.

"Can someone come double-check this seal?" Kellan asked his team. He grabbed the roll of polyimide tape and added a couple more layers of it to each end of the duct just to be safe, and Aris came over.

"You already do a pressure puff test?" she asked.

"Yeah, I just want a second set of eyes on this."

He thought he saw a flash of sympathy from inside her helmet, and then she picked up the oxygen canister and repeated the test Kellan had just done. "It looks good. Do the flush."

"Okay," Kellan said, his heart fluttering. "Here goes nothing."

He retrieved the flushing solution from the robot and hooked it up to the duct, repressurized, and then all there was to do was wait while the entire unit was bathed in much the same chemicals that he got doused with every time he came back from outside.

"Time?" Aris asked.

Kellan checked using his overlay. "Twelve minutes remaining on the flush."

"It'll take me about that long to disconnect power from the old unit. I'm going to get started so Ronan can connect to the new one as soon as the flush is over," she said. "Quinta, walk me through it."

"Your first step is to disengage the safety switch," she read off the documentation. "You need to remove the access panel and locate it just above the power line."

"Found it," Aris said. "And... disengaged."

"Okay, next you'll need to–"

A sharp hissing sound cut through her words, followed by a violent burst of pressurized air. Kellan turned just in time to see the ductwork from the old unit breaking free, the thick rope of it slashing through the air.

"Move!" he shouted to Iska, but she was too slow, her suit too clumsy.

The jagged edge of the duct smacked her dead in the chest, knocking her down.

"What happened?" Ronan demanded.

"Is everyone okay?" Aris asked.

"The duct was still pressurized," Kellan said, abandoning his post. "It snapped off the old unit."

"Seal it!" Ronan roared, running over from the new unit too. "The hab–" He wrenched the emergency seal shut, his breath heavy in the comms.

"Yank the old power," Aris said, and Kellan reached over on instinct and wrenched the cord out of the old unit, protocols be damned.

"How long was it open?" Quinta asked, her voice nervous.

"Seconds," Aris said.

"Long enough," Ronan answered. "Valence help us."

If regolith had infiltrated the unit… if it'd had time to travel through the converter and leak into the hab…

"Iska!" Kellan called, seeing her on the ground, a dark slash across her chest. "Her suit's been breached."

He dropped to his knees in front of her. He still had the roll of polyimide tape in his hand. He ripped off a piece and slapped it onto the rip, his hands shaking.

"Her pressure's dropping," Dr. Anya's voice came through the comms.

Kellan pulled off another piece of tape, layering it on top. "Somebody help me lift her. We have to get her back to the hab."

"Who skipped the depressurization?" Dex demanded through comms. "There shouldn't have been any pressure in that duct when you started disconnecting the old unit!"

"We're going to bring her back now," Aris said, crouching with Kellan to lift her, but the suit strained against his tape job. The cut was big and they set her back down, not confident it'd hold.

"We can't just stop in the middle of this," Ronan said. "The old unit's off and the new one still needs to be flushed."

"Scrap the unit, get her back here!" Dex demanded.

"Ronan's right," Aris said. "We're past the point of no return. If we don't connect the new unit, the nearest modules will begin feeling the effects within the hour."

"I'll go," Quinta said, appearing at Kellan's side as he was applying more tape, cross-ways this time. "You two keep working."

QUINTA

YEAR: 2179

"Her blood pressure's dropping," Dr. Anya warned through comms. "Likely the beginning of decompression sickness."

"Oh Deimos, Deimos!" Dex was near tears.

"Somebody turn off his comms," Dr. Anya ordered. "Dex, you don't need to be hearing all this."

"Like hell—"

And then his voice cut out, and it was just Quinta, Kellan and Iska in the decon chamber. "Stay with us," Quinta begged.

The young woman's dark skin had gone dull, and her eyelids fluttered occasionally, but she was unresponsive. There was nothing Quinta could do about her blood pressure without access to meds, and the damn decon protocol felt like it was taking an eternity and a half. Quinta's mind was split in two.

One half was flipping through everything she could find in the medical protocols for decompression injuries. The risk was always present, but it was rare.

The other half kept going back to what Dex had said when she was outside. Was he right? Did she skip a step in the documentation?

She looked up at Kellan, holding Iska in his arms. His face was a mask of worries. "Does she have it?"

Yeah, that was the other thing – the thing Quinta didn't even dare leave room for in her mind. "I don't know," she said honestly. "Don't take off your pressure suit when we get out of here. Wait for me to seal the tent first."

The inside team had been frantically working to erect an emergency containment tent right outside the decon chamber and they were loading it up with medical supplies. Through the tiny window, Quinta could see Dex pacing, running his hands over his hair, saying something inaudible to Dr. Anya.

"Quinta, don't forget to do your own decon procedure," Castor cut into her comms. "Raise your arms, turn around, make sure the mist is getting everywhere."

She did, distracted, then looked at Kellan again. "What about you? You need to put her down."

"No," he flatly refused.

"You have to decontaminate," she insisted, then after an uncertain pause, held out her arms. "Give her to me."

"You can't hold her."

"I can. Trust me."

So Kellan transferred Iska to Quinta's arms, turning her facedown in the process because they needed to decontaminate her suit too. Quinta widened her stance and braced herself, and Iska was about as much weight as she could manage, but she held her while Kellan spun in slow circles, waiting impatiently for the mist to stop.

"Okay, I'll take her–"

Just as Kellan reached for Iska, she started to shake and flop and Quinta started to lose her grip. "She's seizing."

Dr. Anya was instantly on comms again. "Lay her down. Protect her head if you can."

"Get her out of there!" Dex roared again. "She's dying, oh my god!"

"She's not dying," Quinta gritted out as Kellan helped her to her knees and they set Iska on the floor. Relief washed over her as the tremors subsided. "Seizures are a common response in decompression sickness."

What she didn't tell him was that the literature also said they were likely due to brain swelling. She wasn't sure what she could do about it in this sun-forsaken module when she couldn't even properly set a few measly metatarsals for Jace.

When the decon chamber door finally popped open, she and Kellan got Iska into the new med tent. Dr. Anya had been suited up and ready to join her, but Quinta held her back at the door. "Somebody has to stay out here for Jace."

We need a doctor who hasn't been exposed to Glass, she added mentally, but wasn't about to say that out loud.

"Okay. But you need someone in there helping you," Dr. Anya insisted. "You can't treat her alone."

"Me," Kellan said without hesitation. "I've already been exposed."

And so that was how Quinta came to be trapped in a room three steps wide by four steps deep and packed with medical supplies, a little stack of meal kits, a single bed, a patient, and Kellan Reilly.

The NPC who'd killed her father.

Who'd stolen antibiotics seven years ago and set her fate in motion.

Who'd refused to take comfort in her rabbit when they were just kids and life was so much simpler. At least for Quinta.

There was no time to dwell on any of that in the beginning. They cut Iska the rest of the way out of her suit, then Quinta's next priority was to reduce the brain swelling so she didn't seize again. Kellan made a good assistant, despite not knowing forceps from his forearm.

"I can't start an IV in these gloves," Quinta said after a few minutes of trying. It was Terra all over again, except the biosuits she and Cydra had worn were nothing compared to the pressure suit she was in now. Those were big and clumsy. This was... untenable. "I have to take my suit off."

"But Glass–" Kellan began to object, but Quinta was already yanking her helmet off.

"Keep yours on," she ordered. "I'm just going to have to take the risk. I can't take care of her with this thing on."

Quinta noticed Dex outside the tent while she quickly stepped out of her suit, discarding it in a heap in the corner. He'd been pacing up and down the length of the tent since they laid Iska on the bed, and Quinta didn't need her comms to hear him now.

"Save my girl," he was begging, over and over, to Quinta or Valence or whatever god he prayed to.

Quinta picked up the needle, deftly sliding it into Iska's bare arm and then pushing a cocktail of steroids and diuretics to stop the swelling. Yes, Iska could have Glass. Quinta could have just exposed herself to it. But if this was her fault, if she was the reason Iska got hurt...

She owed it to her.

LIRA
YEAR: 2083

ira found Gaurav and Tamika in the geology lab, continuing their study of V. martialis in the hopes that something helpful would reveal itself. Lira made the introductions to Hoyt and his crew, and explained the urgency, and the geologists volunteered anything in their lab that would be useful.

The evening stretched into night and Hoyt barely looked up from his work to do so much as chug a cup of Mars mud. Lira watched the autofeeder level tick down to 2.7%, then 2.6%. Hoyt's first attempt at a resin was too soft, and the second was too porous. Waiting for it to dry enough to be tested, even with heaters and fans beneath the fume hood to speed up the process, was excruciating.

"They'll figure it out," Tamika tried to reassure Lira. "Science takes time."

"The rabbits don't have time," Lira told her. She'd been steeling herself to watch them be destroyed, but now that Hoyt had dangled a solution in front of her, not making it in time might kill her.

There had to be hope for *something* in this colony, if only that a hundred innocent rabbits would get to live a bit longer.

"How's your research going?" Lira asked, looking for a distraction. "Is there a cure yet?" she teased.

Tamika sighed. "Gaurav and I are no microbiologists, but we're trying to isolate exactly how the bacteria has mutated."

"What are you finding?"

"The structure is different," Tamika explained. "The cell walls are thinner, and there are these strange filaments we can't identify."

Lira felt a chill run down her spine despite the fact that the hab was perfectly temperature-controlled. "Are you sure it's the same bacteria?"

Tamika nodded. "We compared it to samples that were taken last year. Our best theory is the radiation from the solar flare did something to it. Activated it, or turned it into a more aggressive strain."

"What about the regolith that was never irradiated?" Lira wondered. "The stuff in the rabbitat... it could still contain the dormant strain."

"Or it could have mutated when it came in contact with the new variant," Tamika said. "We just don't know enough yet."

Lira fell asleep in a pair of chairs pushed together in the corner and she didn't know how long she slept, but she woke to someone shouting her name.

"Lira," Hoyt called from the fume hood. "I think we have something."

She bolted over to him, completely abandoning fears of mutant bacterial strains – for now. "It worked?"

"I think so," Hoyt said, pointing to a handful of samples set up under the hood. His first two failed attempts sat off to the side, and three more were centered beneath the exhaust fan – little cups of regolith sealed beneath thin layers of clear resin. "We needed something that would both penetrate the regolith and harden so much it couldn't be damaged."

"We also needed it to be effective in a thin layer," Ellis added. "The thicker it is, the longer it'll take to harden and the more off-gassing it'll do."

"That's our winner," Hoyt said, pointing to the cup in the middle. "Gaurav helped me test for permeability, and Ellis made sure the fumes won't harm the rabbits. I'd like to take the rest of the morning to run some more tests to be absolutely sure–"

"We can't wait that long," Lira said, checking her overlay. "The autofeeder is down to 0.3 percent."

"They can go a few more hours without eating," Hoyt said. "I haven't slept. We need to gather supplies, prep the application site. If we rush this–"

"You or I could go a few hours without eating," Lira interrupted him. "The rabbits can't. Their digestive tracts aren't built like ours. If they go empty, they enter GI stasis, which can be deadly. Hoyt, I'm sorry, I know you're just trying to do this the right way, but either we do this now, or we don't bother."

"Okay," he said after a moment, letting out a breath. "We'll start now. But we need to be careful. If we mess this up, we could kill the rabbits faster than starvation would."

LIRA

YEAR: 2083

The scissor lift and gurney were repurposed as supply carts full of resin components, mixing tools, and large sheets of plastic. For the first time since she was evicted from the rabbitat, Lira was decked out head to toe in protective gear, as was everyone else, and Hoyt insisted they all wear respirators once the chemicals came out.

The rabbitat door looked almost as Lira had left it, a big digital warning sign plastered across it: *QUARANTINE ZONE – Unauthorized Entry Prohibited.* Only, in addition to the sign, Lira found a few flowers and notes in her overlay as well.

The rabbits made me feel less homesick, one read.

Another said, *Rover looked just like the bunny I had as a kid. Love you, boy.*

A third was a beautiful watercolor of a sable-coated lop, which Lira guessed was meant to represent Scout.

"They memorialized the rabbits," she said in awe. "Do you think they even know they're not dead?"

"You can reintroduce them when this is all over," Chen said, then retrieved a chisel and hammer they'd gotten from the sector supply room. He started on one side of the door and Hoyt began on the other, chipping away at the seal Yusuf and Moses had applied.

It came away in brittle chunks and bits of dust. About five minutes later, the crack of the pocket door meeting the wall was visible again.

"Go ahead, Lira, try," Hoyt instructed.

She brought up the rabbitat door's controls in her overlay and triggered it open.

Nothing happened.

She hadn't really expected it to work.

But Valence had worked with her in the past, when she wanted to relocate the bodies. It had given her unfettered access to everything in the med clinic and the dorms once it realized what she was doing.

"Valence," she said, louder than was strictly necessary, "we're here to feed the rabbits and seal the regolith. We've taken all necessary precautions and this will render the rabbitat safe. It'll save the rabbits' lives, and they'll die if we don't do this right now."

Then she tried opening the door again.

It didn't budge, and Valence used a speaker nearby in the hall to respond, "Warning: breaking the bioseal on the quarantine zone may release contaminants. This action requires authorization from the administrator."

"The administrator has deserted his post," Gaurav said flatly. "Override protocol. This is an emergency."

"Override denied. Please return to your assigned quarters."

"We're going to have to break it open," Chen said, picking up a pry bar and wedging it into the crack in the door. Valence's warnings continued as it cited various parts of the colony manual, but they all ignored it as Chen threw all of his weight into the pry bar.

The flimsy pocket door popped open, and Lira's heart leaped at the sight of dozens of rabbits scattered across the grassy play area. They looked up at the intrusion, ears perked and alert. Not a single one of them appeared to be in GI distress.

"They're okay," she said, rushing inside and scooping the nearest rabbit into her arms. Its impossibly soft angora fur brushed her face and its whiskers tickled her nose. "We got here in time."

"Let's keep it that way," Hoyt said, navigating the scissor lift through the door. "We have a lot to do."

Lira snapped back to focus. "Right. We need to get them all into the wall cages. Everybody know how to pick up a rabbit?"

She demonstrated just to be sure – no point risking injuring them while they were trying to save them. She set the angora in a cage, then scooped a little Dutch rabbit nearby into her arms.

"We brought food," she told them, "and I'll go to hydroponics when we're done here and get you something fresh, too."

The team worked surprisingly well together. Some of the rabbits were more willing to be held than others, but it didn't take Gaurav and Tamika long to figure out how to corner the more skittish ones without startling them too badly. Lira noticed Ellis taking a few extra moments to pet each rabbit before placing them in the wall cages.

"The fur behind the ears is impossibly soft," she cooed, cradling a gray mini-rex to her chest as she walked him out of the play area. "I never thought I'd get to touch a bunny again."

"Tim's wrong about them," Chen said, then laughed as Houdini tried to climb out of his arms. "They're not just comfort, they really are therapeutic. It's like being home again, if only for a minute."

"We wouldn't have two pregnant colonists if the rabbits hadn't proven it viable first," Lira pointed out.

"Two?" Ellis's eyes bulged.

"I'll tell you about it later," Lira promised.

After they'd secured the last rabbits in their cages, Lira refilled the autofeeder system with pellets and made sure the water recycler was functioning properly as well. The others started hanging the plastic sheeting from floor to ceiling, creating a barrier between the cages and the play area.

"Make sure you tape it down well," Hoyt was instructing them.

"The fumes have to stay on that side of the room or we could make them sick."

Lira slipped through the barrier just before it was sealed. While the engineers prepared the resin, Lira, Gaurav and Tamika cleared all the toys, tunnels and hutches off the grass.

"Respirators on, everyone," Hoyt announced after a few minutes. "We're ready."

QUINTA

YEAR: 2179

ska lay on the bed, an oxygen mask on her face, the flow cranked up as high as Quinta could get it.

Dex wouldn't look Quinta in the eyes.

She'd gotten Iska stable, then explained that the first-line treatment, hyperbaric oxygen, wasn't possible while they were stuck inside this module. "That doesn't mean she won't be okay."

"But it's Jace all over again," Kellan had said. He was out of his pressure suit now too. Quinta had argued against it, but his oxygen tank wasn't meant to last longer than a few hours and he was sweating so much his hydration warnings had started going off. "They need more care than they can get here, but Valence won't let them leave."

"It's too dangerous," Quinta said. "Iska's suit tore. You realize the two of us are stuck in the tent for three days too, right?"

She pointed to the stack of meal kits, and Kellan sank down to sit on a low shelf of supplies behind him. His curly hair was plastered to his forehead. "I know."

Quinta rooted around and found a water pouch, handing it

across the small space to him. "I promise I'm doing everything I can, for both of them."

Kellan sucked on the water pouch. Dex went back to pacing. After a while, Kellan said, "I'm afraid to ask where the toilet is."

Quinta pointed into the corner opposite the meal kits, where she'd discarded her pressure suit on top of a conspicuous bucket. "At least it has a lid."

Not long after, the decon chamber hissed to life and started doing its thing, and then Ronan and Aris emerged looking exhausted but triumphant.

"It's done," Aris announced, grinning. "The new atmo unit is online."

It should have been a celebratory moment. A week ago, not one of them would have said they felt totally confident that they were even going to survive the mission, let alone complete it. Now, the colony was safe again, with clean air to breathe for decades to come, all because of what they'd accomplished.

But nobody felt much like celebrating as long as the ominous medical tent sat taking up all the free space outside the decon chamber.

"Are you sure it's all correct?" Torrent asked. "If the unit malfunctions because you had to rush the installation–"

"We didn't rush anything," Ronan said, his voice taking on an edge. "The valve blew because the pressure wasn't purged, but nothing broke and we followed the documentation to a T after that."

"But before that, someone skipped a step," Dex said, his eyes locking on Quinta through the thick plastic of the med tent. It sent a chill down her spine, even though he had to be right. How did she miss an entire step in the documentation?

Her mind had been on other things, pretty much since the dig began.

She'd been preoccupied, and she never had understood the schematics.

Still, all she'd needed to do today was read from a list. How had she screwed it up this badly?

"Stop," Castor demanded. "If they say they installed it right, then they did. You all saw the readings. The new unit is online and functioning normally."

"For now," Dex said. "And how convenient that *another* NPC got injured."

"What's that supposed to mean?" Aris demanded.

"Six of us, two injured," Dex said. "Four of you, all completely unscathed! We knew from the start you'd take the safe jobs, you'd look after your own people first, and we'd be left taking all the risks."

"Hey, Quinta's in there with her suit off, exposing herself to take care of your daughter," Castor argued back.

"She should be, she's the one who got my Iska hurt!"

"We're all on the same team," Aris shot back. "We were all equally responsible for knowing the steps. It was an honest mistake."

She looked haunted, and Quinta knew it must be eating her up inside even more. How many hours had she spent memorizing the diagrams, only to forget a fundamental step?

"Honest," Dex grunted. "A word I wouldn't apply to you people."

"What are you trying to say?" Aris asked.

Quinta looked to Kellan, who was just sitting there watching the anger boil over. He wasn't hurling accusations but he wasn't defending anyone either.

"You NPCs always do this," Castor's voice cut through the rising tension. "You blame everyone else for your problems. You have a persecution complex the size of Olympus Mons. If you spent half as much energy contributing to the colony – the *whole* colony – as you do coming up with conspiracy theories, maybe it wouldn't seem like the whole hab is against you."

"Okay, enough!" Ronan shouted before anyone else could retort.

He held his hands up, and his face was as stony as Quinta had ever seen it. "Everyone needs to cool off. We're stuck in this module for three more days and I won't spend it listening to you all screaming at each other."

"Another Blinker thinking he can tell everyone what to do," Dex said, but then the cluster broke up. Aris and Ronan headed off to the decon showers. Castor came over to the side of the tent, carefully avoiding Dex, who'd pulled up a chair to sit near Iska's head. Dr. Anya went to check on Jace.

Quinta looked at Kellan, sitting with his arms crossed in front of his waist. He looked as uncomfortable as she felt, trapped in this airtight bubble with no escape and the weight of accusation pressing in from all sides.

"I missed that step, didn't I?" she whispered.

He gave a tight nod. "You did."

KELLAN

YEAR: 2179

What had very briefly and tentatively started as a sort of truce between the two groups during the dig turned into an unbridgeable chasm by the first full day of quarantine.

Kellan watched it all through the window of the med tent, the NPCs staying at their table and the Blinkers segregated to theirs, neither group talking to the other.

They independently monitored the performance of the new atmo unit.

Iska woke and was able to eat some of her breakfast, but then she'd started complaining of chest pain so Quinta laid her down and put the oxygen mask back on.

Castor kept coming around, shooting dirty glances at Kellan and asking Quinta if she was okay. As if Kellan was going to make an attempt on her life in here, or worse. He wanted to point out the bucket and say, *Sooner or later I'm going to be forced to poop in front of her. You don't have to keep coming around, marking your territory because I can assure you when that happens, she'll want nothing to do with me.*

For her part, Quinta was fussing over Iska, tweaking her meds in minute increments, taking her blood pressure every hour, asking if she was comfortable enough, as if there was anything Quinta could do if Iska said no.

Kellan recognized it. Guilt.

After about the fiftieth time that Quinta fluffed Iska's pillow while she tried to sleep, he said, "Now we've both made mistakes."

Quinta looked up at him. She didn't answer, just stared back with those dark, tortured eyes.

"You don't get to dig to make up for yours," Kellan went on. "But it was an honest mistake, and Iska's going to be okay. Right?"

Quinta nodded. "She should be out of the woods now."

"Sit," Kellan said. "You haven't rested since yesterday."

They'd slept overnight, of course, on the uncomfortable floor, but Kellan kept waking up every few hours to noises that turned out to be Quinta getting up to check Iska's vitals and refresh her IV bag.

He sat at the head of the bed – the furthest corner from the bucket. Quinta looked hesitant, but she slumped down across from him, hugging her knees to her chest. His hair had dried sort of stringy and unkempt after the heat of the pressure suit yesterday, but hers was still silky and smooth-looking. She tucked a strand behind her ear in a gesture he was starting to notice was habitual, then said, "I don't think I deserve to rest."

"What does Valence say?" he couldn't help asking.

Quinta rolled her eyes, but then they momentarily went distant as she checked her Exchange dashboard. "Ten credits if I drink some water and take a twenty-minute nap," she reported back.

Kellan reached up behind him, feeling blindly on a shelf, then came down with two water pouches. He tossed one to Quinta and opened the second one for himself. "Halfway there," he said.

"*You* want credits?" Quinta asked in a slightly mocking tone.

Kellan shook his head. "Can't have them. Valence keeps

awarding and then revoking them for everything I do. It's really annoying, but I can't figure out how to shut her – it – up."

Quinta grinned, the first genuine smile he'd seen all day. "You can't shut her up, it's sort of the point. But you can mute the notifications. Do you know how?"

He shook his head, so Quinta crawled over to his side of the tent, sitting with her shoulder next to his. "Easier to walk you through it if I don't also have to mirror it. Okay, look up to the top right corner..."

She walked him through it, way more steps than should have been necessary unless the purpose was to discourage you from doing it. Finally, they got rid of at least some of the pop-ups, and Kellan breathed a sigh of relief. "Thanks."

"Are you going to have to keep that after we're done?"

"I don't see how I can get rid of it," Kellan said. "I like my eyeball, and my vision."

"It's going to be weird for you," she said – not a question. She was turned a little sideways so she could look at him, and their height difference was obvious even while seated. She had to tilt her head up to meet his eyes. "Being the only NPC with an implant... Will they treat you different?"

No, Kellan thought immediately, but something held him back from saying it because how could he be so sure? No NPC had ever had an implant before. It was the thing that made them NPCs. "I don't know."

"I'm sorry they did that to you," Quinta said. "It wasn't right."

Kellan couldn't think of anything to say to that, so he just sat still for a while, feeling Quinta's body heat radiating off her in the small space. Iska's bedframe blocked the view of most of the module, and for the first time since they sealed themselves in, it didn't feel like his prison cell.

"Do you remember the day I brought a rabbit to your sector?" Quinta asked out of nowhere.

Kellan smiled. "Of course. I had to rescue you from getting your ass kicked by my entire Parallax team."

Quinta laughed, then sobered. "It took me a really long time to figure out why all those NPC kids were so mad at me." She turned, her whole body facing him now, her legs crossed, no longer defensively tucked up against her. "I just wanted to share something that was important to me, something that gave me comfort. Back then, I had no clue just how different your life was from mine, or that one rabbit was never going to fix anything. I was raised believing NPCs chose their life."

"We do," Kellan said.

"But the system isn't neutral like they say. It's rigged against you," Quinta said. "They teach us that you get the minimum supplies necessary to survive, and if you want more than that, you're welcome to become a citizen. That that's the fairest way, and the best way to allocate resources. But it's not that simple, and that's not the whole story."

"What is?" Kellan asked, his interest piqued.

"I don't know yet," Quinta said. "But I'm going to find out."

She took another pull on her water pouch and Kellan glanced over Iska's bedframe at the tables. He found Castor staring daggers at him, and couldn't help grinning back at him just to rile him further. Should he wave? No, that'd be too much.

LIRA

YEAR: 2083

I t was close to midnight by the time Lira and her crew left the rabbitat.

The resin was still hardening and they wouldn't know for sure if it had worked until Hoyt could run his tests again in the morning. Lira had been able to convince Valence to recirculate the air in the module so that the rabbits' side of the partition wouldn't suck up the fumes, and there was nothing else to do for now.

Lira was the last out, reluctant to leave the rabbits yet again, and when she stepped into the hall, the first thing she saw were her friends standing awkwardly still. Then she looked beyond them and saw Tim and a half-dozen of his new lackeys blocking their path.

"What's this?" Lira demanded, the hair on the back of her neck rising.

"I came to ask you the same thing," Tim said, the veins standing out on his thick neck and giving her chills. He gestured to the door. "One of my systems friends got an alert the containment seal had been broken. Are you trying to kill the few of us who are left?"

"No, I'm trying to save the rabbits," Lira said, anger beginning to make her body shake. "We just finished applying a resin that–"

"Risking the entire hab for a bunch of pets," Tim spat. "That's what you just finished doing. I knew we couldn't trust you to be on your own, doing God knows what."

"They're not pets–"

He cut her off again, but this time, he swiveled to the six people standing behind him, looking at him with complete and utter trust. "This is exactly why I've been advocating to turn control completely over to Valence. Humans can't be trusted right now – they're too emotional. But she has all the data to make the best decisions for us."

She. Like the AI was a person, some wise leader and not just a computer program running math problems with the colony's statistics. Yes, Valence had a human voice, but Lira had never heard anyone refer to it like one before.

Tim whirled around and pointed accusingly at the dents in the door frame. "They're blatantly disregarding the protocols put in place to protect us – and not just from the bacteria. We have a colony manual for a reason, and we allocate resources carefully for our own survival. We all agreed to live by those guidelines, and this group is putting us all at risk for their own selfish, nonsensical desires."

He locked eyes with Lira.

"They *are* pets, and the sooner this colony is rid of them, the better protected our resources will be."

"You eat rabbit meat," she spat back at him. "You benefit from the research we're doing with them – I assume you want us to be able to procreate here, and if we're going to find a cure for this disease, we'll need animal research subjects. If you ever want to wear something other than your coveralls–"

"I ought to go in there and kill every single one of them right now," Tim snarled. "They're eating our food, they're breathing our air and wasting our energy, and every single one of them is covered in regolith because *you* let them roll in it. I don't care if you epoxied that entire module from floor to ceiling, the rabbits themselves are tainted. And *you*. Don't think we haven't been watching you move those bodies out of their approved quarantine locations. It's incredible! Like you *want* to get sick and take the rest of us down with you."

"They're no risk to us," Gaurav said, stepping even with Lira in the narrow hallway. "We don't know why yet, but everyone here has some sort of immunity, otherwise we wouldn't still be standing."

"We just wanted to give the dead the dignity they deserve," Hoyt added, coming to stand on Lira's other side. The three of them were shoulder to shoulder now, and she could feel the others at her back. "You claimed in your own messages that you wanted that."

"He didn't want to give them dignity, he wanted to clear them out of *his* disease-free sector," Lira corrected. "How did that work for Administrator Voss, huh, Tim? Have you checked lately to see how sector three is doing?"

She hadn't had the heart to look, but if the rate of transmission held, it wouldn't be pretty. Dmitri himself could be dead by now for all they knew, or Una and the baby. All of them.

"Voss has abdicated his responsibilities," Tim said, and the tone of his voice proved there were no lingering loyalties there. "He fled at the earliest signs of trouble, so what's going on in sector three is no longer any concern of mine. My worry is for the people behind me in this hallway, and all the ones who are working on making sector one a safe haven. And you better believe they're using all the protective gear available to do it. We're not fools, Salonga, and we don't suffer them, either."

"They're not fools, but they are scared," Lira said. "And you're taking advantage of that. Manipulating them, using this horrible situation to prey on their emotions and get them to follow your every whim."

Tim laughed loudly, and the sound echoed in the narrow hallway. "Not my whim. Valence's. She's the only one who can save us now. You're the perfect example of why emotional decision-making is going to damn us all. I won't allow that to happen."

Lira's back turned to steel. "Yeah, what are you going to do?"

Tim's numbers might be equal to hers in this hallway and in this moment. But he'd spent the last week steadily sending out messages and holding meetings and amassing a following. Who knew how many he had now, who were willing to do what he said.

"We're sealing off sector one," he announced, and his people began to murmur. "I didn't want to do it without trying one last time to reason with you, but now that I see with my own eyes what you've been doing here, we can't be connected to sector two any longer – it's far too dangerous. And sector four is out of the question. With those regolith walls, the entire thing is a tomb. We're seceding."

Lira barely held back a snort. "So you're doing what Dmitri did."

"No, I'm taking everyone with me," Tim said. He looked past her to the geologists and engineers behind her. "Any of you who want to follow the protocols and abide by Valence's decisions are welcome to come with us. We could use more scientists – smart people who understand the consequences of their actions." His eyes fell on Lira. "As for the rest of you… good luck."

Less sincere words had never been spoken, and yet Lira's heart climbed into her throat as she imagined, one by one, everyone standing behind her pushing past her to join Tim's group.

It didn't happen.

For a few long, painful seconds, he stood there with his hands on his hips, confidently waiting to steal all of Lira's friends from her, and when they didn't budge, he nodded his head tightly and said, "So be it."

Then he turned and walked through his parted sea of followers.

They all scurried after him, looking relieved the more space they put between themselves and the rabbitat.

Or maybe it was not the rabbitat but that insane veterinarian, the one who'd fallen in love with the criminal. The one who was moving bodies with her bare hands, who must want to give everyone regolith-covered rabbits like the American colonists had given smallpox-infected blankets to the natives.

Once Tim and his followers had disappeared around a bend, Ellis asked quietly, "Can he actually do that? Give Valence total control?"

"Not without sys admin privileges," Tamika answered.

"Even if he did, it's a colony management system," Gaurav added. "Not a dictator."

Lira nodded, trying to believe them, but the looks on the faces of Tim's followers was a new addition to the things that would haunt her when she tried to go to sleep at night. They were all so fearful, so desperate for someone who was confident. Someone who could protect them.

"All he has to do is say Valence told him to do something and it'll be law to them," she said. "And he's not done with us yet."

What better way to consolidate power than to unite around a common enemy? He was following the authoritarian's playbook exactly, and it was working.

KELLAN

YEAR: 2179

y the third day of quarantine, the med tent was dense with condensation from their breaths. The latrine bucket had been made use of. The meal kits were all empty. Kellan was stiff from three nights of sleeping on the floor, and he hadn't changed his coverall or even his underwear once because no one had thought to include any.

He was dying for a shower, but even more than that, he was dying to get out of this module.

Quinta told him that word on the Exchange was that there was a big party being planned in the atrium, sort of the reverse of the big goodbye that the Blinkers had had on day one. She said her mother had been messaging her, asking her which of her outfits she'd like to change into and what foods she wanted on the menu. Apparently, Castor's parents had spent a good deal of their credits to hire his favorite band for the occasion.

"What do you hope is on the menu?" Quinta asked while she removed Iska's IV and applied a bandage to the site.

"You think they're going to want us there?" he asked.

"It's for the entire dig crew," Quinta told him.

"But nobody's asking us for our input," Iska pointed out. "At least, nobody out there."

"I just want Iska and Jace to get whatever medical attention they still need," Kellan said. "With the good equipment, the right medications. Not whatever we can make do with at home. They dug, they deserve decent care."

"They do," Quinta agreed. "I submitted requests this morning for both of them to be seen by citizen doctors as soon as possible."

"And the response?" Iska asked, wincing as she sat up. She was still having what Quinta called girdling pain across her midsection.

"Pending," Quinta said. She and Kellan helped Iska to her feet, and the three of them walked to the sealed flap of the tent.

Dex was waiting impatiently. Aris and Castor were there too, along with Dr. Anya.

"Are we sure the risk of Glass has passed?" Aris asked.

"If it hadn't, none of us would be getting out of the module today," Dr. Anya pointed out, then added, "All of their vitals have been stable for forty-eight hours, Iska's included. If they were infected, we'd know by now."

"Okay, let's get them out of there, then."

As soon as the tent flap was pulled aside, Dex surged forward, taking Iska out of Quinta and Kellan's hands. "My girl, how do you feel?"

"Like I got hit by a rover," she said. Her complexion still had a clammy sheen to it, but she'd be okay.

Quinta was holding a portable oxygen tank for Iska, but that didn't stop Castor from throwing his arms around her. Kellan peeled off to go find Jace, whose bed was now a more or less permanent fixture beside the tables.

"You lived," Jace said, sounding impressed. "How was it in there?"

"I need a shower. I feel disgusting."

"You've smelled better," Jace agreed.

"Oh, look who's talking. When's the last time you took a shower?"

"Okay, we both reek," Jace said, then nodded to Quinta, who was following along with the oxygen tank as Dex carried Iska over to a chair. "Saw you talking to her in there."

"Not much else to do," Kellan said. "I'm gonna hit the showers."

It was about three hours later, just late enough in the evening that a couple of them started to consider one more prepackaged meal, when a new alert popped up, a notification in the corner of his eye rather than a screaming message taking up his entire vision this time.

The dig mission is complete, as is your mandatory quarantine period. The doors will unlock in fifteen minutes. Congratulations and thank you for your service to the colony!

Torrent let out a whoop and Ronan's hand went to his tattoo. Kellan laid down the cards in his hand, and Jace abandoned his as well, a round of poker that would never be completed. "This is it, we're done!"

"Help me up," Jace said.

"You sure? We can go get a wheelchair for you as soon as the door opens," Kellan offered. It'd be nice if whoever was organizing this bash thought to provide them for the two injured crew members, but Kellan wouldn't bet on it.

"Scrap that, I'm walking out of here," Jace insisted. "Or at least hopping."

They didn't waste time. Everyone gathered whatever belongings they'd brought with them – Dex's cards, Castor's HoloPong paddles, Quinta's old leather book – and they all went to stand at the door. Iska leaned heavily on Dex and Jace had his arm slung over Kellan's shoulder for balance. Kellan noticed Castor taking Quinta's hand.

There were still a little more than five minutes before the door would open, according to the clock in Kellan's overlay, but they were all lined up and ready – probably would have pulled the door open on their own if they could.

But then Torrent stepped forward. He produced a small glass bottle from his coverall pocket, clear liquid sloshing around in it.

"I traded my favorite painting for this bottle of vodka when I drew a straw for this mission," he said. "After the last few days, I wasn't sure if I wanted to share it or take it home and have a few drinks with Eddy." He ran his thumb over the smooth curve of the bottle. "But we all completed this mission together. We risked Glass. Two of us were injured out there. We sweated and cursed and I don't know about anyone else, but my arms were as sore as they've ever been after a long dig shift."

There were a few murmurs of agreement from both sides of the group.

"I doubt we'll all be sending each other birthday cards after this, but we pulled off an impossible task together. And for that, I think we deserve a drink."

He cracked open the bottle and took the first swig, then held it out to Aris. She hesitated, looking down the line for approval, and when no one objected, she took a sip, grimaced, and held up the bottle. "To mission completion."

She handed it off to Ronan.

"To survival." He passed the bottle on down the line.

When it was Kellan's turn, he took a long swallow and the vodka burned down his throat. He'd only tasted it a few times, a rare treat. The experience of drinking it was never pleasant, but the warmth that spread in his belly immediately after was worth it.

They kept passing the bottle around until it was empty and all the animosity of the past couple of days melted in proportion to the growing warm feeling, and then the module door abruptly slid open in front of them.

QUINTA

YEAR: 2179

The atrium looked nothing like it had the day they went into the fabrication module.

For one, it was packed with people, some she recognized and some she didn't. She spotted her mother immediately, standing beside Administrator Weyland near a stage that had been built in one corner. Castor's parents were already running full-speed toward him.

The room itself had been transformed with streamers and colorful banners fit for a Day of Renewal, which maybe this was, in a way. A celebration of the colony's will to survive, its determination to keep going in the face of every challenge the hostile planet could throw at it.

And the food... Quinta was inhaling the mouth-watering aromas of fresh fruit and hot-out-of-the-oven baked goods when her mother threw her arms around her. Her algae perfume that always reminded Quinta of the hydroponic gardens filled her nose, and a knot immediately formed in Quinta's throat.

"Mom," she squeaked. "I missed you."

"I was worried every second you were in there. I thought for sure I was about to lose my whole family," Havana said, drawing back to cup Quinta's cheeks in her palms. "You look tired."

"I am," Quinta confessed. "I could sleep for a week."

The crowd surged forward, reclaiming their loved ones, and for a moment Quinta felt lost in it, anchored to her mother, her free hand still instinctively searching for her father.

Then Administrator Weyland stepped up to the podium and boomed through the room speakers, "Welcome back, heroes of the colony! On behalf of Valence, the administration, and every citizen, I extend our deepest gratitude for what you have done."

Havana squeezed Quinta's hand, a silent *I'm proud of you.*

"Please, eat, drink, enjoy yourselves," Weyland continued. "In a little while, the ceremony will commence."

"Ceremony?" Quinta asked her mom.

"To honor you," Havana said. "Come on, let's get some food. I know it's dinnertime, but I had them make pancakes and strawberry jam, your favorite."

The next few minutes were a blur of flatware clinking and food being piled on plates and familiar faces getting too close to Quinta, thanking her for digging and marveling that she wasn't dead. If there were any whispers and rumors flying around like before, the room was too chaotic for her to notice.

Quinta spotted Aris once, briefly, surrounded by her fabrication team.

She saw Ronan taking a baby from the arms of a young woman, who lightly pressed two fingers to his sternum, a Chosen gesture Quinta had seen many times in the clinic when people were grateful for good outcomes.

She wound up at a table with Castor and his parents, a plate absolutely heaped with food in front of her, and Havana sitting beside her, ignoring her own food to ask question after question.

"Was it difficult work? Were you terrified? Did you have to work with… the NPC boy?"

"Kellan. His name is Kellan Reilly," Quinta said. "And he paid his debt to the colony."

"We were worried sick that something would happen to you," Nita Marcellus said. "After what the NPCs already did to your father… But Valence wouldn't allow him on the crew if there was any chance of it, of course."

"There were plenty of us there to keep an eye on him," Castor assured her.

"He worked just as hard as everyone else," Quinta said. "He never hurt anyone on purpose."

She looked around the room again. In the upheaval of the doors opening and everything happening all at once, she'd lost track of the six NPCs, and she couldn't see a single one of them now – neither her crewmates or any of their loved ones.

Was this just a citizen party?

"Oh, I've got good news for you," her mother was saying. "I spoke to Dr. Nilsen and he said he would take you on for the last six months of your apprenticeship. I didn't think you'd want to go back to the sector one clinic with all the memories it holds. Isn't that great?"

"Yeah…" Quinta trailed off, checking the hab map. Kellan was the only one of them who'd show up on it, but just as she suspected, he was nowhere near the atrium. He was in a hallway, making slow progress toward sector four.

She opened her messages and sent him one. *Where are you going?*

He didn't respond right away, and her mom was telling her about the strings she'd had to pull to get one of Dr. Nilsen's apprentices to agree to switch places with her. Quinta switched over to the clinic system. Jace really needed an MRI to check for tendon and ligament tears and then a proper realignment. And Iska needed imaging to figure out that lingering girdling pain in her chest, and more drugs than she could get in sector four, at least legally.

She pulled up Jace's request. It was no longer pending.

Current symptoms do not meet thresholds for immediate care. A standard appointment has been placed in the patient queue; notification will be issued when the scheduled date approaches.

Quinta's mouth dropped. She switched over to Iska's request. Same exact message.

Valence had asked them to take an incredible risk digging for the colony, and now she was going to bury them in the queue, which often stretched weeks out for NPCs, just because they weren't actively dying!

Quinta dashed off a fast appeal message to Jace's request, although she didn't expect it would do much good. *If the patient doesn't receive treatment now, his body will begin healing around the broken bones and he'll likely end up with a permanent limp.* She thought for a moment, then added, *This will impact his ability to contribute to his sector.*

"What's wrong?" Castor asked when he saw her stern expression.

"You haven't seen any of the NPCs, have you? Did anyone bring a wheelchair for Jace?"

He shook his head. "I didn't notice."

Quinta looked around again and saw that most people had found chairs. Administrator Weyland was heading for the podium again. It looked like the ceremony was about to start, whatever that entailed.

"Valence is denying Jace and Iska immediate medical attention."

"Well, Dr. Anya can treat them."

"But she doesn't have the right equipment."

"Doesn't she?" Castor asked. "I thought that was the whole point of..." He trailed off, not willing to say it where he might be overheard.

Quinta shook her head. "He didn't smuggle an entire MRI machine."

"May I have everyone's attention, please?" Weyland boomed through the speaker system. The crowd quieted, and Quinta couldn't whisper to Castor anymore without drawing attention so she turned to the administrator. "Let's have a round of applause for our heroes! Please stand, dig crew!"

Across the room, Aris and Ronan popped up at separate tables. Castor got up, then held out his hand and pulled Quinta up too.

There wasn't a single one of the NPCs still in the room, and Kellan was ignoring Quinta's message. She shouldn't have shown him how to minimize the notifications.

It was like they'd been erased, as swiftly and efficiently as the incinerators burned up any waste that couldn't be reclaimed.

Just like Kellan said would happen.

"These courageous people exemplify the finest qualities of citizenship," Administrator Weyland went on. "And in recognition of the work they have done, I am pleased to announce that Valence has awarded them each… ten thousand Exchange credits!"

Gasps and applause erupted from the crowd.

Castor staggered.

Across the room, Ronan touched a hand to his tattoo.

Quinta felt sick, her stomach rebelling against the half a pancake she'd eaten.

Ten thousand credits was an astronomical sum – more than most colonists earned in a year. A trip to the rabbitat cost fifteen credits without a prescription. A cup of Candor dark was five credits. An hour in the pleasure gardens was ten credits, plus whatever you ate while you were there.

How much fruit would you have to gorge on to use up ten thousand credits?

And the NPCs, who had no implants and therefore no way to access the Exchange, went uncompensated for doing the same dangerous job. If Kellan had gotten the credits, he was the richest

NPC in history, with no way to spend his wealth except to stop being an NPC.

Quinta felt her mom take her hand, and looked down to see Havana beaming at her.

Castor's mouth hung open.

And suddenly Quinta's chest felt tight and she couldn't stand to be in that room one minute longer.

She wrenched her hand out of Havana's grasp and stomped toward the exit, even as the rest of the room was still cacophonous with applause.

"Where are you going?" Castor called.

Even Administrator Weyland saw Quinta leaving and there was a hitch in his voice, a temporary pause in the lavish praise he was raining down on the four citizen members of the dig crew as if they were the only members of the dig crew. She kept walking until she reached the hallway, out of sight of the cheering crowd, and then suddenly adrenaline surged through her veins and she had to catch herself against the wall, gasping for breath.

"Quinta," Castor said, appearing behind her. "What's wrong?"

She spun on him. "Everything. The whole damn system. Can't you see that?"

Quinta got a notification, hoping it was Kellan, and saw that Valence had already responded to her medical appeal for Jace.

Estimated impact on sector contribution remains within permissible limits. The patient queue appointment remains in effect.

She almost lost her mind. She started kicking the wall and Castor had to put his arms around her waist and pull her away from it before the noise could echo back into the atrium. When she finally stopped fighting against him, he let her go and she started crying.

"Castor, this isn't right." She sent the appeal decision to him. *"Estimated impact is within permissible limits?!* His foot is totally fixable if we just do *something* now, instead of nothing! This is the medical supply distribution all over again. How could it be best for the colony to let Jace lose function in his foot?"

"I don't know what she's thinking," Castor admitted. "None of us do, exactly, but that's because she's responsible for so many variables, so many lives, that there's no way we could understand the big picture like she does."

"We can't decide to fix someone's foot so he can walk normally again?" She started pacing, struggling just to suck in enough oxygen as the adrenaline surged again.

His cricket-brown eyes contained a storm almost as powerful as the one Quinta felt twisting her guts. "All I know is that there are other aspects that we're not seeing. Valence has her own math, and it's way more advanced than we–"

"Wait a minute." Quinta stood upright. "You said she keeps logs that we can read for a few hours before she compresses and archives them."

"Yeah…"

"I want to see the math."

"What?"

"If she's making calculations about Jace and Iska… and my dad and Elise and Owen… and who gets what resources…" She was already marching in the direction of the computer lab, one sector over. "I want to see the calculations."

"Quinta…" Castor objected, but he jogged after her. "It's not as simple as just requesting a raw data file. It has to be done directly from the server, and it'll probably be encoded–"

"But you can access it?"

"Theoretically."

Quinta whirled on him, tears streaming down her cheeks. "Please, Castor. I don't know what to make of any of this, but I'm not going to be able to sleep tonight – or ever again, honestly – if I don't prove to myself that what it looks like is not what's actually happening. Because it looks bad."

"You think Valence's math is bad. That she's making the wrong choices and hurting people."

"I think…" *I think the math is just fine, but the equation isn't the one we thought she was using.* Quinta couldn't stay that out loud – not with all the cameras in the ceilings, not with so much adrenaline coursing through her veins and making her pulse audible in her own ears. "Please, just help me look up the logs for Iska and Jace's medical requests. You think everything is fine and I'm overreacting, right?"

He looked pained. "Probably?"

"Okay, prove it to me. Please."

Castor drew a deep, uncertain breath. "Okay."

QUINTA

YEAR: 2179

The server room was quiet except for the low, constant hum of the fans that cooled it. They'd had to walk past one of Castor's coworkers, who'd tried to pump them for information about the dig but also seemed like he wanted them to keep a good distance from him.

Perhaps why he'd taken the shift that kept him here instead of at the party with everyone else.

He asked why Castor needed in the server room, and why he'd brought Quinta Voss with him, but backed down easily when Castor said it was for Administrator Weyland.

"Technical difficulties, you can't get away from them," Castor had joked, then he took Quinta's hand and pulled her inside the cool, dark room.

Dozens of server racks softly hummed, green and blue lights twinkling all over the linked machines. They went back row after row, with cables tied neatly from one to the next like a spinal cord.

"This is Valence," Quinta said, awed. "I'm standing inside her mind."

"Not quite," Castor said, and pointed to a door at the end of the row. "The servers that run her algorithm are on dedicated machines in there. This is more like… her nerve system, collecting information to feed to her."

Quinta felt an almost irrepressible urge to reach out and run her fingers along the bundled cables in front of her… and an equal revulsion to the idea.

"How do we get in?"

Castor went to the end of the first row and pulled a keyboard out of a little nook between two servers. He unfolded a monitor next, propping it up against the rack. "It's old-school in here, less opportunity for corruption if the human data inputs only come through one terminal." He logged in, then paused with a glance toward Quinta that attempted humor but looked more like nerves. "That's why my dad would kill me if he knew what I was doing right now. He always insists on the buddy system in here, one to type and the other to check the work."

"Should we go get your friend out there?" Quinta hooked her thumb toward the lab.

For the first time, worry etched Castor's brow as he looked toward the door. "Let's just do this."

He worked for a few minutes, typing rapidly while Quinta hovered and looked over his shoulder at the screen. It was all a bunch of gibberish to her, the same way the atmo unit schematics meant nothing to her because she'd spent the last three and a half years learning the language of medicine.

"I don't see Jace and Iska's requests in the medical data logs…"

"What? How's that possible?"

"I told you Valence has an idiosyncratic way of categorizing things," Castor said. "There's so much data, it's not all logical to us. There are vectors and relations… It's one of the reasons we don't bother trying to look at the raw data very often. The requests exist… we just have to figure out how Valence is labeling them…"

He trailed off, chewing on his lower lip while he worked. Quinta thought about sending Kellan another message, maybe initiating an audio call this time to be sure he saw it, but they hadn't come across any of the NPCs on their way through the central commons. That meant they were home by now, and they didn't want to be bothered anymore.

"Does she segregate the requests by sector?" Quinta asked. "NPCs versus citizens?"

"Sometimes…" Castor trailed off again and Quinta wanted to strangle him for the suspense he was creating. His fingers were moving as fast as she'd ever seen him type, but some part of her was waiting for someone to burst through that server room door and stop them in their tracks.

She was imagining Dr. Liang, as improbable as that was.

Your father was just as bad as I said he was and you have to live with it! You can't make this go away with some community service and a little hacking! Quinta pictured her saying.

Or maybe it'd be Administrator Weyland, come to drag them back to the party and force them to be celebrated the way Valence wanted.

Could Valence herself stop them now, kick Castor out of the system–

A window popped up and Castor said, "There!"

Quinta grabbed his arm. "What did you find?"

"They were lumped in with the dig mission," he explained. "This file is… huge. It goes all the way back to when the old atmo unit started acting up weeks ago. But it hasn't been compressed yet so I can read it."

"First bit of luck I've had since… well, you know," Quinta said. She still didn't like uttering the words *my dad died.*

"I can search for Jace or Iska's name and jump to what we need," Castor offered. "Who do you want first?"

"Jace." Iska needed further medical attention too, but Quinta could make the better argument for the long-term consequences if Jace's bones weren't set properly right now.

Castor made a few more keystrokes, then stepped aside so

Quinta could read the screen. He read over her shoulder.

There was her original request and Valence's reply, as well as her answer to the appeal. It was all exactly how Quinta had seen it in the medical system – no confusing code, nothing extra at all – and she started to deflate until Castor reached around her and scrolled over, revealing a whole second column of text.

"That's the algorithm," he explained. "What she's doing behind the scenes to come up with the response she gives us."

"'Subject classification: Non-participating Colonist,'" she read. "We already know she uses that as a data point... 'Intervention pathway produces greater than three system adjustments.' What does that mean?"

"The domino effect," Castor said. "Treating Jace's foot would impact at least three other systems. Maybe a citizen's treatment would get delayed, supplies would be used up, stuff like that."

Quinta kept reading.

Deviation in sector output if no action taken: ≤ 0.3%

Colony survival outcome: unchanged

Individual outcome: non-critical

"What does that mean?" she asked. "It sounds like there were too many variables and not enough negative consequences, so Valence didn't want to bother."

"I told you we can look at the raw data but it's not always useful. She did a calculation and decided it was best for Jace to go in the patient queue."

"Find Iska's," Quinta demanded.

Castor pulled it up. It said a lot of the same stuff. She's an NPC, there would be no change in colony survival odds if she didn't get treatment.

There would be only two system adjustments if she got treatment, and the following lines:

Progression risk: stable within acceptable variance

Projected recovery trajectory without escalation: adequate

"She's saying it's too much trouble to treat these people because their health will be 'adequate' without it!" Quinta said. "I thought the algorithm was only supposed to make those kinds of calls in crises, like when it was save one person or save the whole colony." Or save three people versus a dorm full. She started scrolling up on the touchscreen. "You said everything from when the unit first started malfunctioning is in here?"

"What are you doing?"

"I want to see the algorithm notes from the day my dad died."

"Quinta, I don't know if you should see that."

"Why not?"

"It could be traumatizing."

"I'm a doctor, I can handle it." She kept scrolling. There really was a ton of raw data – everything from each crew member's vital signs throughout the dig and how many calories they each consumed every day to exactly how much weight the lifter robot carried during each dig session. "How do you search?"

"Here." Castor showed her, and a few seconds later, Quinta was reading what she'd asked him for days ago.

The raw data from the night her father died.

The first column started months ago with the first documented decline in function of the old atmo unit. Every time it hiccuped, every time its capacity deteriorated was meticulously recorded.

But then: *CO_2 purge initiated. Concentration rose unexpectedly in Dorm 3A. Emergency sequence initiated and rescue teams dispatched. Post-event analysis revealed manual airflow panel adjustment in sector four.*

"CO_2 purge initiated? By who?" Quinta asked.

Castor reached over Quinta and swiped the screen so the algorithm logic was visible.

Subjects: Hadrian Voss, Elise Chandra, and Owen Markovic

Classification: Unstable, routinely produce multiple system adjustments due to repeated unauthorized supply redistributions, in excess of 7 system adjustments per month

Probability of sector-wide destabilization if continued: 0.41

Probability of colony survival reduction: 0.08

Intervention pathway: Remove sources of destabilization to restore homeostatic equilibrium, ≤3 system adjustments to achieve

---

Quinta was shaking when she turned back to Castor. "Okay, here's the part where you tell me I'm reading this all wrong and Valence didn't kill my dad because he was introducing uncertainty into her calculations."

Castor looked from her back to the screen and to her again. "I don't know what this means. It's not... it's not data I normally look at. I don't know how to interpret it–"

"But that is one way you could interpret it," Quinta insisted, vaguely wondering if she might puke here and now. How would Valence's calculations like that, vomitus in her nerves or whatever Castor had called them?

"Oh my god... we have to tell people," Quinta realized. "Valence killed three people and we don't even know why her programming told her–"

She heard the distinct, soft but crystal-clear sound of the tumblers falling into place in the door. She turned to Castor.

"Did you do that?"

"No." He looked just as freaked out as she felt.

"Your coworker?"

Castor shook his head. "I doubt it."

"Open the door," Quinta said, trying to make it sound like a suggestion rather than the terrified demand that was bubbling up her throat.

His eyes went distant for a second, then he came right back. "I can't."

"What does that mean?"

"It means the door control's been deactivated for me," Castor said, and he dove into his overlay again. "So are all my work systems. It's all gone."

Quinta looked at the computer screen, now blank but for the VossCorp logo, a sharp V with a rocket taking off from its center. "The display's down."

Castor jabbed it with a finger, trying to wake it up, but nothing happened. "It's locked too."

"Do you believe me now?" she asked. She tried her own overlay. The video call button, all her old messages, everything she could use to tell someone where she was... it was all gone. She could still get to her Exchange dashboard, where a new task awaited her.

Remain in place until your status has been re-evaluated, five credits.

LIRA

YEAR: 2083

t had been close to a month since Tim sealed himself up in sector one, along with his followers, and life had settled into a new sort of normal.

Lira was in the rabbitat doing her routine wellness checks on the warren. It was almost peaceful in here today, although the ache of knowing Ada would never walk through that door again hit her in the ribcage at the most unexpected times.

The resin had hardened perfectly, creating a smooth, impenetrable surface over the flattened grass and regolith. The rabbits had lost their digging area and Lira had been working on solutions to make the surface less slippery. But at least they still had hutches and toys and 3D printed tunnels.

At least they were still alive.

She ran her hand over Flash's silky white fur. It was no longer bandaged and regular X-rays showed it was healing well against all odds, although it still ached if she moved it just the wrong way. The angora male sat still on the stainless steel exam table, tolerating the prodding as she checked for abnormalities because he knew a fresh carrot top treat awaited him.

Tim's campaign for power, under the guise of wanting to give it all away to the colony AI, had continued even after his sector sealed itself off. He still refused to speak to Lira directly and he'd stopped trying to reach her friends, but his messages leaked out of his precious, pristine sector one and she saw most of them eventually.

Lately, he'd been touting an alliance of sorts with Administrator Voss, claiming to have gained his support from within the silent sector three. If it was true, Dmitri's sys admin privileges would give Tim all the power he needed to remake the hab in his image.

The module door slid open and Lira turned to see Hoyt entering. His expression was tight, his steps rapid. Something was wrong.

"Hey," she said, putting Flash down on the epoxied play area. "What's up?"

"I saw the sign outside the door," Hoyt said. "Did you make it?"

"Yesterday, when Natalia and I went to the fabrication lab," Lira said. "Do you like it?"

They'd gone to try to make more storage containers for the produce they were frantically harvesting from hydroponics. There was far more than their small population could use, but when it was gone, they'd be facing shortages because there weren't enough of them to tend the new crops. The best solution was to figure out how to save it and make it last as long as possible. While their containers were printing, Lira had used an etching machine to make the sign. It was decorated with delicate Arabian jasmine flowers around the edges, and in the center, it read, *Ada and Dana's Place.*

"I love it," Hoyt nodded rapidly, blinking away a tear. "Thank you for including Dana."

"I wanted them to have something physical, just in case..." *In case Tim and Dmitri did something to Valence to erase the memorials.* Lira couldn't bring herself to say it out loud. The colorful shrines lit up most residence hallways in the sector, and some other doors like the ones leading to the clinic and microbio lab. You could hardly turn a corner without finding one, and Lira worried about how tenuous they were. "I made one for Jamila, too. I'm going to hang it outside hydro next time I go."

"I think that's a great idea."

"But you didn't come in here to compliment my etching skills," Lira said.

She bent down and picked up the nearest rabbit – Trouble, who'd very nearly not survived launch when he chewed through his wires in the first hour in the shuttle. She put him in Hoyt's arms. The rabbits were meant to be a comfort, and now that the bulk of the Glass crisis was over, she was determined for them to get back to work, too.

"What's going on?"

He stroked Trouble's long black ears. "Tim claims to have received intel from Earth."

Lira's mouth was suddenly dry. "Bullshit. The satellites are down."

"Well, these are just images," Hoyt said. "Tim says it's the comms that are broken, and on Earth's end, not ours. He found these images in Valence's logs. They're not pretty."

Lira picked up a rabbit too. She intended to keep herself busy by continuing her health checks, but she ended up just standing there cradling the juvenile angora against her chest. "What images?"

An alert popped up in the corner of her vision. A message from Hoyt, linking to the photos. She pulled them up.

They were satellite photos of Earth, except it was barely recognizable. There were storm systems everywhere, casting large yellowish hues over large portions of the land masses. A lot of what used to be green, especially around the equator, was now brown or even blue, reclaimed by the ocean.

"Oh my God. These are real?"

"As far as we can tell," Hoyt said. "Gaurav and Tamika spent all morning pouring over them. They say this kind of damage is possible if the methane hydrate release finally reached a tipping point and turned into a feedback loop. If it's real, it happened almost as fast as Glass spread through the colony."

"It's not possible…" Lira trailed off, searching through the images for one that had a good view of Southeast Asia.

Things had been getting bad on Earth for years. Some colonists said before the outbreak that they were lucky to be here because Earth wouldn't be inhabitable much longer. They claimed there wouldn't be any more Exodus missions because Houston would no longer be a suitable launch location. Lira hadn't believed any of it, not deep down.

She found the Philippines hidden beneath another big, thick storm system, little bits of the islands poking out from under the clouds. But the shapes were all wrong, with too much water between them.

With horror, it dawned on her that the flooding she'd been warning her mother about for years had finally happened.

Manila was under water.

Lira closed her overlay. "This can't be real. Tim doctored the images. This is just another power grab."

"Gaurav and Tamika looked at the angles, the timestamps," Hoyt said gently. "These are real, Lira."

"My mother," she whispered, the words barely audible. She'd never been able to convince her to leave her house.

Hoyt set Trouble back on the play area and he hopped away, oblivious. "I'm so sorry."

"And your sister."

He nodded.

Lira set Scout on the exam table, keeping a hand on her back to keep her from trying to hop down, but also concerned with being able to brace herself against something in case her legs gave out. She trusted Gaurav and Tamika and they wouldn't say the images were real if they weren't absolutely sure. She managed to think beyond her mother, the individual people they'd all left behind, and the full consequences began to crash over her in waves.

There would be no resupply missions.

No communications from home.

No return trips, even in an emergency.

"We're on our own," she said, feeling like her mind was floating somewhere near the ceiling. "VossCorp isn't ignoring us... they're dead. Are they *all* dead?"

"Maybe not," Hoyt said, trying to be comforting even though his eyes were distant and haunted too. "There could be survivors. A shuttle could have lifted off before things got too bad. There could be people in bunkers..."

Lira barely heard him. Her mind had turned to survival. Things were already looking dire for them with more than half the colony wiped out and those remaining split into groups needlessly fighting with each other. In the back of her mind she'd been counting on another Exodus mission coming. New colonists would help bear the load. They would make it easier to rebuild.

Now it looked like they were on their own entirely. No new colonists, no support from mission control, no replacement parts when things broke or ran out.

Natalia and Una's babies had gone from novelties – look, people can procreate on Mars! – to their only hope for long-term survival.

Lira was just beginning to hyperventilate when a new notification appeared in her overlay. She thought it was more satellite images from Hoyt, but he looked distracted by it too. Lira opened the message.

COLONY-WIDE ALERT: Satellite imagery obtained from Earth shows catastrophic climate change escalation. As a result, Voss-Colony will proceed in full self-sufficiency mode until further notice. Administrator Dmitri Voss and Deputy Administrator Tim Robi-

nette have proposed a vote to transfer total colony governance to Valence to ensure optimal use of supplies and allocation of human resources for the colony's survival. Voting begins now and will conclude in one hour.

Lira got a second ping to alert her to a new task in the Exchange. She rolled her eyes, already knowing what it would say before she opened it.

Vote to transfer colony governance to Valence, five credits.

"Well, at least we can buy a cup of Candor dark for the price of letting the machines take the wheel," she snarked. "This is all Tim needed to get exactly what he wanted. He's going to win."

His new title had not escaped her, and she wondered how long the 'deputy' part would last before he usurped Dmitri. Would the administrator even put up a fight when it happened?

"Let him be king of sector one," Hoyt said. "We have hot meals and fresh veggies and all the geologists in the hab. We'll be okay."

Lira nodded, looking around at the perfectly healthy, happy rabbits hopping around her. She'd fought to keep them alive. She'd worked until her muscles ached to move the dead to refrigerated rooms, and was still trying to come up with a respectful way to permanently dispose of them. She'd sat by Ada's side all day and all night when there was nothing else she could do to help, and then she'd done the same for Jamila, and a handful of strangers after that.

If – when – Tim got his way with this vote, he still wouldn't control her. But he'd be making it damn near impossible to override Valence, no matter what sector she was in.

It felt like she was floating on the ceiling, looking down, quickly running out of oxygen up there. She opened the poll and cast her vote, one no in a sea of yes votes.

The End

THE STORY CONTINUES IN UNWORTHY

Every Eye Reports to Valence

Quinta survived the dig. She learned the truth. Now comes the hard part: living with it.

Available on all retailers.
https://bestdystopianbooks.com/unworthy

WANT MORE FROM THE WORLD OF GLASSBORN?

Join my reader newsletter and get a free copy of *Children of Glass*, a companion novella set before the events of *Glassborn*.

Inside you'll discover:

• Why Ada was imprisoned

• How Quinta and Kellan first met

• The mystery that shaped the colony generations before the dig

You'll also receive twice-monthly updates featuring dystopian book recommendations, new articles and videos, behind-the-scenes series updates, and exclusive *Glassborn* content.

Get a free copy at

https://bestdystopianbooks.com/childrenofglass